W9-AHH-377

Coup de Grâce

Also by J. S. Borthwick

Coup de Grâce

MISS
MERRITT'S
SCHOOL

1861

J. S. Borthwick

ST. MARTIN'S MINOTAUR ❧ NEW YORK

F

Although the town of Carlisle is real, Miss Merritt's School, and the characters and events in this work, are entirely fictional.

Library of Congress Cataloging-in-Publication Data

Borthwick, J.S.
    Coup de grâce / J. S. Borthwick — 1st ed.
      p. cm.
    ISBN 0-312-25313-3
     1. Deane, Sarah (Fictitious character)—Fiction. 2. Women detectives—New England—Fiction. 3. English teachers—New England—Fiction. I. Title.
    PS3552.O756 C68 2000
    813'.54—dc21

                                    99-056354

First Edition: February 2000

10 9 8 7 6 5 4 3 2 1

To Les Girls: musical, medical, and motherly, the lovers of animals, the huggers of trees and workers of gardens, the artistic, the academic, the sporting, the freewheeling, and those who are always ready with a cup of tea and two aspirin.

Acknowledgments

Thanks are due to granddaughters Clare and Kate, who brought me up to speed on some of the details of end-of-the-millennium life in boarding school. Also my gratitude to the Town of Carlisle chief of police, David T. Galvin, for taking the time to answer questions on police procedure in cases of homicide. Any errors in describing the handling of the murder investigation are on my head, not his. And a belated nod to all those French teachers in my past who worked me into the ground, ruined my weekends, but to whom I am indebted when I find myself in a French Café at ten-thirty P.M. wanting to know the whereabouts of the Avignon railway station. Finally, for giving me her valuable suggestions, a special *salut* to Julia Schulz, president of the Penobscot School of Languages and instructor in French who in no way resembles the formidable Madame Grace Marie-Henriette Carpentier.

Cast of Principal Characters

Instructors and Students at Miss Merritt's School

SARAH DEANE—Instructor in English
GIDDY (GRACE) LESTER—Cousin of Alex; Instructor in Art, soccer
FREDA COHEN—Wife of Joel; house parent in Gregory House
JOEL COHEN—Husband of Freda; co-house parent with Freda
JOANNA SINGER—Head of Miss Merritt's School
BABETTE LECLERC—Instructor in French
CARLO ANTONIO LEONE—Instructor of Italian and European Literature
ADRIAN PARSONS—Assistant head of the Language Division; teacher of Classics
GRACE MARIE-HENRIETTE CARPENTIER—Head of the Language Division; Senior Instructor, French Department
ANITA GOSHAWK—Instructor of History of Art
HANNAH HOYT—Senior student
ROSEMARY STREETER—Senior student
ZOË FOUNTAIN—Senior student

With

ALEX MCKENZIE—Physician; husband of Sarah
GEORGES THIBODEAU—Sport shop owner

Police

JAKE MARKHAM—Security guard at Miss Merritt's School; officer,
    Carlisle Police Department
HILLARY MUMFORD—Detective, Carlisle Police Department
DR. HAROLD ZIM—Forensic pathologist
FRANK O'MARA—State police investigator, forensic team

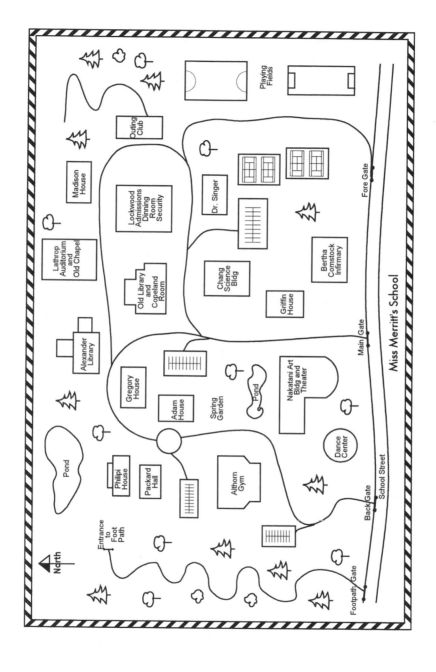

Coup de Grâce

1

You may charge me with murder—or want of sense—
(We are all of us weak at times):
But the slightest approach to a false pretense
Was never among my crimes.

—Lewis Carroll, *The Hunting of the Snark*, Fit IV

THE immortal words attributed to Marshall Petain concerning the defense of Verdun—*on ne passe pas*—they shall not pass—could apply, in a less dramatic sense, apply to Madame Carpentier's French classes at Miss Merritt's School in the small town of Carlisle.

This school, catering to young women in their high school years, had from its founding put a strong emphasis on foreign language instruction, and today this remained a cornerstone of the school's academic structure. And Madame Carpentier was an admirable representative of such a stone; she had sharp corners and was as hard as any chunk of granite.

Miss Merritt's had been founded in 1861 by an intrepid Miss Claudia Merritt, who believed that American women had better shape up and learn something to help them survive in a contentious modern world. The school, however, was now generally referred to by the more acceptable name "The Merritt School" or more simply "Merritt's." A Merritt girl, when graduated, would combine, it was hoped, the tenacity of its founder with the contemporary sensibility of the new millennium. Unfortunately, among the impediments blocking this aspiration stood Madame Carpentier.

Semester after semester, Madame Carpentier, with a stroke of her Mont Blanc pen, blocked students from honor rolls, free weekends, extracurricular activities, varsity teams, and, in several notable instances, from graduation itself. It was said with some truth that an auditorium could have been filled with students whose hopes of Stanford or Harvard had been blighted by a few sharp remarks inserted into their college applications by their French instructor.

However, as the years went by, the presence of Madame in the lives of the Merritt students became in a curious way a sort of bloody badge of honor, something the equivalent of making it through some excruciating tribal rite of passage. Her black-browed, sharp-nosed self, wrapped in her favorite cold-weather garment—a black wool, high-collared cape—was pointed out with a certain amount of pride by students to visiting relatives and prospective applicants. In short, a kind of cachet began to be attached to Madame Grace Marie-Henriette and by association to those girls who had taken, endured, and passed—or been removed from—one of Madame's classes. As one of the former Merritt students remarked—she now a practicing physician at the Brigham and Women's Hospital in Boston—"not even my medical school exams could compare in horror to one of Madame Carpentier's two-hour finals."

And such was Madame's reputation that former students could always command an audience if the subject was a tale of some noted Old Girl who had been done in by Grace Carpentier. A renowned pianist from Oregon had failed two semesters with Madame, a Virginia governor's wife, an attorney, had fled in tears from a French Three classroom; a noted biologist defied Madame to her face and spent a large part of her senior year on detention; and a First Lady had failed to graduate because of her French grade and had to be tutored all the following summer, *grâce à* Madame.

And when a certain Sarah Douglas Deane, a newly minted Ph.D. from Maine's Bowmouth College, was offered a temporary teaching slot at Miss Merritt's School—there being no immediate opening in her own English Department—all she could think of was being on the same turf with the woman some of her friends called Madame Coutou—Madame the Knife.

"Letter from your cousin Giddy," called Sarah. She waved a sheet of paper in the face of her husband, Alex, who had just arrived home from a long day of seeing patients at the Mary Starbuck Hospital, an institution called by the Camden, Maine, Chamber of Commerce brochure, "a major teaching health facility."

Alex McKenzie, a tall man with black brows, dark hair, a notable chin, and a thin, long mouth—all in all, a formidable presence when he wanted to confront something disagreeable—threw himself into one of the dilapidated upholstered chairs in the McKenzie-Deane kitchen. He was tired, wanted a cold beer, and didn't wish to hear much about cousin Giddy Lester—a loose family cannon if there ever was one.

"Giddy," said Alex, "isn't coming here, is she? I thought she was safely employed by that girls' school, what's it called, Miss Muffin's?"

"Miss Merritt's, or just Merritt's. And don't be condescending. It's a good school, rigorous, strong on women being strong—that sort of thing."

"I think that's the place where one of my cousins was thrown out of French class and switched to Italian."

Sarah flopped into a chair next to Alex. Before answering, she looked around for a moment and sighed. The kitchen, indeed the whole house, showed the unmistakable signs of one of its tenants having just emerged from the academic threshing ground of a thesis defense—of "The Use of Early English Folk Tales in the Novels of Charles Dickens." The room was, to put it bluntly, a wreck—an overflowing, unwashed, undusted wreck. Sarah, the early ebullience of finally finishing her doctorate having faded, found the kitchen scene a desperate one. She also saw her husband looking frayed—too many very sick patients, too many nights on call. At the same time she knew herself to be hollow-eyed, sleep-deprived, and altogether lean, mean, and very hungry.

"So," said Alex, "what does Giddy say, and how about pizzas while you tell me? No, wait, I'll get them started myself. We've got frozen crusts in the freezer, and all I have to do is sprinkle the junk on them. Then I'll give you a hand with the housekeeping. And what happened to your hair? It looks like something that Patsy finished chewing." This with a nod toward Sarah's enormous Irish wolfhound, who now laid his shaggy head across her shoes.

Patsy, on hearing his name, rolled on his back, lashed the rug with his tail, and bared his teeth.

"I could even eat Patsy," said Sarah, looking fondly at the dog—a rescued beast found on a memorable visit to the Texas border. "And I haven't had my hair properly cut in months, my skin feels like sandpaper, and I know I look like hell, but never mind, just listen, and I'll read the letter." And Sarah smoothed the long, yellow-lined sheet.

Hey, Sarah and Alex:
Just a note from the upscale side of Boston—Miss Merritt's School for young female monsters. First, congrats on the Ph.D. Second, want a job? I know you're unemployed because Alex's mom—Aunt Elspeth—spilled the beans. You see, Dr. Himmelfarb—she teaches three lit classes—had her baby early, only it was twins, so she's taking the rest of the year off to cope with things, and there's this hole made to order for you to fall into. My dorm—Gregory House—has faculty space, and you can have the room above mine on the third floor—it's a sort of mini-apartment. It's a five-day teaching week, so you could get back to Maine on weekends. Most of the faculty are sane, a few eccentrics, one or two paranoiacs, an inflated ego here and there, and of course, La Carpentier, or Lady Guillotine. Let me know and I'll give the head Dr. Singer—the good news. As for me, I'm fine—teaching art plus coaching soccer. Say hello to cousin Alex.

Ciao, Giddy.

P.S. They might let you bring Patsy; what's one more dog in this zoo.

5

Alex, having unwrapped a frozen pizza crust, was now industriously slicing mushrooms. He paused, knife in hand. "So would you think of taking the school up on it? You and Patsy, leaving me lorn and lonely."

"Without me around, you can see more patients," said Sarah. "Start making a lot of house calls. Remember the olden days when the beloved doctor was often invited to share in the family meal? You could save a bundle by mooching free dinners."

Alex, now twisting open a jar of tomato sauce, looked up. "Seriously, would you go?"

"I'd miss you, I'd miss our house—disheveled though it is—but Bowmouth doesn't want me, not until next year anyway. I need a job, and all the colleges around have their faculty in place for the next semester. It's December after all; Christmas at our throats, New Year's sneaking up on us."

"How about sub teaching in the local high schools?"

"A thankless job. New sets of kids in different classes ready to destroy you every week. Having to use other teachers' programs. I'd do it in desperation, but I'd rather grab something a little more permanent. Like for a whole semester. Besides, I don't mind Giddy."

"I also don't mind Giddy, especially when she's in Massachusetts and I'm in Maine. But she wears me out even looking at her. And she usually has some god-awful sleaze of a boyfriend in tow who doesn't wash and uses controlled substances."

"Giddy's boyfriends won't be on campus, and she can do the boyfriend scene after hours, none of which will bother me as long as I have my own space."

Alex, one of the world's optimists, shook his head. "Don't jump on it until after Christmas. That's in five days. Something around here is bound to turn up. It always does."

But as the determined jollity of Christmas, the faculty parties, the hospital eggnog events, the Christmas pageant featuring assorted nieces and nephews, the family gatherings and dinners arrived, briefly flourished, and vanished, no other job offered itself, and Sarah called Giddy and accepted the offer from Miss Merritt's School.

Carlisle, Massachusetts, is one of those towns within the Boston orbit that managed to maintain a semi-rural character and so attracts those citizens who admire lichen-covered stone walls, white or buff-colored clapboard houses, and narrow, winding roads shaded by mature oaks and maples and conifers. It is a town that somehow has held its commercial presence to two auto repair services, a couple of real estate offices, and a small deli named Daisy's Market. A riffling through the pages of the Carlisle phone book informs visitors that although the town has not sullied itself with fast-food drive-ins, low-life cafés, or warehouse merchandisers, it is possible to engage the services of a calligrapher, a film maker, a choreographer, several graphic designers, a poet, a storyteller, a maker of handcut wooden jigsaw puzzles, as well as a cellist, a teacher of the bassoon, the flute, and a specialist in decorative embroidery. For those who wish to eat out or have a need to visit a hardware store or a hospital, the Carlisle traffic circle—actually an irregular triangle of granite and grass below a sloping green—sends the driver spinning off toward the markets of Concord, Acton, Westford, and Chelmsford, or to Billerica and Bedford. Or beyond, to those magnets of culture, history, and inner city turmoil, Boston and Cambridge.

Beyond this traffic circle, at respectable distances, stand the Gleason Public Library, the firehouse, the town offices, the post office, a public school, a police station, a Congregational church, a Unitarian church, and St. Irene's Catholic Church. The town newspaper, the *Carlisle Mosquito*, diligently reports on the events and personalities in the town, and the *Boston Globe*, the *Boston Herald*, the *Wall Street Journal*, and *The New York Times* keep some of the townspeople in touch with a wider world.

And this wider world included Miss Merritt's School, established, as the sign outside of the administration building—Lockwood Hall—announced, in the year of 1861. And because of this fateful date the entering class of thirty-five girls, housed in a red brick, three-story structure—formerly a tavern—would always remember that part of their extracurricular duties included the rolling of bandages and the knitting of socks for the Army of the Potomac. Now the girls came from all of North America, from Mexico, South America, the islands of the Caribbean, and several from European and Asian countries—all of them lending, as they walked about town, by reason of accent and color, a diverse and global look to a New England village.

Sarah, arriving slightly after one o'clock on January the third, Sunday, felt a sense of coming home. She had lived in Carlisle through her early teen years, lived in fact on School Street, the Congregational church on one side and the woods that marked one edge of the Merritt School property on the other.

But proximity, for children, often means if not contempt, at least boredom. Sarah had seen the girls going about the village in their navy blue school jackets, had watched them pound up and down the field hockey and soccer fields, but had not wanted to be part of a too familiar scene. She had gone to the local public school and, when of high school age, begged to go away to boarding school—please, please, don't send me next door to Miss Merritt's. Her mother had just landed a big contract in New Hampshire—she was a landscape architect—and would be much away from home, and her father, now an environmental consultant for the Department of Interior, was always traveling, so both agreed, and Sarah had spent four reasonably contented years at a school very much like Miss Merritt's.

Now she took the time to drive slowly past her old family house, found it enlarged by a porch, painted yellow, and on the snow-covered lawn saw and heard three shouting children and a barking golden retriever. For a moment, overcome by a wave of nostalgia, she toyed with the idea of revisiting her childhood. But no, time was wasting. She tramped on the accelerator, drove down the curving road, and, after a quarter of a mile of leafless shrubbery and trees, turned into the main school gates—two tall stone columns, each marked with a brass plaque, and nearby a sign sticking out of a melting mound of snow that announced a speed limit of fifteen miles per hour. It was really, she thought, like seeing the whole place with new eyes, coming as a stranger who would be soon earning part of her daily bread as part of the preparatory school machine.

She took her time and drove slowly around the school, noting four green-shuttered, white clapboard dormitories, the two brick Greek revival houses, the new Alexander Library, the glass and steel science hall, and the Nakatani Art Center, as well as a number of smaller shingled and semi-shingled houses scattered haphazardly among the more imposing buildings. Circling about, turning behind and beyond buildings, Sarah decided it was almost a film setting: a town within a town.

In this, Sarah was not much off the mark. Over the years the school had, by hook and occasionally by crook, gobbled up a fair amount of property, complete with houses, barns, fields, and streams, and now sported some thirty acres on School Street (named for the public grammar school that still held sway a short distance north of the Congregational church). Miss Merritt's acres now held not only the school buildings but a variety of playing fields, plus a large wooded section complete with pond. That the pond played host to breeding mosquitos and that the small, roving deer herd supported a population of Lyme disease ticks was a frequent subject of friction between town and gown, among anxious parents, animal lovers, and the environmentally sensitive biology faculty.

On Sarah's third whirl around the campus, through the tangle of narrow roads that wiggled between buildings and past odd plots of ground decorated with heaps of melting snow, Giddy appeared in a parking space by one of the brick buildings. She was waving her arms and shouting a welcome. Sarah pulled to a stop and Patsy let out a howl of joy—Giddy was an old friend. Giddy waved a mittened hand in greeting.

Giddy, tall and broad-shouldered, was a woman built for kicking balls, lifting weights, and hoisting kayaks. Today, in a navy quilted jacket her neck wound about with a yellow and black striped scarf, she looked more like the chief of a wrestling team than the art instructor, the job for which she was hired. But Giddy both coached sports teams and produced minute and delicate woodcuts of a botanical nature—a recent shift from her early oeuvre, heroically sized oils featuring tormented land-scapes and frenzied oceans.

"Hey, Sarah," shouted Giddy—Giddy often shouted. "Pull over there." She pointed to a parking space marked with a "Re-served for Faculty" sign.

Sarah pulled into the space, and Giddy wrenched her pas-senger door open and grabbed a duffel bag. "I'll take this," said Giddy, "and you grab the rest of your stuff. I've got half an hour until I have to go over to the art building and set up for tomor-row. Life class—well, just large sections of the human body. You can't get away with total nudity in boarding school because some parents would raise holy hell. Here's Gregory House. It's not bad. High ceilings and a lot of windows. A laundry in the basement. Kids do their own clothes these days, or at least they're supposed to, but from the look of some of them I'd say that some of the jeans and T-shirts will rot on their backs. Freda Cohen—she teaches math—and husband Joel Cohen—he's

10

photography—are the house parents. Both pretty mellow."

"Wait up," called Sarah as Giddy began striding in the direction of a three-storied building complete with Doric columns and green shutters. "Patsy needs to sniff. And pee. Get his bearings."

Giddy turned around and grinned. "Patsy will fit in just fine. Lots of dogs around. Particularly Madame Guillotine's animal. He's called Szeppi, which isn't exactly a French name. Actually, one of the best things about Madame is her dog. He's kind of neat."

Sarah, after a brief tour around a stand of spruce trees with Patsy, caught up with Giddy. "Do I have classes tomorrow? After all, it's Monday."

"Right, so pull yourself together. The first day of the semester is a little chaotic. Okay, here we are. Use the side vestibule door, everyone does. Kids come in here or through the back. Classrooms are in the basement along with the laundry and heaven knows what else."

Giddy jerked open the door, and Sarah walked in pulling Patsy, her wheeled suitcase bumping over the threshold of the glass-enclosed entry.

A sudden screech. A third party had arrived.

A black, curly-coated hurricane on four legs flung itself onto the scene. Was pulled back by red leash and a second screech. And then, restraining the excited animal by repeated jerks on his leash, the black-clad figure of Madame Grace Marie-Henriette Carpentier appeared.

Sarah hauled Patsy to the door of the vestibule, and Giddy reached for the collar of the newcomer. "Miss Lester," said the woman, "where did this dog come from? We do not need any more dogs in Gregory House."

"Hello there, Madame Carpentier," said Giddy cheerfully. "Meet Patsy. He's a sort of Irish wolfhound, and he belongs to

Sarah Deane. She's a cousin or a cousin-in-law of mine, and she's taking Rachel Himmelfarb's classes for the rest of the year. Sarah, this is Madame Carpentier. She runs the Language Division."

Sarah, listening to Giddy, was able to make a quick examination of the famous—or infamous—Grace Carpentier. The black cloak, seen at close quarters, turned out to be a handsome wool cape, decorated on its collar by a cameo brooch. It was, Sarah thought, the sort of cape that Bela Lugosi might have worn when on the prowl as Dracula. The cape's owner wore a dark purple wool hat that set off a face for which the term "sharp" was entirely inadequate. The nose was a beak, the lips were thin and colorless, the eyebrows dark, the chin pointed, the eyes brown and now shooting sparks in Sarah's direction. Around the face, with its high cheekbones and wide forehead, appeared a rim of black hair pulled back under the hat's protecting brim.

Sarah advanced with her hand extended. "Hello, Madame Carpentier." Seeing the frown that appeared, she throttled a remark about having heard so much about her and ended weakly by saying how nice it was to meet one of the faculty before she'd even had time to unpack.

Grace Carpentier ignored Sarah's outstretched hand. "So, you are keeping that animal on campus?" she demanded crossly.

"Why, yes," said Sarah, taken aback. "I was told there were other dogs at the school, and Patsy is perfectly harmless. He's just big. He was a stray I found in Texas and about to be put to sleep. He'd been abandoned." This story, Sarah had found, won minds and softened hearts.

But not the heart of Madame Carpentier. "We have already at this school enough dogs," she snapped. "I suggest you find out if you will be allowed to keep this animal here." Madame Carpentier gave another jerk at her leash, said in a softer voice,

"*Alors*, Szeppi, come," and strode off in the direction of a rise of ground that in the spring must have been a garden, but now showed a wasteland of brown shrubbery and a snow-frosted, trellised archway.

2

SARAH looked after the retreating black-caped figure and shrugged. "So welcome to Miss Merritt's."

"Hey," said Giddy, "that wasn't the full treatment. Grace must not be feeling up to par. She's capable of going over to the office and demanding Patsy be made into a carpet." Then, seeing Sarah's worried face, she added, "Listen. Forget it. By tonight she'll have something else to be mad at. But one thing you should watch out for."

"Which is?"

"If you're assigned to one of the rooms she uses, be sure you leave the place as you found it, board erased, chairs in order. I know it sounds like third-grade stuff, but if you want peace you'll do it. Now let's get you settled. I'll take your duffel. The apartment's on the third floor, which means climbing stairs, but you won't have a lot of students barging up and down the hall. Only a few seniors on the third floor. I've talked one of them into giving you the grand tour before Sunday tea."

"Tea? We have tea?"

"Ancient custom. Radnor Hall. In the Old Library. Not *the* library—Radnor's just a place for school archives and old books. Victorian Gothic, paneled walls, portraits, casement windows. It's a time for mixing it up. Faculty and senior girls. Selected people from the town, like one of the ministers or the fire chief or a Girl Scout leader. One of the town librarians."

"Is there a reason for all this?"

"Oh, Merritt's has a reach-out community program. The girls sign up to work in the nursery schools or the day-care centers or with the Scouts. Or visit the infirm."

Giddy led the way and Sarah followed, up the three flights of stairs to a hall punctuated by several closed doors decorated with decals, banners, logos, and questionable quotations, then down the corridor, this carpeted with some industrial-strength material the color of cow dung.

"There you are," said Giddy. She pointed ahead to a white-painted door unadorned except for a small brass knocker in the shape of a fish. "Your apartment looks over the side parking lot. It belonged to Mrs. Varcaro, who did European history, but she's on leave this year, so it was up for grabs." Giddy dropped the duffel with a thump on the floor. "Here's your key. The outside doors are locked at night, and everyone is supposed to lock their room door, too. Your key works for both. Everyone has keys, and God help you if you lose them. I did, and you'd think I'd opened up the school to Iranian terrorists. Or rapists from Boston."

"And Madame Guillotine? Is she a neighbor?"

"Nothing's perfect. She has the apartment at the end of the hall. Looking over the garden. Senior faculty get things like that. Views of gardens."

Sarah took the key, inserted it into the lock, and pushed the door open. Walking in, she found herself in a square room with two long windows, a small oak desk, two chairs upholstered in green vinyl, a two-cushion sofa covered in a floral pattern, and against a window an oak gateleg table surrounded by three pine chairs. Beyond this window stood a curtained alcove from which could be seen the end posts of a bed. A second alcove to the left of the living area featured a small, four-burner electric stove and a waist-high refrigerator, plus a row of painted shelves protected by a green gingham curtain. The living room rug was multi-colored with frayed ends, and the walls featured faded geometric paper in rose and green. All in all, Sarah decided, the room looked as if it had been furnished by means of yard sales, but was on the whole perfectly comfortable, if not for an entire teaching life, certainly for a semester's sojourn.

"Cozy," announced Giddy, hauling in Patsy and unfastening his leash. "Now, if you need anything, I'm underneath on the second floor. I've left coffee, tea, sugar, and other stuff until you can shop. But keep an eye out for Szeppi. He runs up and down the corridor for exercise and likes to hide under beds."

"Like my bed."

"Exactly. And . . ." At which the black, curly-coated dog rushed into the room, whirled, barked, rolled on his back, barked again, grabbed hold of Patsy's ear and tugged, and then let go and shot into the bedroom alcove and under the bed.

Sarah plunged after him, threw herself down, reached under the bed, detached Szeppi's teeth from the hem of the bedspread, and brought up a struggling bundle of black, curly fur. Keeping a grip on the dog, she hoisted the animal on its back two legs and looked it over.

"God," said Giddy. "Speak of the devil. It's worth your life if you hurt him. Just shove him out of the room."

"Actually," said Sarah, turning the wriggling dog around for a better look, "he's kind of cute. Sort of a Portuguese Water dog type crossed with a black lamb."

"Put him down," said Giddy between clenched teeth.

"You've already made an impression on Carpentier. Don't over-do it."

But at that, the door opened wider and in came not Grace Carpentier but a small, round, and rosy woman bundled in a coat. Giddy gave a sigh of relief. "Oh hi, Babette. I'm glad it's you. Szeppi's loose. This is Sarah Deane, who's taking Rachel's classes. Sarah, this is Babette Leclerc. She's the French Department."

"Not *the* French Department," said the woman. "Just an underling. I ran into Grace on the way to the library, and she told me to take Szeppi home, that it was too sloppy out. He got away when I was closing the vestibule door. He's a real escape artist."

"It's a day for dogs," observed Giddy. "That's Patsy, over there. He's an Irish wolfhound." She pointed to one of the upholstered chairs over which Patsy had draped himself.

"Goodness," said Babette, backing up a step.

"He's perfectly harmless," said Sarah for about the thousandth time in her life. She took a tight hold of Szeppi, who seemed to be ready to go on with the wrestling match. "And he doesn't even seem to mind Szeppi."

"Yes, Grace told me to beware of a new dog. You know how Grace talks. She doesn't think about the effect of the things she says."

"She is," said Giddy stoutly, "a teacher of languages, and she knows exactly what's she's saying, and don't you deny it."

Babette paused, and Sarah thought she was on the edge of agreeing with Giddy but had thought better of it. Instead she reached over to a now quiet Szeppi and took hold of his collar. "Szeppi isn't a bad dog, just a little wild at times."

"I'm glad to meet you," said Sarah. "Do you have a room, an apartment in this building?"

"No," said Babette in what seemed to both listeners a thankful voice, "but I teach in the basement. French One and French Two. And Intro French lit."

"Are you French?" asked Sarah.

"I'm from Montreal, but I did study for a year in Lyon. And, after all, Grace herself was named for her mother, a Grace Briggs from Maine. She's only half-French, but she'd never admit it." She turned to Sarah. "Will I see you at the Sunday Tea this afternoon? It's a good chance to meet the rest of us."

Sarah was about to say yes, she was looking forward to it, when heavy footsteps sounded in the hall, followed by an explosion into the room. Grace Marie-Henriette Carpentier. Disguised as a mud pie. Wet and muddy from top to toe. From the collar of her black wool cape to the pointed toes of her black boots. Her wool hat was gone, her black hair astray, and she was in a major rage, sputtering and stamping her feet. Babette rushing to her began ineffectually to brush at the bits of grit and sand and melting lumps of snow and wet leaves stuck to her sodden person.

Grace turned on Babette. "Get away, you're making it worse. You are rubbing the dirt in. Look at me. *Regardez ici*. Students with snowballs, and then I was pushed. From behind. Into the mud and the snow. And give me Szeppi this very minute." She seized the dog's collar, whirled around, started for the door, and spied Giddy. "Your students. Your art students. And I saw you with them out in the snow last week. Teaching sculpture, you said. A fine thing. Sculpture in the snow. Playing in class time like children. I will find them, those students, find out who they are if it takes a hundred years, *je vous assure*."

Here Madame Carpentier stopped, inhaled, marched over to the door, and departed, the sound of her boots making a soft tattoo down the carpeted corridor.

"Oh dear, wouldn't you know!" exclaimed Babette, clasping her hands together in distress. She looked at the open door and took a step forward, but halted and made no further move to follow her fellow instructor. Sarah, during Madame's rather dramatic entrance, had used the time to take the measure of this second French teacher. Round as a teapot, rosy of face with a double chin, china-blue eyes, and the sort of bunched, blond hair that threatened to escape from a number of barrettes. She still wore a mottled-green oversize raincoat pulled together with a belt and now fluttered her hands to emphasize her distress.

"Relax, Babette," said Giddy. "She can't eat you. I suppose she just slipped and fell into the snow and then decided to blame the students."

"No," said Babette slowly. "I don't think she made it up. I think it's the sort of thing the students do. I have some of the ones she had in first-year French in my French literature class, and they're—what's the word—traumatized."

"Is she," asked Sarah, choosing her words carefully, "an effective French teacher? I mean, do her students actually learn anything? Because how could they if they're quivering wrecks the whole time?"

But Babette had begun nodding before Sarah finished. "That's the thing. She pounds French into their heads. If the students stay with her, they actually do amazingly well. They begin to think in French and get advanced placements, honors, and scholarships to study in France. But of course a lot of them can't stand the heat."

"And you," said Giddy, "are the kinder, gentler teacher?"

"Who doesn't get half the results Grace does," said Babette reluctantly. "I'm too easy, I don't *demand* results so I don't get them." And then, listening to a call down the hall, she said, "I'm coming, Grace."

"I thought so," she told Giddy and Sarah. "She wants help. And a little compassion. And to take her things to the dry cleaners."

"Are you her slave?" said Giddy.

"I need this job," said Babette. "I need Grace, and I'm used to her. It could be worse. Carlo Leone might be the head of the

Language Division. I'll see you at tea, Sarah. Welcome to Miss Merritt's."

"Carlo Leone?" said Sarah, turning to Giddy. "Is that someone else I'll have to watch?"

But Giddy was looking at her watch. "I've got to get over to the arts building. Forget about Carlo. He's a maverick who wants half the faculty hung up by their thumbs. He's on the shifty side, but he does have a sense of humor. There are worse people."

"Don't tell me about them," said Sarah. "This is my first day."

"Yeah, right. Listen, I've got Hannah Hoyt coming over to lead you around and point out Radnor Hall for the tea scene. Hannah's a senior in my art class, quite talented." With which Giddy strode to the door and almost walked into a girl who had a hand lifted to knock. She was very tall, auburn-haired, with a splash of freckles across her face—the sort of freckles that do not fade in the winter. She was wearing rubber boots, had a blue and white striped scarf wound around her neck, and wore a navy sweatshirt with "Merritt Soccer" writ large across its back.

"Oops," said Giddy, backing up. "There you are, Hannah. Listen," she said, adopting a teacherly frown, "you didn't by any chance just try to shove Madame Carpentier into a snowbank? Don't even answer that question, but tell your no-good, lousy friends if they even thought about doing it—well, to cut it out, or the whole Arts Department will be under the gun, and you guys will be on detention until you graduate. If you graduate." Giddy shook her fist at Hannah for emphasis, turned to Sarah, made a brief introduction, and took herself off.

After Patsy had been settled on the comforter at the foot of her bed and her door carefully locked behind her—as instructed by Giddy—Sarah found herself conducted by Hannah Hoyt on a whirlwind campus tour—the Althorne Gym with its workout room, basketball courts, indoor track and swimming pool; the Chang Science Building; the assorted dormitories; the infirmary; the admissions office; and finally the glory of the Nakatani Art Center. Hannah was a cheerful and efficient guide, prattling about this and that, and lingering only once in the doorway of the largest of two art studios. "I'm working on a set of images to go with some poetry," she announced as they stood gazing at a forest of tables and easels.

Fatigue was beginning to set in, and although Sarah didn't want to sound discouraging, she settled for a murmured "That sounds interesting" and turned to leave.

"Don't worry," said Hannah. "I'm not about to hit you over the head with a fifty-page epic. I'm into satire. Stuff with an edge. Just a few lines of my own and some cut-outs to go with it. Paper shapes, blues and purples and burnt umber. A slash of yellow. Sepia. Not exactly realistic. More like, what's the word, provocative. Suggestive. Now I'll take you back so you can change before tea."

"This tea is formal?" asked Sarah, running over her low-key wardrobe, one designed more for utility than fashion.

"Students—the seniors—are supposed to be clean and neat and not be in jeans and T-shirts or sweats. The men mostly wear jackets and ties or turtlenecks. Except for Mr. Leone, who turns up in any old thing. The faculty women go in for dresses, skirts, or stretchy pants with some kind of top thing."

And Sarah, wondering if she even owned a decent pair of pants with a "top thing," hurried after Hannah, who now that they were out of the arts building was striding ahead. "We'll take a shortcut through the garden," she called over her shoulder.

Leading the way, Hannah ran up a flight of flagstone steps, crusted and icy now that the skies had darkened to slate and the late-afternoon January temperature had dropped. Pressing forward, shivering, Sarah almost ran into Hannah.

The girl had stopped and was standing under the trellis.

"Jesus H. Christ," she said. And raised her hand. Pointing.

For a minute, Sarah couldn't see anything. The trellis was built as an arch, over which roses or clematis or honeysuckle presumably climbed in the summer and died back in the winter, leaving a straggle of brown, snake-like twigs and branches. And then she saw it.

Hanging down from the center of the arch was a figure. A black, witchlike shape about twelve inches long. A cut-out made of stiff material formed a rudimentary cape with arms protruding sideways, and the head of the figure was topped by a purple paper headpiece. But that was not the whole of it. Around the figure's neck a dead twig of a climbing plant had been twined. As if it had been hanged. Or had hanged itself.

"Christ," said Hannah again. Softly, almost reverently. Then she reached up, carefully pulled the circling twig loose from the figure's neck, and brought the object down to eye level.

Sarah, who had been holding her breath, now exhaled and extended a hand. "This should be reported," she said.

But Hannah shook her head and pulled away, putting the paper figure behind her back. "No, no. Absolutely not. Listen, they'll nail me on it for sure. Everyone knows I've been doing cut-outs. I did one of the varsity field hockey coach just last week. Only it wasn't nasty. I mean, I didn't hang him. And everyone knows I've been put on restriction for the next three weekends by Madame Carpentier. They'll think I'm threatening her."

"Never mind, just go to the head or the dean—someone—and tell the truth," Sarah urged.

"Please. Please, no. Listen, this thing is awful. Disgusting. Completely disgusting. I'm tearing it up." And before Sarah could stop her, Hannah pulled the figure into two pieces, and then four pieces. Tore the head from the shoulders, the arms from the body, ripped the cape in two, and crushed the whole between two angry hands.

"Disgusting," she repeated. And then seeing Sarah's

shocked look, she said, "Listen, Miss Deane. Or Dr. Deane, who-ever you are, well, forget it. Some people have this sick sense of humor. It's meant to be a joke, only it's not funny. Probably a freshman. They do things like this because they're still kids. Fourteen and fifteen. And hey, it's not as bad as shoving Madame Carpentier into a snowbank, which I heard happened this afternoon. I mean, that was like an assault. You can get arrested for assault. This stupid thing is a kind of scare tactic. Look, I'm going to get rid of it." Hannah took the pieces of black paper and pushed them deep under the soft snow and into the half-frozen mud at the edge of the garden steps, and then stamped on the snow with her thick boots.

"There," she said with satisfaction. "The pieces can just rot there, and by spring, when the snow melts, there won't be any-thing left." She straightened her shoulders and resumed her role as a tour guide. "Now you've got to get ready for the tea. Meet the crowd. The town movers and shakers. Dr. Singer wants us all to be one huge, happy Carlisle family."

"You aren't?" asked Sarah.

"Not quite. I mean, the school needs to get along with the town, and the town needs the school. Taxes and stuff like that. But a lot of people who live in the town think the school is a breeding pit for snobs. Which isn't exactly true. Forty percent of the girls are on some sort of financial aid or get scholarship help."

"But the word doesn't get out?"

"We don't have that much interaction. We've got our classes and schedules, so we can't spend a lot of time making friends outside. Then Alumnae Day comes around, or Parents' Week-end, and in roll those SUVs and Saabs and Volvos, and then these groups of Old Girls go flashing their school rings, clicking around in their alligator shoes, and clanking their gold brace-lets, and some local people are, like, totally turned off."

"But," Sarah pointed out, "half of Carlisle drives expensive cars, and the houses in town aren't exactly tents made out of boiled Yak wool. Or Lincoln log cabins."

"You have a point," said Hannah. "A lot of the Boston suburbs don't have what you call affordable housing."

"Do you think that someone from the town might have strung up that paper puppet of Madame Carpentier?"

Hannah considered the question and then shook her head. "I don't think so. She's really more an in-school ogre than a town one. In town she gets along. At least I've heard she does. Plays bridge with some ladies' group in Carlisle, and she speaks to the Carlisle High School PTA about language classes and goes to Saint Irene's—the Catholic church—and helps with their rummage sale. I'd say this was as inside joke. And other teachers get picked on, too. Like Ms. Goshawk in History of Art. Someone last year did a scanner thing of Goshawk's head imposed on that Titian painting of a nude Venus. But look, I've got to get along." Hannah turned and raised her mittened hand and pointed. "See that pointed roof over there, that's Radnor. The Old Library's in the back. See you later."

Checking her watch, Sarah found that she had twenty minutes in which to take a quick shower and change. Time even to consider how much weight to give two incidents involving an unpopular but noted teacher. Did this sort of thing happen commonly, as Hannah seemed to suggest? Good God, Madame Carpentier had been at Merritt's for, what was it, seventeen, eighteen years, so she couldn't be *that* bad. As Babette Leclerc had testified, she sent superbly trained—if battle-hardened—students out into the world, ready to win honors and ready to speak, if needed, flawless and idiomatic French—a teaching record not to be sniffed at.

Yes, she decided, no school with an eye to increasing school applications in today's competitive secondary school world would hang on to a female Iago if she didn't have some powerful redeeming qualities.

24

All through her unpacking, her satisfying shower, her dressing in what she decided was an adequate "Sunday tea at school" costume—long, black wool skirt, linen vest, white turtleneck, and long silver earrings—Sarah remained troubled. Even as she examined herself in the mirror hanging over the low bureau and even after deciding her new, very short haircut made her look sharp and academic, a chic but serious woman—she had qualms.

Sarah, through association with her husband, Alex—physician and one of Maine's medical examiners—and through occasional excursions taken with assorted family members, had been mixed up in a number of untoward incidents and so had come to be highly suspicious of anything that even distantly smelled of trouble.

And this paper puppet of Madame Grace Marie-Henriette Carpentier found hanging by the neck in the school garden smelled to high heaven of hazard and violence—in short of trouble. Well, it didn't really do to shove these signs—Sarah balked at the word "evidence"—of trouble under the snow. Hiding the shredded pieces of the puppet, not giving it publicity, might well encourage more of the same. Possibly something considerably nastier.

Thoughtfully Sarah locked her door, slipped the key into the deep pocket of her skirt, pulled her winter coat about her, and headed down the stairs, out of Gregory House, and leaning into a rising north wind, she struggled along the icy brick walk toward Radnor Hall. By the time she reached the heavy front door with its well-shined brass knocker in the shape of either a peculiarly ugly angel or an impish gargoyle—school opinion was split on this—Sarah had made up her mind. The paper puppet fragments would not be resting under the snow and frozen mud until the spring. She, Sarah, would see to that.

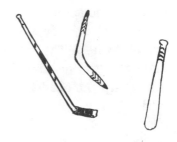

3

SARAH, shoving the matter of a shredded paper puppet aside, braced herself for a period of sociability that might give her a feel for life in an all-girl boarding school at the beginning of a new century. After the rage for secondary co-education had somewhat subsided, single-sex schools emerged from being considered places of unnatural confinement to institutions that nurtured confidence and independence. Well, there was no lack of these qualities here if her recent tour guide, Hannah Hoyt, was any example. Of course, this tea affair, packed with faculty and visiting VIPs and only senior girls, could not be expected to serve up a real sense of the place. For that she needed to experience the school at exam time, dormitories after lights-out, the frenzy after a soccer game, and the classroom ambience on a dreary winter Monday morning and its opposite, the same classroom on any Friday with a weekend shimmering on the horizon.

And then there was the problem of being a newly arrived

person and so an object up for inspection. There would be names and faces to remember, in-jokes to smile at politely, and under-currents eddying about that she would sense but not understand. A boarding school, like any closed community, has its own private vocabulary, its villains, its factions and counter-factions, and its own arcane ethos, and these would only be revealed to the newcomer after a certain amount of time had passed. Sarah had never forgotten her early days as a lecturer in Bowmouth College's English Department, when she had invited two mortal enemies for dinner. While she and Alex tried to be cheery, they watched one glower and disfigure her food with an angry fork while the other, a more sensitive flower, drank himself via a succession of martinis into a stupor and had to be assisted home.

And now, like some newly arrived tropical fish, Sarah would be dropped into the aquarium to make her away among the guppies, the mollies, and the fighting fish; and in her turn to swim about, she would be dodging and circling and, while she was at it, perhaps getting some sort of sense of Madame Carpentier. Certainly that lady would now show herself to a much better advantage among her peers—or subordinates—than when Sarah had seen her in Gregory House, dripping with wet and dirty snow.

Sarah hung her jacket in what was designated on a polished brass plate as the "Cloak Room"—a relic from the days of Miss Claudia Merritt, when women actually wore cloaks—and edged her way into the Old Library. This proved to be a rectangular room, carpeted with ancient orientals in red and dark blue and paneled in oak. Two marble fireplaces faced each other across the room, and low, glass-fronted bookcases marched around the walls. The whole chamber was lit by a trio of chandeliers whose oval glass globes resembled nothing so much as a series of lighted hanging breasts.

Sarah, removing her fascinated gaze from these last wonders, began to consider at what point she should insert herself into the crowd and begin to mingle, and then she saw that Giddy had joined her.

Giddy pointed at the chandeliers. "Those are the hanging tits. The ones in the faculty lounge are the hanging boobs—they're completely round—and the ones in Dr. Singer's office have little gold crowns and are called the crowned tits."

"Does Dr. Singer call them the crowned tits?" asked Sarah, wanting a clue to her new boss.

"Well, she's careful, because you never know about some of the sensibilities around here. Someone's grandmother lurking. Okay, ready to mingle?"

Sarah squared her shoulders. "As ready as I ever will be. Who are the sharks, and who are the harmless bottom-feeders? Start with Dr. Singer. I only had a phone interview with her."

"Dr. Joanna Singer," said Giddy, "plays her cards close to her chest—make that breasts. Anyway, plays it cool. Not exactly a person you get intimate with—at least I don't—but she keeps the school on an even keel and somehow manages to hit it off with fascist parents and congressmen daddies from D.C. Plus, she manages to keep all those Old Girls happy, because some of the ones from the forties and fifties are shocked shitless at kids wearing jeans and tacking up pictures of naked rock stars on their walls. It's a real balancing act."

"Okay," said Sarah. "I've got the picture. Who's the one you called a loose cannon?"

"Oh yeah, that's Carlo Leone. He's a joker. Sometimes. And you never know, he can be a real pain in the ass. Teaches Italian, though not that many kids sign up for it. He really comes out of the English Department and teaches one freshman English section and European lit—comparative lit, they call it. You'll be bumping into him—he's hard to avoid. Or you'll be bumped *by* him. And over there, under the portrait of our lady founder, Miss Merritt, is Babette Leclerc—you've met her rescuing Grace's dog. And here's Dr. Singer."

And Sarah, who had accepted a cup of semi-warm tea and a cucumber sandwich, found herself spun in a half circle and presented to a tall woman with a neat, upswept swirl of bronze hair, a long face with high, arched eyebrows, glasses on a beaded chain, and a long, taut body nicely fitted into a gray jacket and matching skirt, the whole finished off with a high-necked, fluted white shirt. An academic costume, Sarah thought in a split-second examination, for all seasons.

"Oh yes," said Dr. Joanna Singer. "We've met over the telephone. How nice. Dr. Deane. Sarah Deane. I'm Joanna, and thank you, Giddy, for bringing her over. We are delighted that you could help us out until Rachel comes back." She turned to Sarah, and Giddy melted away to the other end of the room.

Sarah, feeling like someone being interviewed for a slot in an especially competitive college, found herself delivering a quick sketch of her past life and acknowledging her unfamiliarity with an up-to-the-minute, state-of-the-art girls' boarding school.

"I was at Miss Morton's a million years ago," said Sarah, "and I taught grade school for a couple of years, and since then I've been at Bowmouth. Boarding school is fuzzy in my mind, and so I'll have to start from scratch."

"I'm sure our girls will keep you on your toes," said Dr. Singer, "but I'm sure, too, that after suffering with college students who often revert to a second childhood, you won't have too much trouble. Now, I'd like you to meet some of our faculty. Oh, Babette." Sarah found her teapot-shaped acquaintance of the afternoon, now in sober green silk with a knitted matching vest, summoned, and in a deft combination of introduction and farewell, Sarah was cut loose and found herself escorted to the tea table.

"It must be hard, Sarah," said Babette, offering Sarah a tea cake, "keeping us all straight."

"But I certainly remember you," said Sarah. "Szeppi and Madame Carpentier. And Dr. Singer is impressive. She'd make a good senator."

"Or special prosecutor," said Babette. "She runs an efficient school, but I wouldn't want to cross her if things got serious."

"Do they ever?"

"Don't they always?" returned Babette. "We need a tough nut as the head of school. A boarding school is simply seething sometimes, and the faculty, well, they're human."

Sarah grinned. "I'll bet that's an understatement."

"Drink your tea because I'm supposed to introduce you at least to the heads of the divisions."

"You mean departments?"

"No. The school is divided into major divisions. The Language Division, the Art Division, Science Division, History, Performing Arts, which includes Music, the Athletic Division, and so on."

"And underneath are the departments, like the English Department is under the Language Division."

"Right. And Grace Carpentier wears three hats. She's head of the Language Division and the Foreign Language Department and runs the French classes."

"Good God."

"Don't jump to conclusions, and don't listen to whatever Hannah Hoyt told you. Hannah was kicked out of French the first semester and then was taken back into the class—special request of her mother—so Hannah acts like she's having her fingernails pulled during every class."

"But you get along with Madame Carpentier?"

"We have our little moments, but I make it my business to get along. As I think I said. And some of the things that have been happening are, well, there's no excuse for them."

"You mean hitting Madame with snowballs."

"And the scarecrow and the effigy on the school sign."

"What!" Sarah had an instant flashback of the black paper doll hanging from the garden trellis.

"Oh, both were stupid jokes. You'll hear about them. The latest was just before Christmas vacation. A choir robe, taken from the costume room—we don't have a choir anymore, and the girls use the robes at Halloween—was hung up on the school sign—the one that says "Miss Merritt's School, Established 1861"—with a sign tacked on that said 'Home of the Witch.' "

"A little more than a stupid joke," observed Sarah. She put down her empty teacup on a marble-topped table and turned her head slightly, looked about, and almost immediately caught sight of the lady in question. Grace Carpentier was in conversation—animated and cheerful, if expressions could be trusted—with an elegant-looking man who sported a bottle-green jacket with what appeared to be, at that distance, a velvet collar.

Babette followed her gaze. "Grace just shrugged it off, but I think she was hurt. Although it would take an earthquake to make her admit it. That's Adrian Parsons she's talking to. He thinks very well of himself. Number two in the Language Division and seems to get along with Grace."

Sarah gave Adrian an appraising glance and then returned to the matter of the choir robe. "But this scarecrow, the effigy business?"

But Babette had lost interest in the subject. "Come on," she said. "Dr. Singer—Joanna—said to hustle you around. You can meet Adrian Parsons and have another shot at Grace, who may not remember meeting your dog." She tugged at Sarah's sleeve, and together they joined the Parsons-Carpentier couple.

"Hello, Adrian. Grace. Here's Sarah Deane, who's filling in for Rachel. Grace, I thought you'd like to meet Sarah Deane. Formally in a proper school setting."

Adrian Parsons, equipped with a high forehead, an aquiline nose, a long mouth, a firm chin, and gray hair smoothed across a notable skull, extended an elegant hand—the sort of hand that popular literature associates with playing long passages of Debussy—and for a moment, Sarah thought he was going to raise it to his lips. But he held it for one millisecond more than necessary and then returned it to its owner.

"What a pleasure. Professor Deane. Or is it Doctor Deane, or simply Ms. Deane? Help me."

"Just plain Sarah, please. How do you do, and hello again, Madame Carpentier."

"This is the one with the very large dog," said Grace Carpentier, but in a voice that had lost its earlier edge.

"Grace here," said Adrian Parsons, "is a great dog lover."

"I have met Szeppi," said Sarah. "He's very friendly."

"We will get along very well," said Grace, "if your dog will leave Szeppi alone. Szeppi has a very great sensibility."

"So has Patsy," said Sarah firmly. "And I promise that he won't touch a hair on Szeppi's head." She reached one hand behind her and crossed her fingers.

"Grace tells me," said Adrian Parsons, "that the school malcontents have been throwing snowballs at her, and I told her that only yesterday I found my classroom desk drawer packed with little snippets of Styrofoam. Impossible to clean up. We are all victims." He looked down at Sarah and allowed himself a small smile. "Now, call me Adrian. None of this doctor or professor business. All one happy family," he added with a lifted eyebrow and a look at Grace.

"I believe," said Grace, "that you, Miss Deane, will be sharing a classroom with me. Not my regular language room—that is for me alone—but for my senior seminars in French literature

32

I use one of the English Department workshop rooms. I will show you tomorrow how I wish the room to be left. And how I will leave it for you. The desks in order. The blackboard cleaned."

"Madame Carpentier," said Adrian Parsons, "sets the standard for all of us. Her classrooms are miracles of order. St. Cyr and West Point and Sandhurst could take instruction from her."

Sarah, her ear attuned, wondered if under the compliment lay just the merest hint of sarcasm, but then she saw him reach for one of Grace's hands, this time actually raise it halfway to his lips, and bow his sleek gray head over it. And Grace Carpentier gave a gracious nod, seeming to accept the tribute as her just due.

This moment of gallantry allowed Sarah to murmur her delight at meeting them all and do a two-step sidle toward the nearest exit, but then she found herself blocked by the conscientious Babette, who seemed to feel that Sarah must make a full job of meeting everyone.

A whirlwind tour followed, one that included a hearty handshake from the fire chief, Lester McBride, who reminded her to check her room's smoke alarm. Next, a quick exchange with a woman named Lizzy, who was either the crew or the cross-country coach—Sarah couldn't quite make it out. The tour finally wound up with an encounter with a short, slender woman wearing a woven, heathery garment with a fringed hem. She had a pointed chin, a high forehead, very blue eyes magnified by heavy, rimless glasses, and glossy black hair cut in a square bob. Triple ropes of varicolored beads hung around her neck and chinked gently as she moved. Oddly enough, Sarah thought, even with its echoes of art-in-the-sixties, the effect was somehow one of coordinated chic.

"This," said Babette, "is Anita Goshawk. She's in History of Art and runs a very tight ship."

Anita Goshawk, who appeared on the fragile side, took

Sarah's hand in a grip of iron, said welcome in a cool and modulated voice, and said she hoped to see Sarah at the lecture she was giving Friday at the Carlisle Art Center. "Next to the grade school. Nineteenth-century American painting. It will be open to the town, but I'm hoping for faculty support"—here Anita gave Sarah a meaningful look—"and so I'm asking everyone to come."

Sarah smiled, said "How very interesting" and that she would certainly try, and glided away, taking an exit route that took her along the glass-fronted bookcases of what appeared to be volumes of considerable antiquity. Later, she told herself, I'll sneak in here and see what they have. Sarah had begun a modest collection of nineteenth-century New England fiction and wondered what of that ilk Miss Merritt's Old Library had on its shelves. She had just made it through a side door leading directly to an outside stone walkway when she was stopped abruptly by a large foot stuck in front of her and a large hand holding itself before her face. A man who appeared to be over ten feet tall.

"Halt," said a voice. "Who goes there?"

"What?" said Sarah, startled. She looked up and saw a blond bushy-haired man with heavy eyebrows and a jutting chin. His tweed jacket was rumpled and showed several loose threads, his khakis were creased, and his tie was askew.

"You got away," said the man accusingly. "I saw Babette the Rabbit had you in tow, and I thought you'd be doing the rounds, curtsying to the nobles and simpering at Lord Parsons and cringing before Madame Guillotine, and here you are, sneaking out like the scullery maid with silver spoons in her pocket."

"Who," said Sarah crossly, "are you?" Fatigue, the long day, and the meeting of new people had all begun to catch up with her, and she wanted the peace of her room, perhaps a walk with Patsy, before she faced up to the ordeal of a community dinner.

"I am," said the man, seizing her hand and bowing his head in an exact replica of Adrian Parsons' gesture, "Carlo Leone. Actually, Carlo Antonio Leone. Not 'Doctor' or 'Professor.' A simple 'mister.' Master's degree only. Call me Carlo. Or Carl if you have anti-Italian feelings."

"You teach Italian?" said Sarah, remembering Giddy's briefing.

"Yes, I have a few students who were kicked out of Grace's class, or couldn't fit into the Spanish sections, or hate the Germans, or don't feel up to Cyrillic alphabets or Japanese characters. We start out with *buongiorno* and *arrivederci*, and that's about where we end up. I have these dreams of working up to Dante, but so far no luck."

"But you're in the English Department, too," said Sarah, thinking that here stood the one who was a "loose cannon."

"Correct. I am *in* the English Department. But not *the* English Department. That's John Terhune, but he's off on sabbatical. Under Johnny, we have yours truly and a number of peons, serfs, and varlets spreading the word and stamping out the sentence fragment. Of which you will now be yet another one."

"But the Language Division?" began Sarah, who wanted to find out to what extent Grace Carpentier would control her own teaching program.

Carlo Leone shook his head. "The English Department is not a free nation. We are but an abused colony of the Language Division, on which the sun never sets. Grace the Knife is our chief, Sir Adrian Parsons is number two, Babette Leclerc, bless her soul, is number three. We would like to have a little revolution, but those things take time. Rounding up the partisans, the *popolo* taking to the barricades. All that takes energy, which I haven't got. Besides, our leader, Dr. Singer, probably doesn't need a shake-up from within. She has enough on her plate with the alumnae wanting things to stay just as they were when Grover Cleveland was in the White House."

Sarah mentally shook herself. It was time to break loose from this man, entertaining as he might be. She extended a hand, began to thank him, but he stopped her.

"Yes, I'll let you go. But remember me on these Sunday night tea party sessions." Here he pushed his jacket aside, fished in a back pocket, and brought out a flat silver container.

"Brandy," he announced. "I do this as a service to my fellow workers. I bring cheer and warm feeling, and I have a large following. Just spiked our head librarian's teacup."

"And you don't get caught?"

"Corrupting the morals of minors? The senior girls who are allowed in on the festivities? They are all about as innocent as Lucretia Borgia. But I'm circumspect. I am swift of hand, and the attendance at these tea affairs would drop like a stone if I were not circulating with my flask."

Sarah smiled in spite of herself. "You'd better go on back then," she said, "and get on with the good work."

It was dark by the time Sarah took Patsy out for a tour of the winter gardens and around the perimeter of a small frozen pond, returned to her room, finished unpacking, and braced herself for dinner. But this passed more pleasantly than she had expected. Babette and Giddy called for her, the dinner was cafeteria-style, the faculty chose small, round tables at the end of the dining room or, if they were in a democratic mood, joined a student group. Before long, Sarah found herself back in her room after Patsy had been given one more airing and had not even ruffled his neck fur at the distant sight of Szeppi being walked.

And then it was time to think about digging up those scraps of paper. Sarah decided that she would wait until the senior girls' lights-out—eleven P.M.—and then slip out into the night and do a hasty job of disinterment. There was even an implement available; she had spied a rusty trowel lying partly hidden under a motley collection of rubber boots and lacrosse and field hockey sticks in the vestibule of Gregory House.

Everything worked as if Sarah had planned and rehearsed the event for weeks. She pulled on her green windbreaker and a navy blue pair of pants, pulled on her boots, and jammed a black polar-fleece cloche on her head. Then, moving with the stealth of a practiced felon, she stole down the stairs, slipped through the heavy, locked inner door, laid hold of the trowel, opened the glass storm door of the vestibule, and padded quickly up the small rise of ground and flight of stone steps that led to the Spring Garden and the trellis. Although it was a cloudy, moonless night, the houses and dormitories and the parking lots were all ringed with lampposts, and these lent a soft bloom to the night as well as added eerie shadows to the dark shrubbery that edged the roads and the garden path.

To be sure, there was a problem finding exactly where to dig, and Sarah spent a certain amount of time on her knees, exploring with stiffened fingers the half-frozen, inhospitable soil. But after some futile scratching and probing, she came upon a slightly jagged stretch of disturbed soil and began to dig with her trowel. And, to borrow a phrase, hit pay dirt.

Only five minutes of thrusting and scrabbling and she was rewarded with a number of half-frozen, muddy scraps of paper. Carefully, she lifted one tiny piece after the other and put them in a pile by her side. She regretted not bringing her flashlight, conspicuous as that might have been, because she couldn't be sure if she had rescued all the pieces—too many of them had already partly transformed themselves into scraps that looked like small, dead leaves. But after a few more minutes of probing, she gave it up and began pushing the soil back in place, smoothing the surface, and pressing down hard on the place of excavation.

Carefully she gathered her booty, transferred the muddy pieces to her windbreaker pocket, and then, straightening a now aching back, she got quietly to her feet.

And faced directly into a sudden explosion of light. A light that blinded her, a light that only around the edges gave her the hideous news that a figure, a figure with a heavy-duty flashlight, was only ten inches away from her nose.

The light was lowered, a hand reached out and took firm hold of her arm, and a gruff voice sounded.

"What," said the voice, "do you think you are doing?"

4

"OH, shit!" That summed up Sarah's feelings, but did nothing to make the person move the blinding light out of her face. Sarah shielded her eyes with one hand and backed up.

The flashlight was lowered to shoulder level, but the hand on her arm remained firm. "Could I ask again," said the voice, the tone calm and reasonable, "what you are doing? I'm Officer Jake Markham. Security at Merritt's School and also with the Carlisle police. So please answer my question."

Sarah had used those few seconds to pull her frantic thoughts into some sane and coherent form. "I'm the new English teacher," she said, trying to keep her voice level. "I'm taking Rachel Himmelfarb's place. Her English classes, I mean. She had twins, and so she's staying home this semester." Sarah somehow felt that if she loaded her narrative with a few bits of domestic trivia, it would all sound credible.

"Have you any identification with you?" demanded Jake Markham.

Sarah reached around her windbreaker, felt around her body. Her pants. Nothing. "No, I'm afraid not. I mean, I just came out for a few minutes. To get some air. It's stuffy up there on the third floor. Gregory House. I'm in Gregory House."

"I've been standing behind that bush ,watching you there on the ground for over five minutes." said Jake. "You've been down on your knees. Is that how you usually get air?"

"Oh, no," said Sarah, trying to keep the exasperation out of her voice. "It's just that, just that when I was out here earlier I, well, I dropped an earring. A gold earring. And I thought it might be here. Because I was out talking—you know, having a conversation, this afternoon—just about where that trellis is."

"And you thought that eleven forty-five at night was a great time to go looking for it?"

"I was worried. I couldn't go to sleep. It was my mother's. The earring, I mean," said Sarah, digging herself ever deeper into a snake pit of lies. The trouble was that the truth, which had at first seemed much too complicated, now seemed to be entirely reasonable. But it was too late.

"I see," said Officer Markham. "And did you find this earring?"

Sarah shook her head. "No. No, I didn't." And that, she thought, is at least the plain and simple truth.

"If you are living at Gregory House, then you have your key."

"Key?"

"Yes, key. The outside house doors are locked at nine o'clock. Everyone has to have a key. Faculty and students. Even me. I have a key."

Sarah patted her jacket frantically. No key. No key because it was resting on her bureau, next to her handbag. The handbag with her faculty confirmation letter and her collection of identification documents. "I think," she said in a low voice, "that my key is up in my room. On my bureau. Third floor. Gregory House."

"I see," said the officer again, still in the gruff but reasonable voice. "And how did you come here? I mean, arrive at the school?"

Sarah gave an exhalation of relief. "My car. The Jeep. Actually, it's my husband's. It's my husband's Jeep. He's taken my car, a Subaru, because it needs work. He thought the Jeep was safer, I guess. I drove down from Maine this afternoon. The car's over in the faculty lot. A 1996 Jeep."

"And you have the key for the Jeep? And the registration? And a driver's license?"

Sarah again patted her windbreaker pockets. A futile gesture, since each of these items was safe in her handbag. On the bureau. In her room. On the third floor of locked Gregory House.

Officer Markham again ran his flashlight briefly over Sarah's person and then delivered that time-honored police statement. "I think," he said, keeping his hand steady and strong on her arm, "that you'd better come along with me."

Sarah had been in several police offices in Maine. In fact, one of Alex's oldest friends—and now hers—was Sheriff's detective Mike Laaka, and she and Alex had spent a certain amount of time in his office discussing questionable activities. These small-town places had a certain sameness about them. Calendars came from the local oil supplier, file cabinets came in olive, chairs in splintered oak, and there was always a scratched-up metal desk presided over by a highly colored photograph of the U.S. president or the governor of the state, although rarely of the current incumbent.

The Security Office at Miss Merritt's School was in the lower back reaches of Lockwood Hall, an impressive brick building that housed admissions offices, Dr. Singer's rooms, the school dining rooms, cafeteria, and kitchens. Jake Markham's office was on the lowest level, tucked between a huge food-delivery door on one side and the school laundry on the other. The laundry ensured warmth and noise, and the delivery doors invited intermittent blasts of January air. Comfort in Jake Markham's office depended on the location of one's chair.

Sarah was at the same time numb with cold and heated with the embarrassment that comes from letting oneself be caught in an ignominious activity. Now Jake released her arm and indicated to her a wooden chair—one that happened to be on the laundry side. The laundry was manifest not only by the radiant warmth but also from the distant vibration caused by machines working away at the week's sheets, tablecloths, and towels. The room itself exactly matched Sarah's memories of other such spaces. Except in a small area between two tall file cabinets and a shelf holding a collection of flashlights and a battery radio, the expected photograph of a political leader had been usurped by a reproduction of the self-portrait of Vincent van Gogh in his straw hat.

Jake Markham saw Sarah looking at it with some surprise. "Old Vincent makes me keep my wits about me," he said. "And now, Ms. whoever you claim your name is, what have you to say before I get on the horn with the Carlisle police station."

But Sarah had pulled herself together. "Please call Miss Lester. Giddy Lester. My husband's cousin. She teaches art and coaches the soccer team, and she's the one who told me about the job opening. Her room is in Gregory, second floor."

Jake Markham raised his eyebrows slightly, checked a printed list hanging over his desk, reached for the phone, and punched in a number, waited, listened, and then hung up. "No answer," he said. "Any other ideas?"

Sarah frowned and then remembered Giddy leaving to check a kiln. "Please try the art building—what's it called—the Nakatani Arts Center." Sarah was pleased that even in her agitated state she could pull this name out of the hat.

But Officer Markham did not appear impressed, thinking, no doubt, that any stranger up to no good on the school grounds would have familiarized herself with the buildings and general layout.

No one answered at the Nakatani Arts Center, and Sarah had a cold sense of abandonment. Giddy had undoubtedly turned down the telephone ringer and was sound asleep, or she was off campus.

There was no help for it. "Look," she said. "I'll tell you what really happened. Why I was down there on the ground."

"I don't really need another scenario," said Jake. "Have you any other person who can identify you?"

Sarah, with a sense of desperation, ran through the slender cast of characters. She could hardly drag the distinguished Dr. Singer out of bed. Madame Carpentier? Good God, no. Babette what's-her-name? Sarah somehow didn't want to have a worried Babette fluttering about her. Who else was there? Certainly not suave Mr. Adrian Parsons, who probably wouldn't remember meeting her. Nor that tight-jawed history of art teacher whose last name she had already forgotten. Anita somebody. But what about that joker in the hall? Carlo, Carlo Leone. Okay, bite the bullet. She grimaced and said, "You could try Mr. Leone. Carlo Leone. I met him at that tea party over in the Old Library."

The changed expression on Jake Markham's face suggested a knowledge of Mr. Leone, and he punched in the numbers. Making contact after several rings, he described the problem of a strange female found digging in the garden who said she had met him and could he come down and identify her. There was a pause, and Jake Markham said, "Okay. See you in a minute."

"I hope he lives close by," said Sarah.

"Hey, you're supposed to know the guy," said Jake. "He's got an apartment in Packard Hall, and he's on his way."

The confrontation took place. Carlo Leone, a bit tousled in what must have been a hastily assembled costume of jeans and a sweatshirt, took one look at Sarah and burst out laughing. "A lady of the night," he said. "What's the line, 'She walks in beauty, like the night/of cloudless climes and starry skies.' Only," he added, "you look a little worse for wear. Byron would disown you." He turned to Jake Markham. "Yes, Jake, I know the lady. She's going to be another slave of the English Department. But I think she owes us one. Sarah Deane, what in hell were you doing in the garden? It's January, and even if you were having a horticultural fit, it's too cold to plant anything."

Sarah took a deep breath and then told her story. "I've been stupid. I should have stepped in before Hannah Hoyt buried it, but it was only my first day, and I wasn't sure about throwing my weight around over what might have been a school joke— disgusting, but still a joke. Then, later, I began thinking it might be serious. A cut-out from black paper, obviously meant to be Madame Carpentier, cape and all, hung by the neck. So, I decided to dig it up at night. And maybe take it to the school office tomorrow. Or somewhere. Anyway, here are the pieces of the puppet, and you can both do what you want with them. I quit. I just want to go to bed."

Carlo, who had helped himself to a chair, shook his head. "As one of my students always says to get a rise out of me, you done right. These things shouldn't be hidden, though I'm sure Hannah Hoyt was just trying not get some student in trouble. Or herself, for that matter. And now, look, you've thrown Jake's patrol schedule on it's ear, and someone may be sneaking into the gym to steal the swimming trophies. And I must tell you that pulling Madame Carpentier's chain is a popular extracurricular activity. Last semester—"

"Yes," Sarah interrupted, "I was told about a choir robe on the school sign. Just before Christmas vacation."

"Right. And earlier this fall, the scarecrow on the soccer

field. Made out of hockey sticks, dressed in a black raincoat. The head was carved from a squash. The sign said something like 'I have brains but no heart' and was signed 'The Wizard of Oz.' "

"But don't you think," Sarah persisted, "that this puppet hanging by the neck is more than a joke? It seems pretty sick."

"I'll keep an eye out," said Jake Markham. "The girls do stuff like this, but the hanging job is a little meaner than most. I'll take these pieces to the dean tomorrow—that's Mr. Greenwald—and maybe he'll get the word out for the kids to can it."

"Please," said Sarah. "I feel like a damn fool." Looking over at Carlo Leone, she added, "And don't say, 'if the shoe fits.' "

"I wouldn't dream of it," said Carlo.

"I'll say it was found by a responsible teacher," said Jake. "Torn up by persons unknown."

"Yeah," said Carlo. "I think this is some kid's lousy idea of a joke. Dr. Singer and the dean have more important things on their minds. Last semester, for example, one of the day girls brought some drug paraphernalia to school and was expelled. A senior. Honor student. Played French horn in the orchestra. Believe me, this puppet thing can't compete."

"And," said Sarah to Jake, "if you let me into Gregory House, I promise never to go out again without that goddamned key."

"A lot of people—including faculty—wear it on string around the neck," said Jake Markham, rising and opening the door.

But Carlo Leone did not return to Packard House and his bed. Instead, he waited in the security guard's office until Jake returned.

"Goddamned nuisance," said Jake. "Not the woman. Sarah Deane. She probably meant well, and she's right, the puppet should have been turned in. And Hannah Hoyt should have known better than to bury the thing. A senior is supposed to be almost an adult. Out in the world by next year."

"Don't bet on the adult part. And Hannah is in deep shit with Grace Carpentier. Those two shouldn't even be in the same town."

"You have her in class? Hannah, I mean."

"Yeah. For the last three years. English. Not Italian. She wanted to switch languages but was forced by her parents to go back into Grace's French class, and the two just sizzle when they see each other. Hannah may just be the lady who wants to see Carpentier swinging from the end of a rope."

"Hannah does well in art," said Jake thoughtfully. "I've seen some of the school art shows. Her stuff—cut-outs, paste-ups. What's the name, découpage. Very clever. People mostly, not abstract shapes. Miss Merritt's answer to Matisse." By which remark Jake Markham revealed himself a man of dual preoccupations: policeman-*cum*-aspiring artist.

"Matisse wasn't really into satire," said Carlo. "But some of Hannah's stuff has a bite. A real edge." He stood up and stretched. "*Buonasera. A più tardi.* Glad I could help. Ms. Deane would not have enjoyed a night in the Carlisle police office."

Sarah had washed hastily and fallen asleep almost as soon as her head hit the pillow, and only the most insubstantial of life-sized paper puppets blowing on a clothesline disturbed her dreams. Morning came, and with it would come her new classes. And as she sluiced her face at seven-thirty, she swore to leave the students and their little jokes to themselves. She had overreacted by her nighttime digging expedition because she had forgotten how the teenager often finds little difference between the humorous and the cruel. From now on, she would stick to the teaching of English.

Fortified from the ample cafeteria spread by orange juice, tea, and oatmeal, and pleased not to run into Mr. Carlo Leone,

Sarah, working her way through the streams of girls pouring out in all directions, found herself, after several wrong turns, at nine o'clock in the basement of Adam House, facing fifteen freshman girls. Here she discovered just two signs of Madame Carpentier, with whom she would be sharing the space. Only a chalk quotation in French, "*le temp fuit*," with "SAVE" written below, haunted the room.

The introduction of *Macbeth* to Rachel Himmelfarb's freshman lit section went smoothly—the students were still taking this new instructor's measure—and then she launched *Bleak House* at a sophomore group at ten. Both Will Shakespeare and Charles Dickens, Sarah reminded herself on the way to the faculty lounge for a fifteen-minute breather, had plenty of edge—and just maybe the kids, through a stringent set of readings, could begin to judge and weigh some of the finer points of evil. At eleven-thirty she would shiver the timbers of a small senior honors class with the likes of Wilfred Owen, William Butler Yeats, and T. S. Eliot. These were poets whose works could marvelously concentrate the mind. And if by any chance the maker of that hanging puppet happened to be in the class, well, the works of these gentlemen might divert her from further scissor work.

These ideas Sarah expressed to Carlo Leone on finding him joining her at an empty table for a late one-thirty lunch.

"You, Sarah Deane," laughed Carlo, "are some kind of idealist. You've forgotten about boarding schools. Tight little islands. Worlds of their own. The girls—most of the girls—have two compartments in their heads. One is for the world outside—the environment, the destruction of the rain forest, their parents, their outside friends, the far East and the state of the Union. The other compartment is for the school. Make that 'The School.' And, believe me, the effect of, say, an impeachment of the U. S. president does not make the fact that the soccer coach chose Katie Stephens over Becky Stein as starting goalie any less of a dire event. Nor can an earthquake in the Punjab overwhelm the terrible fact that Madame Grace Carpentier put the captain of the ice hockey team on restriction for a month and that Anita Goshawk is keeping Heather Morgan away from play rehearsals because she failed her last history of art exam."

Sarah finished the last of an egg-salad sandwich and shook her head ruefully. "I suppose I'm always hoping that Macbeth doing in Macduff's children and poor Jo dying will lead to serious thinking about life—as well as literature."

Carlo put down his coffee cup and shook his head. "They'll think about life, but as life-in-a-book. A paper to write, an exam to prepare for. They may even weep real tears over Jo dying. They will be very sorry about what happened to children in nineteenth-century London. But it probably will not cross-fertilize nor change their view of what's important in school."

"In other words, no matter how gripped they are by their reading, there'll be more paper puppets or things like that."

"Sure. But Dean Greenwald knows, and he'll tell Joanna Singer, and there'll probably be an announcement or house meeting on the subject. Now, how about some out-of-this-world coconut cream pie."

"Really?"

"No, it's only slightly above average. But it rounds out the meal."

"I'll stick to fruit," said Sarah. "But I guess what's worrying me is that senior, Hannah Hoyt. She told me about working up some poetry and doing cut-out illustrations. Hannah was pretty vehement about burying the puppet pieces. Afraid she was going to be blamed."

Carlo Leone reached for his briefcase and rose. "Hannah's a bright kid. I'm not sure she'd stoop to making puppets. See you around, Sarah, and stay out of the garden." And he strode off through the dining room, dwarfing half its population with his lean, six-foot-four presence.

48

He was almost immediately replaced by Giddy, who plunked herself and a plate heaped with spaghetti down at the table. "Hey there, Sarah. How's it going? Get through classes in one piece?"

Sarah admitted to survival. "I'd forgotten that high-school-age students are just like first-year college students—hard to distract from their own points of view. Except, I suppose, these Merritt girls aren't completely hung up on what guy they're sleeping with next week."

"No, they're hung up on what guy they *might* sleep with on spring break. They like to speculate about possibilities."

"Anything new with you?" asked Sarah in what she hoped was an offhand tone.

Giddy wrinkled her nose. "As a matter of fact, yes. Someone got into one of the studios early, before the first nine o'clock class—the kids are allowed to do this to finish up projects—and left a drawing sitting on an easel. In color—pastel—of Madame Guillotine as a rattlesnake, with a black cape and a French flag, hung up like laundry, on its fangs. I've no idea who's behind it. I'll make a fuss in all my classes, but there won't be a confession."

"You threw the picture away?"

"Not yet. It was very well done, so I thought of Hannah Hoyt, but she claims she was working out in the gym after breakfast, so who knows? There are other gifted art students."

"What about someone sneaking into the building in the middle of the night?"

"That," said Giddy, "takes keys. I have a key, and the other art teachers have them. So do the security and the maintenance people. But that's about it. I doubt if even Joanna Singer has one."

At which point they were joined by Anita Goshawk, commander of the History of Art Department. Anita, thick glasses gleaming, moved Sarah's teacup aside and placed her briefcase front and center before the two women.

"I've had the notices of my Friday night lecture printed," said Anita. "I hope it's going to attract some of the Carlisle population." She unlocked the briefcase and handed out two bright green announcements printed in an exotic font.

"Take one, each of you," she said. "Then you can't possibly claim not to have known about it." She turned to Sarah. "Faculty must stand together, and you'll be expected to go to all the faculty affairs, piano recitals, seminars, roundtables, even demos of judo and karate. Students are always on the alert for breaks in the ranks. You know, Mr. Hodgepodge skipped out on Mrs. Melody's harpsichord concert. Anyway, if nineteenth-century American painting isn't your bag, I don't want to hear about it. Captive audiences are what I'm after. My students will be there because their grades will depend on knowing the material I cover."

"About Friday night," began Giddy. "I might have a friend—"

"Bring him," said Anita, "but no bare feet."

"I was going back to Maine," said Sarah. "See my husband. Check on some loose ends."

"Oh, husbands," said Anita, dismissing the subject with a wave of her hand. "Husbands can be put off. I know, I've had two. They're a nuisance." Anita stood up, snapped her briefcase closed, and said she'd see them Friday evening. "And don't forget the reception afterward. Radnor Hall, Old Library. Food and drink. A reward for attendance." And Anita was off, heading for another table, a sheaf of lecture notices in one hand.

"That lady won't take no for an answer," said Giddy. "Nothing wrong with *her* ego. All that fuss about us going to the reception. Does Anita expect to be crowned queen?"

"She knows her stuff?" asked Sarah, thinking that there were entirely too many chiefs among the faculty she had met and that Babette Leclerc loomed as a positive oasis. Friendly and modest and easygoing. Even Giddy could be a strenuous companion.

"Oh, yeah. Sure. As an art critic would say, she's well regarded in the field. Anyhow, she drives her students, keeps their noses in the books. Next to Madame Grace, I suppose she's the toughest teacher around."

"How about Adrian Parsons? He gave off an odor of power."

"He's a smoothie. Doesn't throw his weight around. Sort of glides through problems. The girls like him well enough, and he has his share of honor students signing up for Virgil and Horace and the rest. Or the *Iliad* in Greek, God help them. Adrian used to have a thing for Anita once. A few years back. Went to art openings and concerts together. And, I guess, to bed together. But they broke up about the time I came to the school. Listen, Sarah, I have to go. We have indoor soccer until February, and I'm going to put the kids through some ball passing in the gym. See you at dinner."

Sarah hesitated. Should she include Giddy in the paper puppet affair? But then she decided no. If there was to be a house meeting or a bulletin on the subject, well, that should take care of the matter. It was time to think about preparing for tomorrow's classes. Sarah returned to her room, snapped on Patsy's leash, and took a healthy walk in what was now a fall of heavy, wet snow, and then she returned to her room and hit the books.

Shortly after four, Sarah shoved *Macbeth* aside and rose to make tea, and just as the kettle began to rattle and shake, there came, as had happened to Mr. Poe, a knocking at her chamber door.

It was Hannah Hoyt. Red-faced, in a state of fury.

"Ms. Deane," she shouted.

Sarah, sensing that the disinterred puppet was now a matter of public record, braced herself for a student session in which she might be called a traitor, a snitch, someone unworthy to be a teacher or a confidant of trusting youth. Sighing, she opened the door wide and found herself confronted not just by Hannah but also by a slim, tall, very severe-looking black student and a short, stocky girl with a head crowned by tight, yellow curls.

They scowled, they glared, their hands curled in fists, and they thrust their chins forward in a belligerent way.

And Sarah, always a victim of the irrelevant, could only think that in case she wanted to put on scenes from *Macbeth*, well, she had found the perfect three witches.

5

SARAH opened the door and told the three to come in.

The three girls pushed into the room, looking, in their hiking boots, worn blue jeans and ragged sweatshirts, like members of an underpaid militia.

"Come and sit down," said Sarah. "And how about some tea?"

They would not sit down; they would not drink tea.

"Not with someone we can't trust," said Hannah. "But we have to talk." She pointed at the tall black student. "This is Rosemary Streeter. She's our class representative for the student council. And this is Zoë Fountain. She's Rosemary's roommate. And I'm Hannah Hoyt, remember? We're all in Gregory, third floor. All seniors. And we're all mad."

"We can't really talk if we're standing up," said Sarah. "Go on being mad, but sit down. Please."

Reluctantly the three found chairs and perched themselves on the very edges. They sat up straight. They glowered.

"Okay," said Sarah. "Out with it."

The two strange students looked over to Hannah and nodded.

"Okay," said Hannah. "Miss Deane, if you'll forgive my language, what you did about that paper puppet no one was supposed to know about, was, I think—we all think—a pretty shitty thing to do."

Sarah nodded. This was hardly the time for a chat about appropriate language. "Go on," she said.

"You saw me find the cut-out puppet in the garden, and I said if it was made public I'd be screwed because I've been in trouble with Madame Carpentier. Or they'd blame one of my friends. I told you things like that happen all the time. So we agreed—I thought—to keep it quiet. You let me bury it. You watched me while I tore it up and shoved the pieces under the snow and into the dirt. And that was supposed to be the end of it, but now . . ." Hannah faltered, biting her lip and looking straight at Sarah as if what she really wanted to do was throw some heavy object at Sarah's head.

Then Hannah, after a visible struggle with her temper, went on. "And now there's going to be a house meeting about it. So that's what you've done." Here Hannah ground to a halt and looked around at her confederates for support.

"Do you two girls agree with Hannah's summary of the problem?" Sarah asked.

They did. Absolutely. Totally.

"Okay," said Sarah. "I don't blame you. I did stand there and let Hannah bury the puppet. I should have stopped her when it was found and taken the thing to the school office. But I had just arrived at school, and I was feeling that I wasn't yet a part of the school machinery. I should have found Hannah later—when I decided I couldn't let the matter drop—and explained that I had to do something about it. Hannah, I was wrong, and

I'm sorry. And if it would help in the least, I can say that from your reaction when you found the puppet, you were as surprised as I was."

"Hannah told us the thing was really gross," said Zoë. "I mean, I'm not wild about Madame Carpentier, but that's going too far."

"Can you accept my apology, Hannah?" asked Sarah.

Zoë and Rosemary turned to Hannah, who stood up frowning, apparently unsure whether to stamp out of the room or loom over Sarah in confrontation. And as sometimes happens in the annals of human events, a dog made the difference. Patsy, who had been suffering from the state of affairs in which not one of these new people had offered to scratch his head or exclaim over his size and beauty, now walked over, tail wagging, to Hannah, reared up, placed his front paws on her shoulders, and, since they were close to the same height, extended his wire-haired, gray head into her face and began to wash her forehead with his long tongue. Hannah pushed Patsy away, and her frown turned to a smile. And then a laugh, and she ruffled Patsy's hair. Then she sat back down in her chair, reached for one of Patsy's paws, and nodded.

"Okay. You're new, and I suppose every teacher should be given one chance. I don't think it's all such a big deal, but I can see that the faculty might think it was."

"Like Hannah says," added Rosemary, "these things happen. You've got a bunch of kids—freshmen and sophomores who are not even half grown up—and they do incredibly dumb things."

"So," said Sarah, "can we go back to square one? Hannah, I saw that you were on the list for Mrs. Himmelfarb's poetry class, but you weren't there this morning. I'm taking over that class now, and I wondered if you dropped it because of me. I hope not."

Hannah colored. "I didn't want to listen to you go on about

a bunch of over-the-hill poets. I mean, I've never even heard of this Wilfred Owen. But I guess I'll stay. Did you mark me absent?"

"No," said Sarah. "I was waiting to talk to you."

"So we can just forget about this puppet business," said Zoë. "After tonight's house meeting, that is."

"I think," said Sarah slowly, "that there seems to be a kind of acceleration of the Madame Carpentier attack. Not just the scarecrows from last term and this cut-out, but today a drawing of Madame Carpentier as a rattlesnake turned up in the art building. You'll probably be hearing about it at your meeting."

"Damn," said Hannah. "Not the art building again. I think someone's after me, only they're doing it through Madame Carpentier. Everyone knows I just about live in the art building. I've even borrowed the key a couple of times."

Sarah tried to compose her face at this piece of news. She did not want to suspect Hannah, with or without the key. Or, for that fact anyone for a hundred miles around. "Let's just leave it," she said. "We all agree a paper puppet hanging by the neck is too much like a death threat. It's scary and shouldn't be ignored. Now, let's have tea. What kind? I've got black and herbal and decaf. Even something called Super Soothing."

"I think we can distract everyone," said Zoë. "Rosemary here has an idea for freaking out the new girls."

"I pretend I'm into black voodoo and that I've taken Zoë's little white soul," said Rosemary. "It really spooks them."

"I'll bet it does," said Sarah, heartily glad to be rid of the previous topic and willing to be initiated into the mysteries of student jokes. She went over to her mini-kitchen and began arranging four mugs on a tray.

"And it spooks some of the faculty," Rosemary said with satisfaction. "Zoë and I've been called in to the dean—that's Mr. Greenwald—and given these serious talks about being sensitive to ethnic and minority differences. And the dangers of making jokes about racial and religious matters."

"I told him," said Zoë, "that I didn't miss my own soul and that Rosemary was working to give me a real out-of-body African experience."

"Good grief," said Sarah. "You'll end up having to give a seminar and write a term paper on it."

"Or be put on probation," said Zoë cheerfully. "Like we're not raising other students' consciousness about race in a thoughtful and conscientious way."

"I'm working on getting possession of an Hispanic soul right now," said Rosemary. "Maria Cordero has promised me her soul, but she wants to borrow and use my drums in her room for the whole semester, and that's too long. I need my drums, it's part of my mystique. But I think we've really freaked out the Cohens."

"The Cohens?" asked Sarah.

"Our house parents," said Zoë. "He's Joel and does photography, graphic arts, and basketball. And Freda does math—trig and pre-calc. They wear matching sweatshirts and fake Tyrolean clothes because Freda was born in Austria."

"Point is," said Rosemary, "they're very serious about being house parents, and they have us in for talks about the human community and religious diversity. And when I talk about voodoo—I don't know much about it, but they don't know that—it makes them nervous, and then I go into some tough, African-American street rap, and they break into a sweat, and sometimes I'd like to shout 'hey, come on you guys, lighten up.' "

"You know," said Zoë thoughtfully, "it might be fun to say you're working on getting hold of Madame Carpentier's soul. Sucking it out."

"No," shouted Hannah. "No way. At least no voodoo dolls with pins in them. Or puppets."

"I mean psychologically," said Zoë. "Let her know Rosemary's working on the project."

"Leave me out," said Rosemary. "I've got to pass French Four this year. Besides, I'm getting interested in the Druids."

"I like the voodoo-club idea better," said Zoë. "Have rites and ceremonies. I'll look it up. Make it seem authentic. I'll be president because my soul is already in—what's the word—in bondage."

And so the afternoon meandered toward five o'clock. The three girls sprawled on the floor, tickled Patsy, and had second cups of tea and Pepperidge Farm cookies that Sarah unearthed from her grocery supplies. And as the shadows lengthened and the girls chattered, even a voodoo club or a plunge into the world of Druids seemed to Sarah an acceptable idea.

This, however, was an opinion that Sarah was not able to hold for any considerable length of time.

Tuesday, January fifth, except for the sixteen-degree temperature and an early-morning bluster of snow, was uneventful. At least as far as Sarah knew. Giddy, at breakfast, reported that the drawing of Madame-as-rattlesnake had been duly exhibited to the proper authorities and then destroyed.

"I must say," Giddy added, "that the whole thing has stimulated an interest in drawing snakes. The kids looked at me yesterday with these absolutely straight faces and said they've always had a thing about snakes. Any snakes. Vipers, asps, mambas, constrictors, copperheads, bushmasters, coral snakes, you name it. You should hear them go on. Snakes are so cool. So awesome. Snakes are basic, sexual, phallic, colorful, mystical, mysterious, evil, biblical, part of our inner selves. And can they do an art project of painting, weaving, sculpting, or making collages of snakes? Oh, God."

Sarah, in her first class, remembering Giddy's remarks, decided that although never personally attracted to snakes, she would, when Act IV of *Macbeth* rolled around, rouse her students by featuring the contents of the weird sisters' cauldron. In the meantime, she kicked off the nine o'clock session by spending a few moments on the Elizabethan penchant for witches. This made for a successful class, since witches were very "in," while kings and thanes were not. Sarah, packing her briefcase at the end of class, felt that by the time they came to Lady Macbeth—always an attention getter—she would have the class ready for anything. Particularly adders and newts and toads.

Bleak House went well, although the length of the novel seemed to have stunned some of the students. As for the honors class, following a video of World War I trenches, mud, barbed wire, and bodies, the students seemed braced and ready for Wilfred Owen. Hannah had attended and had paid attention, so the peace treaty appeared to be holding. The end of this last class was marked by an encounter with Madame Carpentier, who pointed out that Sarah had not properly cleaned her blackboard, for the words "Cawdor" and "Battle of the Somme" were clearly visible. And that Miss Deane should be mindful that the students wriggled about and thus disturbed the perfect ranks of chairs.

"You are, of course, new, but that can only be an excuse for a very few days," Madame reminded her.

Sarah allowed the words—and more of the same—to flow over her head while she examined the Carpentier person. Black hair streaked with gray dragged back over her skull, fierce black eyebrows, and snapping dark blue eyes—or were they purple?—hard to tell with those thick, horn-rimmed glasses. A small, dark mole beside the thin lips, and a wedge-shaped chin that was usually seen in the thrust-out position. For her teaching costume, Madame featured black. First the black wool cape. Beneath, black with purple accents: black velvet vest, purple silk blouse, black wool skirt, and high black boots. The only ornament was a cameo broach on the collar of her cape that featured what appeared to be the profile of some Roman emperor—probably Caligula, Sarah thought.

Grace Carpentier's strictures on classroom order finally wound down, probably from the lack of her victim's response—Sarah having decided early on that least said was soonest mended. She left, thanking Madame Carpentier for her interest—she was not asked to call her Grace—and the last glimpse of the French teacher showed her vigorously working over the blackboard, an eraser in both hands.

Sarah met Giddy for lunch, and they were joined by Freda Cohen, house parent with her husband in Gregory House. The cafeteria was particularly busy with the hearty noise of students who had come in from the cold, stamping their feet, shedding their heavy jackets, and dropping their enormous backpacks with a thump on the floor. From the cafeteria line came the clatter of trays, the chink of heavy china, and the rising voices of students greeting each other or calling from one table to the next. And over everything hung the mixed odors of wet outdoor clothing, damp leather boots, and wet wool gloves, as well as the faint scents of deodorants, moisture creams, lip salves, and menthol cough drops.

"Of course," said Giddy over the featured special, minestrone soup and garlic bread, "about that snake drawing, any kid with half a brain who was pulling a job like that would do it in a different style than her own. You know, delicate lines if she usually uses a thick dark line. I heard that Dr. Singer was going to call on the so-called experts, Goshawk and Adrian Parsons, to make a sort of guess about the artist, but . . ."

"Hold it," said Sarah. "How did Adrian Parsons get in on this? I thought he was classics."

"Oh, don't you know," put in Freda Cohen, making her first remark since lunch had begun—she was a noted eater—"he's an artist himself. He's even had a show of pen-and-ink sketches in Concord. Or was it Acton? Somewhere around." Freda Cohen was a brown-eyed, brindle-haired woman of some breadth. She wore her hair braided and circling her head, and her sweater with its silver buttons and her long, woolen skirt and woolen stockings gave off whiffs of the Tirol.

"Adrian," Freda went on, "thinks of himself as a critic. He judges the Concord-Carlisle high school art show every year and every now and then writes up some art event for the *Carlisle Mosquito*. You'd think they'd ask Anita, but she's apt to say exactly what she thinks and hurt feelings. Adrian is very diplomatic."

"Let's hope," said Giddy, "we have no more of this crap. The seniors, at least, should start worrying about college admissions."

After a satisfying few minutes of soup and bread, Sarah decided on a change of subject. "Are you both going to Anita Goshawk's lecture on Friday?" she asked.

Giddy made a face, and Freda put down her spoon and sighed lustily. "The trouble is," said Freda, "that when she goes on about the faculty supporting each other, she's right. We stand behind each other. I'm supposed to be helping with a faculty music recital, and if not a single teacher showed up, it would be noticed. Joanna Singer can skip it every now and then if she's got some speaking engagement, but we all do try and go."

"Anita and I," said Giddy, "don't always see eye to eye on teaching art. And she's pretty sharp when you disagree with her. For me, sitting through her lectures is sometimes like sitting on a patch of thistles."

Sarah moved her empty soup bowl to one side and poked a fork into the center of a lump of peach cobbler, removed it, and feeling virtuous, scraped away the whipped cream. "I was going back to Maine," she said. "Just to touch base, remember what normal life was all about. Tell Alex all the things about the house I forgot. Like when the oil comes, and when to pay the trash pick-up guys. But now I think I'll persuade him to come to a lecture on nineteenth-century art. Freda, can he stay in my apartment, or shouldn't I introduce an unknown man to Gregory House?"

"Unknown married men joining their wives is acceptable," said Freda primly. "But your room has only a twin bed. I'll ask maintenance for a roll-away cot."

"Cohabitation even with unmarried men," said Giddy, "is not an unknown phenomenon to the teenage female. In fact, Alex would be a lot more welcome if the kids thought he was on the loose. He's not entirely over-the-hill and might give the old building a whiff of new testosterone. Not that Joel," she added, turning to Freda, "isn't sexy, but the girls are too used to him."

"You have sex on the brain," said Freda, reaching for her dish of tapioca pudding.

Giddy rose, grinning. "No, Freda, that's not where I have it."

"But what about the reception?" asked Sarah. "If the faculty has to support Anita, we'd better go the whole distance."

"I suppose," said Giddy reluctantly, "you're right. Sherry in tiny glasses or a punch bowl full of tangerine-colored fluid. I could ask Josh, but the way I feel now, he's history. He took me to a strip bar last week, and I was the one who almost got stripped."

"Josh?" said Sarah, thinking it was time to get a handle on this new boyfriend—boyfriend number one thousand and one, probably.

"MIT," said Giddy. "But not one of those engineering types who walk around with his glasses on backwards. Josh teaches in the drama department. He's does interactive stuff. Electronics interfacing with human DNA. Bare stage, actors in wetsuits.

Minimal dialogue. But I think he's turning into a real grouch, so it's time a goodbye scene came up. I'd take you to one of his things, but I'd say you and Alex are really nineteenth-century types. I'll bet you've seen all those Jane Austen movies."

"You'll win your bet," said Sarah, for whom Jane Austen, by written word or movie, was a sacred figure.

And they went their way, Freda Cohen humming "Edelweiss," Giddy pouncing on a student sliding by her table and demanding where the girl had left her portfolio because it was overdue, and Sarah heading back to her apartment to collect Patsy for a rigorous walk. She did not like to admit to herself that part of the walk might take in a view of the garden trellis and its environs. It was always possible that lightning—or in this case, the puppet maker—might strike twice.

But the first part of the walk with a delighted Patsy was uneventful. The snow had ceased, leaving a thin layer of white on the ground, and the garden was properly empty of threatening objects; the only matter for concern was the occasional patches of ice over which Sarah managed twice to skid, the second time falling to her knees and losing her grip on Patsy's leash.

Patsy, rescued in Texas by Sarah from a life of vagrancy, like many former tramps when unexpectedly set free heard distant trumpets and calls of the wild and took off. Sarah, her knee bloody and bruised, called, hooted, clapped her hands, and whistled. And Patsy, ranging wide, rushed here and there, around the pond and across to the tennis court as Sarah limped after him, swearing, picturing Patsy rearing up, putting his paws on the shoulders of some visiting prospective parent or student, someone with a profound fear of or allergy to dogs. An Irish wolfhound is a notable presence, and human reactions to a shaggy dog the size of a small horse are not always favorable. Then, of course, there could be an even worse scenario: Patsy meeting Szepppi and devouring him.

Capture came from an unlikely quarter. A distant scrabbling noise sounded followed by a series of whistles, and the elegant Adrian Parsons emerged from the shrubbery by the tennis court, one end of the leash in a gloved hand, Patsy trotting at the other end.

"Ah, our new arrival. Ms. Sarah Deane, I presume. And this wonderful creature is yours? Or else, why would you be out in the cold calling for a 'Patsy'? An appropriate name. I do admire the Irish wolfhound. An ancient and honorable breed and quite amiable, appearances to the contrary."

Sarah, as she received the leash, felt that the encounter was at least worthy of some lesser nineteenth-century novelist and was profuse in her thanks. "I had terrible visions of him charging out of a bush and frightening some important visitor. Or Szeppi," she added, remembering her previous tea party encounter with Adrian and Madame Grace.

"Szeppi," said Adrian, "can take care of himself very nicely. And any VIP visitor or a trustee with an endowment plan in his pocket would not be skulking around the tennis courts in the middle of January. Now, I have a suggestion. There is a pleasant old eatery in Concord. Just down the road from Carlisle. Why don't you leave Patsy in your apartment, and I will pick you up for dinner. Say around six. I'll ask Babette Leclerc to come; I think she needs a change of scene. Working under the admirable Madame Carpentier does, I think, exact a toll. We could be a threesome—always a good number for dining because no one splits off. Yours is the new face, Ms. Deane, and a new face among the old and weary is always refreshing. You can recite your life story, and we will listen and ask suitable questions."

Sarah hesitated. "I do have three classes to prepare. And a quiz to put together."

"This will be an early affair," said Adrian. "Just an hour or so of non-academic ambience to reinvigorate our jaded selves.

One should not eat always in the school dining room. That way, madness lies."

They parted, and Sarah watched Adrian Parsons, clad in— of all things—the sort of camel-hair topcoat that she imagined retired 1920s movie stars wore when taking strolls. And his conversation—it would have been laughably antique if she had not heard sly undercurrent of mockery. Mockery at what he was saying, mockery of the whole Miss Merritt scene.

She spent the following hours dealing with the next day's lessons, checking the exact ingredients of the three witches' cauldron, and bringing her knowledge of the lives and deaths of nineteenth-century English crossing-sweepers up to date. And then, after a quick shower and change into a sober blue wool dress, she walked down the hall, knocked on Babette's door, the door opened, and Babette, swaddled in a maroon knitted coat, emerged.

Together they descended the stairs to wait for the arrival of Adrian's car. Sarah tried to picture this vehicle and had just about settled on a silver-gray Saab when she became aware that Babette had been speaking at some length.

"So you see," said Babette, "this isn't like Adrian. He's not the kind of man to go out for dinner on an impulse. You must have been extra charming this afternoon."

"He rescued Patsy for me, that's all," said Sarah. "And I thanked him. Tell me about him. Married, single, divorced, gay, or what? Or does he have a demented wife locked up over in the Old Library?"

"Former wife. I've heard she was incredibly beautiful, but I don't think they got along that well. She was killed on I-290, outside of Worcester. Drove over a guardrail. Six or seven years ago."

"Oh dear," said Sarah, then thinking what an inadequate remark it was—suitable for everything from rain on the Fourth of July to sudden death on the interstate, she added, "I suppose he would have a beautiful wife. I can't see him with a bag lady at his side."

"That's what I mean," insisted Babette. "Taking the two of us out for dinner—not that you're not quite presentable, and I'm not repulsive, but he doesn't do things like this. If he goes out or brings someone to a concert, it's usually the likes of Queen Nefertiti. Actually, for a while back, Anita was his number-one woman, but it didn't last. Both too opinionated, I'd say."

"Anita Goshawk would be suitable," admitted Sarah. And then, peering through the glass of the vestibule, she said with disappointment, "I pictured him in a Saab. Or maybe a Lexus."

"Nothing so fancy," said Babette, pushing open the door. "He drives a dark blue Ford Taurus. Like Carlo Leone's, but Carlo's is a wreck, and Adrian's always looks perfect. Just like Adrian."

Sarah, as the new arrival, was given the place of honor—or at least as Adrian presented it—the front passenger seat, and Babette sat behind. Adrian, turning the car this way and that through the tangle of intersecting paths and roads on the Merritt campus, paused now and then to recite the histories of the buildings, with comments on the styles—Dr. Singer's house (Greek Revival), Philipi House (Cottage Gothic), Radnor (Queen Anne), Adam House (Shingle). Sarah leaned back and let her mind drift back to *Macbeth* and tomorrow's class. She came properly back to life when she realized that Adrian, now free of the school grounds and sweeping past the Congregational church, the Carlisle Art Center, and the Unitarian church, was in full flood giving Sarah history of the town of Carlisle, with special reference to its place in colonial history, its ties to other towns, and its recent renovations and commercial arrivals. Sarah listened with something like despair. Why had she tuned out when she should have stopped him right off the bat?

66

Now it seemed awkward to point out that she had grown up in Carlisle, went to the public school, roller-skated to the library, and played grade-school field hockey against teams from Concord, Bedford, Acton, and Chelmsford.

But truth should out. Sarah cleared her throat, ready to derail the lecture, however as the car took a left turn onto the Concord Road, Adrian Parsons, being a man who obviously loved the sound of his own fine baritone voice, moved smoothly from Carlisle to a short history of the town of Concord. Sarah subsided and did not interrupt to tell him that her fourth-grade class had walked over the Rude Bridge that Arched the Flood and gone twice through Louisa May Alcott's Orchard House, had written compositions on the subject of the minutemen, taken pictures of Nathaniel Hawthorne's house, and in seventh grade had been bussed over to Walden Pond to stand restlessly as their homeroom teacher went on—and on—about the not-so-interesting (at least to the seventh graders) ideas held by Henry David Thoreau.

"You must," said Adrian Parsons, "take time to get a deep sense of Concord. Old Concord. Bronson Alcott might be a good place to start. Then branch out. Go and visit the physical places. There's nothing like being on the spot. At the exact site."

But Sarah had tuned out again. Now she stared in fascination at the Ford's ignition key, one of several keys on a chain from which dangled a familiar form. Made of some dark plastic—or metal—slowly rotating from the motion of the car, swung the tiny figure of a black-caped woman. She wore the hat of a witch and hung from the end of the key chain. By the neck.

6

LIKE a creature hypnotized, Sarah stared at this tiny replica of Madame Grace Marie-Henriette Carpentier. Was this business of making Grace figures some sort of general school joke? A game anyone could play? Or Adrian Parsons' private response to his boss in the Language Division? Was it a totem? What exactly was a totem anyway—something to do with animals or families? A Native American tribe in the north used them, some tribe beginning with an "A." Algonquian—or was it "O" for Ojibway? Or both? Sarah stared harder at the little hanging figure now trembling at the end of its chain as the car rose and bumped over a rough patch of the road.

Maybe totem wasn't the right word. How about fetish? Something having magical powers. Used in rites and devotions or curing ceremonies. But what in God's name did Adrian Parsons have to do with fetishes, or with fetishes that looked like Grace Carpentier? Was Adrian Parsons putting a spell on the woman? Or was the figure really supposed to be Hecate? After all, Adrian was a teacher of classics—Latin and Greek—and he might have found Hecate, the sorceress, the earth goddess of the night, an amusing appendage to his key collection. Or it could be a memento given to him by a friend for some arcane reason, even by his wife, and so of sentimental value now that she was dead.

And then, Sarah realized with a start, it was only this very afternoon that Rosemary and Zoë were going on about a voodoo club. Weren't fetishes part of voodoo practice? My God, Rosemary was taking French Four with Madame Carpentier, and Adrian Parsons was number two in the Language Division. Now if these things were connected . . .

"And if you take that turn at the street up ahead you'll go right past Orchard House," said Adrian as he slowed the car at an intersection.

"What?" said Sarah, coming to with a jerk.

Adrian frowned. "The Alcotts," he said in an aggrieved voice. "I've been talking about Bronson Alcott. Fruitlands. His education theories. Here you are, teaching in a Massachusetts school in the Concord area. Concord, as you and Babette must know, has made significant contributions to the practice and theory of secondary education." Adrian seemed to finally realize that he had not captured all of Sarah's attention. "I hope I am not boring you," he said. "I thought you'd be interested. As a new teacher to the area."

"Oh yes, I am, I am," said Sarah in an unseemly gush, at the same time biting her tongue to prevent herself from telling him that she had taught for two years in a Massachusetts secondary school before moving to Maine and had taken her master's degree at Boston University. Then, aware that the car had come to a stop facing a large, familiar gray clapboard building, she added, "But I thought you said 'bistro.' But this," she waved at the building, "isn't exactly . . ."

"I thought better of the idea," said Adrian complacently—

a man again in charge of his audience. "This is the Colonial Inn. I thought since you are new to the area, we'd start in with an eighteenth-century atmosphere."

Oh God, breathed Sarah to herself as she crawled out of the front seat, let me get out of this mess. She shook her head and followed Adrian as he bustled ahead to hold the door open for Babette.

Adrian was apparently well known because in almost no time the three were settled at a table near the end of the room, and each was handed a menu boasting that they would be served the "Finest and Freshest New England Fare." Fortunately, the pleasant business of choosing dinner distracted Adrian from Sarah's lack of response to the history of the Alcott family. By the time the Salmon Picatta (Adrian), Grilled Chicken Tuscany (Babette), and the Scallops St. Jacque (Sarah), had been ordered, along with an all purpose Chablis, Sarah just about decided that after a certain amount of wine had gone down the hatch—Adrian Parsons' hatch, anyway—she would confess that she had been born in Concord's Emerson Hospital and had spent formative years in Carlisle. She would ask for mercy. Plead distraction on the drive over. She would boldly say that his key-chain figure had reminded her so strongly of Madame Carpentier that she had not properly attended to what he was saying about Bronson Alcott. Then she would assure him she had never properly studied the history of the Concord-Carlisle area. "You know, Adrian," she would say, "you never properly learn about the place in which you're living." This he could accept or reject, but her role as an alien to the area would be put to rest. And perhaps over the crème caramel, when they were all chummy together, he would laughingly admit to the practice of voodoo. That he kept a Carpentier doll stuck full of pins under his bed pillow.

With this unlikely thought fixed in her head, Sarah bent her head over her scallops and concentrated on listening, glad that Bronson Alcott had been shunted aside, her companions now sharing their irritation over Anita Goshawk's ursurpation of two language shelves in the Alexander Library for her Byzantine architecture references.

"Anita is a tough cookie," said Babette, who was into her third glass of wine.

"Miss Merritt's Academy has a number of tough cookies," said Adrian.

"I suppose that's better than the place being stuffed with a faculty of wimps and jellyfish," said Babette. "I know. I'm a jellyfish. Grace keeps telling me to sharpen up."

"Grace Carpentier is a woman of many virtues," said Adrian, attending to the last morsel of his salmon. "But she is not always, how shall I say, politic in making her opinions known. Her standards are very high. A laudable thing."

"Her standards are too damn high," said Babette, spearing a tiny parsley-topped potato with a thrust of her fork.

Dessert orders were taken, and now it was confession time. Sarah ran through a quick resume of her happy but heedless childhood in Carlisle and her superficial familiarity with Concord, explaining that she knew almost nothing about Bronson Alcott and how useful Adrian's comments had been. And then she pointed out what had riveted her attention. What had prevented her from interrupting Adrian's conversation. That keychain figure. So suggestive. It had given her a sort of shock. Madame Carpentier all over. The cape, the whole gestalt.

Sarah's explanation managed to cast a chill over the early part of the dessert course. A man of Adrian's learning and conversational skills does not like to feel that he has wasted fifteen minutes of erudition on an undeserving ear. But finally, in the interest of civility and perhaps to drown out Babette's exclamation of surprise and interest in the key chain, he gave her a thin smile and said that he withdrew his earlier welcome to Carlisle. Would Sarah accept instead his wishes for a happy homecoming?

Sarah allowed that she would, and before she could turn the conversation back to the key chain, Babette did it for her.

"You mean, Adrian, you have this little model of Grace Carpentier hanging from your ignition?"

Adrian looked at Babette reproachfully. "Not Grace," he said. "The figure—a witch, I'd say—simply came with the key ring. The end of October. This past Halloween. One of my students left it in my mailbox. I get—we all get—funny jokes like this. But my key chain, as it happened, had just broken, so I began to use this one. And Sarah, you have a lively imagination, but my key chain bears no relation to Grace Carpentier."

"Well, I did think of Hecate," Sarah murmured.

Adrian smiled again, a broader, warmer smile. "I shall think of it from now on as Hecate." He cocked his head slightly to one side, and Sarah could almost hear the academic machinery cranking up. "Hecate has commonly been represented as a daughter of Perseus or Perses. She is a wide-ranging goddess, but one associates her activities particularly with the hours of darkness." Adrian fixed first Babette and then Sarah with the sort of look that brooks no interruption. Sarah, tired as she usually was at the end of a teaching day, tried to concentrate as Adrian informed his listeners that the approach of Hecate was said to be announced by the whining and howling of dogs, and that proper sacrifices to the lady included dogs (no wonder they howled, thought Sarah), libations of honey, and black female lambs.

The arrival of the waitress with the bill, the polite argument that followed over its responsibility, and Adrian's insistence that it was his party all put an end to Hecate, although Sarah, wishing to solidify the peace, told Adrian on the way home that she would use Hecate and some of the things he had mentioned in her class discussion of Macbeth's weird sisters. This led to a spate of information on Elizabethan witches, and by the time Sarah crawled out of the car with Babette, she was so sick of the subject that she had begun to wonder if it was too late to shelve *Macbeth* in favor of *A Midsummer's Night Dream.*

"That Adrian, he's something else," said Babette when she and Sarah reached the third floor of Gregory House. "We might as well been out with the *Encyclopaedia Britannica.* I wonder that Grace can stand him being number two in the Language Division and knowing everything on God's green earth."

"I suppose," said Sarah, "it works both ways, and it evens out. I mean how does he stand *her*?"

"Oh, he's all deference and just flows past her, like water around a stone. And now I'll try and make points with Grace and take Szeppi for a walk. I really like that dog, and I do need some fresh air."

Patsy greeted Sarah with a pleased woof, and Sarah promised him a walk as soon as the area was clear of Szeppi. In the meantime, there were her classes to prepare for and the poetry quiz to make up. And Alex to call. She needed to tell him that a lecture on nineteenth-century American art lay in his future.

Alex, happily not on-call that weekend, gave only token resistance, particularly when Sarah pointed out what a good opportunity it was to look up old friends and relive the glory days of medical school. Only later that evening, Sarah in bed, Patsy settled beside it, did she wonder if local stores really carried key chains featuring witches. But wouldn't Adrian, who seemed so careful about his attributes, car, topcoat, and doeskin gloves, want something classier than a plastic Hecate hanging in his car?

The rest of the week rolled by on greased wheels. The temperature, as sometimes happens in January, rose into the fifties, and a mild and distant sun came out, melting snow and turning the brick paths into little rivulets. Students gave up their heavy jackets, and in cut-off jeans, T-shirts, and sneakers tramped to and from classes shouting to each other about being too hot.

Sarah, taking comfort from Alex's approach and the prospect of visiting some of the Boston and Cambridge bookstores, got through her Wednesday classes with something like dispatch. And success. She found that things really moved after one student's suggestion that poor Macbeth, suffering from low self-esteem and a bad self-image, had been pussy-whipped by his wife. This created an outcry from the feminist stalwarts, who said that Macbeth was a deadbeat and that Lady Macbeth had the guts in the family and was the one who should really be the Thane (Thane-ess?) of Glamis and Cawdor.

Sarah's Thursday classes continued in this lively vein and by Friday, Lady Macbeth was having trouble sleeping, Macbeth was on his way to dusty death, the *Bleak House* students were united in a loathing of courts and lawyers, and the honors group climbed out of the trenches of World War I and made ready to meet T. S. Eliot.

Lunch that Friday was a noisy affair. Trays clattered, students waved and called, feet stamped in and out. "Weekends," said Giddy as she joined Sarah, "always get the adrenaline going."

"Even without any males in sight?" asked Sarah.

"Males will turn up to visit, and there's a dance at Middlesex Saturday. But aside from sex, there's a basketball game and tryouts for the Drama Club production of *Antigone*."

"Shall I join the ladies?" It was Carlo Leone, tray laden with a bowl of beef stew and a piece of French bread the size of an NBA basketball sneaker. "Yesiree," he said as he arranged his plates. "I'm helping with the production. The kids wanted to do *Who's Afraid of Virginia Woolf*, but I told them not to push it. They can rent the Elizabeth Taylor and Richard Burton movie and get it out of their systems. Rosemary Streeter wanted to do the play as a black versus white affair—the black students in whiteface and vice versa—but I told her that it's been done. Which it has. "

"She and Zoë mentioned a voodoo club," remarked Sarah.

Carlo shook his head. "If they start something like that, we'll probably find that a local Haitian association will want to take the school to court for slandering religion. Those two just want to get a rise out of the faculty. Like Grace Carpentier."

"Did you know that Adrian Parsons has a black witch charm that looks like Grace hanging from his ignition key chain?" said Babette. "What do you think of that?"

"I don't," said Carlo. "Babette, you're as bad as the girls. Forget this witch business. And since you're up there in Gregory House with Rosemary and Zoë, tell 'em to cool it."

"I think both those girls are ripe for the big world," said Babette. "A twelve-hour job on a construction site wouldn't hurt either of them. Hannah Hoyt, too."

At which remark Sarah saw Carlo rise slightly in his seat and fix his attention on the dining room entrance. In the doorway, making an entrance, stood Rosemary, dressed, from what Sarah could see, in a brown and black bedspread. This, wrapped around her tall, lithe body, suggested robes from some African or Asian country. On her head was a turban, made from, Sarah guessed, a pillowcase in a "One Hundred and One Dalmatians" pattern. Beside her stood short Zoë, wrapped in what must have been in its normal life a beach towel—Sarah could make out a pattern of starfish and seahorses—and on her head a small, bluc tcrry turban, on her feet rubber thongs, and in her hand a gong. Which she sounded.

The clatter of dishes subsided, and the dining room became silent.

"Hear ye, hear ye," called Zoë in a high-pitched, unnatural voice. "A new club to join. Formed under the new moon by Her

Royal Mystery, Pharaoh Rosemary of the Upper Nile."

"The Nile!" exclaimed Babette. "What happened to voodoo?"

Zoë resumed her natural voice. "Hey, listen, you guys. This is January, the time we all get to feeling a little depressed. So how about a new club devoted to the ancient Egyptian mysteries? Rosemary is our Pharaoh, and I am Tut-Tut, her scribe and Minister of Supply. Which means food. Like seniors and juniors who are interested can meet in our room tonight at five. We don't know yet about sophomores and freshmen, but we may need slaves to build our tombs. Wear your robes." And Zoë beat her gong and took off her turban and waved it.

Giddy shook her head. "That's better than voodoo, which is a little tricky, all those animal parts and blood. Let's hope a fake ancient Egyptian society is safe."

"It may be safe, but I'm about to put a stop to it. Utter nonsense." Anita Goshawk appeared at Giddy's side, her face blazing like a firecracker.

The firecracker went off in the faces of Rosemary and Zoë. The two students came into the dining room in smiling triumph, stopped near Sarah's table, and were accosted by an exasperated Anita, who pointed out that both girls were being childish, a nuisance, and didn't they have better use of their time?

"Honestly, both of you. Seniors. You probably both have drivers licenses, you'll be voting in the next election—you're adults, for heavens sake. And Zoë, you're close to a 'D' if you don't get that paper on Monet in by Monday. An Egyptian club. Right now, I have two classes up to their eyebrows trying to get a grip on the complexities, the religion, and the art of the ancient Egyptians."

Anita paused for breath and then finished by telling them that, please, could they forget, right now, the whole idiotic Egyptian idea. Hadn't anyone noticed, she said, that there were too many clubs on campus as it was? And so she, Anita Goshawk, was going to the dean to discuss the matter.

"And take off those ridiculous costumes. You look like fugitives from a second-rate movie," she added as the two gathered their robes and, with heads held high, departed the room.

Anita Goshawk turned to Sarah's table and grimaced. "You really have to put your foot down when students go off the rail like that. Mysteries of Egypt. The next thing we know they'll want to embalm something." And she marched off in the direction of the cafeteria line.

"Well, aren't we having a crabby day," said Giddy softly. "She isn't usually so totally lacking in humor. I think someone should do a cut-out of her, too. She's giving Grace a run for her money."

"Isn't Anita way off base?" asked Sarah, worried. She herself had almost encouraged the voodoo idea.

"Way off," said Carlo. "Christ, let the kids have some fun, the winter term needs something offbeat, a little kinky, maybe. Think what those two *could* be into. But I'm surprised. Anita doesn't usually go around like a bear with a sore paw."

"A bear? Who is a bear? I shall join you, yes?" It was Madame Grace herself; Madame in something approaching a cheery mood. Perhaps, Sarah thought, she enjoyed Anita Goshawk losing it.

Madame Carpentier, not in her usual black ensemble, wore layers of rust and gray. Now she sat down and arranged a salad and pasta to the left and a bowl of soup front and center. This done, she addressed the three. "Anita Goshawk is very angry, yes, about this Egyptian idea. I myself never bother with student activities, and Anita is foolish to let herself be involved. If student activities begin to disturb the classroom, one has only to put the girls on restriction. Or one plays into their hands. Anita is acting without thinking."

Madame Grace then turned to Sarah. "You have become

better about cleaning my blackboard, but yesterday one of your students left a not-so-nice message—'out damned spot' it said—so you, the instructor, must be the last to leave the classroom so this does not happen again."

And to Carlo she said, "Good afternoon, Mr. Leone. I hear you are planning to do *Madame Bovary* in translation in your comparative literature course this semester. I think you must cancel your book order, because I am using the novel for my advanced students, and since you also have some of these students, they will be confused. The social tension in the book will be better understood, *voyez vous*, in the language in which it was written."

"Not all my students," said Carlo, "read French."

But Grace was now confronting Giddy. "Miss Lester, I have your note asking about the lifting of Brianna Zeiss's restriction so she may play soccer in the game tonight, but again I say no. Brianna's average is below a 'C.' One must hold the line on discipline, or one is trampled by such students." And Grace returned to her soup.

Sarah, Giddy, and Carlo, steaming in silence, waited until Madame finished her meal and departed, and then Sarah turned to Giddy and Carlo, who had progressed to second cups of coffee. "Madame Carpentier must have invented that quote on the blackboard. I erase everything after each of my classes."

"Some kid sneaked in after you left the classroom," said Carlo. "*Macbeth* is served up every year, so the girls know the quotations."

"Well, damn," said Sarah.

"Ignore it," said Giddy. "Besides, Grace scored off Carlo and me and got in a good jab at Anita Goshawk. No love lost between those; they're too much alike."

"I'll be very happy," said Sarah, "to see Alex. He can be annoying at times, but I love him, and even if he tried for a hundred years, he couldn't match those two ladies."

"Alex," said his cousin Giddy, "is a pretty good guy. I used to think he was on the stuffy side, you know, totally rational, but he's had his moments. One minute he's Dr. Friendly, the next he's running around with a knife in his teeth." She turned to Carlo. "Alex missed his calling. He should have gone on the stage as Captain Kidd, because he looks the type. You know, black hair and a chin. And a long mouth."

"Alex," agreed Sarah, "as Giddy claims, may have his moments, but the trouble is that he always thinks I'm the one who keeps bringing trouble home."

Carlo put down his coffee cup. "Sarah has already made her mark here by digging up a paper puppet at midnight. No, Giddy, I'm not telling tales. Things have a way of getting out."

"You probably leaked it yourself. Jake doesn't go around gossiping," said Giddy. "I see him from time to time because we've both been helping out in an evening community arts program at the grade school. I told him I heard he almost arrested Sarah. He got a good laugh about it."

"Well, I certainly didn't," said Sarah crossly.

"Hey," said Carlo, "it's the weekend. Rejoice and be glad. Everyone can go into the big city and hit some hot spots."

"You've forgotten the lecture," said Giddy. "We are tied to the stake. What's that quote, Sarah? About going the course."

"That's Gloucester with his eyes put out," said Sarah, "and I don't think the lecture's going to be that bad. Everyone says Anita Goshawk knows her stuff."

"You can hit the reception, tell Anita she was wonderful, and blow the whole thing," said Carlo. "If you can't make it to Cambridge, there's always Acton. Or Bedford. Chelmsford. Even Concord, though Concord's too upscale for the likes of me."

But fate, always hovering over the affairs of academe—even in the lesser form of a boarding school—had already arranged for Friday evening to end in a facility far removed from a place of gracious dining: the Middlesex County morgue.

7

ALEX was not expected until well past five, leaving barely enough time for a quick dinner before Anita Goshawk's lecture. Sarah, trying to fit the afternoon together, planned to split her time between working on next week's lesson plans and excursions with Patsy. To this latter end, she took Patsy in hand and then stopped at Babette Leclerc's next-door apartment to suggest that she join her in Patsy's airing, perhaps borrow Szeppi so that the two animals could get to know each other when both were under proper restraint. "Otherwise," said Sarah, "I'll be a wreck every time I see Grace's dog outside. Patsy will be okay once he knows Szeppi."

But at that moment there was a thumping on Babette's door and in came Rosemary and Zoë, divested of their robes and now in cut-offs and T-shirts. Hannah Hoyt stood to one side, presumably dressed for the upcoming lecture in a short plum-colored corduroy skirt and black boots.

"Hannah's called a meeting," announced Rosemary, "because it's time we did something about Madame Carpentier ruining the soccer program. And while we're at it, to get a grip on Goshawk before she turns into a real ogre."

"Academics come before sports," observed Babette mildly.

"Okay," said Hannah. "We know that. But it's like Madame Knife is trying to recreate whatever prison school she went to in France—probably some convent where they all wore black pinafores. And I don't know what's gotten into Goshawk. Maybe she really wants us to spend all our time talking about Donatello and Ghiberti. Me, I can only remember that the Medici went around poisoning each other—or was that the Borgias? And Michelangelo got a stiff neck painting the Sistine Chapel ceiling."

"Stick to the point," said Rosemary, "which is that we'd like to try out Hannah's ideas on you both because you're not important faculty, if you know what I mean."

Sarah and Babette nodded in agreement with this sentiment, and Rosemary walked down the hall and flung open a door heavily decorated with a collage of X-rated movie posters.

The room was packed. Girls everywhere. In jeans, in bath towels, in skirts, in soccer shorts, in ski pants, and in warm-up dance leggings they were draped on the floor, the beds, leaning against the radiator, straddling a chair, flopped over a stuffed laundry bag. Sarah, familiar as she was with the dormitory "look," wondered for the hundredth time how any of these girls could pull themselves together, unearth their textbooks and notebooks, clear a space on the jumbled desks, and actually do the work required for finishing an assignment. Most student rooms throbbed with music—rock in all shapes and forms, reggae, ska, mood music, hip-hop, recorded animal noises, and even the chanting of Benedictine monks. The cacophony of noise was duplicated in a visual sense by the wall decorations— rock stars, Hollywood favorites, political rascals, and unsuccessful revolutionaries.

Babette, viewing the scene, took a step backwards. "Hold it," she said. "Call Freda and Joel. Get a house meeting going. If you want advice, I'd say cool it. Sarah and I aren't going to stand here and listen to student plots. Even as trial listeners."

"It's Hannah's revolution," called a short, sandy-haired girl in a purple sweatshirt who peered out at them. "But it's time we stood behind her and manned the barricades."

Hannah turned to Sarah. "How about you, Miss Deane. Sarah. Are you at least sympathetic?"

"Look," said Sarah firmly, "I'm new, I don't know the ropes, but for what it's worth I back up Miss Leclerc. Go and drag your house parents in here before something gets out of hand."

"But," said Zoë, "this is serious. We need some teachers on our side. Starting with you two."

"And right now we abstain," said Babette. "Work it out with Freda and Joel and the higher-ups."

With which Babette and Sarah, with Patsy in tow, retreated, found Szeppi not to be at home, and headed down the stairs and out into the late-January afternoon. And as luck would have it, they met Szeppi and his mistress coming from the direction of Lockwood Hall.

"Aha," said Madame Carpentier, drawing herself out of reach of an interested Patsy. "Babette, I have not time for a longer walk, and if you are going out and can avoid that wolf dog belonging to Miss Deane, could you . . ."

Babette agreed. "It can be a training session," she said. "Szeppi will be properly introduced to Patsy."

After a number of cautions, Madame Grace allowed Babette to take Szeppi's leash, and the two dog walkers took off in the direction of the tennis courts. Patsy gave Szeppi several sniffs, and Szeppi gave a halfhearted growl, then both decided it was a draw and trotted along in an equitable manner.

Sarah broached the subject first. "Is this student thing serious? And are Anita Goshawk and Madame Carpentier treading too hard on student toes? Particularly Hannah Hoyt's toes?"

"One packed dorm room—twenty girls at the most—well, that doesn't make a revolution," said Babette. "But if the idea spreads, it could be nasty. Grace is always tough if she thinks classroom discipline is in danger, but I don't know what's gotten into Anita."

Sarah shook her head. "Schools don't usually encourage students trying to unseat teachers. Particularly teachers who get such good academic results."

"You just wait," said Babette. "The students will probably decide they're being harassed. It's the 'in' thing to be. But our good head, Joanna Singer, is nobody's fool. She'll put the fire out and probably have a quiet word with both Goshawk and Carpentier that will make them pull in their horns."

Here Babette pulled Szeppi loose from a piece of sugared doughnut that had been dropped on the path and fearlessly grabbed another piece out of his snapping jaws. "Anita has me wondering. Maybe she's in the middle of a midlife crisis. More than just menopause. Maybe she didn't get a pay raise this fall. And here's a tidbit. I heard a rumor that Grace wants to take over Anita's big classroom. The language labs are crowded, and more space is needed. Of course, Anita has settled in for life. The room has a bunch of cabinets and a lot of storage for all those millions of art slides and videos she's collected."

"If she loses her art room," said Sarah, "we'll probably find Anita cutting out paper puppets of Grace."

"And," continued Babette, for whom gossip seemed to be her life's blood, "I heard that Adrian Parsons isn't that enchanted with Anita's lectures on Greek and Roman art. Adrian likes to incorporate little snippets about sculpture and architecture into the literature when he's doing his classics thing. Anita claims he's moving onto her turf. Of course, the fact that they used to go out, or sleep together, doesn't smooth the waters. Also, I think that Adrian must really hate being under

Grace in the Language Division. Being number two doesn't become the man."

"One big happy family," said Sarah. "So what about Carlo Leone? He seems to be above the strife."

"Don't you believe it. He's quite a con man and that cool attitude is an act. He's spitting nails because Anita's added Italian lit reading to her Italian art course, and she's been dipping into his reserved bookshelf in the library, telling her students they can check 'em out, so when Carlo's students come for a book, they find it's gone. Carlo told me that if Anita tries that again she's history."

"You, Babette," said Sarah, "are a sacred pool of information. Now all I need is to hear that Grace is doing *Macbeth* in French."

"Hello, hello," called a voice. A voice from a blue Subaru pulled to the side of the path.

"Alex!" shouted Sarah. Dragging Patsy through a melting pile of dirty snow, she reached the car. "Am I glad to see you." She leaned into the driver's window and gave him a quick kiss. "Look, pull in up there, that's the parking lot by Gregory House. I've got you a roll-away cot in my room and all the comforts of home."

Alex parked, emerged, greeted Babette, and reported on his drive down from midcoast Maine. "Not too bad. A semi overturned on I-495, that's about all."

"Let's go out for dinner, right now," said Sarah. "Time's short. Babette, you come with us. The lecture starts at seven-thirty, the reception is afterwards, and then we're on our own."

"Shall I take my things in?" Alex indicated a small duffel bag on the passenger seat.

"No. Gregory House is in turmoil with a bunch of students wanting to decapitate a couple of teachers."

Alex grinned. "High school has not changed, I see."

"Nor will it," said Babette.

"Never mind the students," said Sarah. "Let's hit the road. I've done the research. There's Ciro's, a pasta and pizza place in Chelmsford, off I-495, or Makaha for Chinese, in Acton."

Sarah's sense of pleasure and general euphoria at a weekend free of school, a weekend with Alex, was so strong that when she came upon a small file card tacked to a tree at the edge of the parking lot, she read it, frowned, and shook her head. More of the same. Disgusting. Certainly something to be dealt with, to be turned in later. After dinner. Right now they had plans, dinner and a tight schedule. She glared at the object once more and then folded the rather damp card and stuffed it into her coat pocket. Awkwardly lettered in black marker, it read in its entirety, "MME. GRACE CARPENTIER YOU PIECE OF SHIT. GO ROT IN HELL."

Dinner away from the school, without the shuffling of feet, the banging of trays, and the crescendo of weekend voices, was balm for the weary teaching soul. At Ciro's, Babette positively sparkled over her *Tagliatelli con Salsiccia* and revealed she had a new male friend from Korea, by way of Boston University. A math wizard who had been making suggestions about cohabitation. Alex, who suffered a brutal week of on-call evenings that featured a rising number of flu cases, relaxed with two mugs of home brew and shared with Sarah a dish of shrimp, olives, onions, and mushrooms over fettuccine called *Gamberi con Putanesca*—which sounded, Sarah said, like a sort of Italian gavotte. It was not until the three were discussing the virtues of the various desserts that Sarah, with a guilty thump, remembered the card in her pocket. She reached her hand in and fingered the thing. The folded card, once limp, had dried and now felt stiff. Should she bring the thing out and so throw a pall over the conversation? But why? Neither Alex nor Babette could do a damn thing about it. No. She would simply

85

leave the card at the school office and head for the lecture.

But time was against her. Babette, halfway through her cappuccino, brought her wrist into view, squinted at her watch, and let out a small yelp. "Fifteen minutes. The last thing we need to do is come in late. Anita would make an issue of it, and I already have enough trouble with Grace. Come on." And Babette put down her fork, stood up, and reached for her handbag.

But Alex, in the guise of Sir Galahad, beat her to it. The bill was paid, the tip left, and the three entered the lecture hall in the basement of the shingled, white-pillared Carlisle Art Center with exactly three minutes to spare. And the folded cardboard message still in Sarah's pocket remained undelivered, unread—except by its finder. Or at least she fervently hoped that she was the *only* finder and reader. Surely the file card had not been there earlier in the afternoon when she had taken Patsy for the first of his several outings. Nor when she and Babette set forth on their two-dog walk. The card must be a very recent arrival, and Sarah wondered which discontented student had slipped away from the Gregory House meeting and stuck the thing on the tree.

Alex and Sarah, followed by Babette, settled into their seats, and a tall, red-haired man rose from a front row, proclaimed that the Carlisle Cultural Council was delighted with what was to come. He then read off a long list of Anita's academic honors, and handed her up to the lectern.

Anita had chosen the perfect costume for showing works of art. After all, the lecturer could hardly want to distract from the slides she would be showing. Tonight she wore an ankle-length number in a rich bark brown. The lights dimmed, the screen in front of the stage lit up with Frederic Edwin Church's canvas *Twilight in the Wilderness*, and Anita was off and running, ready to zip through a century of American painting in something like a little over an hour.

After the first few moments there occurred a communal

exhalation of breath, a sitting up and taking notice. Because Anita was damn good. Her speaking voice was low and clear and crisp, and her demeanor gave no sign that she had been recently in a state of high irritation. Her material was well organized and well chosen, and her remarks were to the point, qualities that blessed any lecture. The introduction was followed by a slide, followed by two slides for comparison, followed by a talk on the subjects of European influences, study abroad, the Western experience, and the Hudson River School, and before the audience knew it, landscapes had given way to portraits, to still lifes, to scenes of domestic pleasures, and to worlds of rocky shores and oceans.

Sarah watched as the world of Winslow Homer flashed on and off the screen—croquet, crack the whip, the grim *The Life Line*; saw Homer give way to Albert Pinkham Ryder and his *Moonlight Marine*, who yielded to Thomas Eakins; and as she inspected the placid *Max Schmidt in a Single Scull*, she found her hand again touching the file card. It felt almost hot in her hand, and Sarah began to shift her focus to matters other than art.

Fingering the card, she began to contrast the styles of the first two threats to Madame Carpentier—the two large, black-robed figures discovered in the fall, and the cut-out black paper puppet on the garden trellis and the snake drawing found in the art center. And to compare all these with the message on the file card.

If she were to write an essay on the subject, Sarah would have said that the first two figures were crude, effective, simple-minded—showing, perhaps, a student sense of humor. And the second two efforts, the paper puppet and the snake, showed artistic ability—a sense of design. Whoever had done the last two showed a skilled hand. Hannah Hoyt? Despite her protestations, her denials, Hannah's forte was art, and her recent art project involved cut-outs. Hannah had been the one to find the hanging figure. And Hannah hated the guts of Madame Grace Marie-Henriette Carpentier.

To sum it up, even accounting for differences among these efforts, all suggested a working, if misguided, black sense of humor, with the puppet bordering on the sinister. But the file card slammed one right in the face with its heavy, black capital letters and its brutal message. It seemed unlikely that the delicate scissor work of the paper puppet or the skilled drawing of the rattlesnake had been done by the same awkward hand that printed the file card. Unless. Unless the angry file-card writer had simply grabbed a magic marker and scratched out the thing, marched outside, stuck it to the tree, saying to herself, so there. Up yours. Take that.

Sarah pulled her hand out of her pocket with the sense that her fingers had been soiled by the contact. And, looking up at the screen in the front of the room, became aware that time had passed and Anita was winding it up with William Merritt Chase's peaceful landscape, "Shinnecock Hills"—was he a relative perhaps of the redoubtable Miss Claudia Merritt, Sarah wondered briefly.

Refocusing, Sarah again had the sensation of comfort and order. Anita Goshawk was finishing with a last few, crisp sentences, and listening, Sarah was reminded of the students of Gregory House, their hodgepodge rooms, the disorder, noise, and confusion that seemed to define their lives as much as did their humor, their energy, and their remarkable frankness. And, yes, their honesty. But somehow, tonight, Anita Goshawk's soothing and intelligent presentation seemed remarkably welcome. Perhaps it was not to be wondered at that the lady found the prospects of voodoo clubs and spurious Egyptian ceremonies a bit hard to take.

The red-haired man rose again like some genie from the front of the lecture hall, allowed the audience to propose exactly five questions, cut the sixth off in mid-sentence, and waved his long arms over his head. "Don't forget," he called, "the reception." This, he informed the audience, would take place at the school, Radnor Hall, in the Old Library. And since parking was limited at the school, those with cars should leave them at the art center and take the school footpath to the campus. "After all," the man pointed out, "we're in the middle of a January thaw, so we might as well enjoy it. The path," he added hastily, "for those of you from other parts, is marked with a blue sign and goes into the woods one house beyond the Congregational church."

With that, the audience unraveled itself with a rustling of coats, thumping of footgear, some people surging forward to congratulate Anita, some rising to greet friends, others to head off to the reception. Merritt School receptions were popular affairs with many people in the town, this having less to do with honoring dignitaries than with the presence of a festive table of cold meats, cheeses, homemade biscuits, and cake, as well as a fruit punch or a choice of dry or cream sherry. Besides, for those in the know, there was always the hospitable flask concealed on the person of instructor Carlo Antonio Leone.

Another attraction that Babette pointed out to Sarah and Alex as they made their way down the steps to the walk was that many in the town had a strong curiosity to view the gown on its home turf.

"You know," said Babette, "for some people, it's the school they love to hate. All that feeling about public versus private education comes bubbling up. But others just love Merritt's, think it sheds a kind of a classy glow over the whole town, puts it on the map. And besides, there's always a couple of girls in the school from some famous family, and people hope to bump into them. Last year we had Franklin Roosevelt's great-great-niece and Oprah Winfrey's goddaughter. This year we have a girl who might be related to Houdini."

"I can't wait," said Alex. "Listen, I'll drive the car back to

Gregory House and meet you at the reception. Yes, I can find the way—Scout McKenzie. We can whirl around the crowd for twenty minutes and then hit the road. Okay, ladies?"

This was pronounced satisfactory, and Sarah and Babette, taking their time and letting the crowd swarm past them, began the walk down School Street to the blue sign proclaiming "Miss Merritt's School—Footpath" and took the left turn into a narrow, tree-guarded entrance.

"We'd better move it," said Sarah. "This so-called January thaw is about over. It's starting to rain. Or sleet, and the temperature's taken a real nosedive. I'm glad we both wore coats."

"I don't want to rush," said Babette. "There'll be a mob lined up to shake Anita's hand and tell her how wonderful it was . . ."

"But," interrupted Sarah, "she *was* pretty damn good. Most of the time I just rafted along and enjoyed it. But we can walk fast and then linger under cover later."

The footpath, constructed through the gift of grateful parents whose impossible daughter had managed to ingest a small slice of secondary education before running off to Delray Beach with her boyfriend, ran a serpentine and narrow course through pine, hemlock, and a second growth of birch and oak. At several turnings, other parents and alumnae had presented the school with rustic park benches as well as small, plastic signs that identified specimens of trees and plants. In good weather, the path made a pleasant walk by day and remained navigable at night by the placement of street wrought-iron lamps designed to look like nineteenth-century gaslights. These now shed a limited but adequate glow on the pathway and on the bordering growths of rhododendron, azalea, and laurel, as well as illuminating expiring lumps of snow and small black puddles of water.

The lamps also shed a dim light on a distant figure who was shouldering her way against the flow of foot traffic, away from the campus and toward the School Street entrance.

90

Sarah nudged Babette. "Someone's forgotten something."

"It always happens," said Babette. "You go to a lecture and forget you took your gloves. Or your briefcase."

But now they were in the semi-dark between the lights, and the figure, a woman, approached at a trot. She was bent forward, wrapped in some dark winter garment, intent on moving ahead.

Babette stepped in front of her and peered. "Is that you, Anita? I can hardly see you. Is there anything wrong?"

"You're damn right, something's wrong." It was Anita Goshawk, her face the palest of ovals, showing only a tiny glint from her thick glasses, her figure muffled in black. "Not all of my slides got put back. Adrian said he would do it, and I suppose he forgot. I can't leave them at the art center."

"Pick them up tomorrow," urged Babette. "You're supposed to be at the reception. Besides, the temperature's going down, and it's turning really nasty."

"Fifteen minutes won't make a difference," said Anita. "People will be hanging up their coats, getting something to drink."

"Look," said Babette, "Let me go. You head back. You're the feature attraction."

"No, those slides are not replaceable. I don't want anyone fooling with them. Not even you. Thanks anyway."

And Anita Goshawk, head bent, rushed back down the path and disappeared around a dark corner.

"So much for the guest of honor," said Babette. "She should right now be standing next to Dr. Singer, shaking hands and saying 'Thank you for coming' and 'I'm glad you enjoyed it.' The school spends a bundle on these affairs."

The two women emerged from the path and joined a flow of people heading for Radnor Hall. Of the three men just ahead, Sarah recognized her captor of last night, Jake Markham.

And as luck would have it, Jake, perhaps feeling eyes on him, swiveled about, saw Sarah, and grinned. "Are you prowling at midnight tonight or staying in your coffin and resting?"

"Very funny," said Sarah. Then, turning to Babette, "You know this man, I suppose."

"Jake Markham," said Babette, "helps guard all of us virgins so we may sleep safe in our beds. And by day, when he's not playing policeman, he paints large, erotic oils that have shaken the town to its roots."

Jake dropped back, and as he and Babette engaged in mild repartee, Sarah, seeing Alex ahead, waved and ran up to join him.

"Twenty minutes," said Alex. "Then we are out of here. Girls schools have their place but not on a perfectly good Friday night."

But the crush of people, the leaving of coats, the greeting by Sarah of those teachers she had met, and the introduction of Alex, who was favored by Carlo Leone with the promise of a snort of really great Scotch—all of this took time, and Alex, glancing over at the grandfather clock by the door, saw that twenty valuable minutes had slipped by. And there were still more hands to be shaken.

These were indeed shaken, pressed, clasped. But not the hands of the guest of honor, because—Sarah craned her neck, searching the room—there was no guest of honor.

8

NO Anita Goshawk stood by the fireplace, shoulder to shoulder with Dr. Joanna Singer, to receive the congratulations of the community. Good Lord, how long did it take to jog back to the art center and return? Twenty-five minutes at least had slipped by. And there was Dr. Singer, standing by herself in front of the fireplace. She smiled, inclined her head, shook offered hands, but just as often lifted her head each time a newcomer appeared in the doorway.

Sarah, seeing Jake Markham approach with a plate of tiny rolls filled with slivers of ham, stepped in front of him. "Where's Anita Goshawk?" she asked. "Because," she added, "we're trying to do the proper thing and shake her hand and then get away."

Jake shrugged. "Oh, Anita's somewhere fixing her face, getting ready to enjoy her public."

"I meant," said Sarah, "why isn't she here by now? We met her charging back to the art center to pick up some missing slides. But that shouldn't have taken more than fifteen minutes."

"My thought," said Alex, "is that we greet Dr. Singer, blow the joint, and tomorrow, if we run into Lady Goshawk, we tell her how great the program was."

"Good idea," said a voice. It was Giddy, unnaturally dressy in a two-piece, faux-leather black suit. "Hello, cousin Alex. What are you doing tonight? Want to join me and a few choice friends?"

Alex eyed his cousin. "Giddy, your choice friends are usually enough to kill a horse. How about dinner tomorrow?"

"Well, one particular friend is moving out of my life," said Giddy. "So how about you, Jake? Can you get loose? Jake," she informed Alex, "is a really hot item. Great new series of oils."

Before Jake could reply, Dr. Singer was among them. "Jake," she said, "would you please go over to Anita Goshawk's apartment? Second floor, Lockwood Hall. See what's holding her up."

At which Sarah explained about Anita's return trip for her slides. "I suppose she might have gone back to her apartment to change her shoes. The pathway was on the sloppy side, and it's really coming down now. Rain and sleet. Look, Dr. Singer, Alex—he's my husband, down for the weekend—well, we have to go. We'll take the footpath and see if we can run into her and speed her up."

"Good idea," said Joanna Singer. She turned to Alex and extended a graceful hand. "And how very nice to meet you . . ."

"Alex," said Alex. "Alex McKenzie. The lecture was wonderful. But Sarah's right. We have to move on."

Joanna Singer gave a distracted nod of her head and headed back toward her station by the fireplace.

Amid a welter of wet garments in the cloakroom, Alex and Sarah found their coats and departed, Alex pointing out that his car was at Radnor Hall, so why walk back toward the art center. They could drive over and check from there.

"We should take the footpath," insisted Sarah. "Anita could just have easily slipped on some of that wet snow and be crawling here on her hands and knees because she's broken her ankle."

"And after that, see if Anita has fallen down the art center steps or been electrocuted by her slide apparatus. There are times," said Alex with a sigh, "that being married to a teacher of fiction is a bloody nuisance. Okay, we take the path. And if she's broken her ankle, don't offer my services. I'm an internist and don't know a thing about bones."

"Kind and generous, Dr. Welby," said Sarah, and she strode off in the direction of the footpath's campus entrance.

No Anita Goshawk, on all fours or upright, appeared. Not on the footpath. Not at the art center, which was dark, apparently put to bed for the night. Not on the return down the same pathway. In fact, just as they emerged from the path into a small parking space between two dormitories, Packard Hall and Philipi House, they ran directly into Jake Markham. Who was clearly annoyed.

"She isn't in her apartment. Not even hiding in the bathroom. Jesus, this is my weekend night off-duty, and I'm playing hide-and-seek. Okay, you two, exactly where did you meet her on the path when she was heading back for the slides?"

"About midway," said Sarah. "She was practically running."

"I don't care if she was playing hopscotch. Come on and show me, because if she doesn't turn up in the next few minutes, I'm calling the school security guard on duty and the police station for backup. To help with the search."

But the trip down the path, now slick with snow and rain, and the tour inside and out of the art center—one of the directors having been contacted for a key—proved nothing more than that both areas were uninhabited.

"Hell," said Jake Markham as they reached the halfway section of the path on their return trip. He turned to Sarah. "Is this close to where you last saw her?"

But Sarah didn't answer. Instead, she bent her head and studied the side of the path. There, half-submerged in a dark puddle, one finger resting on a small lump of wet snow, was a glove. Black.

She reached to pick it up but was jerked upright.

Jake shook his head at her. "Not the way to pick up things when you're out looking for a missing person," he said. He reached in his pocket, fumbled, and produced a small plastic bag.

"You carry evidence bags around on your day off?" asked Alex.

"Nope," said Jake. "But I promised to take a slice of cake back to my mother. She couldn't make the reception, and she's crazy about the carrot cake the school makes." With that, Jake broke off a small branch from a rhododendron on the other side of the path, reached down and nudged the glove into the plastic bag, sealed it, pocketed it, and then stuck the branch into the ground close to the glove. "To mark the place," he explained.

But Sarah, her eyes somewhat adjusted to the dim pathway light, had, even in the now pelting rain, seen something else. A trampled and broken section of azalea. She wiped the water from her eyes and squinted. Yes, beyond the broken azalea lay a muddy, disturbed bit of shrubbery, and next to it was a pile of mushy snow with a dirty, depressed center, as if a foot had come down on it. Without hesitating, without thinking, she plunged a short distance into the woods and was rewarded by another trampled piece of undergrowth. Her very next step took her forward and down a small decline, catching her by surprise so that she stumbled several more steps before coming to a halt. Now she stood almost at the lip of what looked like a tree-rimmed pond, though a pond whose black surface barely caught the meager yellow glow of the footpath lamp.

"Hey, come back here!" It was Jake Markham calling. Angry.

"Sarah, damnation, what do you think you're doing?" Alex, yelling.

But Sarah didn't answer. She stood rigid. Frozen in place. Because beyond her feet, right by the water's edge, lay an enormous shape. The shape of a bat, wings wide and black. But this bat had arms at the end of its wings. Dark arms and black hands. No, correction. One black hand. And one hand pale and clenched. A hand without a glove. And beside the hand, faintly gleaming, was a cracked lens from a pair of glasses.

Sarah later wondered whether she had called out or simply stood there making inarticulate noises. Whatever she did, her voice brought Alex and Jake crashing through the undergrowth. And then, as Sarah, without speaking, pointed ahead at the dark, unmoving shape, both stopped. Exhaled. And swore.

Jake: "Jesus H. Christ, what in hell is that?"

Alex, quietly, grimly: "Jesus is right." He took a short pause, a deep breath, and then, "Okay. Let me have a look."

Jake, taking charge: "I'll come with you. But watch what you walk on. Sarah, you stay put. Don't move an inch."

Sarah about to protest, remembered. If a human, a human flat on its face, an unmoving human, appears—anywhere, be it forest or pond or drawing room or lecture hall—leave it be. Leave it be unless you are called on for CPR or other heroic measures involving rescue and comfort. But now, as two certified helpers, Alex and Jake, the doctor and the policeman, pushed through to the edge of the pond, Sarah told herself to stand still and shut up.

Shut up and leave them alone, leave them to get on with it—whatever "it" was. But her every muscle and bone and nerve wanted to push forward, forward to . . . to do what?

To stare down at this bat-like person. Unless the person was not a person anymore. Just a body? Or was it a body? Sarah crazily thought about the hockey stick figure and the scarecrow of Grace Carpentier in the black choir robe—could another like object been dumped in the woods? Perhaps to be used at some auspicious occasion. She hoped hard that "it" would prove to be a scarecrow, and the more she hoped, the less likely this seemed. And so she had to do *something*. She raised her hands to her mouth and shouted, "Alex, Jake, I'll go and get help. The rescue squad."

And Jake roared back, "Hang on. Stay put. Don't move. I'll lead you back in a minute."

And Sarah understood. The human form, if living, must be dealt with. Right now. Pronto. Stat. But if it were dead, just a body, well, a body must be left untrampled. And everything around the body—if it was a body—must not be violated. But it didn't even seem to be a body with a proper head, just a dark, mangled-looking, misshapen lump. Oh God, she felt sick to her stomach. But she couldn't be sick. *Repeat after me, everything around a body—if it was a body—must be left exactly, exactly . . .*

Sarah put her head down and breathed through her nose, then slowly straightened and tried to focus ahead to the edge of the pond. Three dim shapes. Jake standing. Alex kneeling on the ground, kneeling by the black bat shape. Not a bat, more like a stingray. Those triangular wings. And no one was moving. No one was doing CPR. No one was trying to save a life, clear a passage for air, bring back breath, start up a heartbeat. Then Alex stood up and shook his head.

And Jake, picking his way carefully through the brush, came back to Sarah. He didn't waste his words. "She's gone. Must have happened within the last hour. She's still warm."

"But what, what happened?" Sarah's words stumbled out.

"Severe head injury. I mean *severe*. She couldn't have survived. Not even with all the doctors in Boston working on her."

"Do you know who, what?" Sarah stopped, incoherent.

"That can wait. Listen, I'll walk you back to where you left the path. Then you stay right there. Alex will stay with the body. I'll go back and call the police station and get things moving, call the ambulance. No arguments." This as Sarah began to shake her head. "Just make sure," Jake continued, "that no one goes into the woods here. Send anyone who comes along back to Radnor Hall and tell them to stay in the building until the police come. Any trouble, you've got Alex close by. Got that? Good."

And Jake took Sarah by the arm, steered her carefully past the tramped-down underbrush, and pointed to one of the park benches a few feet away where they had emerged from the woods. And then he was off at a run.

Sarah at first tried to compose herself and her jittering mind. Tried to force her mind to calming subjects. Work. Teaching. Her students' assignments to come. Like the dark and deathly affairs in *Bleak House*? Like *Macbeth*? Like Wilfred Owen and the dying soldiers? No, forget it. There were no calming subjects, not tonight anyway.

Sarah, unable to sit still, stood up and began to pace the path. Up twenty steps, back twenty steps. Like that children's game. What was it? Mother may I. Mother May I take twenty giant steps? Twenty umbrella steps? Twenty baby steps? Oh, goddamnit to hell. And *who* was that lying like a wet, black stingray by the pond? Who always wore a handsome black wool cape?

And then, as if to force out the answer she already knew, Sarah, on her sixtieth step back to the trampled-down entrance to the woods, caught in the corner of her eye the glint of something. Something metal. In the dim light, something with a dull gold rim. Without thinking, she reached down—as she had with the glove—and picked it up.

A pin. No, a brooch. Cold, heavy. Slowly she turned it over and held it under the lamplight. And, despite a smear of mud over its surface, the face was clear. The emperor Caligula. Or someone similar. In cameo. As recently seen fastened to the collar of the distinctive black cape worn by Madame Marie-Henriette Carpentier.

And Sarah, as if it had been a hot coal, dropped it back on the ground.

Then, chiding herself for irresponsible behavior—she had already covered it with fingerprints—she picked the object up between thumb and forefinger. Dropped it into her coat pocket, betook herself to the bench, sat down, locked her hands over her chest, and planted her feet on the path. And waited.

And waited.

And the waiting—waiting in a state of suspended horror—defined the night.

Waiting is, of course, part of the homicide game. And Alex, perched uncomfortably on a large fallen pine log close to the spread-eagled body of the woman, tried to force his thoughts away from any self-centered regrets. Regrets at having driven down from Maine to spend a quiet weekend with Sarah, visit old friends, old haunts, take in a show, go on a hike along the Esplanade. What was that old saying, "age before beauty"? Well, this was death before pleasure. A true thought if there ever was one.

And this was death in its most vile aspect. When he and Jake, finding the woman's skin still holding some warmth, had examined her head to judge if CPR was a possibility, they found her skull and her face beaten, clubbed, pounded not just with a killing blow or two, but with an extra measure of violence. Repeated blows. Blows to the mouth, the ears, the eyes, the chin, the brow, the cheeks. Blows that reduced what must have once been a face into a pulp of splintered bone, macerated tissue, shards of teeth, and matted strands of blood-soaked hair.

100

Alex closed his eyes, as if for a moment trying to prevent the likeness of this gory atrocity from becoming part of memory, but knowing that even as he tried to erect a barricade, it was now being imprinted on his memory, there to join with other past images of the sick, the grievously injured, the dying, the dead. It was all part of the physician's baggage, Alex reflected, kicking out at a broken branch next to his feet. And what had this person done to incite such a spasm of homicidal wrath? For one thing was certain; this death was no chance affair, no accident. This must have been intended as a killing from first blow to last. There was little doubt that the life and last moments of the person over whom he kept vigil had ended most wretchedly.

Had it ended in blinding pain? Had the first blow, crashing down on her skull, done its work, knocked her out? Knocked her out so that she collapsed, arms flung out, senseless, to the ground? He most ardently hoped this had been so. The alternative, that she was conscious for any part of the rage-driven battering, was awful to think about. So he would try not to. Not now, anyway. Later, under the business-like eye of some forensic pathologist, it would all be dealt with and presented, a physiological puzzle laid out on an autopsy table.

Alex shifted on his log—the damp was sinking into his trousers, the mixed snow and rain was beating down his neck, and his feet felt as if they had been wrapped in ice chips. He recrossed his legs and swore aloud at nothing in particular except the sheer insanity of much of what passed for ordinary life.

Jake Markham did not have the discomfort of waiting by a corpse and swearing, nor, like Sarah, of sitting on a bench fighting demons; he could move. He had people to call, systems and procedures to activate. Half-jogging, half-running, he pounded along the footpath toward the school. Twice he paused to order

some startled walkers back to Radnor Hall, back into the Old Library. "Where that reception is going on," he said. "An accident—tell anyone you see to go there. And stay put."

Then off he went, cursing because he was out of uniform, had no cellular phone, no service revolver, not even a whistle. Reaching Philipi House, the dormitory that stood closest to the path entrance, he hurled himself into the common room, grabbed a telephone, called the necessary assistance, and headed for Radnor Hall. Arriving breathless, he herded straggling students, faculty, and townspeople who were retreating from what was proving to be a non-reception back into the Old Library. There, spotting Joanna Singer, who had long since given up her stand at the fireplace, he strode across the long, Persian carpet and delivered six succinct sentences. Joanna, no stranger to sudden mishap—only last year a student, run amok, had pushed a campus visitor in front of passing car—took in the story, nodded, and held up her hand and called for silence.

Jake, leaving the headmistress to handle her end of things until the forces of law and order took over, raced back past Philipi House, charged along the slippery surface of the footpath, and found Sarah sitting on her bench like someone frozen in time.

"Sarah," he shouted. "Come to. The ambulance, the police, the works will be here any minute. And it's going below freezing, so get up and walk around. You'll get stiff sitting there."

And Sarah, trying not to associate the word "stiff" with the horror in the woods, stood up a little unsteadily. And then felt in her pocket.

"I found this," she said. She held the cameo brooch under the lamp, turning it so that its gold caught the light. "By the edge of the path. I didn't dare leave it down on the ground. Someone might have stepped on it. Got fingerprints all over it."

"But you," Jake said in a hard voice, "have gotten *your* fingerprints all over it."

Sarah felt a rise of anger. "Damn it, I'm sorry, but at least I saved it from being stepped on. Or pushed into the mud."

Jake cocked his head. "They're coming. I hear the siren. Give me the thing, and I'll turn it in. Do you," he added, almost as an afterthought, "know who it belongs to?"

Sarah nodded. "Yes, to Madame Carpentier. You've probably seen it, too. On the collar of that black cape she wears."

"Like the sort of cape on the person back there in the woods?"

Sarah's answer was made almost inaudible by the sound of heavy engines and running feet. But Jake was able to make out a muffled "Yes, like that."

And they came. Men, women, boxes, bags, cameras, a wheeled stretcher, and two men and a woman from the Carlisle Rescue Squad. Sarah retreated to her bench. The bench had, she now noticed, a dimly lit brass plaque that proclaimed this particular bench dedicated to the memory of one Althea Maxcy, Beloved Teacher of Biology at Miss Merritt's School, 1922–1936.

She sat down again and let the investigating team swarm past her. And, like Alex, she tried not to think about what she had seen. Tried not to think about Madame Grace Carpentier stretched prone on the crumpled leaves and trampled bracken by the pond. Grace Carpentier, chief instructor in French, head of the Language Division, and scourge of the inattentive, the slack, and the reluctant student. Would there ever be a bench set in some green hideaway—by the garden trellis, perhaps—dedicated to the memory of Grace Carpentier? They surely couldn't say "beloved teacher," as they had of Althea Maxcy. Or were past deeds and past reputations forgotten, and with the passage of time, did all teachers become "beloved"?

From such unprofitable thoughts Sarah was rudely jolted by the sudden appearance of Jake Markham. He stared at her, frowning.

"Sarah! For God's sake, didn't I ask you to go on back to

the school? I meant to. Go on. You'll freeze here and be in every-one's way. They're going to rope off the whole area."

Sarah, realizing perhaps that this was a man under some stress, did not snap back at Jake, which she would have liked to do, but rose to her feet. Then hesitated.

"Is it, I mean, was it Madame Carpentier?" she asked.

Jake shook his head. "Right now, we're saying we have an unidentified victim. Until we can go through the ID procedure."

"But you do know who she is?" persisted Sarah.

"Look, Sarah, go on back to Gregory House. We'll get your statement later. We're making sure everybody we can lay hands on stays put in their houses or dorms or in the Old Library."

"And Alex?"

"He'll probably go on to the county morgue with us. Later on he can report what he found to the medical examiner. But they won't do a post—an autopsy—tonight. Tomorrow morning maybe. I'll tell him where you are. Okay?" Here Jake, thinking that he had been less than civil, patted Sarah awkwardly on the shoulder, and then following the path made by a newly arrived large searchlight, he headed back into the woods.

And Sarah started down the path, her head bent into the increasing sleet. Suddenly she wanted an interval of normalcy. Alex, her apartment, a hot bath, her dog. Despite police pres-ence, despite murder, Patsy would most surely have to be taken out, wouldn't he? Even if his every move, his very act of pissing on a rosebush would be watched and noted. Sarah strode ahead, noting, as she hurried past Philipi House, past Packard House, through the network of pathways, through the parking lot, the police presence—the large numbers of unfamiliar cars, unfamiliar figures in raincoats and dark jackets. A uniformed state trooper was walking purposely toward Radnor Hall. A Concord police car. Did Concord help out with Carlisle crime, she wondered. And was this a matter for the state police or did they just show up to give a hand? In Maine it was the state police CID who took over, but what about Massachusetts?

With these questions buzzing in her head, Sarah found she had reached and entered the glassed-in vestibule of Gregory House. She hesitated in this now-familiar cluttered space, taking in the children's plastic truck, a snowboard, a sled, and, sticking out of a wooden barrel, several lacrosse sticks, a clutch of hockey sticks, a riding crop, and a skateboard. In an open footlocker protruded rollerblades, an abandoned baseball glove, a single sneaker, a frisbee, and a three-ringed notebook. All normal, everyday objects. But by now, the whole house should be throbbing with expectation and curiosity, but perhaps not yet alarm. Because surely the word of the murdered French teacher had not yet been spread abroad. The students and the faculty would have been told of an accident. They would know that for some curious reason Anita Goshawk had not turned up for her own reception. And they would have noticed the absence of Madame Carpentier.

And suddenly, Sarah, as she mounted the stairs, felt a finger of ice move down her spine. Who had been picking fights with Madame Grace for the past few days? Who had heard that her very own history of art classroom, her hallowed collection of cabinets, her state-of-the-art film apparatus, her files, films, and videos were under siege by the powerful head of the Language Division? Grace Carpentier was, Sarah reminded herself, a lady with clout, with seniority, and, to borrow an expression, a lady who had the balls to snatch a classroom of a fellow faculty member. Anita Goshawk was apparently fair game, ready to be shoved aside. So Anita Goshawk, another lady with balls, had taken action.

Sarah, without student interruption, reached her apartment door, unlocked it, entered, and was met by a rapturous Patsy. Absentmindedly, her thoughts still fixed on the awful sequence of events she just put together, she poured out five cups of kibbles for the dog, walked to her refrigerator and assembled a piece of bread, a pot of marmalade, a package of tea, and plugged in her electric kettle, an object she had brought with her from Maine. She was strangely hungry, hungry for simple, comforting food.

Fifteen minutes and two cups of tea later, Sarah had fashioned a script. Anita Goshawk, who had left the art center as soon as she was free of questions and well-wishers, must have noticed that Grace Carpentier was lingering there for some reason, knowing that Grace was probably not eager to be part of a Goshawk congratulatory scene. "Aha!" Anita might have thought. "Here is the chance of a lifetime." So Anita, at some point along the path, would turn around, telling anyone who questioned the direction in which she was traveling that she had left her slides behind—just as she told Babette and Sarah herself. Anita would have continued back toward the art center and met Grace on the pathway.

Anita would have been pleased at the location because, since murder was now her object, the woods would make a more private killing place than the more open areas around the art center or the school. Anita must have engaged Grace in conversation, pretended perhaps to be looking for something, and asked Grace to help her. Grace would bend down. And wham! Bang! On the head. Or the back of the neck. But with what? Sarah pushed that inconvenient question aside for the moment. Anyway, Grace was felled. Or dragged in a semi-conscious condition—she remembered the glove, the cameo brooch falling off at the path's edge—into the woods, toward the pond. Away from the footpath traffic. Then, fueled by hate, jealousy, and fear, the job would be finished. And Grace, in her bat-wing cape, would be left dead or dying by the pond's edge.

And Anita? Certainly not back to the reception. Back perhaps to her apartment to wash. To dispose of bloody garments.

To hide the death instrument. Instrument? Again, Sarah's speeding imagination stumbled, unable to imagine what object had been used to bludgeon the French teacher's head into the bloody pulp she had glimpsed. Never mind, leave that problem to the police. What next? A clean and freshened Anita would then simply not show up at the reception. Would she call Radnor Hall and plead a sudden sickness? A migraine? Yes, a migraine was always useful. But, on the other hand, why in God's name would Anita hang around to be surprised by the sad news of a departed teacher? No, Sarah thought, Anita would pack a suitcase, find her passport—art history teachers must keep up-to-date passports for worldwide museum visiting—climb into her car, and take off. Off into the wild blue—or black—yonder.

Sarah was about to picture Anita entering Logan Airport's International Departure Lounge when Patsy, by paw and howl, reminded her of his pressing need. She left Anita standing at the check-in counter—Alitalia, El-Al, KLM, Air France—Sarah hadn't decided on the final destination, Albania perhaps, or Iran. Some country too busy with civil disorder to worry about strange visitors.

Sarah snapped on Patsy's leash, pulled on her coat, grimaced at the freezing sleet pinging against the windows, and guided an eager Patsy into the corridor and down the stairs. She was fumbling in her pocket for a scarf to cover her head when footsteps and a whining noise arrested her.

Szeppi. Sarah turned and saw that Szeppi, the now ownerless black, curly-haired dog, was nosing his way into the vestibule. But Szeppi had his leash clipped to his collar. And the leash was held by a hand.

And a sharp, entirely too familiar voice said, "*Merde*, what dreadful weather. We shall be soaked. Please, Sarah Deane, keep your dog away from Szeppi. No matter what you say, I cannot trust so large a dog. Szeppi must be allowed to go out safely and do his duty. Even with all this so unnecessary fuss going on. These policemen. Everywhere. Thank you."

And Madame Grace Marie-Henriette Carpentier, swathed in a quilted purple coat and a red and black head scarf, swept past Sarah and out into the night.

9

SARAH, mouth open, turned to a pillar of salt. Or marble. To a lump of uncomprehending flesh. Not until Patsy had half-dragged her out of the vestibule, barking after the receding figures of Szeppi and Grace Carpentier, did Sarah close her mouth and come back to life. And shout.

And Grace Carpentier stopped by the parking lot lamp with enough light on her upturned face for Sarah to see a look of extreme irritation.

"What is it you want, Sarah Deane? Please keep that dog of yours at a distance. Thank you. And speak quickly because this is most foul weather, and Szeppi must not be disturbed when he wets, because he will again ask to go out, which will be not convenient. I do not wish to come outside on two occasions this evening."

What Sarah wanted to say was, "Why aren't you dead?" But somehow this very live and annoyed presence in front of her put a clamp on her mouth, so she faltered, then asked weakly,

"What, Madame Carpentier, is going on? All the police cars. I heard there was an accident."

Grace Carpentier made an expressive and most Gallic gesture with her shoulders and her outspread hands. "I cannot say. We have been told not to ask inopportune questions, so I have not done so. And I suggest that you, Miss Deane, follow those instructions. And now you must attend to the needs of your dog, who is this minute about to lift his leg against the lamppost, which is most improper. I always take Szeppi back into the garden." And Madame Carpentier, head erect, marched off into the driving sleet toward the garden path, Szeppi pulling on his leash and giving out short, sharp barks as he rushed this way and that in front of her.

Sarah was left to totter about the lower garden, struggling with an energetic Patsy, who seemed to have an urge to join Szeppi. Returning to her apartment, her mind reeling with revisions and changed scenarios, she ran a full tub of hot water, bubbling with a gel product that claimed to reduce tension and stress.

She sank in under the foam and let the hot water do its work. Clear her brain. Sweep out the place—Sarah pictured her brain right at that moment as something like an uncleaned cow barn, full of muck, wet straw, and foul odor. Okay, Grace Carpentier was alive. A known fact. Hang on to that. Then where in hell was Anita Goshawk—Sarah's murderer-elect? Now murderer manqué. Or was it murderess? Had the title "murderess" gone the way of "actress" and "stewardess"? Somehow Sarah, who clung stubbornly to a few stereotypes, had always liked to picture the male of the murderer species as a sort of hybrid of Jimmy Cagney, Humphrey Bogart, and Al Pacino. And the female murderess gliding about in trailing, plum-colored velvet, mixing potions, fingering stilettos, and holding bed pillows aloft. Bette Davis and Judith Anderson. Or perhaps Cruella Deville, with her Glenn Close voice. Murderer. Murderess. But

110

how about Murderessa? Like Contessa. Sarah sat up abruptly in her bath. Stop it, she ordered herself. Get a grip. Start to think.

Of course, she could always wait until Alex came home to explain that Madame Grace Carpentier had a clone, an evil twin sister who wore a black cape and a cameo brooch, and that this twin had been beaten unto death by—well, who else? Madame Grace herself.

Sarah, as if to stimulate her thought process, rubbed her sponge over a cake of soap and scrubbed the back of her neck. Okay, her original picture of what happened wasn't too much out of whack. Reverse the picture. If Anita hated Grace enough to kill her—scenario one—then it was equally possible that Grace hated Anita enough to make up scenario two. Which was that Grace trailed Anita down the path when Anita was on her return trip to rescue her slides, perhaps even walked along with her, feigning friendship and forgiveness, waited until the two were alone, and then went for her. Never mind how. That script fitted just as well as the first, given the fact of the vanished Anita Goshawk and the very much alive Grace Carpentier out there in the garden with her dog.

But. Here Sarah slid back under the foam until her only her face was above water—the better to relax and face the fly that just appeared in the ointment. The cape. The cameo brooch. What in God's name was that body—aka Anita Goshawk—doing wearing Grace's cape? The cape was Grace Carpentier's signature garment. With the brooch on the collar. Had Anita stolen Grace's cape? Sarah remembered Anita rushing by on the path wrapped in something dark. A cape? A coat? Who could tell? Sarah—and maybe Babette, too—had been more interested in why Anita was traveling in the wrong direction than in wondering if she was wearing borrowed clothing. Later on, after the body had been discovered, Jake didn't mention the cape as something familiar. But Jake was playing policeman and talking about waiting for a proper ID. What a muddle. Damn.

Sarah reared out of the suds, threw the sponge through the open bathroom door into the bedroom, where it rested damply on Alex's fold-away cot pillow, and said in a very loud voice, "Bloody hell."

"I agree," said Alex. Standing there at the bathroom door, his dark brown hair hanging wet over his forehead, his best gray tweed jacket, donned for the reception, moist and rumpled. He walked slowly over to the bed and sat down on the edge looking very much like a man who had been dragged through several knot holes.

Sarah reached with her toe for the drain, pulled herself out of the tub, grabbed a towel and a bathrobe, and joined him.

"What's happened?" she said.

"Just finished up," said Alex, sagging back against a bed pillow.

"You mean the autopsy?"

"No, that's tomorrow morning. I've been with the pathologist—the medical examiner—going over the details. How we found her, her condition on superficial examination, why we didn't initiate CPR. Stuff they'll need for the death certificate. God, I'm tired."

"But who? Because it wasn't Madame Carpentier. She's alive and well and as nasty as ever. So it's got to be . . ."

"No official ID. They'll have to use dental records for that, I suppose, considering the condition of the woman's head. The headmistress, Dr. Singer, she's driving over to the morgue to make a tentative identification. On the basis of the clothing."

"She was wearing a cape belonging to Grace Carpentier. And the brooch I found along the path, and maybe even the glove, is Grace's. I suppose they came off in some sort of struggle. But how anyone got that cape away from Grace in the first place is beyond me."

112

"Never mind the cape. There's no real mystery about who it is. The victim is the art teacher. Anita Goshawk. As soon as we turned the body over, I recognized the dress. After all, she stood up in front of us for more than an hour giving a lecture. A dark, reddish brown one-piece thing with a high neck."

Sarah took a deep breath and then nodded. "Yes, since it wasn't Grace, it had to be Anita Goshawk. She'd been missing since after the lecture. Babette and I may have been the last ones to see her when we bumped into her on the path." Sarah looked up at Alex and gave him a wan smile. "As to your identifying Anita Goshawk's dress, I would have sworn in court that you never notice what any women wear. That Anita could have worn a shower curtain at the lecture, and you wouldn't have batted an eye."

Alex gave a tired grin. "I don't usually. But Anita had lopsided breast works. One breast was higher than the other. It gave her a skewed look. I wondered if she'd had a mastectomy and her bra, her prosthesis, had slipped down. So, you see, I looked at her a little more intensely than usual."

Sarah shook her head. "You know, Alex, you should be bottled and put on a shelf. You are something else. Only a totally obsessed doctor would come out with that statement. I'll bet you don't even know what the poor woman was lecturing on."

"American painting in the nineteenth century, portraiture, landscape, the move away from romanticism, the influence of European impressionism, early hints of abstract expressionism. Et cetera, et cetera. Want me to take a quiz?"

Sarah looked at her husband with something like active dislike. "There are times, Alex McKenzie, when I truly hate you. Okay, I'm sorry, very sorry about Anita Goshawk. Maybe she wasn't exactly a cozy character—in fact, from my few encounters, I'd say she was pretty prickly. But I've also heard she was a damn good teacher, and the school will be hard put to replace her."

"Amen to that," said Alex. "But don't blame me for noticing physical oddities. It's part of the job. If I see blue fingernails or hear someone breathing like a steamboat whistle, I pay attention."

Sarah sighed. "Life lived in a clinic. Okay, how about tea, even if you never touch the stuff. Herbal? Or just a beer. I put in a supply because I am aware of your needs. Let's hope we have a rest period before someone knocks on the door and starts asking questions." Sarah rose, and followed by Alex, padded into the kitchen alcove and turned on the kettle.

Alex reached over her shoulder, opened the refrigerator, and removed a green bottle of Heineken's best. "You have the tea, I'll go with the brew. I think we're safe from the police. Until morning, that is. Tonight they'll be working on the physical evidence, taking preliminary statements, and setting up procedures."

Sarah was silent, busied herself over a cup of herbal peach tea, and then, mug in hand, she joined Alex in the little sitting area. "Have they found what was used to hit her over the head?"

"There's a team working over the whole area—a god-awful job with this weather. Tomorrow, when it's light, they'll send more people into the woods, check the pond and the school grounds. The playing fields. Then the school dormitory houses and classroom buildings."

"You mean the works?"

"Right. From top to bottom. So let's hope . . ."

But the sentence remained unfinished. Instead, a heavy double knock sounded at the door. It was Hannah Hoyt and, behind her, Rosemary and Zoë. All were now remarkably neat in skirts and jackets, their going-to-lecture costumes.

"We won't stay," said Hannah, coming in and plopping herself into the nearest chair. "But we wanted to know what you know, because someone said you knew something."

"Alex," said Sarah, "these are three senior students, who are supposed to be staying in their rooms."

"No," said Hannah. "It's okay. We've given a statement to some plainclothes cop. He wanted to know where we went after the lecture, and did we see anything peculiar at the reception. But none of us went to the reception because all we had to do for our history of art grade was go to the lecture."

"So what can we do for you?" asked Alex. "I'm Alex McKenzie, and Sarah is my wife."

Rosemary chuckled. "She'd better be, or our house parents would have you expelled. Gregory House is very moral."

"You can tell us what's going on," said Zoë, looking up at Alex's six feet from her five-feet two. "We know you're a doctor, and we saw you with Jake Markham. What accident are they talking about? Is it Miss Goshawk? Because we heard she didn't turn up for the reception."

"What Zoë is asking," said Hannah, "is whether someone like Miss Goshawk has been murdered. I mean, whatever happened must be something pretty major."

Alex shook his head. "You'll hear about it tomorrow from your school people. But, yes, there's been an accident. And no, there has been no positive identification of the person involved. So good night, ladies. Thanks for coming in."

"You mean," said Rosemary, "get lost."

"You took the words right out of his mouth," said Sarah. "We're sorry we can't help, but please put a lid on the speculation and go to bed."

"So I shouldn't tell you that Zoë and I saw Miss Goshawk running past Philipi House wearing Madame Carpentier's cape?" asked Rosemary.

"And I'll bet," said Zoë, "Madame Carpentier will have her head when she finds out. If someone hasn't gotten Miss Goshawk first."

"Lately," said Hannah, "Miss Goshawk has been on some sort of campaign, like she wanted to beat Carpentier at her own game. But I guess we'd be sorry if anything happened, because she's a good teacher. I mean, she really made you think, even if it hurt."

"Thank you, Hannah, for those thoughts, and good night to all of you," said Sarah. "You should add what you've told us to your statement tomorrow. But now, outta here."

The door closed, the three could be heard banging down the hall, and Sarah returned to the little gateleg table that served as a dinner table, sat down, and picked up her cup of tea.

"Probably," she said, "those girls know more now than the police will at the end of two weeks."

"I," returned Alex, "will finish this glass of beer, take a shower, and then, because I am feeling lonely, will join you in that twin bed for part of a night's sleep. Patsy may have the roll-away cot with my blessing."

It was a tribute to the extreme fatigue of both parties that, despite the restrictions of a twin-sized bed, both Alex and Sarah slept heavily and without undue interruptions of nightmares, something Sarah was prone to after a day of agitation. It wasn't until Patsy placed his gray bearded chin across Alex's throat that either woke.

"Damn that dog," said Alex, shoving Patsy away.

"He wants to go out," mumbled Sarah, pulling the pillow over her head.

"Your dog," said Alex, sitting up.

"Trade-off?" said Sarah. "I don't feel up to the school cafeteria scene, but I've got food here. I'll get your breakfast, and you walk Patsy. Maybe you'll meet Madame Carpentier with Szeppi. Begin your day with a bang."

116

Forty minutes later, over orange juice, tea, coffee, and instant oatmeal, Alex told Sarah he had met a charming French woman with a black, curly-haired dog. "A lot cuter than Patsy. So was that the Madame Medusa I've been hearing about?"

"I suppose," said Sarah nastily, "she likes strange men and was all grace and favor with you."

"*Mais oui*," said Alex. "We exchanged dog news—Szeppi has been a bit on the constipated side, and he fears Patsy. For which I don't blame him. Madame hopes that I have a visit the most pleasant."

"I suppose you chatted it up in French."

"*Certainement*," said Alex, helping himself to a slightly burned piece of toast.

"I don't want to cast a shadow on your day, but Jake Markham called. The autopsy is scheduled for eleven o'clock. Also, the whole school community is to meet in the Lothrup Auditorium at ten. A briefing, I suppose, to let everyone know what's happened before the media hits the school. Already the word's gone out from the office asking that no one talk to anyone from the press. The police don't want the investigation trashed by some reporter, and parents mustn't be riled up by seeing their daughters talking up a storm on the evening news. But of course all of this is going to happen anyway. You can't keep the whole school population quiet forever."

Alex drained his coffee cup and looked at his watch. "Right, then. I'm off. I said I'd meet with the pathologist and go over my statement."

"But you don't have anything official to do?"

"God, no. I'm just a witness. An after-the-fact one. I say my piece, sign my statement, and get out."

"We can go into Boston this afternoon, do you think? Put a little distance between all this and us."

"We'll see," said Alex. "I think the weather's going to go on being lousy. Snow, sleet, and rain. But I'll meet you back here around one, and we can grab lunch somewhere."

The Lothrop Auditorium was a brick addendum to what had once been the school chapel. The Merritt School chapel—dark, scalloped shingles and dark red brick—had been built in a particularly hideous combination of Queen Anne and Gothic revival at a period when chapel services were an integral part of the school program. The dark woodwork and the rather murky, stained-glass windows—each of these given in the name of a departed student—encouraged little in the way of positive thinking, and after chapel attendance ceased to be compulsory, the space was only used for such traditional occasions as the Christmas program, the awarding of honors, the graduation ceremony, and, of course, memorial services for the recently deceased members of the school community.

Sarah, wrapped in a slicker against the blowing snow, skirted the chapel entrance and headed toward the auditorium door. She couldn't help but think that in a matter of days the chapel itself would again be called into service. On the lower steps of the auditorium, she found herself swept into a moving stream of students, a stream punctuated here and there by a faculty member.

"So, what do you think's going on in our little community?" said a voice behind her. Carlo Leone, straw hair combed flat, and looking unnaturally somber in a gray pin-striped suit.

"I gather," Carlo went on, "that Anita is either in intensive care or in the morgue, but no one has shared much information, not even with the faculty." He reached for the door and held it open.

"Isn't that the point of this assembly?" asked Sarah, squeezing in between two students.

But Carlo was now holding the door as Dr. Joanna Singer

118

pushed through. She looked, even to the casual eye, as if she'd gone through a rigorous night, her face pinched, her eyes shadowed.

Sarah looked back and found her elbow seized and herself guided. "Faculty usually sits off to the left," said Carlo, and in short order Sarah found herself wedged between Carlo and a large, walrus-like man who was, she remembered, one of the musical faculty and director of the school chorus and glee club. A Mister—or was it Herr—Mittendorf? She had only a few minutes to marvel at the building, a structure made of huge panels of glass, arching steel supports, and rows of blue, upholstered theatre seats, and to spare a brief thought that perhaps the old chapel was the better place for dispensing grim information and sharing dark thoughts. Then Dr. Singer was on the stage, neat as ever in a navy suit. She put her glasses on the table by her side and spoke without notes.

The message was given without flourish. "Thank you for coming," said Dr. Singer. "I very much regret to tell you that our colleague and friend, Dr. Anita Goshawk, whom many of you either have known through her classes in history of art or have met during school activities, died last night in an incident that took place on school property. In the woods on one side of the footpath. Her death is presumed not to have been an accident, and the police have cordoned off the footpath area, and you are asked to avoid the area. The police have begun taking statements from members of the school community. If any of you saw or heard anything, or remember something that you have not already mentioned that might pertain to Dr. Goshawk's movements last evening, please let Dean Greenwald know, as he will be in touch with the investigators."

Here Joanna Singer paused, and a shadow seemed to pass over her face, and her mouth took on a grim, straight line.

"It is always better to be safe than sorry. So, although we dislike the idea, a curfew will be in effect this weekend. Students are to be in their houses by eight-thirty this evening. Also, we are asking that during the day you do not leave the school grounds. And that on campus, you go from place to place in groups of two or more. I know many of you, teachers and students, have weekend plans, or expected to take part in team sports. I'm afraid these will have to be canceled. For those of you who are troubled by this event—and it is indeed a very disturbing one—and wish to talk about it, Dr. Kretikos, Miss Holz, and Mrs. Johnson, our school counselors and psychologists, will be in their offices all day and through the weekend."

Another pause, and then Dr. Singer seemed to straighten her shoulders. "And now let me say that Anita Goshawk was the pillar of our History of Art Department, a loyal and most valuable member of the school. She was an inspired and rigorous teacher who always asked the very best of her students. She will be sadly missed. I ask you now all to stand and bow your heads for a minute of silence in her memory. Thank you."

And with a shuffling of shoes and rustling of coats and jackets, the school rose as one body and bowed its many heads. And then, subdued, made its way out of the auditorium.

And Sarah, almost as soon as she had reached the door, was surrounded. By Hannah, Rosemary, and Zoë, the first two in yellow slickers, the latter in her hooded green slicker, looking for all the world like a figure from an Irish folk tale.

"It's like this," said Rosemary, looking down on Sarah from her three-inch advantage. "We, none of us, really know the psychologists, the counselors, and . . ." Her voice trailed off.

"Like, the three of us haven't had a nervous breakdown, or a major family thing like a father running away with the Avon Lady or a mother drinking and deciding she's really a man," put in Zoë.

"So, we really haven't had a chance to try the counselors out," finished Rosemary. "I thought once about going in and saying that I'm being harassed by all these no-good, white folk trash like Zoë and Hannah here, but I never got around to it."

"What we're saying is we know you, sort of, anyway," said Hannah. "So we'd like to talk about this. Just for a little bit. We thought we'd get pizzas and meet in my room. Or your room, if you don't mind. Your room hasn't got so much junk around."

A true statement if there ever was one, thought Sarah. She looked at her watch—ten forty-five—looked at the three expectant faces, and nodded. "Okay. But I am supposed to meet Alex at one."

"Then you don't want a pizza?" asked Rosemary.

At which suggestion Sarah's stomach gave a sudden twitch, and she smiled. "One medium. Loaded."

Identification of the homicide victim comes high on the police list of "things to do." When visual identification is made difficult by the condition of the corpse, proper procedure requires that the forensic pathologist, with the aid of blood samples, dental records, and DNA determination, pronounce on the matter.

But as Alex had explained to Sarah, there had not been any real question of the identity of the woman found by the pond. And if he had not himself recognized the slight figure in the long brown dress, any number of persons from the school community who had attended Anita's lecture could have named the victim. And once the identification had been pretty well arrived at, there was little outward mystery pertaining to the life and times of Anita Goshawk, B.A. and M.A. University of Maryland; Ph.D., Boston University. She was a known item. Her references and her academic achievements had been followed up by her current employer, Miss Merritt's School, and not found wanting. What remained for investigators was to dig beyond these statistics to see what hitherto unknown forces had been at work that made her the target of such an act of violence. Why had Anita Goshawk, at this time, in this place, had her head pounded to a pulp? The Carlisle detective, the police, and the whole crime team would continue to delve and sift through the victim's life and her recent movements until some sort of answer rose to the surface.

In the meantime, the autopsy process went forward to try to answer other questions. How did she die, how long had she been dead when found, what had been used to kill her? Time of death? That one was easier to answer. The lady had been seen alive on the school footpath back toward the art center shortly after her lecture, about eight-forty-five P.M., and found dead by three witnesses shortly after nine-thirty the same night.

How did she die? Two hours after Anita Goshawk had been measured, photographed dressed and naked, physical characteristics noted, and external abnormalities, signs of abuse, struggle, or injury remarked on, and after the chest, the abdomen, the pelvis, and finally the head was opened and their contents viewed, weighed, and sent for analysis, forensic pathologist Dr. Morris Zim had come to the conclusion. It was one that most spectators might have reached with a simple glance at Anita Goshawk's battered head. She had died from a series of heavy blows to the head—massive head trauma. And, further, that she had probably been stunned and helpless after the first blow, lost consciousness after the second or third, and died shortly thereafter. The blows numbered, Dr. Zim suggested, between seven and ten, but a closer examination of tissue and bone fragments would be needed before the final count could be calculated.

And what was used to kill her? Not a question easily answered.

"I'll be damned if I know," said Dr. Zim to a watching Alex McKenzie and Jake Markham, and to Carlisle detective, Hillary Mumford, a small, sharp-eyed person whose blond hair was pulled back into a long, tight braid. "All I know," he went on, "is what it wasn't. Not a firearm or anything long and sharp-edged. Or pointed—no puncture wounds. No sign of poison, but the lab's still working on the stomach contents. And she wasn't strangled or suffocated."

"A baseball bat?" suggested Jake.

Dr. Zim was a stout and balding man with a drooping gray mustache of great thickness—the sort of facial hair that suggests it was grown to compensate for loss on the scalp. He was a cheerful and bustling man and found his work all that he needed to keep him happy. In his spare time he was working on a magnum opus, a compilation of herbal poisons used in unsolved murders.

Now he frowned, pulled the sheet away from what was left of Anita's head, and pointed a finger at an area above the right ear.

"Don't think so," he said. "Look at this indentation. And the one above it. The angles. Baseball bats are more or less round. They leave different wounds."

"What if the handle of the bat was used?" suggested Jake.

"Well, maybe. Maybe not. And why use the handle? The bat itself makes a much better weapon."

"Hammer?" said Jake. "Splitting maul, crowbar? Shovel handle?"

"I don't think so. I suggest you and the CID guys see what you can come up with. Girls' schools are probably loaded with tools to beat each other up with. And there's nothing else to attract attention. She's had a radical mastectomy, she wasn't pregnant, no sign of ever having a child, no sign of rape. Okay, all of you. Keep in touch."

"But then," said Alex, "there's the question of why Anita Goshawk was killed."

Dr. Zim turned away from the eviscerated body on the table, pulled off his apron, and peeled off his surgical gloves. "That ball," he said, "belongs in Jake's court. The police play the motive game. I'm just a simple sawbones."

Alex and Jake Markham left the county morgue together.

"Nothing surprising there," Jake remarked. "And nothing so far in the woods. She was a lightweight, not more than one hundred and twelve pounds, so that first blow probably sent her down. Just off the footpath, we've found blood and hair. We guess, she was hauled down toward the pond—there were scrape marks, indentations, disturbed leaves, and broken brush, her broken glasses. Killed with repeated blows near the edge of the pond. The forensic team guys have come up with bone and tissue fragments, clumps of hair, threads from her dress, plus widespread blood spattering."

"That sleet and rain mix hasn't helped," said Alex as the two men fought their way to the parking lot, their heads bent into the wind and snow.

"Can say that again. A lot of the site is pretty well compromised. Snow washed away, ground turned to mush and then frozen. But we'll keep at it and begin dragging the pond this afternoon."

They reached the car, and Jake stopped and confronted Alex. "Of course, the question isn't why anyone wanted to kill Anita Goshawk, is it? It's why someone decided to beat Madame Carpentier into a bloody pulp."

Alex nodded somberly. "The cape."

"Right. That goddamn cape."

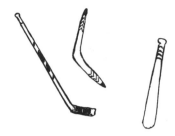

10

JAKE brushed a wet forelock out of his eyes and climbed in the car. "God, what shitty weather. But it's January, so we should be grateful it's not twenty below. Anyway, why in God's name was Goshawk running around in Carpentier's cape? From everything I've heard, those two females weren't exactly buddy-buddy."

Alex shrugged. "Anita Goshawk borrowed it. She asked and got permission."

"Why not wear her own coat?" demanded Jake.

"Try this. Anita doesn't wear a coat to the lecture. After all, it was unseasonably warm—the January thaw—and not raining when she leaves for the art center. She's thinking about her lecture, not about what the weather's going to do later."

"Okay," said Jake. "She gets to Radnor Hall for the reception, finds some slides are missing, and decides she has to go back."

"But by now the weather's turned. Anita is in her best lecture costume, doesn't want to get soaked, hits the cloak room, and lifts the cape. Or Madame Carpentier graciously—or grudgingly—offers it."

"Even grudgingly is out of character," objected Jake. "From what I know of Madame Knife, she wasn't into lending her things."

"Come on," said Alex, "the lady's human. I met her this morning, and she was positively jolly."

"So she thinks you look French. That smoldering, dark-haired type."

Alex grimaced and started the engine of the Subaru, switched on the headlights—a necessity for a stormy, dark, January morning—and shot the car out into traffic.

"You know," he said to Jake as they reached Carlisle and turned toward School Street, "there's no point wasting time trying to make sense out of this cape business when all we have to do is ask Madame Carpentier. Did she or didn't she hand the thing over?"

"I like the idea of Anita snatching it," said Jake.

"A cape is a good choice to snatch. An all-purpose outfit. One size fits all."

Jake nodded agreement, and Alex slowed the car—the hill was slick with ice—and drove past the Unitarian church, the Red Balloon Nursery School, the grammar school, the art center, the Congregational church, and past the footpath entrance and through the Merritt School service-entrance gates, these given, according to the bronze plate, in loving memory of Sophie Pettingill, Class of 1917.

Alex pulled into the faculty parking lot nearest to Gregory House, the area now thickly infested with cars from the local constabulary, and checked his watch. "I'm ahead of time, but I'll go in anyway and see if Sarah's there, then get back to Radnor to go over my statement, add anything I've forgotten. And then try very hard to get both of us out of here around one."

"Well," said Jake grinning, "why not have an escort? Here comes the Madame Knife you claim is so damn jolly. Not wearing a cape, I may add. Why not join her? She's heading your way."

Alex really had no choice. Grace was approaching slowly, struggling to bring her black umbrella under control. Her purple and black wool hat, or helmet, reminded Alex of something that might have been worn at Agincourt. And, having lost her cape, she wore a purple quilted affair that hung to her ankles, so that from the neck down, the general appearance was of an ambulatory duvet.

Alex, feeling he should properly swing a cane and doff a top hat, moved into the Carpentier orbit. "Good morning, again," he said, trying for a cheerful note.

Grace raised her head, her black brows contracted. "Ah, it is the husband of Miss Deane who has the much too large dog."

"Much too large," agreed Alex, falling into step.

This response seemed to go over well. Madame Grace relaxed her brows. "I have just heard," she said, "that you are the one who found Miss Goshawk who was dead. This is, of course, a tragedy for the school. Miss Goshawk, I think, was not so beloved, but I believe she was very competent. Also, she kept her students in order, which is very much the way it should be."

Alex slowed his step. Here was, if not the major player in recent events, an important supporting actor, and one with information regarding a certain black cape. "It must be very upsetting to all of you," he said. "The faculty, the whole staff, and of course the students . . ."

Grace interrupted with an upward thrust of her umbrella that delivered a small storm of drops down the back of Alex's neck.

"Ah, the students," she said, her voice sharp with scorn. "The students—I do not think any of them will be overcome with grief. As I have said, Miss Goshawk was not so very popular a person. I am a realist, doctor, so I say if one of these rock star persons died somewhere a thousand miles away, then there would be upset. There would be goings-on in the cafeteria and in the dormitories."

"Popularity is not a good thing?" said Alex to keep the lady talking. He took the umbrella from her not-unwilling hand and held it over her head.

"*Mais non.* If the victim had been myself, I do not think the students would be stricken down. Their eyes would be quite dry. To be popular is for incompetent instructors—I name no names. I try to teach a most beautiful language to students, many of whom have—what is the expression—an ear of tin."

Alex came to a halt at the flight of stone steps leading to Gregory House, and since he had the umbrella, Madame Grace was obliged to stop beside him. "Have you been threatened, then?" asked Alex casually—he had been filled in by Sarah in the matter of paper puppets and effigies.

Madame Carpentier narrowed her eyes so that her very dark brown eyes looked like tiny slivers of coal. "Have I not! Surely Miss Deane and the others will have told you about the scarecrows wearing choir robes. And the drawing of the snake. And now Dr. Singer tells me there was also a cut-out paper doll. It is not in the least a joke, no matter what the students say. I think it must be a student plot against the strong teachers here at Merritt's." Here Madame paused, and Alex felt that if she had been a horse she would have been switching her tail and stamping her hooves.

"You know, do you not, doctor, that Miss Goshawk wore my cape in which to be killed? My black wool cape. Without it I am quite uncomfortable, and I have ordered another from this little shop in Albany, New York."

Alex raised his eyebrows in an inviting gesture, and together they moved up the last few steps, and with the umbrella lowered, Alex opened the door to the cluttered vestibule of Gregory House.

"Of course," said Madame, taking control of her umbrella and shaking it vigorously, "I am in distress concerning this most tragic accident. Violence in America. Blood everywhere, gangs and shoot-ups. Drug wars. Children without discipline. Even in the best schools. These are most characteristic things about your country, I think. I have kept my French citizenship, but I have taught in the country so many years that I may say freely what I think."

"And you certainly should," said Alex encouragingly.

But Grace had taken a step toward the inner door, caught the end of her long, quilted coat on the handle of a bicycle, and plunged forward, only to be caught from falling onto the flagstone floor by Alex's quick grab.

"*Merde*," said Grace, straightening herself and disentangling the hem of her coat. "These students. Always so much of this junk. Why," she exclaimed, her voice rising, "must we have bicycles and these sport things, these bats and sticks crowding this place. It is winter, so these objects have no place. No person rides a bicycle in the middle of the winter. The girls do not play field hockey or baseball or lacrosse, or go on their skateboards or their rollerblades, at this time of year. I went to a most proper convent school, L'Église de St. Cuthbert, and we were not allowed to spread our things all over the school like little pigs and run about in torn blue jeans and T-shirts through which one sees there is no soutien-gorge—what you call the brassiere, being worn. I am going to call maintenance. Now, this minute, and have these things taken away."

And suiting words to action, Madame Grace wrenched open the inner door and stepped to the house telephone that hung on the wall just inside. And Alex, leaving her to it, began the climb to the third floor and Sarah's room, hearing as he went the angry voice of the French teacher demanding that maintenance "arrive at once" and remove the contents of the vestibule. "I do not care," she shrilled, "where you take any of it, but I suppose you have receptacles or storage buildings for such things."

Alex, thumping each stair to give some sort of warning to wandering nude students that a male was in upward progress, reflected that Madame Grace had missed her calling—the IRS, perhaps, or some assertive branch of government. Sarah, he told himself with relief, had never been obsessively neat—an understatement if there ever was one—and at times, her immediate surroundings resembled a pack-rat home site. Sarah would never have had the contents of the vestibule hauled away; she would have stepped over it. Even added to the mess. And also, hearing Madame on the telephone imitating an outraged parrot, he conceded another point in favor of his wife: Sarah's speaking voice was usually soft and low, an excellent thing—as a certain royal father had observed—in a woman, or a man for that matter. He looked forward to a period of peace in Sarah's room before heading back to Radnor Hall to reexamine his statement.

Reaching the room, Alex hesitated. Sarah was not alone; in fact, the sounds coming from the room sounded very much like those from a slumber party; a party, judging by the smell, fortified by fully loaded pizzas. Obviously, this was not going to be a haven of quiet. Bracing himself, he rapped loudly on the door, which was jerked open to reveal a tall, slender black woman with a firm chin and snapping dark eyes. She was wrapped in what appeared to be a patchwork bedspread and was flanked by a small stocky personage with a mop of yellow hair, a snub nose, and a wide mouth, wearing cut-offs and sporting bare feet.

"Give the password," announced the tall woman—it was Rosemary.

"We shall overcome?" suggested Alex.

130

"That's old stuff," said Rosemary. "Try again."

"*Honi soit qui mal y pense?*"

"You got it," said Rosemary. "Come on in."

"But don't stay," said Zoë. "We're hashing out some things."

"Things like are we sorry about Mrs. Goshawk getting murdered," said Hannah, rearing out of Sarah's armchair.

Sarah uncoiled herself from a floor cushion, straightened her back, and waved. "Hi, Alex. You're early, it's just past noon. Have you gone over your statement already?"

"That's where I'm headed, but I thought I'd check on you first. Meet you then at one."

"Make it one-fifteen. Radnor. Front hall."

Alex looked around at the three girls. "I suppose," he said, "that you've figured out this whole business."

"Right," said Zoë. "We'll be on top of it. School violence is becoming pretty common."

"She," said Rosemary pointing at Zoë, "doesn't know a thing about school violence. Zoë is a protected child of the middle-class suburbs. We've been trying to bring her up to speed for the last three years. Tell her about the real, inner-city street world where things like finding Miss Goshawk dead happen every day."

"Yeah, tell me about it," said Hannah. "Rosemary," she informed Alex, "grew up in Hanover, New Hampshire, and her daddy taught at Dartmouth. And Carlisle isn't Roxbury or the Bronx. This little town doesn't teach much about street life."

"Right," said Zoë. "Rosemary, you're as bad as I am. You don't know anything about life in the streets except what you see on the tube."

Rosemary tossed a loose corner of her quilt over her shoulder and looked down at Zoë. "Hey, I know what I'm talking about. It's in my blood. My ancestors keep me tuned in. Generations of enslaved families in my head. So close your mouth, girl, and let's get on with what we're supposed to be doing.

Which I think is helping all these adults who are trying to solve the murder. Dum dee dum dum."

And Alex quietly closed the door behind him and cautiously made his way downstairs, hoping to escape another encounter with Madame Carpentier.

He did not escape the lady, but fortunately two men from maintenance had arrived with a small Ford pick-up, and under the imperious direction of Madame, were at the moment adding the bicycle, skateboard, and the motley collection of sticks and bats to the bed of the truck. Alex nodded hastily at Madame, who gave him a brief but gracious smile, and returned to her supervisory duties.

Sarah, in the role of listener, had settled back on her cushion. She was only too aware that the trio of senior students were not so much pouring out their angst and sadness, or even terror—was there a stalker on campus?—as trying to stifle a certain relish of the whole affair. Not just the violent act but the whole interesting process—the police, detectives, state troopers, scene of the crime people with their familiar (from TV) yellow tape, the giving of statements, and all those questions about what they had seen, where were they when. Sarah imagined that each girl was well equipped with a quiver full of gossip, innuendo, bizarre school incidents, and which student or teacher or coach had it in for which other student, teacher, or coach. Sarah almost pitied the police for when this bucket of refuse would be dumped down on their heads.

"Like this murder isn't just something weird about the faculty, or a student getting picked up for shoplifting," said Hannah. "This is really gruesome."

Zoë took a thoughtful bite out of a triangle of pizza. "God, I can see it," she said. "Someone hiding in the woods with a baseball bat, waiting. Talk about creepy."

132

Sarah opened her eyes wide, an image of two hands grasping a bat floating in front of her. Then she shook her head. "Wait for the police report—although they may not hand out information like that to the public."

"We're not the public," objected Zoë. "We're involved. We may even be suspects, especially after those two scarecrow things. And the other stuff. The trouble is those were meant for Madame Carpentier. Not Goshawk."

"You're all being stupid," said Rosemary. "You forget, Goshawk was wearing Carpentier's cape. It's perfectly simple, and it's right under your dumb noses. A case of mistaken identity. One of Madame's six million enemies followed her into the woods and nailed her in the dark. Thinking Goshawk was Carpentier. End of case."

"Okay," said Zoë, "that makes sense, but whoever did it will know by now they got the wrong person. So won't they try again? To get the right person."

"Which means," said Hannah with poorly concealed enthusiasm, "that Madame's life isn't worth shit."

"Unless," said Rosemary thoughtfully, "they can pin the murder on Madame the Knife Couteau herself."

"Hey, that makes sense," said Zoë. "Madame Grace couldn't stand Goshawk. They were always stepping on each other's feet."

"Too complicated," objected Hannah. "I say it was raining, and Goshawk snatched the cape and got nailed by someone in the woods. Someone hiding drugs maybe. A total stranger."

"Shut up and listen," said Rosemary. "This is very subtle, but you know, no matter what we think about the old witch, Madame Grace has a good brain. She sees it's raining, and she lends the cape to Goshawk, hoping the person who's been threatening her will see Goshawk wearing the cape and think it's her. It's dark, and the killer finds Goshawk alone in the woods and thinks it's Carpentier. He murders her, and saves

Madame the trouble of doing it herself. It's like the murderer is an assistant, an accomplice of Carpentier without knowing it. What's the word, an accessory."

"No, I've got it," said Hannah. "Carpentier saw Goshawk swipe the cape from the cloak room and took off after her. Goshawk making off with her cape was the absolute last straw because Madame just loved that cape, she about lived in it. So Carpentier flipped her lid, followed her, and killed her."

"I think," said Sarah, pushing herself off the floor, standing up, and looking seriously at the three, "you should all sit down and write a sympathy letter to Anita Goshawk's family and forget about working up a scenario of this murder or any other crime you have in mind. The police are on top of it—it's what they do for a living—and I'm sure they'll keep an eye on Madame Carpentier. They're perfectly capable of realizing that Miss Goshawk may have been mistaken for someone else."

"You think so, too," said Zoë. "I mean, it's one of the options, isn't it?"

Sarah, who had been trying hard not to express any opinion, to just be a sounding board for the girls, nodded agreement. The identity mix-up was too obvious not to acknowledge.

"I think," said Hannah, "if we have to choose, I'll bet someone from the faculty did it. They all hate Carpentier as much as we do."

"Not true," said Rosemary. "Dr. Singer likes her, for one. And likes the results that Madame gets in her French classes. Face it, the girls who hang in learn French. The hard way, but they learn it. What I'm saying is that Dr. Singer doesn't go in for hating faculty. She keeps her cool, and if the teacher is just plain no good, well, they don't come back. Remember when Miss Sanchez—you know, that Spanish teacher that left after one semester—when Miss Sanchez lost her temper in the dining room and threw a bowl of Cheerios?"

"And," said Zoë, "Adrian Parsons acts like Sir Walter Raleigh with her. As if he was about to spread a coat under her feet."

"He should," said Hannah. "She's Parson's boss."

"So maybe he wants her job," said Zoë.

"It's hormones," said Rosemary. "The men don't mind her because she likes men and isn't so horrible to them."

Sarah moved to the door. "It's time for you ladies to hit your rooms or work out in the gym and for me to head out. I don't think any of you are going to have a nervous collapse over this business, but if it starts to get to you, please go and talk to your house parents. Your advisor. The psychologists. And write those condolence letters. It will make you think you're doing something responsible. From what I've seen and heard, even if she wasn't always Miss Sunshine, Anita Goshawk was a pretty terrific teacher. Okay? And thanks for the pizza."

Sarah reached for her coat, grabbed Patsy's leash, stood aside for the three students to leave, closed and locked her door, and, with Patsy pulling at his leash, started down the hall.

Alex was standing with Jake Markam just inside the heavy oak doors of Radnor Hall, both men dripping water on the tiled floor from their raincoats. Both, in their olive green slickers, with their damp hair—Jake's light brown, Alex's dark—plastered against their foreheads, looked to Sarah for all the world like fugitives from a fishing trawler that had foundered in heavy weather.

"Pizza party over?" said Alex. "I've signed my statement, but I think Jake has another question for you."

"I closed the pizza party," said Sarah. "At the moment, those three girls are not really candidates for grief counseling because they're really into the investigation process."

"I'll bet they are," sighed Jake.

"They've already concluded that it was a case of mistaken

identity, what with the cape and all, that the hit was meant for Madame Carpentier, that whoever did it is probably on the faculty at Merritt's Academy and will strike again at the real target. To quote Hannah Hoyt, 'Madame Grace Marie's life isn't worth shit.' "

"Christ Almighty," said Jake with feeling. "How did I get mixed up with school girls and a homicide at the same time?"

"Some of the girls in this place," said Alex, "are ready to run IBM, manage a seraglio, and direct a Himalayan assault team."

"Point is," said Jake to Sarah, "they're on target. About the mistaken identity. That's what I figure, that's what Hillary, Hillary Mumford—she's our town detective—and the state police guys are thinking. And that's what I'm supposed to ask Sarah. When you saw Anita Goshawk heading back to the Carlisle Art Center to pick up her slides, did you mistake her at first for Carpentier?"

Sarah hesitated, remembered the small woman, head bent, half-running down the footpath, a dark figure wrapped in some sort of blanket-like coat. Saw again her thick glasses blurred with rain. "No," she said slowly. "She caught up with us near one of those pathway lamps, and I could see her face. So I guess I didn't confuse Anita with anyone else."

"Okay," said Jake. "We'll have you put an addendum to your statement about that. Not now. Later will be fine. We've still got half of the students and the staff to wade through."

"Two of the girls did see Anita in Madame Grace's cape when she was heading toward the footpath," Sarah said. "They thought it was funny. Hoped she'd swiped it and that there would be a wonderful confrontation they could all enjoy."

"The school is a jungle," said Jake.

"Well," said Sarah, "they've already run through some of the suspects and discarded the men," said Sarah. "Madame likes men. But their favorite candidate is Madame Carpentier herself, although they can't quite explain how the cape business works."

"What the entire student body needs," said Jake with feeling, "is an announcement that there'll be two-hour exams in all subjects starting tomorrow."

"Good idea," said Sarah. "But what about the idea that Madame Carpentier needs a little protection? Someone to ride shotgun if she goes out?"

Jake grimaced. "Putting a tail on that lady isn't going to be a favorite assignment, but we will be watching her."

"You should give Alex the job," said Sarah. "He thinks she's rather charming."

"*Mais oui*," said Alex. "*Elle est une femme la plus agréable.*"

Back on the third floor of Gregory House, a council of war was taking place in Rosemary and Zoë's room. This space, like its fellows up and down the corridor and throughout the dormitories of the school, was decorated, along with the usual posters and blow-ups of John Travolta, Michael Jordan, Leonardo DiCaprio, with a unique collection of headless Barbie dolls hung upside down along the ceiling molding. The three girls were sprawled across the bed.

"We can't just sit around waiting for something gruesome to happen," announced Hannah.

"Just what," said Zoë, "do you have in mind? Ask the police to swear us in as deputies?"

"The trouble is," said Rosemary, "that the police don't know how this school works or what some of the teachers are like. We could keep our eyes open. Be on red alert."

"That's sort of boring," said Hannah.

"Boring," said Zoë with feeling, "isn't all that bad. What I think . . ." But Zoë never finished. From outside their room came a scrabbling noise and a scratching on the door's woodwork.

Rosemary pushed herself off the bed and opened the hall door and in bounded Szeppi, an excited bundle of curly black fur. He let loose with an excited yelp, pounced on a pizza crust that was resting on the cover of the *National Enquirer*, clamped his jaws closed on the morsel, leaped to the center of Zoë's bed, whirled in a circle, and settled down to chew.

"Oops," said Hannah. "Szeppi must have smelled the pizza. Oh boy, we'd better not be found with him in our room."

"Maybe," said Zoë, "Madame forgot to lock the door, and he got out. I'll go and check her room. Keep the dog here." And Zoë departed. And returned almost immediately. "Madame's door is wide open. I knocked and called but no answer." Then Zoë stopped as the implications of what she had said became clear.

The others got it.

"God," said Hannah, "do you suppose . . ." Her voice trailed off.

"Someone got into the room," said Rosemary slowly. "Broke in and went after her. And left the door open, so Szeppi got out."

"Should we call someone?" asked Zoë. "Security. Or maybe 911?"

"But if she's in her bedroom taking a nap and the police come charging in, God, wouldn't she be steamed."

"One step at a time," said Rosemary, taking charge. "We take Szeppi down the hall, call again. If there's no answer, we go in with Szeppi. If Carpentier gets mad, we'll point out we're returning her dog. That he might have gotten outside and been hit by a car. She should thank us."

"What if she's not in the apartment?" asked Hannah.

"Then we shove Szeppi back into the room and close the door," said Rosemary. "You guys worry too much. Come on. Zoë, you grab Szeppi's collar, and we'll go to her apartment together. She won't dare put us on restriction when we're doing a good deed."

"That's a laugh," said Hannah. "Nothing she'd like better than to have our scalps hanging from her belt. She loves to get hold of seniors and ruin their lives."

Zoë reached over and lifted a small wedge of pizza from her bureau top. This she held over Szeppi's nose as she grasped his collar in her other hand.

The door to Madame Carpentier's stood ajar. Repeated calls, knocks, and Szeppi's whining brought no answer.

"Okay," said Rosemary. "We go in and look. Who knows, maybe there's evidence just sitting around in the apartment."

"You mean a bloody baseball bat or an automatic rifle?" said Hannah with heavy sarcasm. "Look, I'll try the bathroom. If she's taking a shower, we beat it. Then Rosemary looks in the bedroom. Zoë, stay right here at the door and hang on to that dog. If you hear anyone coming up the stairs or down the hall, yell."

"If I see Madame coming, I'll go down the fire escape," said Zoë, pointing to the window across the room. "And," she added, "if you find her body anywhere, we can all go down the fire escape."

Walking with careful steps, Rosemary headed toward the bedroom, and Hannah moved toward the bathroom.

And Zoë stood at the door, biting her lip and swallowing with difficulty. And keeping a death grip on Szeppi's collar.

11

MADAME Grace Marie-Henriette's living quarters were, as anyone would have agreed, a wonder of neatness. It was the space of someone brought up in a convent school and who brooked no nonsense from furniture and furnishings. Chairs, covered in a geometric gray-and-white needlepoint, and several small, polished tables stood squared as if at attention. Two reproductions of French landscapes, each with a polished brass label on the bottom of the frame, hung evenly spaced across the white wall.

"It's like a museum," marveled Rosemary, making the rounds. She read from the labels, "Monet, *Vetheuil in Winter*; Cezanne, *Mont-Sainte-Victoire.*"

A bookcase along the far wall held neat rows of French textbooks and a number of contemporary French novels in paperback. Beyond the little living room, the kitchenette gleamed, the tea towel was crisp and clean, the kettle shone, and several immaculate copper saucepans hung in a row over the stove.

Hannah emerged from the bathroom first. "No body in the

bathtub," she announced in a sort of giggle that suggested a serious case of nerves.

Rosemary tiptoed into the bedroom and came out almost immediately. "Empty," she announced in a relieved voice. "At least she's not on the bed or under it."

"Did you look in the clothes closet?" called Zoë. "That's where people hide bodies."

Rosemary hesitated. Then said, "We'll look together. Zoë's right. In the movies, bodies are always falling out of closets."

The bedroom reflected the same tidy hand as the rest of the apartment. A Nativity scene hung over the bed and a small wooden crucifix was fastened over the bedside table, on which stood a brass lamp, a box of Kleenex, a cut-glass water jug, and a ceramic mug imprinted with the likeness of Victor Hugo. On the bureau, a silver-backed brush and comb kept guard over a lavender satin pincushion and a double-framed photograph of a man wearing a frock coat, striped trousers, and a sash fashioned diagonally across his chest. This gentleman looked severely across at the second photograph of a woman dressed in beaded black, holding a fan in gloved hands.

Hannah, after a brief inspection of these items, squared her shoulders, took a deep breath, walked over to the louvered closet doors, took hold of the handle, and pulled it open.

No body plunged forward. No body lay atop the neat row of black leather and gray suede shoes. No body slumped against the hanging dresses and skirts, many that were all too familiar to the two girls who had almost four years of dealing with Madame.

"She's not here," said Hannah unnecessarily.

"So let's beat it," said Rosemary, who was now feeling increasingly queasy about the visit.

Returned to the living room, they met an equally anxious Zoë, who stood by the door clinging to Szeppi's collar.

"It feels really weird being in here," she complained. "And

anyway, there's nothing to see. Come on. I'll let Szeppi go, and we'll get out of here." And Zoë released the dog and gave him a push toward the center of the room.

But Rosemary, who was in forward motion, took a step at the exact moment Szeppi bounded free. Szeppi shot toward the kitchen toward his water dish, but Rosemary lost her balance, stumbled forward, and saved herself by grasping at the top of a small desk that stood close to the hall door. The desk was a delicate thing, bird's-eye maple with curved legs and a slant top, and as Rosemary grasped the top for balance, the top fell open and a sheaf of papers, envelopes, and cards slid to the floor.

"Damn," breathed Zoë. "Now see what you've done. Carpentier will have us in front of a firing squad."

But the other two girls were on their knees; Hannah scraping letters and envelopes into one pile, Rosemary stacking the postcards.

Hannah rose and pushed the papers into a an open cubbyhole. But Rosemary stayed kneeling. It was, Rosemary explained later, as if her name were Alice and each postcard labeled "Read Me." Slowly she stretched out an arm—it seemed to have a will of its own—and turned over the first card, a view of a stone bridge over a wide, blue river. For a moment she stared at the inscription. Then, gathering the cards, she stood up and placed them on the open desk. And with Hannah and Zoë watching open-mouthed, not yet protesting, Rosemary turned over a second card, a third. Then two more. Then, as if her fingers had been suddenly scalded, she slapped the postcards back on the desk, squared the edges, then turned and grabbed Hannah and pushed her toward the door.

"Move it," she commanded. "Zoë, don't let Szeppi out." And with the door closed and the lock snapped into place, the three raced down the hall, flung themselves into the first safe haven—Hannah's room—slammed the door and, breathing hard, collapsed against the wall.

"What was it?" demanded Zoë when she had caught her breath.

"Makes me feel sick," said Rosemary, shaking her head as if to rid herself of a swarm of flies.

Hannah stiffened. "This whole business is giving me the creeps. We won't graduate, and Madame will probably personally ruin us for college. She'll know someone's been at her desk, and she'll suspect students. She always suspects students."

"She'd be right," said Zoë. "It usually *is* the students." And to Rosemary. "Okay now. What'd you find?"

"What I found," said Rosemary, "is pretty awful."

"How awful?" demanded Zoë. "They looked just like ordinary postcards. Cathedrals and gardens. Stuff like that."

"Not the pictures. What was written. It was so gross. I mean, no wonder."

"No wonder what?" yelled Hannah.

"Total yuck, is what I mean." Rosemary went over to the bed, flung herself down on it, and pulled the pillow over her head. Then she reared up and faced the other two.

"This whole shitty mess is a lot more complicated than just Anita Goshawk being killed." She sat up and pushed her hands through her close-cropped black hair in a distracted gesture. "Okay. First of all, they're just postcards. Ordinary postcards."

"If you turn this into a shaggy dog story," said Zoë, "I'll strangle you."

"The postcards I saw," Rosemary went on, "were the sort people buy when they take trips to Europe. You know, instant history of art. Florence and some palazzo, Venus on the half-shell, the Sistine Chapel, one of those Roman bridges. A couple of Leonardo things I recognized, and a picture of that statue of David by what's his name, Donatello, that Miss Goshawk raves—raved—about."

"And that's what was gross?" demanded Hannah.

"What they said was gross. Just short messages. Printed.

One said something like, 'Go to hell you fucking French bitch.' "

"Ouch," said Zoë, while Hannah just shook her head.

Rosemary nodded. "Ouch is right. Anyway, another one said, 'You lying piece of French cunt,' and another said something like, 'Get out of here or'—I didn't get the last word. It was smeared. And one called her a motherfucking piece of boiled shit."

"This stuff was written right on the postcards? I mean, *postcards!*" exclaimed Hannah. "Postcards for everyone to read. People in the Carlisle post office, the school office staff? They sort the incoming mail and stick it in the school mailboxes."

Zoë held up her hand. "Wait. Did these postcards have stamps? Maybe they weren't sent; maybe they were stuck in envelopes first right here at the school."

Rosemary frowned. "All I can remember are the words. Black ink, like a marker with a thin point. I didn't look for stamps. I suppose," she said doubtfully, "they might have had stamps. But not unusual ones, like big commemoratives. Those I might have noticed."

"Say they didn't have stamps," said Hannah softly. "Do you think it's like Zoë said, that they weren't mailed at all. That they were stuck into Carpentier's box? Not by the school secretaries, but by another teacher. Or by a student. Anyone. We open our mailboxes using our number combination, but I suppose someone could come around to the back of the boxes and stick in a postcard. The faculty get those announcements and invitations that way. They send stuff to each other about meetings. Students leave notes asking for appointments. It wouldn't be hard to slip a postcard into Carpentier's box with the writing side down and just a picture of the Mona Lisa showing."

Silence. Heads shaking.

Then Zoë walked over to the window. "I need fresh air."

"Look," said Rosemary, "remember when we were guessing that someone like Madame Carpentier killed Miss Goshawk?"

"Yeah," said Hannah. "And if Carpentier got those messages, well, wouldn't she feel like killing whoever sent them?"

"Those two scarecrows and the cut-out puppet hanging in the garden and the snake drawing—they all seem pretty tame after this stuff," said Rosemary. She paused and studied her friends, Zoë at the window, her back turned, Hannah in the middle of the room, her hands on her hips.

"So," said Rosemary, "what do you think?"

"You mean," said Zoë the practical, "are we actually going to tell someone about these disgusting postcards we shouldn't have seen—or that Rosemary shouldn't have seen?"

"What we're *not* going to do," said Hannah, "is all go tiptoeing into the school office and say, 'Guess what, we were breaking into Madame Carpentier's apartment just now, and you'll never guess what totally revolting postcards we found on her desk.' "

"So," said Zoë, trying to sum things up and get it all straight in her head, "we shut up? We button our lips. Right?"

"Right," said Rosemary and Hannah in one loud voice.

Jake Markham was not having a happy day. Taking statements always gave him a headache. And taking statements from the students—variously confused, defensive, a little frightened, or in many cases entirely too eager to tell what they did, and for the most part, did not see nor hear—was a real chore. As for the faculty, for the most part, thought Jake, they were an even tougher lot to deal with than the kids.

With the faculty, Jake and the others had to deal with articulate, educated adults, many of whom were doing a splendid imitation of, in Jake's words, "a goddamn clam." A concerned clam, a wanting-to-be-helpful clam, but, nonetheless, a clam. A clam that snapped closed and warily viewed the assorted members of the constabulary through a tiny slit between their half-shells. But even worse than the clams were the squids, those persons who, from nervousness or a wish to guard their privacy, sent out clouds of murky and irrelevant misinformation.

Jake, along with Hillary Mumford, kicked off the morning with the redoubtable Madame Carpentier.

"We'll take her first, ask about the cape business and her relations with Miss Goshawk, then haul her back at the end of the day and run through her statement again. Ask her if she's remembered anything else to help us," said Hillary.

"You mean, let her dangle. Give her time to start worrying, in case she's fudged around with the truth," said Jake.

Jake liked working with Hillary. A classy lady. And smart, too. Five years' experience with the Springfield police in uniform, a law degree from B.U. and then with the CID, plainclothes. And now she lived in Carlisle, along with her husband, a contractor, and two kids, six-year-old twin boys. Jake looked at her appreciatively. A slight build, fair hair pulled into a braid, green-gray eyes, a wide and friendly mouth, and a cascade of freckles down her small, straight nose. This morning she was all business in her turtleneck, blue windproof jacket, and wool slacks tucked into a pair of waterproof high-laced boots. If she hadn't been so thoroughly married Jake might have been more than interested.

The session with Madame Carpentier set a pattern that did not vary much with subsequent faculty interviews and statements, although probably Madame took the prize for minimal cooperation. One of the clams, Jake decided. Or perhaps a snapping turtle.

"Yes, indeed, I am so very much shocked by this which has happened," said Madame, sitting bolt upright in a straight-backed oak chair, her hands laced together and placed on her lap. The police were settled in the Copeland Room (gift of Lois Mills Copeland, class of '89), a long, rectangular room with somber portraits of school notables hung against dark, paneled

146

walls and thick, rather faded Persian rugs. This space, opening as it did directly from the Old Library, had become the repository of a few remnants of last night's non-reception—several punch glasses on a ledge behind a curtain, a crushed napkin, and a large silver urn sitting forlornly in a corner next to a bronze vase of drooping yellow roses.

Madame Carpentier, dressed that morning in plum and gray wool, not only expressed her shock at the recent sad events but claimed to regret the loss of a colleague. "Miss Goshawk kept a strong discipline, and her students did not run about squawking like chickens with their heads chopped off. This, *voyez vous*, is a condition that is often seen in the American classroom."

Jake looked hard at the woman and for a moment allowed himself to be distracted by a drop of moisture at the end of Madame's sharp, chiseled nose. Then, bracing himself, he asked if she had always been on good terms with Miss Goshawk.

"But of course," said Madame. "One does not let a small personal difference enter into the practice of teaching. We were not, how shall I say, the very best of friends. But we respected, each of us, the work of the other."

"I heard," said Jake quietly, "that you wanted to move your French classes into Miss Goshawk's history of art classroom and that this had upset Miss Goshawk."

"Do not listen to gossip, Officer Markham. Yes, I wished to exchange classrooms with Miss Goshawk, and I believe that she was a little distressed with the suggestion. It was, I should tell you, a plan that had the support of Mr. Adrian Parsons, who is the assistant director of the Language Division. It was a plan the most sensible because I now must teach in three separate classrooms, one of which is used in a disorderly manner by the English Department. My reference books and my teaching library is split into different rooms, which is quite inconvenient."

"But," said Jake, "wouldn't Miss Goshawk have found it also

inconvenient to move her art stuff—projectors, her slides, all those big, heavy art books—in and out of separate class-rooms?"

Madame Carpentier shrugged. "The French Department has a great many more students than does the History of Art Department. History of Art is a small part of the Fine Arts Division, and the French Department is a very great part of the Language Division, of which I am the head. History of Art is not a subject necessary for graduation. It is an elective. A charming and useful one, one does not doubt, but not of the first importance. Of first importance is the study of a foreign language. And I try to cover, *en français*, all the aspects of the art of France in my advanced classes—the architecture of the Roman period, the Medieval, the Gothic, the Renaissance, and the Baroque. The treasures of the Louvre. The Impressionist movement in France, which so changed the art world."

Here Madame paused for breath and allowed the increasingly impatient Jake Markham a thin smile. "Your concern about Miss Goshawk and myself must be put aside. These most trivial agitations happen in an academic community. *Vous comprenez, n'est-ce pas*, that one is not always at peace in the school about the little things, but time, it goes by, and the dust, it settles, *et voilà*, we are all again sensible adults, and things are arranged for the good of all. And now, I must insist that you let me depart. My little dog, Szeppi, he has the need to go out for his walk."

Jake held up his hand and fixed what he hoped was an ingratiating expression on his face. "It's still raining hard, Madame, so I think your walk will have to be postponed. Besides, we have other questions. First, the police have heard about the jokes, the scarecrow on the soccer field, the one in the choir robe at Halloween, the cut-up puppet, and the drawing of the snake—all of which I've been told you know about. We've also heard about the snowball attack by students outside the art building. So now, can you tell me whether there've been any more of these incidents. Incidents that might be stupid jokes. Or threats."

Madame visibly bristled and her dark eyebrows drew together. "I do not call them jokes. And not threats. I am not laughing. I do not feel threatened. These things came, I am certain, from the students. The ones who have not had a good grade and have perhaps been disciplined by me. Some of these girls have not good sense. They have been badly brought up by careless and perhaps divorced families. Families with too much money for their own good."

"So you don't know about any more incidents?"

"No," said Madame, opening and closing her mouth with a snap.

"And you don't think any one of these incidents could have come from someone on the faculty? Someone on the staff of the school? From someone outside the school? A parent, perhaps."

"No," said Madame again.

"Okay, then here's my last question. The cape, Madame Carpentier. We are confused about the cape. We need you to tell us about why Miss Goshawk was wearing your very good black wool cape." God, Jake thought, I'm beginning to talk like her.

But Madame Carpentier had finished. She rose, pulled her gray vest down over her hips, brought her dark brows even closer together, and looked down at Jake over her beaked nose. "I have already told many people, including the police, that I did not lend, give, or force upon Miss Goshawk my cape. She took it without asking me. This action I forgive, because after her lecture it had begun to rain and sleet, and she needed a *couverture* in which to go back to pick up the slides she so carelessly forgot. I hope to have an accounting from the police of my cape. It was very expensive and made to order for me, and if it has been ruined by your medical team, I wish to have it paid for. Good morning."

And Madame Carpentier turned and marched to the exit.

"God help us all," said Jake Markham, watching her go. "Now who does she remind me of? Besides a snapping turtle."

"I know," said a voice. "I'll tell you if it's my turn to be grilled."

Giddy Lester.

Jake sighed. "Hi, Giddy. You're supposed to talk to Detective Mumford. I know you too well. It might be a conflict of interest."

"You and I only went to a couple of art shows together," said Giddy. "That doesn't exactly constitute interest."

"So we should try another couple of art shows," said Jake. "Someday, after we've got a stranglehold on this case."

"I," said Giddy, "am available. I've broken up with this guy, Josh. It's kaput. He's a genius, but he's also a total slime. Now I need a nice, art-connected relationship."

"So check with me later this afternoon. We could have coffee. Doughnuts. Or hit that Thai place just off campus. I won't have more than forty minutes for dinner."

Giddy grinned. "Be still my heart."

"I'm up to my chin with this crap," said Jake defensively. Then he asked, "Who would you say Madame Carpentier reminded you of?"

"Al Pacino," said Giddy promptly.

"You mean in *Godfather I* or *II* or *III*?"

"Not the mafia. Pacino as Richard the Third. It's a movie. Go see it, it's good." And Giddy headed for a distant end of the Copeland Room, where Hillary Mumford had set up a work corner featuring a table and several uncomfortable, straight-backed chairs.

And Jake found himself facing Carlo Leone. Carlo, his blond

hair raked back, Band-Aids on his nose and across one hand. He wore blue jeans and an oversize sweatshirt proclaiming pride in the Boston Marathon. "Carlo Leone," Jake repeated to himself, mindful of his recent exchange with Giddy. Italian. For several seconds, Jake considered the possibility of a mob infiltration into Miss Merritt's School for young women.

"Wake up, Jake, it's statement time," said Carlo. "Are you ready to arrest someone? Do you carry handcuffs?"

"No," said Jake. "I let the others do the cuffing. Tell me, Mr. Leone . . ."

"Carlo. You know who I am."

"Yeah, okay. So tell me, Carlo, what did Richard the Third look like?"

"Madame Carpentier," said Carlo promptly.

"That doesn't help. How about the real one?"

"Actually, he was rather handsome, judging from an early engraving. Some people claim he wasn't really a hunchback, just had one shoulder higher than the other. But most of us think of Richard looking like Laurence Olivier or Alec Guinness, who played him in the Stratford, Ontario, production. Or, recently, Al Pacino."

"Do you think the similarity means anything?"

"For what it's worth, I'd say Madame, like Richard, plans ahead. A little devious. Doesn't leave things to chance."

Jake nodded, pulled out a pad of paper, and got to work. The results were uniformly unhelpful. Carlo was acting the clam. Yes, he'd gone to the art lecture, which was, he added, well attended. He'd sat at the back so he could get loose at the end. "The lecture was well received because Anita knew what would go down the general gullet and what wouldn't. She didn't get all fancy-dancy with esoteric criticism, and the slides were good and there weren't too many of them. And thank God she knew when to stop."

Questioned about later sightings of Anita Goshawk, Carlo

denied having seen her again. He had left as soon as the lecture ended and hadn't waited to listen to questions because he had the important business of going back to his apartment in Lockwood Hall for his flask of whiskey. There he made himself a drink, picked up his raincoat—it was really starting to come down—and met up with a student on his way to Radnor Hall and the reception and . . .

"What student was that?" interrupted Jake, making a note.

"Senior girl. Smart, good looking, honor roll. African American. Rosemary Streeter. She's in my creative writing class, and we walked together because she had a few questions. About Monday's assignments. She was on her way to the library, the new one. The Alexander Memorial Library. After all, it didn't matter how late I was for the reception. The thing would go on for a couple of hours. Congratulations, chit-chat, circling around."

Jake thought briefly that Carlo was telling him a lot more than he asked for, switching from the clam mode to that of the squid. Why, and did it mean anything? Keeping his voice level, he asked if this Rosemary Streeter had mentioned seeing Anita Goshawk? Before the lecture? During, afterwards?

"Rosemary was at the lecture. The history of art students were required to go. But not to the reception. So she was going to skip it. Said she left as soon as it was over. I didn't ask her if she saw Anita again."

Jake nodded. "We'll be going over the student statements later. Now, were you surprised at Miss Goshawk's absence at the reception?"

Apparently, not at first. Carlo got to the Old Library when it was pretty full. But as time went by, he was puzzled by Anita's non-appearance. But not unhappy. It made it easy to leave. He chatted it up with assorted members of the company, improved their punch glasses with whiskey, and then when it seemed that the guest of honor would be a no-show, he called the whole thing a day and went back to his apartment. And, wouldn't you know, someone had swiped his raincoat. It was always happening. He had a generic khaki trenchcoat and the students—and faculty—grabbed what came to hand. Especially when they'd been caught short and hadn't brought their own.

God, thought Jake. First the cape and now a trench coat. It's like something with the Marx brothers. Aloud he asked Jake if his coat had a name tag.

Carlo gave a short laugh. "You mean one of those sew-on labels the kids are supposed to have but never do? No, no name, no ID. But now maybe I should write my name in it." He shook his head and gave a short laugh. "To be honest, I picked up that raincoat at the end of last year's spring term. One of the kids, or faculty, or some parent, left it after graduation."

Jake sighed deeply, made another note, and asked if Carlo had seen Madame Carpentier at the reception. No, Carlo had not, but he certainly hadn't looked for her. He supposed he might have had a glimpse, but it wasn't one of those things he remembered. A hell of a lot of people, a real crowd in the room. But remember, he left before some of the others. He heard later that Grace had made a fuss about her cape being missing.

"See anything out of the way?" asked Jake, without much hope.

"Hey," said Carlo. "Remember, it was raining like the devil, and so I grabbed a raincoat and lit out of there . . ."

"Hold it," said Jake. "Remember, your own raincoat was missing."

Carlo shrugged. "Well, you know how it is. Pouring rain and sleet, so you look around and grab the first thing you can. It was just like mine, only longer. Anyway, I put it back this morning."

"So," said Jake doggedly, "you wore this other person's raincoat and went back to your apartment."

"Ran all the way," said Carlo cheerfully. "The next thing I

153

noticed was all hell breaking loose, with police cars and people churning around, and then the word got out to stay put. What a night that was. Poor Anita," he added, almost, Jake believed, as a dutiful afterthought.

Jake scribbled a few notes and then asked, as if he'd just noticed something out of place, "What's with the Band-Aids? Someone scratch you?" Like a woman fighting for her life? he said to himself and was pleased to see Carlo look, for the briefest moment, somewhat disconcerted.

But recovery was quick. "Not someone. Not even a cat, and I do have a cat. Tiger. Big monster. Called Joe. Found him at the animal shelter last year. But no, I slipped running back to my apartment—the sidewalks were awash, half-snow, half-rain, and I fell smack into this damn bush."

Again, Jake wondered about this roundabout route to answering the question, as if describing his cat gave Carlo time to think up a reason for the two Band-Aids. But aloud he thanked him and said he'd probably be asked again about some more details of the reception. "We've got to track down who came late, who came early. Who saw whom and when, things like that."

And Carlo thanked him and departed. And Jake entered a fat question mark together with the words "giant squid" next to his statement. Then he made a note to have a chat with this Rosemary Streeter, the smart African-American honor student. Jake knew her and also that she usually had a blond stubby friend, Zoë, tagging along. Both friends of Hannah Hoyt, the finder of the paper cut-out of Madame.

Two more interviews passed. The two maids, Cathy with a "C" and Kathy with a "K," hired for the occasion to help serve refreshments. They brought little light to the subject, not knowing many of the faculty by name and being too focused on getting the job over with in time to catch the late movie in Acton.

The third interview before the quick lunch break produced

Adrian Parsons, instructor in classics, Latin, and Greek, and assistant head of the Language Division, and so second fiddle to Madame Carpentier.

But Adrian Parsons didn't look the part of anyone's second fiddle. Although his face had a ravaged look, and his eyes were heavily shadowed, suggesting sleep deprivation, his whole demeanor was that of high-ranking diplomat forced to deal with some lower member of a rag-tag rebel army. His long, thin nose, centered in a long, thin face—Jake thought of a Russian wolfhound—and his thin lips, dark arching eyebrows, intense blue eyes, and smoothly brushed gray hair—these features, plus the immaculate gray trousers and the muted herringbone tweed jacket, all made other men in view around the room look grubby and unwholesome.

He certainly made Jake feel grubby and unwholesome, which went a long way to fuel the belligerence with which Jake asked his first question. And Jake had the perfect question to strike with. Because Adrian Parsons' distinguished, urbane features were somewhat obscured by the presence—across his nose, down one cheek, and across his right hand—of three Band-Aids. In fact, as far as these went, Mr. Parsons' decorations were almost the mirror images of those of Mr. Carlo Leone.

"What happened," demanded Jake Markham, "to your face? And your hand? Why the Band-Aids?"

12

ADRIAN Parsons' pause before answering was not followed by a description of his cat—if he had one. Instead, giving a wry grimace, he said, "I'm glad the police have the time to worry about the injuries of the people they are grilling..." Here Adrian held up a hand before Jake could break in and protest. "No, not grilling. Asking, as you properly should, questions so you can get at the bottom of this god-awful affair. Anita Goshawk was a very close friend and a gifted teacher. All of us at school are dreadfully shocked. And, it goes without saying," Adrian Parsons' voice trembled and his shoulders rose in a gesture of distress, "that I'll help you any way I possibly can."

Jake, while noting these signs of emotion, felt somehow that his questioning had been preempted. For a few seconds, he glared down at his notes, reorganized his thoughts, and then settled for repeating, yet again, the question about the Band-Aids.

Adrian had pulled himself together. And Jake settled back

in his chair to listen intently to his description of leaving the reception hall, running through the sleet to get to his apartment, the slippery nature of the pathways, and how he slipped, fell, and plunged into a large and prickly bush planted at the edge of the path.

Jake added yet another question mark to his notes and then asked when and where Mr. Parsons had seen Anita Goshawk.

Of course Adrian had seen Anita—Ms. Goshawk. He was on the school lecture committee, so he arrived at the art center early to see if everything was in place—the lectern, the projector, details like that. He remembered he'd been concerned when he saw she'd arrived wearing only that brown dress. Remembered telling her that a warm afternoon doesn't say a thing about the evening temperature and that the weather people were warning about some really foul weather, mixed precipitation. Hadn't she brought a coat? But she laughed off the weather and insisted that they were in a good, old-fashioned January thaw.

Jake let the question of the improperly clad Anita slide by. Later there would be time enough to deal with the knotty problem of the clothes, cape, and raincoat exchanges. "How," he queried, "had Ms. Goshawk seemed before, during the lecture? Anything unusual? Did she seem upset? Wary, looking over her shoulder, something like that? Did you notice anyone in particular watching her?"

At the last question, Adrian Parsons raised his eyes to the ceiling. "Watching her? Of course, everyone was watching her. After all, she was the feature; it was her show, her party."

This made sense, so Jake nudged the classics instructor forward and Adrian summed up the lecture. It had been a good one with slides tailored to the mixed audience. And no, he hadn't lingered after it was over, although he had offered to help her carry her briefcase and her slides on the return trip to the school.

"She just waved me off," said Adrian. "Told me she'd see me at the reception. Anita liked to take care of her own things her own way. Put her slides back in order." Here Adrian Parsons gave a rueful but shaky laugh. "No feminine manifestations of helplessness with Anita. She always took care of her own equipment. I used to see her walking between classes weighed down by boxes of slides and huge art books and video set-ups, but lord help anyone who thought she needed a hand. So I left her with a crowd still asking questions or shaking her hand. Congratulating her."

"It's a woman's world," said Jake, with the idea of inflaming Mr. Parsons, who didn't seem like the type to buy a hundred percent into the New Woman.

"For better or for worse," said Adrian ambiguously. "But Anita never mixed much in feminist politics. Her passion was art history and that took up one hundred percent of her time."

"But why didn't she drive to the art center?" asked Jake. This, to him, was a real problem. All that equipment—did she haul it single-handedly down the footpath? Just to make a point about being independent?

Adrian cleared the matter up. All Anita had to tote were her two boxes of slides; the art center had been the object of a community fund and was well provided. Slide projector, video, audio equipment, the works. State of the art. It was one of the places, Adrian pointed out, where the whole town could meet for mutual enlightenment and social interaction.

"And does mutual enlightenment follow?" asked Jake.

Adrian gave a small thin smile. "Dr. Singer and all of us, the whole school, want to get along with the townspeople. Joanna is a great one for building bridges, but I think that even she can't always manage miracles."

And the interview rambled on to its conclusion, with no reports of sightings of the victim. Although Adrian Parsons had left the lecture hall ahead of most of the audience, he arrived quite late to the reception—he wanted to check the faculty mailroom, pick up a folder in his office, make a phone call. And he left the reception when it became clear that the guest of honor was a genuine no-show. But no, he had not seen Madame Carpentier wearing her cape or *not* wearing her cape. Nor anyone else wearing the bloody thing. Yes, someone had mentioned that Anita had lifted the thing—and how had she dared? It was a sacred object. Here, Mr. Parsons shook his head in mock amazement.

Jake had already marked the cape down in his notes as an object with some of the qualities of an armed nuclear device. However, he ploughed on doggedly. Had there been some friction between Ms. Goshawk and Madame Carpentier? Adrian made a dismissive noise. He heard that sort of thing from time to time, but he never wanted any part of it. What did he think about the business of Madame wanting to move into Anita Goshawk's classroom? Only his opinion, Adrian had answered, but for what it was worth, he supported Madame Carpentier in the move. The French Department was a major bulwark of the Language Division, and it needed a central focus, a home of its own. The classes, with its large library of reference books and big enrollment, shouldn't be scattered among three classrooms like confetti. This history of art, while an important study, could easily be accommodated in a smaller space. After all, none of those classes had more than fifteen students.

"Much as I admired Anita as a teacher, fond as I was of her personally," Adrian said, his voice now faltering again, "it's a matter of priorities. Because the girls are so college-oriented, so busy taking the standard courses with an eye to advanced placement exams and college acceptance, the history of art, like some of the other elective areas—photography, ceramics, studio art, theatre, dance—exciting, charming, even demanding as these are, must take a back seat to the major disciplines."

Jake, irked by the idea that art could be considered a non-essential elective, succumbed to an urge to stick a small needle into Mr. Parsons. "And these days, aren't Latin and Greek, the classics, considered 'charming' but unnecessary?"

Adrian Parsons looked truly shocked. "Good God, no." He shook his head and repeated, "No, certainly not," and said something incoherent about basics and the Western tradition.

And Jake Markham, hearing again the agitation in Mr. Parsons' voice, dismissed the instructor and rose to search out a cup of coffee. It had been a long stretch since breakfast. He had to confess that Adrian Parsons had surprised him. Not the routine answers to Jake's questions, but the emotion, what appeared to be real distress, that kept surfacing during the interview. Funny thing, Jake thought. Of all the adults he'd seen so far, he'd have bet that Adrian Parsons was one cool cat. A snob, too. Like one of those characters in British movies featuring devious members of Parliament. And yet. And yet, if Jake had to make a bet, it would be that Adrian Parsons felt hurt by Anita Goshawk's death, felt it deeply, and had not recovered from the shock of it.

Jake located a large coffeemaker in the Radnor Hall kitchen, set up apparently for the comfort of both the interviewers and interviewees, and filled a mug decorated with the school seal—two quill pens crossed over an open book—and the motto "She flies with her own wings." Wasn't that some western state's motto, puzzled Jake, dumping in a heaping spoon of sugar into the mug. Washington or Oregon? Had Miss Claudia Merritt swiped some state's motto because she had been born out west and later migrated east? Anyway, even if lifted, it wasn't a bad motto for a girls' school founded in the mid-nineteenth century.

Then, bearing his steaming mug, Jake retraced his steps to the Copeland Room and braced himself to take on the two students who were rumored to have spied Miss Goshawk wearing the infamous cape. It was going to be an everlasting day. After those two girls, he was scheduled to talk to the basketball coach, Miss Webster, and the admissions assistant, Mr. Warnke. He sat down heavily in the club-footed mahogany chair just as the clock on the heavy, carved oak mantelpiece was just proclaiming in a soft brassy voice that it was eleven. Jesus, said Jake to himself, I'm going to miss most of the autopsy if I can't clear these kids off my plate in double time.

But the students, Rosemary Streeter and Zoë Fountain, who arrived one after the other, did little to throw light on their sighting. Anita Goshawk wore a cape, *the* cape. Of course they'd recognized it and marveled at her nerve. Ms. Goshawk appeared to be in a hurry and was heading for the footpath entrance. It was a quick glimpse, and neither girl had words with her. After all, the weather had turned pretty foul, so no one was going to hang around making conversation or stop her to say what a great lecture it was.

"Besides," Zoë said, "Ms. Goshawk is, well, was smart enough to know when we were sucking up to her."

"So if you only caught a quick look at the woman," Jake asked each girl, "how can either of you be sure that it was not Madame Carpentier wearing the cape?"

The girls treated the question with scorn. They knew Madame. They would have known her even if she'd been wrapped in a tiger skin. Even if they'd only seen her for a second.

"We know Madame Carpentier," Rosemary insisted. "It wouldn't matter what she was wearing, we'd know her a mile away."

And with that Jake had to be content. He sent the two on their way after telling them not to discuss their statements with anyone. "Anyone, and I mean it," he warned them, knowing full well that in a matter of minutes they would rehash the whole scene with each other and God only knew how many other students, not to mention later telephoning parents, brothers, sisters, and boyfriends. He took a last gulp of cold coffee, packed his briefcase with his notes, and headed for the county morgue and his date with the late Anita Goshawk.

Alex McKenzie felt he didn't need another autopsy in his life. As a visitor to his wife's school, he had only the interest of a physician, who, coming upon a dead body, has a certain curiosity about the cause of death. Well, foul play was almost certain, so let the forensic boys get on with it. But, stepping through the frozen slush on his way to the morgue entrance, he told himself it was more than curiosity; it was the whole damn safety issue of the school and its inhabitants—his wife, the teachers, and the students—and it was setting his teeth on edge. Otherwise, by God, he'd gladly skip the affair.

But a postmortem examination of a woman recently seen alive, seen standing up at the art center in her brown wool dress, heard holding forth about the finer points of American painting, can sharply destroy detachment and command attention.

Without her body covered in the bat-like cape, without her corpse swaddled and zipped into a body bag, the Anita Goshawk he saw now on the autopsy table, lying face-up, feet neatly together, her big toe hung with its toe tag, was a slender thing, almost bony, in fact. Hips, pelvic structure, ribs, clavicle—her skeletal self asserted itself as if to say, see, there isn't much to me, just skin and bones. The word "undernourished" occurred to Alex, and he found his mind reclothing the woman, setting her upright in front of her audience, pointer in hand, bringing her back to life. But an attempt to remodel her ravished face was beyond him. He shook himself. Sarah was the one with the imagination, the one for tours back and forth through time and space; he should stick to the facts in front of his eyes.

To this end, Alex centered his gaze on the business in progress, his ears tuned to the droning of the pathologist as he described the X ray of the head injury, the bone fragments found, and the angle at which the weapon had descended on the skull. The absence on the body of needlemarks or embedded objects, the presence of a two-inch scar along the left femur, the dental work to the lower left bicuspid, and the lack of any foreign material on the hands, the feet, or embedded in the fingernails, all these were noted.

Here Alex interrupted. "Nothing?" he asked. "She didn't scratch anyone, fend them off, Edgar?"

Dr. Edgar Zim shook his head. "Must have been caught by surprise. And she didn't grapple with him—or her—as far as we can tell from a superficial going-over of her clothes and that cape. But the lab will be fussing with those things for a while yet. The only stuff we've found so far is from the woods—leaves, fungi, moss, pond water, mud, and snow residue."

"And the black glove. Plus the brooch that Sarah picked up? The one that Madame Carpentier usually wore on the cape's collar."

"You mean fingerprints? Nothing on the gloves, and as for the brooch, the lab says there was only a partial, and we'll probably find it belongs to Madame. Or your wife. And that it came off during the assault—the clasp is bent. I'd say she was unconscious from the first blow and died soon after two subsequent blows. All from the same instrument. Fragments of fiberglass and wood. The wound is flat on one side and is convex on the other. Penetration more from force than from a sharp-ended object."

Alex nodded, and the post-mortem examination went on its way, with Jake Markham watching, listening intently. But Alex kept tuning in and out so that his understanding was a scattered, patchwork impression of Edgar Zim's exegesis: the oddity of the wound, the force necessary to deliver it, the angle from which the instrument descended to do its work.

Alex came to briefly. "Are you saying that the killer was taller than his victim?"

"That wouldn't be hard," said Zim. "Ms. Goshawk isn't much more than five three and a bit."

"Listen," said Jake. "Most of the people at the school, and in the community, leaving out the kids, were taller than Anita Goshawk."

"Right," said the pathologist. "We can fuss around later with the angle of the delivery and the force needed to deliver the blow, but I don't think"—here he turned to Jake—"it's going to make much difference. Most of the people I've seen around the school could do a similar job of bashing. As for the girls, they have muscles you wouldn't believe. All that soccer and crew and hockey and the fitness center workouts. And most of the faculty and the staff at the school are quite capable of strong-arm stuff."

"You mean," said Jake, "it'll be a hell of a lot easier to find the people who couldn't have done it."

"Like Madame Grace," said Alex. "She's about five three, same height as Anita. And not exactly the muscular type."

"Spare me the speculation," said Zim. "I've enough to do as it is. Now, look here, at the base of the skull."

And the examination moved slowly to its conclusion, and by twelve-thirty, Jake and Alex walked gratefully out into the snow that swirled around the parking lot of the morgue.

"If Madame Carpentier is still on your list," said Alex, "she's a little short to have done all that damage. She and Anita were pretty well matched as far as size went. Can't see Carpentier being able to get away with more than one blow."

"How about the advantage of terrain," Jake reminded him. "The ground sloped to the pond. What if Carpentier got above her?"

"The attack must have come at the edge of the path. That's

where the glove and the brooch were found. And her glasses were just off the path."

"So Carpentier stood on that bench and let her have it with an ax. Or a baseball bat."

"Ease up," said Alex amiably. "You don't buy that."

"Stranger things," murmured Jake. "Let the lab worry about it. But, speaking of which, aren't those guys going to have fun with that cape? My God, Carpentier's been trailing that thing through the school since the Dark Ages. It's probably got the hair and the DNA of kids who graduated fifteen years ago. And dog hairs—not just Szeppi's but some other critters' she's had over the years. Plus the fluff from the dorms, her apartment, the classrooms, and the cafeteria. Put the cape under the microscope and you'll come out with half the town of Carlise."

Jake looked at his watch and stamped his feet free of a gathering mound of snow. "Okay, I've got to get back to the grind. All those statements. And check on the search for the weapon. All those dormitory houses have porches and vestibules crammed with lethal weapons. Bats, sticks, rakes, and skateboards. Even hockey skates. You could do a lot of damage using a hockey skate."

Alex grabbed his arm. "Wait up," he said. "I've remembered something. Did you say 'hockey skate'? And 'bats' and 'sticks'?"

"Yeah, those things can be lethal. I mean, Christ, half the sporting equipment in the world is dangerous."

"I don't mean the equipment. But listen to this. I just saw our friend Madame Carpentier blow her stack about all the stuff stacked up in the Gregory House vestibule. She caught her coat on a bike, got mad, and called the maintenance office to have it hauled away."

Jake stared at him, his eyebrows and forelock turning whitish with the falling snow. "Say that again. Carpentier called maintenance to haul away all the sports equipment?"

"Skates, sticks, bats, rollerblades, the bicycle, baseball mitts. Some pure junk, notebooks, single sneakers, someone's jacket, shin guards. A real jumble."

Jake brushed the snow from his face and shook his head. "Now, isn't that cute? How do you like this scenario? Madame Carpentier and Anita Goshawk have been looking daggers at each other for ages, they've been fighting about who takes who's classroom away, and Madame Knife decides she's had it. Especially when she sees Goshawk has snitched her cape. She grabs another coat, any coat that's hanging in the cloakroom. A man's trench coat, for instance. It's time to act. And what a great opportunity, Goshawk going into reverse on the footpath. Carpentier grabs a stick, a bat, sneaks through the woods, and cuts Goshawk off at the pass—the middle of the footpath. No one is around because they're all gung-ho for the reception. Bangs Goshawk on the head. Does it again and again for good measure. But after she's pulverized her rival, she's got a problem. So tell me, what would you do with the weapon?"

Alex obliged. "After you rinse it off in the pond, you hide it under your coat and take it back to one of the dorms, one of the places you know has a heap of similar bats and sticks, and you mix it in. Then, you profess fury at the disorder, call the maintenance men, and have it all hauled away." He looked up at Jake. "Hauled away to where?"

But Jake broke into a run. "That's exactly what I'm going to find out," he called from over his shoulder.

166

13

SOME corner of Alex's brain nagged him to pursue Jake, to follow him to the school grounds and race from house to dormitory to gym to fitness center, gathering sticks, bats, skates, soccer shoes, anything that could be called a weapon. It was the call, not of the chase, but the call for action. Life as a practitioner of internal medicine demanded an awful lot of sitting and listening and nodding, of quiet probing, ordering tests, and then explaining, soothing, and planning. Sometimes, Alex wanted to get off his tail and move it, and during these moments, he regretted that he hadn't opted for emergency medicine. Or gone in for one of those jobs where doctors are dropped onto an ice flow or lowered into a cave to do something, do anything, and do it immediately. But this fit usually passed, and he saved his energy for dealing with Sarah's occasional plunges into trouble with a capital "T."

Nevertheless, it was with a real twinge of regret that Alex watched Jake's car spin around in a spray of slush and take off toward Carlisle. He drove his own car at a more sedate pace, switching on the radio and letting a flood of Johnny Cash blot out any urges to fling himself into the business of weapon discovery. It was time to map out the afternoon, because he needed the sort of plan that could accommodate his needs (revisiting old medical school scenes, college friends, taking a walk on the Esplanade) as well as those of Sarah (going to museums, shops, and bookstores).

However, in none of these plans did his cousin Giddy Lester figure. But there she was, larger than life, next to Sarah by the entrance to Gregory House. Alex was fond of Giddy, but Giddy's propensity for trouble, usually involving a spaced-out member of the opposite sex, had made him cautious about being involved with her affairs. Allowing himself the luxury of a prolonged exhalation of breath, Alex slowed the car and pulled into a space close to Gregory House's side door. Giddy yanked open the back door of the Jeep and climbed in. "Hey, Alex. Hope you don't mind. My car had cardiac arrest back there by the art building. Now, relax." This as Giddy peered over the front seat at her cousin and decided that Alex didn't exactly resemble a welcoming committee. "Just dump me anywhere near MIT, because I need to pick up my stuff in Josh's apartment now that I've kicked him out of my life. Then I'll get a bus and make it back here."

"Simmer down, Giddy," said Alex. "We'll drop you off somewhere. Sarah and I haven't settled on what we're going to be doing."

"He's saying," put in Sarah, climbing into the front seat, "that he and I will stand in the middle of some parking ramp arguing because he'll want to visit Brigham and Women's and I'll want to go to the Museum of Fine Arts."

"You need marriage counseling," said Giddy. "And happily, I'm available. So enjoy. We have the whole afternoon ahead of us."

168

But the best made plans of mice and men, of husbands, wives, and cousins, gang aft a-gley and by the time the three had settled down to face the death-defying drive into the big city, another personage derailed the afternoon.

Madame Carpentier, to be exact.

Grace Carpentier drove a '94 dark green Chevy Cavalier and, after having filled it at a gas station, wheeled directly in front of the Jeep, and with a spurt of dirty snow accelerated in a southeasterly direction on the Bedford Road.

"Christ!" exclaimed Alex, stamping on the brake.

"It's her," said Giddy. "She always drives like a bat. Or a Frenchman. Full speed ahead."

"It's bloody rude," said Sarah, peering ahead as the Chevy whisked around the curb side of the road, sped by a delivery van, and vanished around the curve ahead. Alex increased his speed, passed the van, and pointed a finger at Madame's car ahead. "It only seems rude," he said judiciously, "if you haven't driven around here lately. I'd say Madame Grace has simply adapted to Boston road rage. She's driving to the manner born."

Sarah peered ahead at the narrowing secondary road. "I wonder where she's off to? She's way off the main track."

"Even Grace Carpentier has a life," said Giddy. "Though I suppose most of the kids at school think she travels by broom."

"With everything happening at school," said Sarah, "you'd think she might stick around. She strikes me as the nosy type, into everything."

"You mean like hauling off the junk in Gregory House?" asked Alex. "That really caught Jake Markham's attention."

"What did you say?" shouted Giddy from the back seat, while Sarah swiveled around and stared at him.

"It's no secret," said Alex. "Madame got maintenance to clear up the vestibule at Gregory House. An executive decision, but probably a good one. That place was a mess."

"And that," said Giddy firmly, "settles the weapon. Anita

was brained by Grace with a skateboard or a hockey stick, and Grace arranged to get rid of the evidence."

"You sound just like Jake," said Alex. He slowed the car slightly. "Our friend Grace is turning. Up there, to the right." He pointed to a yellow clapboard, two-story building with a sign featuring a bounding deer, the animal's outline softened by the falling snow.

" 'True Aim Sporting Goods Shop—Best Value in Sports Equipment, Deer Hunters Welcome,' " read Sarah. " 'Owner and manager, Georges Thibodeau.' So, Madame has a hobby. Or a French boyfriend."

"If you're saying Grace is a closet deer hunter or has a secret lover," said Giddy, "tell me another."

"We'll never know, will we?" said Alex as he drove past the building and began the slow descent into a populated shopping area.

"Hey," shouted Giddy. "Are you just letting her go in there and maybe come out with an assault weapon? Where's your sense of the chase?"

"Jake Markham and the police are taking care of Grace Carpentier. We're going into Boston," said Alex firmly.

"It wouldn't hurt," said Sarah, "just to see what she's up to."

"You're both crazy," said Alex. "What do you want to do, go in and see if she's making an interesting purchase? Or having a dangerous liaison?"

"But," put in Giddy, "she *is* the number-one suspect."

"You don't know that," said Alex. "But have it your way. I'll go back to the shop. If Grace comes out, you can ask her what she's doing with her spare time, and I hope she cuts your noses off for sticking them into her business."

With that, Alex took a left into a gas station, turned around, and drove the Jeep into a parking space by the sporting goods store in time to see Grace Carpentier emerge with a paper-wrapped package clutched under one arm, walk quickly to her car, and with her windshield wipers whisking away the slight accumulation of snow, turn into traffic and speed away in the direction of Carlisle.

"That," said Alex, "is that. Grace probably bought a stopwatch the better to trap late students."

"Wait," shouted Giddy. And she jumped out of the car, slammed the door, and ran up the two short steps into the shop. And returned three minutes later.

"Madame has been buying firearms," she announced. "And a personal protection spray. The guy in there was putting a can of Bear Beware pepper spray—it's like Mace—back on the shelf and locking up a cabinet display of small pistols."

"And he told you, of course, what Grace was buying?" asked Alex.

"Of course not," said Giddy, fastening her seat belt. "I asked if they carried lacrosse sticks, which they don't. And used my eyes."

"As I drive over the speed limit into Boston," said Alex in a weary voice, "you may explain."

"I know what Giddy's saying," said Sarah. "It goes like this. The man in the shop has just had a customer who's been shown certain items. She chooses, she pays, she leaves. And he puts away all the demo stuff—in this case, small arms and pepper sprays."

"You got it," said Giddy. "I mean, there weren't any other customers in the place, so those things had to be connected to Madame Gracie."

"You know," said Sarah thoughtfully, "I don't blame the woman. All those threats and then Anita Goshawk being murdered while wearing her cape. Why not buy a handgun and pepper spray? I might do the same."

"That," said Giddy, "is okay if you don't consider the diabolical mind of Carpentier that came up with a scheme to lend her cape to Anita, sneak after her, and chop her down on the footpath. Then tell the police that Anita lifted the cape without her permission."

"Thank you, Giddy," said Alex. "Let's let the police deal with the lady if she holes up in the chapel bell tower and starts picking off the faculty."

"Okay," said Sarah. "I will cease from troubling. My mind is a blank, a tabula rasa."

"Me, too," said Giddy. "Perish the thought that I'd turn into a school snoop."

All of these heartfelt avowals of indifference to the future movements of the French teacher in fact guaranteed that each of the three, as he or she went about the remainder of their day, would be nagged without mercy about the possible future actions of the lady.

Giddy, left by her request near a Mass. Avenue entrance to the MIT complex, went about the retrieval of her worldly goods. Hauling a canvas sack, she talked her way into the apartment building, found Josh absent, the door open, and his room showing interesting evidence of a new female visitor: black lace underpanties and a cashmere turtleneck.

"Cashmere!" Giddy exclaimed and set to work to gather her possessions, made her way onto the sidewalk, and by dumb chance bumped directly into the Merritt School assistant tennis coach, who was hurrying toward his illegally parked car. Feeling dispirited, Giddy accepted his offer of a ride back to Carlisle, wondering as she climbed into the car whether it might be a relief to have this kind but rather dull man as an acceptable companion for the rest of the school year. After all, Jake Markham was certainly not what one would call accessible.

Alex dropped Sarah at the Museum of Fine Arts and prowled the hospital corridors of Brigham and Women's with an old roommate from his medical school days, but somehow his mind, despite these distractions, kept scooting back to the possibility of an armed and hostile Grace Carpentier.

Sarah's afternoon experience was similar. She was restless in the museum and did not pay proper attention to the recent acquisition of early Japanese prints, nor to the new exhibit of the works of Mary Cassatt. Finally, meeting Alex as planned in the museum parking lot, she suggested forgetting about any special restaurant, instead getting a quick pick-up dinner en route back to Carlisle. Alex, to her surprise, accepted.

"It won't hurt to go on back to the school and just put our feet up and be peaceful," he said.

Giddy, Sarah, and Alex were not the only ones whose day had ended in a decrescendo. Jake Markham and Hillary Mumford had intended to spring into action and begin a collection of the possibly lethal sports items from the houses, dormitories, and field houses of the school. However, signs of a break-in had been discovered by two students using the Althorne Gym fitness room. The alarm was raised, and several computer systems were found missing from the physical education office, as well as a number of stopwatches and other such items.

"Damnation," said Jake to Hillary as late that afternoon they walked through the accumulating snow toward Radnor Hall. "We should be collecting hockey sticks instead of worrying about petty larceny."

"Not so petty," said Hillary. "Those computers—the printers were new. Dr. Singer wants us on top of the business. Thinks it just might be connected to the murder."

But Jake had suddenly stiffened. Tilted his head. Frowned. "What was that?"

"What was what?"

"That noise. Sounded like a shot. Actually, two shots. One after the other."

"I didn't hear anything. Only that car down there, past the art building, revving up its engine."

"No, more than that. Like a shot. Pistol, maybe."

"I think you're hearing things."

"I think it came from over there, past the Althorne Gym."
Jake turned and started off at a run.

"Wait up, Jake," called Hillary. "You know better. Follow procedure."

Jake slowed his steps. "Call in for backup. Don't worry, I'm not going to crash the scene by myself."

Ten minutes later, the school saw the arrival of two squad cars, five plainclothesmen from assorted corners of the campus, a state policeman assigned to the front gate, and Detective Hillary Mumford and Officer Jake Markham. Twenty minutes of searching followed, and the activity most naturally attracted members of the school community, who now emerged out of the swirls of snow into the lighted parking lot only to find further progress blocked.

"What was that noise I have just now heard," demanded Grace Carpentier, the dog Szeppi in tow, arriving breathless at the gymnasium back entrance and finding herself stopped cold by two police cars, several security men, and Jake Markham.

"We are asking," said Jake, "that the school people and the students return to their houses. Or their offices. Their apartments."

"But you are herding us here like a number of sheep. This is most unacceptable." Grace was red-faced, breathless, her black hair disordered, and her purple quilted coat partly unbuttoned. "I was," she went on, "trying to take my little dog, Szeppi, for his walk. He needs his walk every afternoon in every weather."

"Madame Carpentier," exploded Jake, "Please take your dog back to your apartment. The police have work to do in this area. And," he added angrily to several students who had come up behind the French teacher, "all of you go back now. To your houses, your dorms. Away from the gym."

Grace Carpentier eyed him with disfavor. "It is not for me to tell the police that I thought I heard a shot. A distinct shot.

From perhaps a very small revolver. Or a pistol. Which makes one think that things are not so safe at this moment at the school." And she departed, head held high.

A second later Hillary Mumford walked up. "We've cleared the area. Looked under all the bushes, looked in gym rooms, closets, trees. Unless it was someone who came down in a chopper, we can assume that he's out of here. If there ever was a he. Or a she."

"What about the people who were around when you started the sweep?"

"No one. Zip," said Hillary. "Not many hanging around in this weather. Only a couple of students on snowshoes on the soccer field. We checked them for weapons, but we can't start frisking the entire school." Here Hillary waved at the growing crowd behind her. "Later we'll think about warrants and room searches. But I really think it was a car backfiring."

Jake shrugged. "You're the boss."

Hillary grinned. "A boss among many. We'll call for a lab team to go over the area. Look for bullet holes in trees, shells on the ground, signs of firing. To keep everyone happy." She brushed the snow from her forehead and cupped her hands to her mouth. "Everyone, go back where you came from. The Althorne Gym area and the Back Gate Drive will be off limits for a while. Thanks."

And the crowd milled briefly, then broke ranks and began to filter back through the increasing accumulation of snow, lost from sight in the dark because four-thirty P.M. in New England on a late-January afternoon might just as well have been the middle of the night.

"You're not going to find much with this snow," Jake pointed out. "You'd have to bring in searchlights."

"I talked to quite a few people. The only one, besides a couple of students, who thought she heard shots was your friend, Madame Grace."

175

"She just said so because she knew it was going to annoy us," said Jake, who, ignorant of Giddy's theory of an armed and dangerous French teacher, was willing to put Grace down in the category of a damned nuisance.

Two people who had heard a noise resembling, perhaps, the detonation of a firearm chose not to respond by running out into the snow. Each was concerned instead with his physical appearance.

Carlo Leone was daubing Betadine on the long scratch that angled down his cheek and refixing a Band-Aid across the wound on his hand. He was considering a trip, when the weather cleared, to a local pharmacy for some substance that would mask his injuries. One of those make-up compounds women used. He was getting damned tired of all the exclamations of interest and sympathy that his appearance excited.

The other injured party, Adrian Parsons, had by coincidence also chosen Betadine as the antiseptic of choice. His was a crooked scratch that began on his left cheek, angled across the bridge of his nose, and tilted dangerously toward the corner of his right eye. Unfortunately, there was an ominous reddening on the cheek that suggested a possible infection. Grimly, Adrian rubbed in the orange solution for a second time and then gingerly added a squeeze of antibiotic ointment to a folded gauze pad and reapplied the two Band-Aids to his face and the third to the back of his hand. Then he combed his hair, readjusted his shirt collar, sighed deeply, and sank into an armchair. A photograph album labeled "1995" lay open on the table beside him, and the featured photographs showed a dressy Adrian Parsons—dinner jacket, white silk scarf, black topcoat—holding on his arm the diminutive Anita Goshawk, she in layered scarves and twisted amber beads. Behind them, in blurred reproduction, the lights of a theatre. Adrian sighed again, looked at the photograph, grimaced, leaned against the chair back, and closed his eyes.

14

IN communities like boarding schools, gossip may well be said to be the staff of life. If on the evening of Saturday, January ninth, certain members of the Merritt School community had put their heads together and exchanged local gossip, something pertinent to the death of Anita Goshawk might have emerged. But the murder had cast its shadow over the school, and that Saturday was more remarkable for what was not said, or in modern parlance, what was not shared.

This was true for the house parents Freda and Joel Cohen, who, wishing to preserve unstained the reputation of Gregory House, urged their flock to keep speculations on the cause of the murder to themselves, please. This request perfectly suited the senior trio of Rosemary, Zoë, and Hannah, because each girl felt that the obscene postcards they had discovered in Madame Carpentier's room might be a source of personal danger as well as a threat to future prospects. As for Sarah, Alex, and Giddy, all three felt that watching a sporting goods shopkeeper put his wares in order—even if the wares were on the dangerous side—hardly amounted to hard evidence. So, on return from Boston that evening, each decided to keep quiet on the matter.

Jake Markham and Hillary Mumford came to the conclusion that the "shots" or distant "pop-pop" noises could not be taken seriously and school speculations on the matter were to be stifled. After all, a thorough scouring of the area, one that included searchlights, two snow blowers, and a hot-air hose, plus the questioning of those in the vicinity of the gym, all added to a large zero, and the police reluctantly concluded that the so-called shots were indeed, as Hillary had claimed, the backfiring of a car passing down School Street.

Sarah and Alex, on their way upstairs in Gregory House, did hear mention of suspect noises in the vicinity of the Althorne Gymnasium, but this pseudo-information did not stimulate a desire to call the police. Even Sarah's heated brain could not place Grace Carpentier, along with her dog Szeppi, in the vicinity of the gym taking pot shots at trees, bushes, and lampposts just for the hell of it. Even if self-defense was a motive, to be out in the snow practicing her quick draw would be the act of a lunatic.

As for Madame Carpentier, after her confrontation with Jake she retreated from the Althorne Gymnasium scene and continued her airing with Szeppi, her progress slow because of the drifting and whirling snow. Returning to her apartment, she hung up her now-wet purple quilted coat, put on the tea kettle, and poured two cups of kibbles in Szeppi's dish. Then, moving quietly, she went to her door, fixed the chain in place, and then moved aside a wooden chair, rolled up an edge of the carpet, and with the aid of a screwdriver, pried up the loose end of one of the pine planks.

This done, she walked over to her purple quilted coat, reached into an inner zippered pocket, and withdrew a very small pistol and a pamphlet labeled "Instructions for Use and Care." These she deposited in the floor cavity, pushed the board down, tapped the nails in place, rolled the carpet down, and moved the chair back over the area. Next, she removed from its paper wrapping a can of Bear-Beware Pepper Spray, recommended to her as "superior to Mace," and placed it under her gloves and scarf in the drawer of a small chest that stood next to her apartment door—this location chosen for ease of access. Last, she walked to the desk, opened the slant top, and picked up the collection of postcards featuring works of art and places of architectural interest. Selecting a pair of sharp sewing scissors, she cut each card into small pieces, transported the collection to the bathroom, and by successive flushings disposed of them.

Then, hearing the kettle sighing on its burner, she moved to the kitchen, poured a cup of peppermint tea—recommended by her mother for times of gastric tension—settled herself in a small tapestry wing chair, snapped her fingers for Szeppi to join her, and settled back against the cushion, wearing on her face the look of someone who has used her time wisely and to good advantage.

Alex and Sarah, now back in the confines of Gregory House, found that eight o'clock was a little early for hitting the hay, and so they found themselves joining a flow of students, staff, and teachers and heading into the Nakatani Arts Center for a hastily assembled memorial concert by the student orchestra.

Joanna Singer, for the second time that day, spoke of the loss of Anita Goshawk, and of how the students and music faculty wanted to add their particular tribute to a gifted teacher. The program would be a short one, and several favorites of Anita Goshawk had been chosen because she was, as many knew, a faithful attendant at local musical events. Joanna Singer paused, visibly pulled herself together, and said that it had been a sad and difficult day for everyone, thanked them for their cooperation with the police, and said that there would be more statements taken at Radnor Hall during the next few days. A schedule would be posted in the morning.

The singing was remarkably good, although the chorale, *Wer in dem Schutz des Hochsten ist*—Who Under God's Safe Shelter Dwells—showed perhaps more feeling than polish. It was, Sarah thought, a positive way to end the day, although halfway through the chorale Adrian Parsons rose from his seat, his expression an anguished one, and made his way up the aisle and out the exit.

After the program and the silent filing out of the audience, Giddy Lester, increasingly uneasy at the possibility of an armed French teacher in their midst, decided to search out Jake Markham and tell him of her concern. But after twisting her way through the departing audience asking for him, she gave up. Jake was elsewhere. On campus, off campus, in Radnor Hall going over statements, no one knew. Giddy, still uneasy, retired to her apartment. She'd find Jake tomorrow, because surely Madame Grace wasn't going out into the storm to drill someone or do target practice.

Alex and Sarah also returned to Gregory House, climbed the three flights of stairs amid a stream of unnaturally sober students, and unlocked Sarah's apartment.

"Patsy!" exclaimed Sarah. "The poor thing. He's got to go out. I only gave him a quick run after we got home. Can you take him out? I'm so tired I think I'd fall down the stairs."

Alex gave her a resigned look, snapped on Patsy's leash, and departed, and Sarah turned to hang up her coat. And then she remembered. She reached into the pocket, letting her hand close on a folded file card. The message Sarah had found tacked on the tree that desired in crude black print Mme. Carpentier to rot in hell.

She sat down suddenly, coat in one hand, the file card in the other. "Oh my God," she said.

On his return, Alex found her there, sitting, holding the file card. Without speaking, she held up the card.

Alex read the text, scowled, and then, pulling a handkerchief from his trouser pocket, took hold of one edge and checked the blank side. Turned it back. And shook his head. "Pretty disgusting," he said.

"Totally gross, as the girls would say. I found this on a tree. Before we all went out to dinner on Friday."

"And you lifted it?"

"Well, I couldn't leave the filthy thing there, could I? But I meant to turn it in to the school office. It was so obviously another contribution to the Madame Carpentier defamation league."

"It's a wonder it didn't burn a hole in your pocket."

"But you know it's quite different from those other productions," said Sarah. "It's crude. And blunt. The sledgehammer approach."

"So you've got a copycat at work. Or maybe a couple of copycats."

"I'd hate to think there are that many foul-minded people running around the school."

"The copycat angle isn't a wild guess," said Alex reasonably. "I'd say it's very probable."

Sarah shook her head and gave a weary sigh. "Let's go to bed, and I'll do the proper thing first thing in the morning. After all, it's been in my pocket all this time, a few more hours won't hurt."

Alec yanked his tie loose and began unbuttoning his shirt. "I'm not going to talk you into being a good Girl Scout. Let everyone have a night's sleep."

But sleep was not so easy to come by. Sarah was wound up and tense, and Alex, who had planned a loving interlude before sleep, gave up on the idea. He was feeling edgy. Irritable. Sarah's room reminded him of several unsatisfactory bed and breakfast establishments in his past: the radiator clanked, a sharp wind whistled through the marginally open window, and somewhere on the floor below a radio was emitting a strange sort of howl and throb. And now Patsy, usually an easy sleeper, rose from beside the bed like a great gray ghost and was making tentative noises in his throat. The strange sounds probably came from Giddy's room, Alex thought with annoyance. He remembered that her apartment was directly under Sarah's.

Alex was on target. Giddy, trying to banish worry, had put on a new CD promising relaxation through its rendering of "wilderness sounds directly recorded from nature." Giddy fell asleep five minutes into the program, although whether the distant call of a wolf from a mountainside did the trick was open to question. But she left the CD going and set to repeat endlessly.

Also restless, but without the anodyne of a wolf call, Gregory House parents Freda and Joel Cohen were having serious pillow talk on the subject of murder and its effect on students in their charge.

"Of course," said Freda, propping herself up on her elbow, "the girls won't admit that murder is something out of the ordinary. Most of them act as if bodies are found in the woods every day."

"No," said Joel. "I think they're quite affected. Didn't you see them tonight? Hardly speaking after the concert."

"If it had been Grace Carpentier, I think there'd have been dancing in the streets," said Freda.

"Actually," said Joel, "I don't mind Grace that much. She's always civil when I run into her. I've had meals with her at the cafeteria without being poisoned. I think you women can't cope with a strong personality like hers."

"You, Joel," said Freda, "can stuff it. You're being taken in. She probably wants something."

"It's not just me. Carlo Leone tells her off-color jokes, and she laughs. And look at Adrian. He's in a tough position, number two in the Language Division. And yet, he seems to get along fine with Grace. Even when she wanted to gobble up Anita's art history room, he supported her."

"You're saying Grace has this magic way about her that only men can appreciate. But speaking of Adrian, he certainly looked a wreck at the concert tonight. Had to leave in the middle."

"Maybe had to go to the bathroom."

"He was anguished. Positively anguished."

"You mean about Anita being killed? But those two were ancient history. Whatever they had going—and I admit it was pretty hot and heavy—it was over and done with long ago."

Freda pushed herself out of bed, shoved her feet into her slippers, and pulled her polar-fleece dressing gown around her ample waist. "I'm going to make us each a nice hot cup of cocoa, and then we can settle down and get some sleep." She shuffled her way toward the little apartment-sized kitchen. Returning with two steaming mugs of cocoa upon which floated fat marsh-mallows—not for nothing was Freda chosen to be a house parent—she delivered one to her husband and, holding her own mug aloft, crawled in bed beside him.

"And," said Freda, ignoring the nonresponse of her mate, "you can't tell me that Adrian isn't shocked right down to his bones about Anita dying. I'd say it's proof they still had some-thing going or it had started up again. And bang, there she is, dead. Murdered."

"Freda," said Joel. "Don't go passing this theory of yours to the police. They don't need to have you speculate about reviving love affairs. Let them draw their own conclusions."

Freda explored the softening marshmallow with her tongue and then took a long and satisfying swallow of her cocoa. Then she turned and faced her husband. "I don't deal with gossip, but the police may wonder why Adrian's acting like a bereaved fam-ily member. Almost in shock."

Joel placed his empty mug on the bedside table and reached over to pat his wife's free hand. "Take my advice, pussycat, leave the whole thing alone. It will only lead to trouble for all of us."

Freda finished her cocoa, set the mug down next to her bedroom slippers, switched off the bedside light, and wiggled down under the covers and sighed deeply. "Of course," she whispered. "Anita wasn't supposed to be killed. It was Grace."

Babette Leclerc was of a like mind. She had given up on an early sleep and was curled in an easy chair, wrapped in an afghan of a particularly repellent pattern in yellow and brown— a gift from a much-loved aunt and so a sacred object—at least after dark. Babette had turned on the weather channel, thinking it was a relatively nonintrusive form of entertainment—no tornados, mudslides, or floods being reported, only more snow and wind in the northeast. Babette had been an easy convert to the idea that Anita Goshawk had been mistaken for her boss, Grace Carpentier. This being so, Babette reasoned, it was only a matter of time until someone tried again. And perhaps succeeded. In which case, she, Babette, would—at least for the interim— rule the French Department.

The minutes ticked by, and Babette moved from allowing herself a proper period of mourning and distress to the contemplation of how the French Department should be run. Babette didn't aspire to Grace's job of running the whole Language Division—Adrian Parsons could have that and was welcome to it. She would bring to the teaching of French a kinder, gentler regime. And she would not hold the detention system like a sword over the heads of her students. But.

But how would Babette—she of mild temper and easy humor—produce the spectacular results that Grace seemed to get? Survivors of Grace's classes often went on to college glory, at least in their French classes. Nevermind. She, Babette, could handle that. A middle road was needed. Compassion-*cum*-

control. No problem. And Babette pulled her afghan tighter and drifted off to dream of French students playing in a fountain while she stood by holding a large black and ineffectual bullwhip.

To borrow part of a well-known phrase, uneasy lies the head that is filled with ill-gained knowledge. Or in this case, read "heads." These heads belonged to senior Merritt students Rosemary Streeter, Zoë Fountain, and Hannah Hoyt. Their illicit tour of Madame Carpentier's apartment, the discovery of the postcards, and Anita Goshawk's murder were not the stuff of which pleasant dreams are made. Rosemary and Zoë flung themselves down on their beds, got up, went to the lavatory, returned, and flung themselves down again. Got up and rousted out Hannah, who was herself wakeful and pacing. Then the three sat up, speculated, considered, and at midnight decided to reveal the fact of the postcards to the school office in the morning; then at two A.M. decided never to say a word about them; and finally, sometime after three in the morning, one after the other fell into a rumpled and shallow sleep.

Two other members of the school community were wakeful. Carlo Leone sat long after midnight rewording his résumé for employment at a selected group of academic institutions. He then attacked the matter of cover letters. The wording of these required the juggling and shifting of a number of facts and had already caused several rewritings, none satisfactory. Finally, at three-thirty, on this particularly cold and gusty January morning, Carlo fell asleep on the sofa in his small sitting room.

The other person whose behavior needed to be remarked was none other than Adrian Parsons, the number-two man of the Merritt School's Language Division.

As noted, Adrian had left the concert in a state of distress. This condition did not ease, and although he had stood under a hot shower, tossed down a glass of whiskey, done some simple deep-breathing exercises, and then forced himself to ruffle through a clutch of student papers on the *Eclogues* of Virgil, nothing he tried brought any sense of peace. Finally, at something like two-forty-five in the morning, he opened a desk drawer, drew out two keys fastened together by a red string, pulled on his fleece-lined jacket, placed a small flashlight in his pocket, and with great caution opened and closed his door, sidled along the corridor of Adam House, down the stairs to the back door, and with the help of a tiny beam of light, worked his way through the drifted snow to the basement of Lockwood Hall. He unlocked the basement door and soundlessly climbed two flights of stairs. Then, with the stealth of a night-roaming cat and careful to leave the yellow police tape in place across the door, he slipped the second key into the lock and let himself into Anita Goshawk's apartment.

15

THE early-morning hours of Sunday, January the tenth, featured blasts of a north wind and temperature that dropped to slightly below three degrees, with a dry, fine precipitation that whirled and benumbed everything it touched. Miss Merritt's School, the town of Carlisle, and all the houses and shops, playing fields, walkways, churches, road signs, and lampposts were transformed to the ice fairyland so beloved of illustrators of children's books and so loathed by the citizens who had to deal with frozen pipes, non-starting cars, and the miseries of cold feet and frostbitten cheeks. It was, in short, going to be the sort of day in which even the most avid skiers would hesitate before taking off for the slopes and cross-country trails.

Sarah had managed to fall asleep sometime after midnight, only to wake at three, needing to go to the bathroom. The route took her past an uncurtained window and she saw, or thought she saw, a tiny point of light moving and bouncing through the night. Of course, what with the snow, the lamppost light, and the lights fastened to the eaves of the houses, it might have been a false impression. She frowned and pictured some felon sneaking through the snow for reasons unimaginable. But, returning to bed, she shook her head. Of course, someone with a flashlight would be making the rounds. That's what the security people did, didn't they, for heaven's sake. So be grateful, she scolded herself, that someone cares, and stop looking for trouble.

Morning, still dark at six, announced itself in the person of Patsy, who, as was his custom, placed his rough gray head on Sarah's neck and both paws on her chest.

"Your turn for Patsy, remember?" said Alex, turning over and pulling the comforter up around his shoulders.

Sarah nodded dumbly, crawled out of bed, and began the business of layered dressing required for zero-degree weather. Muffled up, with Patsy's leash in one gloved hand, she descended the silent stairs of Gregory House and went out into the wind and stinging snow. And almost immediately ran into the bundled shape of Babette carrying a broom and a snow-scraper.

"I thought I'd better get my car cleaned off," shouted Babette. She pulled down her red woolen helmet, making her look like some sort of crusader posted to an arctic region.

"Good for you," yelled Sarah. "And my dog has to pee."

Babette waved a mitten at the parking lot, an area of indistinct white shapes. "Grace beat us to it. She's got Szeppi, and she's taking off."

And as Babette spoke—or rather, yelled—one of the snow-covered shapes detached itself from its fellows and, revealing itself as green automobile, spun out of the parking area and disappeared in a swirl of snow toward the main gate.

Sarah reached out and pulled Babette into the vestibule, now a tidy space since the removal of the sports detritus.

"Does Grace usually take off in a snowstorm at six in the morning?" asked Sarah.

Babette looked at her watch. "Well, it's more like six-fifteen now. Grace usually walks Szeppi before breakfast, but she doesn't take him driving in awful weather. But she's got studded tires, so I suppose she can go where she wants." She looked after the cloud of snow that marked Grace's departure. "Maybe she's out of coffee. Or wants exercise. Grace actually skies cross-country in the winter—if you can believe it—but she'd freeze to death if she tried it today. Five minutes outside and my face turned to ice. So don't stay out too long, the wind-chill factor is way below zero." And Babette vanished into Gregory House.

Sarah, holding a frozen glove to a frozen leash, knew herself well enough to know that if it had been a bright and shining morning with an acceptable thermometer reading, she might have hopped into the Jeep and followed Grace Carpentier. Just to satisfy an urge to know where a person who might own a new handgun was going.

But the weather argued against such foolishness. And besides, Babette was undoubtedly right. Grace was out of coffee. Maybe she needed a prescription. But then as Sarah, pulled by Patsy, waded into the snowdrift behind Gregory House, she remembered. Of course. And Babette should have known. It was Sunday. Hadn't Hanna told her that Madame Carpentier went to the Catholic church? Therefore, Grace might be off to early Mass. Question answered.

Except why take your dog? No one should leave a dog for more than ten minutes in a car in near-zero-degree weather. How long did early Mass last? Sarah had friends who seemed to make short work of their attendance. But now she, Sarah, would have to start worrying about a frozen Szeppi locked in a frigid car, and she certainly didn't need anything more to fret about.

Returning to her room with a snow-encrusted Patsy, Sarah told Alex, now up and enjoying his first cup of coffee, about Grace Carpentier's departure.

"With her dog. And she loves that dog, so why . . ." Sarah left the question in the air.

"You, my love, are making Mount Everest out of a molehill," said Alex, pulling a piece of toast out of the toaster.

"It's my specialty," said Sarah, shrugging out of her coat. "Anyway, I ran into Babette Leclerc, who pointed out Grace's car leaving. Babette's second-in-command in the French Department and always runs around doing Grace's bidding."

"And you're beginning to think Babette might like to be commander-in-chief?"

"Not me, I don't think," said Sarah, reaching for the carton of Tropicana, "especially before breakfast."

Jake Markham was in a temper. Alex, as recorded, had envied him yesterday as a man of action, hot on the trail of the Gregory House sports collection. Pictured him and his cohorts bundling and tagging the skateboards, the hockey sticks, the baseball bats—the boomerang, hadn't there been a boomerang?—and delivering them to the lab. But events, first the break-in at the Althorne Gymnasium, and then the actions of the Merritt School maintenance crew, had made hash of Jake's plan.

As the two-man crew were wrapping up the loading of the Gregory House vestibule accumulation on Saturday under the supervision of Madame Carpentier, two house parents, one from Packard Hall, the other from Adam House, happened on the removal scene. And so pleased were they at the idea of cleaning up the odd assortment of equipment and cast-off objects from their own house vestibules, porches, and basements that they encouraged the men, Ira and Joe by name—to make a real job of it. Haul all the stuff off from the various dorms and

190

store it out of sight. The girls never took care of their equipment, tossed it around as if hockey sticks and rollerblades grew on trees. Refreshment was promised at the end of the job, and Ira and Joe went to work with a will.

Thus, by the time that Jake Markham arrived Sunday morning at Gregory House to begin his collection, the vestibule was a spotless void. Freda Cohen, when tracked down, reported that Grace Carpentier had initiated the clean-up and that for once, she and Grace were of one mind; it was high time the vestibule was cleared. Where had the stuff been taken? Jake demanded. Here Freda was vague. Probably one of the field houses. Or, perhaps, the Althorne Gym Annex. Or, well, who knew?

Jake had then wasted forty minutes hunting down the crew at first the gym annex, then the two field houses by the soccer and hockey fields, and then the equipment shed by the tennis courts. In clear weather he might have caught sight of the big school pick-up truck, but with the blowing snow and zero visibility, he had not. Finally, after circling the entire school campus three times, Jake in desperation tried the Outing Club building, a structure that sat on the extreme northeast edge of the school property.

And hit pay dirt.

The splendid, new Outing Club building—a gift of the family of Louisa Smythe, class of 1997—was a wooden construction with conference and lecture rooms, kitchen, a loft for overnights, and storage for tents, ropes, axes, backpacks, paddles, and other such items associated with trails, mountains, and rivers. The building also boasted a series of basement rooms for the storage of canoes and kayaks, paddles, and flotation devices.

It was unthinkable, Ira and Joe decided, that the messy heap of oddments they had hauled there on Saturday should stay in this new facility without proper cleaning. So on Sunday morning they returned to the scene of their labors, and with their zeal, supported by overtime pay and a six-pack of Molson, the often mud-encrusted equipment was hosed down and scrubbed in the big basement laundry sinks, sorted and tagged by type, and laid carefully on a series of plank storage shelves.

And here Jake, now in a lather of frustration, found them. "Christ Almighty," he yelled at the two startled workers. "What in holy hell do you think you're doing?"

"Oh, it's you, Jake," said Ira, the milder and older of the two. "We're doing good deeds. Cleaning up a lot of shit from the dorms. We should get a medal."

"Keep your shirt on," said Joe. "We're doing the school a big favor. On Sunday, yet."

"Don't you guys know there's been a murder?" said Jake. "Don't you know that a teacher was banged on the head with something? Not shot, *banged*. With maybe a hockey skate or a baseball bat or a hockey stick."

"Hey, ease up, Jake," said Ira. "None of you guys went around telling us anything about the murder. Except that there was one. And for us not to cross over the scene-of-the crime tape. Which we didn't. And nobody's told us what might have killed her. Hey, she could've have been run over by a truck, for all we knew. That French teacher called us yesterday, the other house parents got into the act, and I think we should be getting more than time and a half."

"We even," said Joe looking aggrieved, "went into town and left a bunch of sweats and jackets at the laundromat. We're to pick the stuff up next week and stash 'em in the lost-and-found. What we are is good citizens, that's what we are. Want a beer? It's still cold."

For a moment Jake stared at the neat piles of equipment. "I don't suppose," he said without much hope, "that you guys know which things came from which building, which house?"

"Nah," said Joe. "We threw everything together in the truck and sorted it and washed it here."

Jake decided to make the best of a lousy situation. "Okay," he ordered, "bag up the sticks and bats and skates. We'll start with those. I'll pick them up later. Say, in about a couple of hours. And use these." Jake reached in his pocket and produced a clutch of surgical gloves. "We don't need more of your fingerprints than we already have. And if you can remember where even one item came from, make a note. Okay, and you're not supposed to be drinking on school property, so get rid of the beer."

"We didn't bring the beer," said Joe virtuously. "Madame, you know, that French teacher, she delivered it herself. She's the one who told us the Outing Club was a good place to store stuff. That the building cost a lot of money and should be used more often. She's not that bad, though I hear the kids can't stand her."

"One thing I remember," said Ira, answering Jake's earlier question. "Most of the stuff, well, it's all the same. Except for the boomerang. From Gregory House. We only got one boomerang. You know, that thing could take a person's head right off his neck."

And with that encouraging remark ringing in his ears, Jake made his departure, teeth clenched, almost hearing the angry lecture that would be forthcoming from the lab team on the subject of compromised evidence.

Sarah and Alex had intended a peaceful late Sunday breakfast in Sarah's apartment, but visions of sausages and bacon and eggs-over-easy began to drift into Alex's head, and the arrival of Giddy coming to escort them to the cafeteria clinched the matter.

"Besides," said Sarah, throwing on her coat, "I have to deliver that filthy file card to someone."

"What file card?" demanded Giddy, alert.

"Some disgusting message I found nailed to a tree. Friday. Before the art lecture."

"Grace Carpentier again?" asked Giddy.

"Yes, although this one is particularly vile," said Sarah. "Anyway, I found it in my pocket last night."

"Give it to Jake," said Giddy. "He'll probably be at breakfast; he likes the food. Besides, he likes to look over the suspects. That means us."

Jake, just returned from his visit to the Outing Club, was indeed in place at a centrally located table, hunched over a mound of scrambled eggs. He greeted them without enthusiasm. "Yesterday was shit, and this morning is turning out the same."

"Did you get all the Gregory House things collected?" asked Alex, joining the table with a plate of pancakes and two dark and smoking hot sausages.

Jake scowled, jammed a fork of eggs into his mouth, chewed, swallowed, and shook his head. "Every odd piece of sports equipment from here to Boston is stashed in the Outing Club basement, hosed, wiped, and probably sand-blasted. If the lab finds anything with Anita's DNA on it, we still won't know where the thing came from. Thanks to Grace Carpentier."

"But," persisted Alex, "you'll be looking for other DNA evidence. Hairs, fibers, maybe blood from the killer—especially if Anita got a few hits in."

Giddy looked up. "Hey, what about the kitchen stuff? Lots of weapons in kitchens. Rolling pins, meat tenderizers, blenders, toasters."

"If you think," said Jake, "that the murderer was skulking around the footpath with a toaster, well, think again. Besides, we've covered the kitchen stuff."

194

"Just trying to be helpful," said Giddy. "Here's another thought. What about Adrian Parsons' and Carlo Leone, both with Band-Aids on their faces. Doesn't that seem funny? Do you think both of them got to Anita?"

"Don't worry," said Jake. "We're not neglecting that. Or anything. Any weirdo event. Or message."

Sarah suddenly started. Reached in her pocket and brought out the file card, now secured in a small plastic bag. Again, she explained its finding, and in general her apologies for late delivery.

Jake held the card in its bag gingerly between thumb and forefinger. Even through the bag the scrawled black print was clearly visible: MME. GRACE CARPENTIER YOU PIECE OF SHIT. GO ROT IN HELL.

"Straight to the point," Jake remarked.

Sarah pointed to the card with her teaspoon. "The printing looks spastic. As if whoever did it had wooden fingers. Or wrote with his feet."

"I suppose," said Jake reluctantly, "that we'll now have to think about getting handwriting and printing samples."

Giddy, who had been uncharacteristically quiet, put down her coffee cup. "Okay, Jake, here's something that's been on my mind. And on Alex and Sarah's, I'd guess. And we may be reaching, but yesterday Grace Carpentier stopped at a sporting goods shop. On the way into Boston."

"Fascinating," said Jake.

"No, listen. We pulled into the store parking lot because we were curious about what she was doing. I mean, somehow or other, she's up to her eyebrows in the whole thing. Anyway, she went into the shop, stayed for a while, not too long, and came out. Holding a small package wrapped in a brown paper. Or in a paper bag."

"Are you saying she went in to buy a hockey stick? Or a baseball bat or a boomerang?" asked Jake.

Giddy reddened. "Don't be sarcastic. I hate people who are sarcastic when someone's trying to help. Listen, will you? I went into the shop after she'd driven away, and the man there was putting away personal defense things, pepper sprays and Mace. And guns."

Jake raised his eyebrows a fraction. "Guns?"

"Guns. Or revolvers. Or pistols. Whatever. Little ones, anyway. A tray of them. All lined up with tags on."

"And you concluded that Grace Carpentier is now armed and ready to protect herself. Or is on the warpath."

"I didn't see anyone else in the store," said Giddy. "So, it looked like she'd been shown some pistols and pepper spray and bought something, because of the package she carried out."

"It isn't a way-out idea," said Sarah. "Here's Grace Carpentier, on the short end of a lot of disgusting jokes and messages, and so why not come to the conclusion that she's beginning to take them seriously."

Jake pulled a pad out his pocket. "Name of shop?"

There was a pause.

"Sporting goods something," said Giddy uncertainly. "Something about being a good value. Or best value."

Sarah frowned. "I think the sign said 'Hunters Welcome.' Or maybe 'Deer Hunters Welcome.' "

"In January?" said Jake. "Deer hunters?"

"Well," said Sarah, "don't people buy rifles and shotguns and cute little pistols all year-round?"

"Especially for Christmas," said Giddy. "We've just had Christmas."

"Come on," said Jake. "Give me the shop name. Think."

Alex, who had been finishing his last pancake, took a long drink of coffee, put down his cup, wiped his mouth, and spoke. "The sign on the store said 'True Aim Sporting Goods Shop. Best Value in Sports Equipment. Deer Hunters Welcome.' "

Giddy and Sarah looked at Alex with dislike.

"I suppose," said his cousin, "you were one of those boy robots who could memorize a page of *Gray's Anatomy* after one glance."

"Oh, he's always doing things like that," said Sarah. "It doesn't mean a thing. It's how you use the information. And besides, he'd have never seen the sign if we hadn't made him follow Grace into the parking lot."

"And," said Jake, "did the sign give the name of the owner?"

"Georges Thibodeau," said Alex promptly.

"Oh, shut up," said Sarah. "You've been obnoxious enough for one morning."

"I'll track it down," said Jake, rising. "Thanks, I suppose, although the idea of Grace Carpentier buying guns, which she can't do legally, is pretty scary. Massachusetts has pretty tough gun laws."

"Couldn't she have bought legally if she went through the waiting time and the record search?" asked Giddy.

"Hell," said Jake. "Anything's possible. Particularly with people owning guns who shouldn't."

"The name," said Giddy excitedly. "The guy's name."

"What about his name?" asked Jake as he began to wind a thick woolen scarf around his neck.

"Georges Thibodeau. It's French."

"So?"

"So, Grace went to a French buddy to buy a gun under the table without having to go through a check or waiting period."

"Detective Mumford and I and the Massachusetts state police will consider that fact," said Jake austerely. "And from now on—I think I speak for all of us—you guys butt out. Okay? No more following French teachers into sporting goods shops run by Frenchmen."

"Yes, Jake," said Giddy. "So how about lunch?" Giddy didn't want to neglect a chance to develop a relationship with Jake. She had given up on the tennis coach, who proved more than a dull companion. Now, even in the middle of a murder investigation, Jake was certainly an improvement over the recently discarded Josh.

But Jake had turned to Sarah. "For God's sake, keep the news about this file card to yourself." He paused and looked around the table. "I mean, to yourselves. You three. And that's really three too many. Alex, are yᵣ . heading home? Not that it hasn't been fun, but then I'll on', have two amateur detectives to throw monkey wrenches into the case."

Alex nodded. "I'm off by noon. Time to face real life. Flu, gastritis, hypertension, and other good things."

"So keep in touch," said Jake. "We'll probably need you back to work on your statement. If you think of anything you've forgotten, or other sporting goods stores you've visited, give us a call."

Alex raised his hand in farewell and found it seized.

"Ah," said a familiar voice. "It is the husband of Sarah Deane. I have at this moment discovered that you are a doctor."

It was Grace Carpentier, her nose red and sharpened by the cold, with frost on her black eyebrows and a mantel of melting snow on her purple quilted coat.

"It is my Szeppi," said Grace. "He has the upset stomach. After his little drive with me, he has thrown up his morning meal. And I cannot get a vet on Sunday morning. Would you come and give me a consultation. I'm sure the disturbed stomach is exactly the same in dogs as it is in the human person. I have saved the throw-up for you to look at."

Alex rose, heaved an inaudible sign, nodded, and followed Grace Carpentier out of the dining room.

Giddy grinned at Sarah. "What's that old saying by somebody or other, 'no good deed goes unpunished.' "

16

JAKE Markham was very much taken with the possibility of Grace Carpentier running around the school, the town, or anywhere with a firearm. This being so, he had little time to think of Giddy Lester as a possible buddy. Or future bedmate. Also, teachers and security guards-*cum*-policemen working at the same school are hardly encouraged, even in this enlightened age, to cohabit on campus. Or even close to the school, where both had to live because of their jobs. Besides, thought Jake, Giddy was a very forceful presence and he, Jake, working two jobs and trying to keep his art life going, wasn't sure he had the energy.

Now Jake left the cafeteria and pushed his way through the swirling snow to Radnor Hall and the Copeland Room, where he confronted Hillary Mumford on the subject of a sporting goods shop and its relationship with Madame Grace Carpentier.

Hillary, her hair still damp from her arrival without a hat, her cheeks red with the cold, listened and then nodded. "So, okay, Jake. Why not make a visit."

"The place is probably closed. It's Sunday, and we're in the middle of snowstorm."

"It doesn't hurt to try," Hillary reminded him. "The owner may live over the shop. Or next door."

"I don't think my car will make it in this snow," Jake said, reaching for an excuse. The idea had little appeal.

"So take mine. The Bronco. Since it's white, this Georges Thibodeau character won't even see you arrive."

"Before I go," began Jake, "what about a room search? Take a look around Grace Carpentier's apartment and see if the lady's got an unauthorized firearm under her bed."

"You prove that she's running around with a gun, and we'll see. And for God's sake, don't get my car stuck in a snowbank." And Hillary slid her car keys across her desk and returned to her notes.

But Jake wasn't finished. He reached into his pocket and produced Sarah's file card in its plastic bag. "Nice little item," he said, slapping it down on the table.

Hillary picked it up and scowled. "Where'd you get this?"

Jake gave a short summary of the file card's discovery and Hillary examined it more closely. "Whoever printed this out had serious coordination problems. Or was faking bad handwriting."

Jake made for the door and turned. "Grace Carpentier's the cornerstone of this thing, you know."

"I know," said Hillary. "She's either the intended victim or the perpetrator. Or none of the above. And she could have manufactured some of these tricks and messages herself."

Jake nodded, crammed on a knitted wool hat, pulled his collar high over his ears, and, bending into the blowing snow, walked down the Radnor Hall steps. He reached the white Bronco, which now resembled a snowdrift rather than an automobile. He opened the car door, reached inside, extracted a brush, and began to clear the windshield with long, angry sweeps. He could have done without driving all over the Boston suburbs trying to find this Thibodeau character. And, for Christ's sake, where was this shop, anyway? He'd forgotten to ask.

Alex returned from his stint as Szeppi's veterinarian to announce that the dog was doing nicely and that Madame Grace would restrict intake to fluids only and administer Pepto-Bismol as needed.

"Should you ask, Madame Grace was gracious and very grateful. Offered me coffee and a croissant, which I declined. She's off to church with, and I quote, 'a great peace of mind because Szeppi is now so much recovered.' "

"You make a nice couple," said Sarah. "Stay for lunch, and you can give Patsy a quick health check."

But Alex, having studied the weather with a judicious eye, pointed out that a small patch of light in the western part of the windy sky suggested that the storm was going to be easing out of Massachusetts and begin working its way to the state of Maine. In which case, he wanted to get out and try to beat it home. He gathered his things into a small duffel and pulled on his jacket. Followed by Sarah and Patsy, he went out into the parking lot and, as had Jake Markham a few minutes before him, began scraping the crust of ice and the accumulated snow from the Subaru.

Alex settled himself in the car and Sarah leaned over for a goodbye kiss and became aware of a white Bronco sliding into place beside them. Jake Markham leaned out.

"This damn car, the motor's running rough."

"Oh, hi, Jake," said Alex, wondering what the remark meant

and hoping it would not slow his departure. He turned the ignition and activated the windshield wipers.

"Alex, you go on and take off," said Jake. "I want to talk with your wife. And maybe help."

Alex rolled down the driver's window, leaned out, and looked hard at Jake. "Whatever you do, don't let yourself get snookered by my beloved wife into some Hollywood chase scene, or a search and destroy mission."

Jake grinned, but Sarah, letting go of Patsy's leash, reached over, grabbed a handful of snow, compressed it, and splatted it against Alex's left temple. "To remember me by," she said. "That was an irresponsible and sexist remark."

Alex laughed, shoved the car into gear, drove out of the parking lot, and was soon lost in the driving snow.

Sarah confronted Jake. "What kind of help? And never listen to Alex. I am the model of good sense and restraint. Speak up. I'm getting cold."

"Simple. Like I said this Bronco—it belongs to Hillary Mumford—well, the motor doesn't sound so great, and I'm supposed to track down your friend Thibodeau. And it occurred to me that not only are you guys responsible for him being in the picture but you also know where the shop is. And you have a Jeep at your disposal."

"And a Jeep goes anywhere," added Sarah. "Through thick and thin, mountain passes and snowbanks."

"You got it," said Jake. "So be my guest. Or let me be yours. Drive me there and sit in the car while I take a look-see and maybe have a chat if the guy is in."

"It's Sunday," Sarah pointed out.

"Hillary says try anyway. He may be around, oiling his guns, or doing his accounts. All you have to do is sit in the car and then drive me home. And I'll buy you lunch."

"You can't bribe me, but I'll drive you there."

"And stay in the car like Papa Alex says. No wild pursuits."

"Listen, Jake Markham. If you go on like that, I'll run you over in my Jeep. I'm reasonably cautious, but if I see Thibodeau chasing you with a machete, I'll do something."

"Like call 911 on your car phone," said Jake.

Sarah let it go. "Hop to it. I'll take you up on a quick lunch, but then I have to get back and spend time getting ready for Monday's classes. Life goes on at school—even with murder."

Jake pointed to the sky. "The weather's easing off," he said, as Sarah turned the Jeep out of the main gate, turned onto School Street, then picked up Route 225 and headed in a north-westerly direction.

Jake looked about with appreciation as they left the town behind them. "It's times like this," he said, waving at a group of white clapboard houses and a church spire, "that I almost like winter. You know, everything glistening."

Sarah nodded, and they settled down for the drive, the only sound coming from Patsy snoring softly in the back seat. Jake made a few entries in his notebook and checked the functioning of Sarah's car phone—"Just in case we have to call AAA," he said. Sarah turned the radio to a Bach cantata, which she kept low, and was glad that Jake didn't object. Actually, she thought, looking over at Jake's big, square head bent over his notebook, Jake is pretty restful. He might be a good balance for Giddy.

At something like eleven o'clock, Sarah worked her way north into the less populated area around South Chelmsford, took a left turn, swerving in the snow, four-wheel drive not withstanding, and turned right, driving north for two miles on roads of diminishing size and maintenance.

After a few miles down a hard-packed icy surface, Sarah slowed and squinted at the roadside. "I'm the visual type. I can't remember route numbers, but I always notice buildings and things, like fortune-tellers and goat farms. There should be an auto parts store up ahead. And then a Wendy's at the edge of a plaza. And after that, a red brick Methodist church."

"Red brick church is up ahead," said Jake, pointing, and Sarah accelerated, took a sharp left, bumped her way down a single track road as yet untouched by any serious snowplow effort, and pulled up into the snow-drifted space that marked the customer parking lot of the True Aim Sporting Goods Shop.

"Deer hunters welcome," remarked Jake.

"Is that going to be your cover?" asked Sarah. She looked at his navy parka, dark gray corduroys, and heavy brown hiking boots. "You need an orange hat and a vest."

"It's Sunday. No hunting on Sunday. Besides, deer season is over. I'm in the door as a customer, then I show my badge, and we chat."

"The shop," said Sarah indicating the windows, "is dark. Except for one light at the end. And one upstairs. So, good luck. Or should I say, good hunting."

She turned off the ignition, unbuckled her seat belt, and leaned back on the seat and watched Jake. He mounted the four steps to the store front and pushed a bell. Waited. Pushed it again. Knocked—Sarah could hear the heavy thumps—and then peered into the two narrow windows that flanked the door.

And then the small lighted window at the end of the shop went out, and Sarah expected to see the whole shop fill with light and the door open.

This did not happen. The shop was now entirely dark, with only the upstairs light suggesting occupancy. He's decided not to open the door because it's Sunday, Sarah told herself. The shop's closed, and he's damned if he's going to let anyone in. She watched as Jake stamped down the steps, waded through a sizeable drift toward the rear of the house, and disappeared from sight.

Sarah yawned—there was something about cold, snowy days that always made her want to curl up in a ball and go to sleep—turned her head slightly, and looked over at the small detached garage that stood to one side of the customer parking lot. Sarah lifted her head just in time to see a slight figure in a dark jacket appear beside the shop steps and begin to push his way through the snow to the garage door. There, standing waist deep in a drift that rose almost four feet, the man wrenched at the door handle. Which did not move. Then, almost frantically, he began with both hands to push the snow away from the door.

Hell, thought Sarah, where's Jake? Here's the guy about to get into his car and leave and Jake's fooling around in the back. She hesitated, seeing that the man pawing at the snowdrift like some sort of burrowing animal had managed to raise the garage door some three feet. He now ducked inside, and returned almost immediately with a snow shovel and began to fling snow away from the door.

And still no Jake. He's probably trying to break in a back door, Sarah told herself angrily, and he'll miss the man completely. Well, not if she could prevent it.

Sarah slid out from the driver's seat into a good two feet of snow and, followed by an interested Patsy, began to wade toward Mr. Thibodeau—if it were indeed he. "Hey," she called. "Hey, there. Could you wait a minute. We're . . ." She paused. Then, louder, "We're customers. My friend and I, and we want to see . . ." She stopped because the man looked up, jerked around, stared at her. And took off. On a run, or what passed for a run, but what in the deep snow was actually a gait that resembled trying to leap through mashed potatoes.

"Hey, there. Hey, wait up," Sarah yelled as Patsy bounded forward. Following the dog, she fought through the snow after the man. But with one frantic look over his shoulder, he redoubled his efforts and charged off toward a small patch of woods that stretched behind the shop.

Sarah, breathless, plunged on, Patsy making small wolf noises. Happily the man and the dog had broken the trail, and all she had to do was leap into his footsteps, so that yard by yard, foot by foot, she gained on him. And by the time he had reached the first row of bushes and snow-heavy hemlocks, she was able to launch herself into the air and with both hands grab him at the knees and send him facedown into a drift.

They both reared out of the snow at the same time, the man spluttering and wide-eyed, gesturing at the dog, and all the time trying to wrestle himself into a sitting position, while Sarah tried for a grip on the man's trouser leg.

"Stop, it!" she yelled as he twisted around to face her.

"What? What?" the man choked. "Call your dog off!"

"Patsy's fine, he's harmless," said Sarah. "Down, Patsy," she called as Patsy leaned over the man as if to begin licking his snow-covered chin.

She tightened her grip on the man's leg. "Please, stay still. It's like this," she began. And then stopped. Like what? she asked herself. The man, making incoherent noises, fists in the air, began to kick his feet as much as Sarah's grip would allow. Patsy, surprised at this show of incivility, sat down, and Sarah had no choice. She reared back and with all her strength pushed the man back into the snow. Then, kneeling on his chest, reaching to hold his flying fists, she tried to fix a pleasant and welcoming expression on her face. "We have to talk," she said.

Jake Markham, hearing inarticulate cries, barks, and grunts from the woods, came on the scene of Sarah wrestling with a snow-covered man. Jake's arrival resulted, after a certain amount of furious shouts and gestures toward Patsy from Georges Thibodeau—for it was indeed he—in a round of incoherent explanations. From Sarah, confused justification of recent actions, and from Jake, "What in hell d'you think you're doing?" Finally, the group unscrambled itself, Patsy was led back into the Jeep, and all parties marched back to the shop's entrance. Then, Jake's hand firmly holding Georges's elbow, the three mounted the stairs and entered the shop.

Two overhead lights inside the True Aim Sporting Goods Shop revealed a linoleum floor in red and blue squares and a line of glass-enclosed cases displaying knives, small firearms, a selection of binoculars, knives, fishing reels, and flashlights. Serried ranks of shotguns and rifles marched along the walls, interspersed with two stuffed heads (a buck and doe), a cow moose, a mounted salmon complete with line and hook in its mouth, and, on a far counter, a stuffed raccoon and a dusty red fox.

At first, Georges Thibodeau demanded the police, pointing at Sarah and shouting something about an unprovoked attack and a rabid dog. But Jake quietly reminded him that he *was* the police, that all he wanted was for Mr. Thibodeau to answer a few questions about a customer, and that his companion, Sarah Deane, was so anxious to secure Mr. Thibodeau's attention for this important conversation that she, well, she just forgot herself. Jake added that Sarah just didn't know her own strength, and the dog was the pet of three small children—this said with a ferocious frown at Sarah, who sat apart from the two men on a small wooden stool.

And Georges, with a malevolent look in Sarah's direction, subsided, grumbling. His jacket now off, he revealed himself as a thin man, somewhere probably in his thirties, with a triangular face decorated by a tiny spade beard. His eyes were dark and wide, and he made busy nervous gestures with his hands, circling them in the air in front of his face. Altogether, he reminded Sarah of a very anxious ferret.

"Yes, yes," said Georges in his high-pitched voice, he knew Madame Carpentier. Grace. A friend. A fine woman. They were both members of the Middlesex County Alliance Française."

"You mean Franco-American?" asked Jake.

"No," said Georges. "I do not mean Franco-American when I say the word 'Française.' America can take care of itself. We are interested in all things French. We, who have been born in France. We are trying to keep the memories of our homeland alive. We have programs, perhaps a French film made by one of the great French directors. We speak only French when we meet. We do not wish to melt into the pot." Here, Georges threw back a forelock of black hair and lifted his chin. His voice rose even higher, and Sarah could hear the note of a true passion. "We are open to any who find themselves, how shall I say, overcome by the American culture. Madame Carpentier supports us in our work."

"But you are an American citizen?" asked Jake.

"Ah, yes, *bien sûr*. Some of us are. And some of us are not and have the green card. It is a convenience, this citizenship business. But it does not touch the heart."

Jake decided it was not the moment to open up what might prove to be a very large can of worms, and instead brought up the subject of Madame Carpentier as a recent customer.

Mr. Thibodeau stiffened. "A customer buying something in my store, that is a question of privacy always. I believe in the privacy of the individual. As you do in Massachusetts."

"Yeah, sure, so do I," said Jake. "But we're trying to find out if Madame Carpentier thinks she's in any sort of danger. And wanted to buy something to protect herself."

"We are very concerned for her safety," put in Sarah. It was time, she thought, to establish Jake and herself as working, in part at least, in Grace Carpentier's interest.

Georges Thibodeau had now regrouped. "Madame Carpentier, I am sure, would not object for me to tell that she made a purchase of a new flashlight. With batteries, of course."

"Of course," said Jake. "Flashlights are always useful. But what about a small gun? Just a tiny one to slip into her handbag. And perhaps something like Mace. Or pepper spray."

"A woman can't be too careful," said Sarah. "Often they are defenseless when out alone."

Mr. Thibodeau eyed her suspiciously. "You are not so defenseless. You did not need a pepper spray when you attacked

208

me. You and that large dog. I was the one who was defenseless. I, who was only trying to clear away the snow from my garage and bring out my car. I am the one who needed a can of Mace."

Jake pounced. Why had Mr. Thibodeau run away, off into the woods? What was he afraid of? The police? Why hadn't he answered the door like an honest shopkeeper instead of acting like someone who had something to hide?

Mr. Thibodeau denied having anything to hide. "This woman," he complained. "Out of nowhere with her attack dog running at me. I thought I must get away from her and the dog quickly. Perhaps it was foolish to run off into the woods, but I did not have time to plan carefully. And," he added in an aggrieved voice, "it is Sunday. The shop is never open on Sunday, so I thought perhaps this woman and the man making the noise at my door were going to make trouble. Someone like me, who sells valuable items—fishing rods, rifles, shotguns—all the best varieties, we cannot be too careful."

Jake nodded. "And you keep records of the sales and conform to the state laws on firearms?"

Georges Thibodeau drew himself up, no more the ferret, now the law-abiding salesman. "But of course," he said. "I obey all the laws of Massachusetts. I am a responsible man. I could not stay in business if it were not so. I sell only the finest sporting equipment."

"I just want to ask you," said Jake, who was becoming very tired of Mr. Thibodeau, "exactly what you sold or gave Madame Carpentier. She could have bought a flashlight at any store for miles around Carlisle. Bedford, Acton, Bellirica, Concord, you name it. Why would she want to come way out here?" What Jake really wanted to ask was why on earth would anyone come into this godforsaken neck of the woods in lousy weather to buy a goddamn flashlight?

When Mr. Thibodeau merely shrugged, Jake pushed. "Madame Carpentier wanted a gun, didn't she? And maybe you just had one you could lend her. Or give her because you're both members of this French club."

Mr. Thibodeau was all injured innocence. "I sold her a fine flashlight." Here he hesitated, and then with a brave show of letting it all hang out added, "She told me about these threats, so, as a little gift, I gave her a personal pepper spray. The sort one uses when one encounters an angry bear. Or a dangerous person." Here Georges Thibodeau, a salesman at heart, waxed enthusiastic. "It is the hunter's model, called 'Bear-Beware,' a natural substance made of Oleoresin Capsicum from cayenne pepper plants. It has a flip-top and fastens on the belt for quick use. This is so Madame Carpentier need not be so afraid at this fine, expensive girls' school she is teaching in." Mr. Thibodeau gave a smile that meant to show that he was a person of rectitude and so could afford the slightest whiff of sarcasm.

Jake held out a hand. "You've got a record of payment? Because this stuff sounds just like Mace, which is illegal without a permit."

Georges Thibodeau shook his head sadly. "Grace gave me cash for the flashlight. I made a gift to her of the bear spray. I make no individual notes about cash sales that are not for firearms. Cash goes into the safe. And then into the bank. I enter it as cash receipt for a certain date. I cannot make a separate entry for each little thing. Each duck call, or fish lure, or flashlight, is not worth the trouble of a separate entry into my journal. I write 'cash sale' and that is that."

It was time to go, but Sarah decided on an act of contrition. She extended her hand, from which Mr. Thibodeau seemed to shrink. "We were all so worried about Madame Carpentier that I acted without thinking. She is an exceptional teacher." A true statement if there ever was one, Sarah thought. "And," she added, "I'm so sorry about the dog. His name is Patsy, and he thought it was a game. Would you like to meet him—he's in the car."

But Georges Thibodeau backed up a few steps and shook a finger at Sarah. "I want nothing to do with your dog, Madame. I have had a very great shock. It is perhaps that I must make a visit to my lawyer."

17

"YOU'LL be lucky," said Jake grimly, as Sarah drove away from the True Aim Sporting Goods Shop, "if that guy decides not to get you for assault, plus attack by a large, unleashed dog. You could be sitting in the county jail by dinnertime. With Patsy in the pound."

Sarah nodded her agreement to Jake's statement and then concentrated on getting back to the Acton Road.

Jake broke the silence as Sarah turned onto Route 225. "I also think he's lying through his teeth about what he sold Grace."

"To prove it, you'll have to catch Grace taking potshots at something with a little Beretta," said Sarah.

"I'd love ten minutes inside Carpentier's apartment."

"She could hide a gun anywhere. It's a big school."

"If she bought the things for protection, she'd have to have them available, not hide them too far away."

"You can get a search warrant?"

"No hard evidence," sighed Jake.

"But we did learn something," Sarah reminded him. "We know Grace has pepper spray—legal or illegal. Maybe a flashlight—which might just turn out to be a gun." She peered ahead at the road. "Weather's easing up," she added.

The snow had indeed abated, the clouds had blown apart, and the sun had made a pale appearance, sending a soft light on the snow-covered little houses and stores that lined these smaller roads. Then, as they reached the outer limits of Carlisle, Jake looked over at Sarah. "I know you're the new teacher on the block, but have you gotten any feel in the school for faculty and student cross-currents, undercover feuds, favorite agendas, stuff like that."

"Because I am the new teacher, I'm the last person you should ask," said Sarah.

"Wrong," said Jake. "All the faculty and staff who have been at the school for a hundred years have vested interests and skewed opinions. Of course, we're going to study the statements and try and factor out personal prejudices, but you haven't had time to develop any particular likes or dislikes. You're just in the first-impression stage. No, wait." Jake held up a hand as Sarah began to protest. "I realize you like some people better than others. I mean, you are human."

"Thank you," said Sarah. "I've wondered."

"No, listen. From an outsider's point of view, what would you say about the people you've met and worked with? Which ones might have an ax to grind?"

"And have a reason to kill Anita Goshawk?"

"Possibly. Have you noticed people reacting oddly to what's happened? Anyone who seems to have a special savvy about events."

"To begin with, I'd ask some of the senior students. Especially that trio, Rosemary, Zoë, and Hannah. They seem to have a good grip on the school scene. Those are the students I know best. We've had talks in my room."

"And the teachers?"

"I'd ask around to see if Adrian Parsons has ever shown the degree of emotion over *anything* in the past that he's showing now over Anita's death."

"He was her lover," said Jake simply.

"Not, I gather, for the past two years. Someone even told me that things were pretty cool between the two."

"A rose is a rose is a rose, and a lover is a lover is a lover," said Jake. "No matter how you try to shove it under the rug, once you love someone, sleep with someone, well, there's all this unresolved stuff waiting to come out."

It was, for Sarah, a remark that suggested Jake had more imagination than she'd given him credit for. "Okay, for what it's worth, here's what I think," she said. "Carlo Leone seems to be, as Giddy told me, a loose canon and not that committed to the school. He's pleased with himself and has a quick, sharp tongue and a roving eye, not so much for women as for pushing down walls and skipping around rules. Joel and Freda Cohen could be stuffed and mounted on a mantelpiece as house parents. I'd say they're more likely to deal in Tylenol and chicken soup than in murder. Babette Leclerc is a very nice person who's the opposite side of the coin of Grace Carpentier, for whom she does kind deeds. Walks her dog, for instance. But, of course, Grace is Babette's boss."

"How about Cousin Giddy?

"Come on, you know Giddy."

"Not that well, though I might try to improve on the acquaintance."

"Well, Giddy's a lot more likely to get physical with a soccer ball or a paint canvas than a fellow art teacher. She'll fight injustice. And if she developed a hate for someone, it would be a fair fight, in an open field with referees. Brooms or hockey sticks at thirty paces." Sarah hesitated and then asked, "Speaking of which, do you think it was a field hockey stick?"

"Possibly. Among other things. The lab is fooling around with a collection of sports items. Which reminds me—may I use your car phone to report my chat with our friend Thibodeau?"

Sarah nodded. Jake punched in the numbers, connected himself to Hillary Mumford—she apparently was still toiling away in the Copeland Room in Radnor Hall—and, omitting Sarah's role, reported the morning's activities and listened to orders.

Hanging up, he turned to Sarah. "Seems someone got into Anita's apartment. One of the lab guys noticed something funny on a visit this morning. And I'm to track down this Alliance Française outfit. Also, you may be psychic—but it seems evidence of blood has turned up on seven of the school's field-hockey sticks. Even with all that sudsing and rinsing that went on."

"My God," said Sarah.

"The weapon had to be something like a field-hockey stick or a baseball bat, although I was betting on the boomerang. They haven't tested that yet."

"But blood on *seven* sticks? Come on."

"Consider where those sticks have been. Hitting shins and thighs and hands and arms. Kids having nosebleeds or maybe a tooth gets loose. That game isn't for sissies. So along with everything else, I'm to spend part of the afternoon researching field hockey sticks. The lab's recovered microscopic fragments from the wound on Anita's head. Looks like fiberglass shreds and wood splinters, so now we have to find out what hockey sticks are made of, and sure as hell there'll be at least sixty different makes."

"But even if you match the hockey stick to the injury, you

won't be able to fix on the place it was taken from. Some of those hockey sticks might have come from the far side of the school property. Madison House or Griffin House or Lockwood Hall, for instance. They're too far from the footpath, aren't they?"

"The time slot is pretty tight," Jake admitted. "No way could the murderer have grabbed one from those houses and raced across the school—it was slippery as hell Friday night—and down the footpath to nail Anita."

"The girls own their own hockey sticks? Or boomerangs?"

"Put that boomerang aside for now. From what I've heard, most of the girls have their own sticks, but the school also provides some. When I'm doing my night rounds, I find sticks all over the school—under benches, in lavatories, under trees. But thanks to Madame Gracie, we'll have a devil of a time figuring out which one came from where. Some girls put their names on the sticks, some don't. And the school ones aren't labeled."

"Are there left-handed and right-handed hockey sticks?" asked Sarah.

"I suppose so, but it wouldn't matter. You're not shooting a ball into a net, you're aiming at a head."

"A nice way of putting it."

"That's homicide for you."

Sarah slowed the car at the turn into School Street and looked over at Jake. "We haven't had lunch. I think I'll just pick up something in my own kitchen."

"School cafeteria for me," said Jake. "So, I owe you one. And, for God's sake, don't go buzzing around the place talking about blood-soaked hockey sticks."

"Look, Jake," said Sarah sharply. "I kept that blasted file-card business quiet, except for telling Alex. And I damn well am not going to broadcast my intimate encounter with that Thibodeau man."

"Just remember," said Jake, "I'm keeping my eye on you as well as Madame the Knife. So no more assaults."

Sarah, with Patsy pulling on his leash, headed for Gregory House, and as she mounted the two flights of stairs she was overwhelmed by a huge desire to go into her apartment and pull the covers over her head. Why had she taken this job anyway? Somehow she had been seduced by long-ago memories of her own Maryland boarding school, memories whose sometimes abrasive moments had been clouded over by Old Father Time. She had actually thought working with high school girls might prove stimulating. And that the school itself would be a caring environment replete with a wise faculty of guides and mentors. Hah! Well, maybe Miss Merritt's might prove to be so in the end, sometime in the spring. But now! For God's sake, a week into the January term they were all living in the aftermath of a horrible murder. And everyone was looking at everyone else as if they carried a concealed stiletto or a flagon of poison.

Sarah unlocked her door, kicked it open, and pushed Patsy into the room. What she wanted now was peace. Oblivion. A nice English novel set in a Cotswold village in which the only question was whether the curate was making eyes at the owner of the sweet shop. That was the sort of reading that soothed the brain. She didn't think she would find refreshment in preparing *Macbeth* or "The Waste Land" or *Bleak House* for tomorrow's classes. Not yet. Talk about literature that sets one's teeth on edge!

First, she would make a little lunch, a salad, and toast, and a dish of some of that ginger ice cream. Turn a few pages of *Barchester Towers* and then take a walk with Patsy someplace where Szeppi and his mistress were not. Later, she'd have an early supper at some quiet café, with the Sunday crossword puzzle. Make a call home to Alex. He would tell her about the decline of one or more of his patients or about a hopeful upturn of another, and this would set the little world of the boarding school into a proper perspective. Then, and only then, would she face the fact that she had three classes to teach on Monday.

Aware that she had been standing in the middle of the living room without moving, she shook herself, pulled off her coat, her gloves, and her boots. Then flung herself down in a chair and leaned back, wiggling her toes in their heavy socks. And sighed deeply. And with that sigh sounded the heavy thud of a fist on her door. These were followed in turn by sharp, welcoming barks from Patsy, who hurled himself toward the door.

Oh Christ, what now? Sarah jerked herself upright and glared at the offending door. Three more knocks. A call. "Sarah, Ms. Deane? Can we come in? We need to. It's important." And three more thumps.

Slowly, with profound reluctance, Sarah walked over and opened the door. Rosemary Streeter, Zoë Fountain, and Hannah Hoyt. Well, who else would it be? Sarah asked herself. She waved them inside. They trooped in, all three dressed rather soberly in dark slacks and jackets.

"This isn't about some new voodoo club or vampires or the Druid thing, is it?" Sarah asked. "Because, honestly, I haven't had lunch."

But Rosemary cut her off. "This is serious, so forget about Druids. It's time for us to stop playing games. After all, we'll be at college next year."

Sarah shook her head. "If you're saying that college freshmen don't fool around playing games, you're in for a terrible shock."

Rosemary gave a brief smile. "Okay. We'll save the games for college. But what I'm saying is there's something that someone—probably the police—should know."

"Then," said Sarah sternly, "you should go and tell them. Or tell your house parents. The dean. Or Dr. Singer. Not me."

"We can't," wailed Zoë. "We'll be suspended or expelled.

You can't let us down. After all, you don't really belong to the school. I mean . . ."

"I get your point," said Sarah. "Sit down. But I won't promise to keep quiet about anything you tell me. For God's sake, there *has* been a murder at the school."

Zoë sank into a chair, and Hannah and Rosemary dropped to the floor.

"That's why we're here," said Hannah. "Even though we agreed to shut up about it, Zoë's in a snit and wants to spill everything. So we decided that since we were all involved, we'd better tell someone. We couldn't go to the faculty because then things get official. We'd be hung out to dry in the middle of the soccer field."

"I can't promise anything," said Sarah. "But I'll listen. And I'll make tea or coffee and hand out some danish left over from Friday. And we'll see."

"That's the best you can do?" queried Rosemary.

"The best," said Sarah, and she headed for the kitchen to deal with refreshments and her own insistent hunger.

Fifteen minutes later, the tale of the entry into Madame Grace's apartment, the rescuing of Szeppi, the search for a possibly dead Madame, the finding of the postcard collection had been told. And what the postcards said.

"I mean, they were, like, totally yuck," said Zoë.

"Postcards," explained Rosemary, "aren't secret. But these didn't have stamps, so we think they were shoved in Madame's mailbox facedown. By someone who hated her guts."

"They were mostly art scenes," said Hannah. "So, maybe they came from the History of Art Department. Or from Miss Goshawk herself, which makes the whole thing really weird."

"Maybe," said Rosemary, "Miss Goshawk was threatening Madame Carpentier with postcards, so Madame loaned her the cape, and then hung out on the footpath and killed her. We think maybe no one knows about the postcards."

"All right," said Sarah. "We'll try to find Jake Markham or the detective, Hillary Mumford, first. That's being responsible, and it doesn't immediately involve Dr. Singer. As for what happens after that, you ladies will have to take your chances."

"You'll go with us?" asked Zoë.

Sarah pushed herself out of her chair. In for a penny, in for a pound. "Yes," she said. "I'll come along. But I will keep my mouth shut. It's your ball game."

Frank O'Mara, a member of the Middlesex County investigative forensic team, had asked to speak with Dr. Joanna Singer, and the meeting took place in Anita Goshawk's apartment in Lockwood Hall. Frank was a stubby, black-haired man, now dressed in a maroon sweatshirt and the sort of trousers that had straps and pockets for holding odd tools and measuring instruments. He had little patience with the niceties of conversation and greeting etiquette with which Dr. Singer had begun their meeting.

"My name's O'Mara, and I haven't got all day," said Frank, making short work of shaking Dr. Singer's outstretched hand and brushing over her opening words about how glad she was to meet him. "Let's get down to it, Dr. Singer. Okay, this apartment was locked right after Miss Goshawk's body turned up, right? And the key turned in to the police, right?"

"That is correct," said Dr. Singer, retreating from anything like a friendly answer. Today, in her beautifully tailored banker's gray suit and pewter gray blouse, she looked ready to deal with the likes of Frank. The fatigue of the previous day had been severely dealt with through the agency of makeup, her light hair pulled tightly back into a knot, and her eyes were fierce, her hands steady.

"And," persisted Frank, "I'm told the school office turned in any extra keys that were floating around."

"If you were told that, then that's what happened," said Dr. Singer in her frostiest voice.

"Nah," said Frank. "There's a hell of a lot that can go haywire between intending to do something and actually doing it. With everything all stirred up, I'd bet the police got half the keys to her apartment, and the other half are God knows where. In the garbage, if we're lucky; in someone's pocket, if we're not. You know what I mean?"

Dr. Singer said she knew what he meant. "A boarding school can't be run like a maximum security prison."

"Never said it could," said Frank. "But I live in the real world. And it seems someone was in this apartment last night. And since Ms. Goshawk's door hasn't been jimmied or tampered with and with no sign that someone's gone up the fire escape or drainpipe and got in a window, I'd say someone used a key to enter."

Dr. Singer bit her lower lip, hesitated, and then nodded. It was clear she hated to expose the workings of the school security system as completely slipshod. "I suppose you're right," she said.

"I know I'm right. Doorknob's been wiped off. When the lab people took the latents—prints, to you—they probably left residue, but now the thing is clean. And there was other evidence of entry. Wet spots on the rug by the desk and by the bedside table. It was snowing last night, so whoever came in had wet feet, with lumps of snow clinging to his shoes. Damn fool, I'd say. Why didn't whoever it was wipe his feet off? Talk about being world-class stupid."

"Burglars can't think of everything," said Dr. Singer acidly.

"We're not talking robbery here," corrected Frank. "We're talking breaking and entering, with maybe an intent to screw up evidence connected with a murder. That's what we're talking about."

"I see," said Dr. Singer, edging away from the man and taking a quick look at the door. "I really have to go now. But I did want to ask the police about when they're thinking about releasing . . ." Joanna faltered, then squared her shoulders and soldiered on. "Releasing Miss Goshawk's body. Her family—actually, it's only her mother, who isn't well—wants to have the funeral as soon as possible. In Chicago. So if you could find out . . ."

Frank broke in. "Sorry. Her mother will have to wait. The pathologists still have some problem with the wound. About matching it up with a possible weapon."

Dr. Singer swallowed hard and nodded. "Thank you, Inspector. And now I don't think you need me anymore, so . . ."

"But I do. I want to know how anyone, after ten o'clock at night, gets into these buildings, through the outside doors."

"Every faculty member who lives on school property has a key to the building in which their apartment is located."

"And you've got more than one faculty member housed in a single building?"

Dr. Singer bit her lip and then nodded. "I'll get you the list of faculty apartments. Lockwood Hall is one of the largest buildings. It has four faculty apartments and no students. Lockwood also houses the admissions offices, the cafeteria, two private dining rooms, and the kitchens. And my office and the dean's office—that's Dr. Greenwald."

"And you all had keys to this building? To all the outside doors into the building?"

"The dean, the dean of Admissions, and I have keys to the side entrance of the building and keys to our own offices. The clerical staff and other faculty members working by day here do not. And the faculty members who have apartments here have their own keys."

"So what about cleaning? The housekeeping people? And the kitchen staff? Don't they have to stay late after dinner to wash up? And come in early to get breakfast?"

Dr. Singer shook her head. "The cleaning staff pick up their keys from the security office when they come in. They usually clean after office hours and finish around ten or eleven. And return the keys to the security office. The kitchen staff and the cooks do the same. Keys from security, keys returned to security."

"Okay," said Frank. "Let's see, you've got regular security shifts day and night?"

Dr. Singer assumed the patient look of a teacher sorely tried by a singularly dense student. "I've given this information in my statement. We have four security guards on at night. They check the buildings and the grounds during the night. At regular intervals."

At that, Frank seemed to lose interest in the matter of multiple keys and lax security systems. He walked across the living room, examined an early engraving of the city of Boston, returned to Dr. Singer's vicinity and gave the living room an appraising glance, the off-white walls, the framed prints, a convoluted bronze sculpture on a table, a massive abstract oil in the dining area, and a thick oriental carpet of deep reds and blues. "Nice place," he said. Then, "Anita Goshawk. She liked to entertain? Have people come in? Drop by? Evening parties after hours?"

"I think Miss Goshawk did entertain friends. We try to let our faculty have private lives, and I've never tried to keep track of a faculty member's visitors."

"Don't keep track of who spent the night?"

"We do not."

Frank looked around the apartment again. "To me, this is pretty elegant. Doesn't look much like a love nest."

Dr. Singer allowed the corners of her mouth to bend slightly upward. "You've seen too many movies, Inspector."

"I've seen too many love nests," said Frank, answering her with a grin. "But not too many upscale numbers. But I guess a love nest could be the Taj Mahal or a cardboard box. And we've already asked around about Miss Goshawk's boyfriends and girlfriends, bed buddies or weirdo friends, but there doesn't seem to have been any real candidate except this Mr. Adrian Parsons, and I'll make a bet that he's still got a bunch of her keys in his back pocket. And maybe decided to use one last night. What d'ya think?"

Dr. Singer remained silent, her face a fixed mask of disapproval.

"Okay, okay," Frank went on. "Sorry, but it seems likely that this Parsons decided to see if any love letters from his past were around. Which they were. We have 'em. They were in a file cabinet. The man was pretty angry about the split-up. Blamed her. That your opinion, from what you know of the guy? What you know of Miss Goshawk?"

"I believe," said Dr. Singer in a distant voice, "that it was a mutual decision not to see each other socially. But they stayed friends."

Frank raised one eyebrow. "Yeah? The letters weren't that friendly. So I ask myself, is Mr. Parsons the sort of guy who gets violent if things don't work out in his love life? If the lady was kind of driving him crazy?"

Before Dr. Singer could answer, Frank O'Mara had changed direction. "I've heard Mr. Carlo Leone isn't coming back next year, that his contract wasn't renewed. So do you think Anita Goshawk, or maybe Grace Carpentier, snitched on the guy, caught him with his pants down? I hear he's not exactly Mr. Law-and-Order around here."

Before Dr. Singer could gather her wits for a final sharp denial of such an idea and sweep out, Hillary Mumford stood at the door.

"Hello, Dr. Singer," said Hillary, stepping into the room. "I hope my friend Frank here hasn't been upsetting sensibilities."

Dr. Singer turned to Frank but did not this time extend a

224

hand. "Thank for your help, Mr. O'Mara. I'm sorry I could not have been of more help." And Dr. Singer departed, her mouth tight, her chin in the air.

"Have you been rattling Dr. Singer's cage?" demanded Hillary. "We need her help on this job."

"Ah, she can take it, although I don't think she wants us to put a finger on this Adrian Parsons. Or any other teacher for that matter. Maybe I wasn't very subtle, but I've been flat out since Friday night. Dr. Singer's a good egg, under that cool managerial style. So what's new?"

"What's new," said Hillary, "is that we may have Madame Carpentier running around with a firearm."

18

"I'VE just had a report from Jake," said Hillary pulling up a chair. And she filled Frank in on the True Aim Sporting Goods Shop, Mr. Thibodeau, and the Alliance Française. "Jake says he's hiding something, but we pulled his file—we keep them on gun dealers—and his shop is clean. No record of noncompliance with gun laws. Store's been around for about eight years. Carries a fair line of sporting goods, shotguns, rifles—the usual. And a selection of personal protection sprays. For bears and for people."

"Popular stuff," said Frank. "My wife's a nurse. She works a night shift at Boston City and carries Mace. Has a permit."

"So," said Hillary, "if you add up the possibility of Grace Carpentier having a handgun and the hearing of shots—or a truck backfiring—off-campus, well then maybe the lady is doing a little target practice. Because—how do you like this? The Great Brook State Park people called about hearing sounds of shots early this A.M. They tried to track the sounds but no luck.

I mean, there was a hell of a lot of snow, and the going was tough."

"Yeah," said Frank. "I'd hate to chase a person down in that park. It's a big mother, trails every which way."

"And," Hillary added, "we had a report that Carpentier took off early this morning, complete with dog."

"What's the dog got to do with it?" demanded Frank.

"From all reports, she doesn't usually take off so early. She walks the dog at school. It doesn't add up to much. We're still at dead center."

"I am about to move you off dead center," said a voice from the door. Jake Markham poked his head in. "I've got something you two should hear."

"Right now?" demanded Hillary. She stepped to the door, looked into the hall, and saw the senior trio of Rosemary, Zoë, and Hannah and, behind them, Sarah.

"Now," said Jake. "I say we go back to Radnor. We don't want to contaminate this apartment. The case is turning dirty. Filthy postcards."

Sarah left Rosemary and company to their fate and returned to Gregory House to reestablish her plan for the rest of the day. Right now she would collect Patsy for a walk along the outer limits of the school property. Perhaps along some of the trails beyond the Outing Club. The tree canopy, with the oaks and the ancient hemlocks, might give some shelter to the trails so that it would not be all slogging through feet of snow.

It was well after two o'clock when Sarah and Patsy set out, Patsy alternately trotting along, sniffing, and lifting his leg. At first all was peace, the sounds of the school, the passing cars well muffled so that Sarah felt blessedly alone. But after a quarter or so of a mile on the twisting, snowy trail had been navigated, Sarah realized that part of her ease in walking was in large part because someone, a small-footed someone, possibly with a dog, had passed this way before and helpfully pressed

227

down the snow. Patsy confirmed this idea by pulling forward and giving out small noises of interest. Hoping to keep her solo status, Sarah slowed her steps, but it was too late. At a turning stood a familiar figure struggling with the dog Szeppi, his leash wound around a bush. Babette. Good-natured Babette taking care of Madame Grace's dog. Well, there was nothing to do but make the best of it, be cordial and hope Babette was on the way back to the school grounds.

But it was not to be. Babette, wrapped as if going on an arctic expedition in scarves, her wool helmet, and knee-high boots, gave a glad little cry and bustled forward.

"Sarah. I'm so glad. I don't mind walking alone, but it's so much nicer with someone else. Besides, ever since Anita—well, you know, I'm just a little jittery about being out by myself, though I can't think why any murderer would bother ravishing or killing me out here. But I did hear through the hospital grapevine—I have a friend in the pathology lab—that Anita wasn't ravished. Raped. Just murdered. Which," Babette hurried to add, "is quite bad enough, isn't it?"

Sarah nodded agreement, thinking that if they were going to make a hiking twosome it might be restful just to let Babette chatter and she, Sarah, could let her mind wander or listen as the mood took her.

"You're wondering about Szeppi, aren't you?" asked Babette, as Sarah let her gaze fall on the small black, dog who was making bouncing overtures to Patsy.

Sarah hadn't been, but she nodded again.

"Grace started out with him. I told you she cross-country skies, didn't I? She's quite a sight when she's in her cape, but of course she doesn't have that anymore. She told me she telephoned an order into that special shop in Albany for a new one and is sending the school the bill. Anyway, that's her exercise. Besides walking Szeppi. She used to go to the gym and use the treadmill, but I think she frightened the students because she didn't like being watched and got very nasty."

"And she turned Szeppi over to you?" Sarah found conversation impossible to avoid. She began walking now more slowly to make certain that the five-foot Babette wouldn't be left behind.

"Yes, he was pulling and being a nuisance, which makes skiing through all this snow difficult. Besides, I don't mind walking with him. He makes me feel safer."

"Madame Carpentier doesn't worry about being alone in the woods? Even after all those threats, the scarecrows?"

Babette shook her head. "I asked her that, but she said she had taken care to protect herself, whatever that means."

Sarah, remembering the sporting goods shop, was sure about what that meant. And this thought in turn brought up Georges Thibodeau and the Alliance Française. So why not ask her friend what she knew about the organization?

"It's a sort of club," Sarah explained. "For French-speaking people. Or French natives. You're French, so I thought you might know about it."

"Oh, I know about it, but it's hard for me to even find time for the things I should be doing at the school. Or even find the time to go to a good movie."

"So you're not a member?"

"Grace did take me to a couple of meetings, but I felt like an outsider, like someone from the colonies. They all went on about life in France. But Grace ate it up."

"So you wouldn't have met someone called Georges—Thibodeau?"

Babette shrugged. "I might have, but I never paid much attention to the names. But I don't think there was anything sinister about the group, if that's what you're asking about." She looked anxiously over at Sarah, and Sarah, as others had before her, found the word "rabbit" slipping into her head. This she banished as unworthy; Babette was a genuinely nice, sweet, person. Certainly not someone who would slug a fellow teacher with a hockey stick. Or a boomerang. Although, Sarah reminded herself with a shiver, rabbit-like people might be thought ideal victims. Maybe it was just as well that she had caught up with Babette and that they walked together.

The two women trudged on in a companionable silence, and the faint sun that had filtered through the trees began a retreat, the sky turned a darker gray, and Sarah felt again, now more strongly, that she really needed at some time that day to be alone. "Babette, I think I'd like to turn back, if it's okay with you. I've got classes to prepare for and I'm thinking of a hot bath."

Babette agreed enthusiastically. "There's something almost spooky about the woods tonight. When I was walking I kept thinking I saw someone, a shadow or something, moving in the trees, and I thought, here I am all by myself, and Grace is way up ahead and out of sight, all by herself, and who would hear us if something happened?"

"The police," Sarah reassured her, "are all over the school property. I don't think anyone, any stranger, would be able to wander around looking for victims."

"Who said anything about strangers?" demanded Babette with asperity. "And the police can't watch the whole school. It covers more than fifteen acres. So," Babette concluded, "I'm glad to turn back. Besides, my feet are about frozen."

Both dogs were hauled into reverse and the two women quickened their steps in the direction of the school campus.

Back in her apartment, to keep herself honest, Sarah ran through the fourth act of *Macbeth*, ran an eye over the first lines of "The Waste Land," and skimmed through two chapters of *Bleak House*. Then she fed Patsy, changed to a favorite long, dark green wool dress with a high neck, pulled on her winter coat, a pair of dry boots, and headed out. First, she would buy a Sunday paper, and next, drive around until she found some out-of-the-way little eatery far from the commotion of school and murder.

Her first object was to find a place completely free of Miss Merritt's School people, so, after securing *The New York Times*, for the better part of forty minutes she circled the outskirts of Concord, Chelmsford, and Bedford before finally coming to rest in Acton and pulling into the Makaha Chinese Restaurant. It wasn't that she exactly felt like eating Chinese, but the idea of thrusting herself into traffic heading into the depths of Cambridge or Boston was not attractive. To be alone and think required a tranquility of mind.

She locked the car and entered, her mind occupied with the problem of choosing between Szechuan or some milder dish more conducive to productive thought. But as she stepped into the entrance, she stopped dead. And if she had been a cartoon character, she would have flung up her hands, cried "foiled again," and slunk from sight.

Instead, she cautiously backed into the shadows and paused. Because, across several rows of white tableclothed tables, leaning toward each other in a booth, his hand lying protectively across hers, sat Instructor in Italian and European literature Carlo Antonio Leone, facing Rosemary Streeter, senior student resident of Gregory House.

Sarah allowed herself only one hard look, then turned and reclaimed her car. Of course, if she had gone in and been shown a table, the two might have called her, probably *would* have called her, to join them. And that would have pleased no one. Carlo was probably Rosemary's advisor, taking her out for some good reason—there were many faculty advisors who took their jobs seriously and treated their students as members of a family—and the presence of Sarah would inhibit both. And, of course, Sarah would lose her chance at a solo meal. Except. Except that Carlo Leone had never struck Sarah as the fatherly type. Quite the reverse.

Anyway, damnation.

Back on the road, Sarah drove out of Acton, headed for Bedford, and after a period of circling, pulled up to Dayla's, a trendy restaurant fashioned in the Tudor style.

But fate, which Sarah was inclined to think of as a hovering and malevolent committee—had apparently decided against Sarah spending any quality time that day with her own thoughts. As soon as she crossed the threshold of the restaurant and was being approached by the hostess, a hand waved from a table against the wall and a voice sounded her name.

Adrian Parsons. Damnation again. She supposed that there must be many restaurants uninhabited by school personnel, but she apparently had a particular knack for missing them. And here, there was absolutely no possibility of hiding or sneaking out. His table was only ten feet away.

"Oh, good," called Adrian. "Well met. Sarah Deane. And I was sitting here thinking that a meal by myself on a cold winter night was not very amusing. Rather glum, in fact. Now we can share the evening." He rose to his feet and gestured to the empty chair across from him.

Sarah, cursing herself for an inability to say no, she was alone and meant to stay so, found herself pushed into place opposite Adrian Parsons. "I only meant to stop in for soup, perhaps coffee," she said. It was a weak effort at best, but might just make the visit a short one.

"Nonsense," said Adrian briskly. "I've just sat down. Just ordered a drink. What would you like? Winter evenings should be shared. It's been a difficult weekend. A terrible weekend. I'm trying to face up to what's happened. Anita, such a loss. Well, I won't go on, but I'm very happy you happened along. I was becoming morbid sitting here by myself. Now, if you like wine, I've found they have a 1993 Bordeaux."

Sarah nodded. Why not. Adrian Parsons looked and acted like the sort of person who would know a good wine. She remembered his air of authority on the matter when she and Babette dined with him at Concord's Colonial Inn. But now—what a difference! Adrian looked like a man on the declining end of a severe illness. His face was pale and positively gaunt. He reminded her of that English actor, Peter—the one that looked like an ambulatory cadaver—Peter O'Toole."

". . . and of course, knowing the school gossip factory, I suppose you know," Adrian was saying.

Sarah had missed something. She tried for an enlightened expression and gave a small nod.

"Although it was over, completely over, in another sense, when you've been part of someone's life and someone has been part of yours, it's never over."

Sarah gave a second, slightly more energetic nod. That remark sounded exactly like what Jake Markham had said as they drove home from the sporting goods store. A lover is a lover is a lover. Adrian Parsons was talking about Anita Goshawk and his relationship or love affair with her.

"It must be a dreadful, a terrible shock," she ventured. This uninspired remark seemed safe enough.

It seemed to satisfy Adrian. He put down his wine glass and began turning it slowly around on the tablecloth. "I haven't been able to talk about it, although I can imagine that everyone is dredging up ancient history. The fact is, a few years back Anita and I really spent a great deal of time together. Of course the police will probably come to some lurid conclusion, that I'm a thwarted lover and decided to kill her. But that's the police mind for you."

"Jake Markham," Sarah volunteered, "seems very intelligent."

"Oh, Jake." Adrian dismissed Jake with a flick of his wrist. "Yes, I suppose Jake has some sense. But there's a dreadful man, Frank somebody. He was badgering me this afternoon for what he called 'a really complete statement.'"

"He's probably badgering everyone," said Sarah. "But he may be focusing on you because he thinks you knew Anita better than anyone at the school. And, of course, questioning would be very painful for you." Really, she thought, I sound like a very low-grade therapist.

But Adrian did not seem to mind. He nodded, took a careful drink of wine, and began a long and careful description of why he had found Anita Goshawk an exceptional person. This tour through the past lasted through the ordering of dinner—haddock for Adrian, soup and Caesar salad for Sarah—the arrival of these dinners, and their consumption.

Half of her mind roving restlessly, the other half forcing its attention on Adrian's narrative, Sarah listened to descriptions of operas, concerts, and art shows he and Anita had shared—a trip to New York for a Braque exhibition at the Metropolitan, medieval music at the Cloisters, *Turandot* at the Met, and, in Boston, a revival of *The Cherry Orchard*, and various exhibits at the Museum of Fine Arts.

Adrian slowly wound down in time for the arrival of coffee, and Sarah was able to look at her watch and mention the morning's classes.

Adrian reached over and laid his hand—a rather bony appendage—over hers and pressed it. "I can't thank you enough for walking in that door," he said. "For sitting here and listening. I know that sounds trite, but you see, you're not part of the school menagerie, and it's a relief to talk to a sympathetic person from the outside world. And yes, I've been monopolizing the conversation and thinking only of myself when there are others who probably feel just as badly as I do."

Sarah couldn't resist. "Who feels just as badly?"

Adrian grimaced. "Anita and Joanna Singer were close, and Babette Leclerc admired her. Giddy Lester, too, even though they crossed swords on art matters. And, although they weren't exactly friends, I'm sure Grace feels Anita's death, particularly with Anita being killed wearing Grace's cape. A case of mistaken identity, some are saying."

Sarah admitted that she had heard talk of just such a possibility.

"Grace, believe it or not," said Adrian with a smile, "is quite sensitive. I know she's considered a bit on the, shall we say, strict side"—here Sarah's eyebrows rose—and he added, "Yes, and often severe with careless students. But she does have a heart. She takes splendid care of her little dog, and I've always felt that the girls are too hard on her. But she gets results, her students learn French, and that's what counts."

"She's your boss, isn't she?" asked Sarah. For her, this was a point to be brought up.

Another smile, this one rueful. "Yes, Grace rules the Language Division with a hand of iron, as indeed I know. But I admire her for it. And her decisions are usually wise ones. And now that I have used you as a listening post—no, more than that, a most sympathetic ear—I hope you'll be my dinner guest tonight."

After a polite wrangle, Sarah thanked Adrian. After all, he had robbed her of her solo dinner, so let him pay. It hadn't been a total loss. The wine, the soup, the salad, and the coffee had been excellent, and Adrian had revealed himself as not only distraught by Anita Goshawk's death—a fact already known—but also as a professed admirer of Grace Carpentier.

Or was it all the act of a very smooth performer?

19

RETURNING to the school and Gregory House, Sarah mounted the two flights of stairs and walked directly into a small knot of seniors pushing into Hannah Hoyt's room.

"Is anything the matter?" asked Sarah, sincerely hoping that the answer would be a resounding no.

Hannah beckoned her in. "The police," she said in an awed voice. "Two of them. In Madame Carpentier's room. The woman detective and Jake Markham."

Sarah looked around Hannah's room. Several unknown faces, two girls in her poetry class, and Zoë Fountain. No Rosemary Streeter, but then she was out with her advisor—if he was indeed that—Carlo Leone.

"Is that all?" asked Sarah. "You know that Miss Goshawk may have been killed by mistake. So the police would want to keep questioning Madame."

"But don't you see," said Hannah. "Those postcards we found. The police know."

"Yes," sighed Sarah. "Of course they know. You told them, remember?"

"That's not the point," said Hannah. "Wait a minute. Let Zoë and me come back into your room and explain. She turned to the other girls. "Sorry you guys, but we weren't supposed to talk about this thing."

Back in her own apartment, Sarah turned on the two. "Okay, out with it."

"The postcards," said Hannah, "showed art scenes."

"I know," said Sarah patiently, "so what's your point?"

"The point," said a voice from the partly open door, "is that the whole art department is on the hot seat." It was Giddy. Giddy looking flushed, in paint-spattered overalls and denim jacket.

"No one has blabbed, but that inspector, Frank what's-his-name, went through the whole Nakatani Art Center this evening. With my help, just when I was trying to work on the scenery for the junior play. He was looking for postcards. Or prints. And, of course, we have do have postcards, along with larger reproductions. The files are full of them. We use them in drawing and painting classes as examples of techniques, subjects, style, things like that."

"And," said Hannah, "the police probably think someone stole them from the art department and stuffed them into Madame Carpentier's mailbox. Someone like Anita Goshawk. Or Miss Lester. Or," she added with a gulp, "one of the art students. Like me. Because I hated every bone in her body."

There was a long pause, and Hannah, her hands rolled into fists, glared at Giddy. At Sarah. And then subsided. "Well, I don't hate her one hundred percent of the time. Just ninety-nine percent."

"Hannah, Zoë," said Giddy, "how about going back to your rooms and getting on with your homework. Classes tomorrow.

And please, just give this all a rest. I'll worry about the art department, okay?"

After the girls had left, Giddy turned to Sarah, her face red with anger. "I didn't want to have a major scene in front of the girls, but you should see what that Frank and his pals did to the art files. And now I've got to go back, pick up the pieces and try to get the place ready for tomorrow's classes."

Sarah nodded, about to plead a similar case when the sound of feet came from the corridor. Hoping it wasn't a return of the three seniors, she went to the door, followed by Giddy. She cautiously opened it in time to see the approaching figures of Jake Markham and Hillary Mumford as escorting bookends to the bundled-up figure of Grace Carpentier, who stopped at the sight of Sarah and Giddy.

"Ah," said Grace. "This will be useful. Please, one of you, tell Babette to keep Szeppi and give him his dinner. Two cups only of kibbles with a soupçon of chicken broth. The broth I have placed in a blue bowl in the refrigerator. I will not be gone long. Officer Markham and Detective Mumford wish to be shown the files in my classroom, the one I have now taken over that belonged once to Miss Goshawk and has art files that have not yet been moved. And also, after this Frank O'Mara person has finished with my room, please to check the lock to make sure it is secure. Officer Markham," she said severely to Jake, "I trust that my room, my things, my arrangements will be left in perfect order."

She paused, and Sarah looked up to see Babette Leclerc scuttling down the hall toward their little group. "It is you, Babette," said Madame Grace. "I have given my instructions to Miss Deane and Miss Lester." Then, peering at Babette's distressed face and fluttering hands, she said, "*Ma foi, Babette, quelle mouche a vous pique*? Nothing is happening. We must cooperate in the investigation. We must make our apartments open to the police." And with her escorts Madame Carpentier set off for the stairs.

After a certain amount of tangled discussion, Babette departed to take care of Szeppi, and Giddy and Sarah retreated back into Sarah's apartment.

"So," said Giddy, "they're searching Grace's room."

"Maybe she refused to turn over the postcards," suggested Sarah. "Or they're looking for the gun and pepper spray. Although Grace made it sound as if she was cooperating. Madame being so helpful."

"Nothing would surprise me," said Giddy, "except finding Grace Marie-Henriette Carpentier completely innocent. I'll bet anything she's got everything hidden and destroyed the postcards."

After Giddy's departure, Sarah, as often happened in the middle of stirring events, found herself inventing excuses to snoop. You see, she informed herself, to be really useful she should not only tell Babette about Szeppi's dinner routine but also should go to Madame's room and fix the kibbles and the broth and bring the dish to Babette.

Madame Carpentier's door was closed but not locked. Sarah gave a firm rap on the door, turned the knob, and entered. And found the dark bulk of Frank O'Mara on his hands and knees examining a cavity under a loose floor board. He straightened and glared at her.

"Hey, who let you in?"

Sarah stared at him, frowning. She then broke into a wide grin. "I know you. You're Frank. Frank O'Mara. You used to live down across the street from our house. The Deane family. I'm Sarah Deane. We had the house next to the Congregational church."

Frank got slowly to his feet. "Jesus H. Christ. Sarah Deane. You were a royal pain in the neck, always following me and my friends around, wanting us to buy you candy corn or sneak you across the street."

"And you used to throw green apples at me when I waited for the school bus when you were six years older than I was and should have known better. And you got my brother Tony to shoplift doughnuts for you from the bakery."

Frank shook his head. "Isn't memory a wonderful thing. Well, you're looking good, Sarah Deane. But, to repeat, how in hell did you get in here? I'm doing a job."

Sarah broke in. "The door was unlocked. And I'm here in a good cause. Madame Carpentier's dog needs to be fed, and I've come to get the food." Then curiosity now overwhelming her, she asked, "Is she under arrest or something? And you're searching her room looking for, well, for what? Postcards, guns, Mace?"

"Sounds like you've been talking to Jake. But this is a fishing expedition, and Madame Carpentier has been mighty cooperative. We can look around as long as we don't slit sofa cushions, tear up toilet paper, or cut up the mattress. She even led us to this hole in the floor like she had nothing to hide. Which means that anything that was in it, well, it ain't anymore."

"Nothing at all?"

"Nothing. Story of my life."

"So, maybe you should start slitting sofa cushions."

"We don't have a warrant. Not yet, anyway."

"And if she was really the intended victim?"

"We've offered her protection off-campus, and she turned us down flat. Which is probably good, because the woman cross-country skis, and there's no way we can outfit a tail with skis. We'll keep an eye on her when she's at school, but that's about it. And now, Sarah Deane, it's been good to see you, but goodnight. And hey, I think all you people at Miss Merritt's la-dee-dah school should stop picking on Carpentier. From all sides I'm hearing the lady's a witch. Or a bitch. But believe me,

240

she was Madame Pussycat just now. Went off with Jake and Hillary like it was an invitation to a fancy-dress ball."

Sarah retreated, not much wiser, holding the bowl of chicken soup and a bag of kibbles. Only two things were clear: Madame Grace was a jump ahead of the police, and she could also apparently charm even the likes of Mr. Tough-Guy Frank O'Mara, who, if memory served, was the absolute terror of their junior high.

Monday morning came and with it a sort of settling down and smoothing of what that weekend had become a fractured school routine. Counseling was still offered to those students (and faculty—many thought Adrian Parsons seemed to be a good candidate) upset by Anita Goshawk's violent death. The school grounds remained host to a number of state police and Carlisle police investigators. Jake Markham had requested leave from his night security shift to devote his energies entirely to the murder, and his place was taken by a huge chunk of a man who could have doubled for Governor Jesse-The Body-Ventura.

Sarah, cheered by the news that Alex could join her again the next weekend, made her way through the bright sun and now crusty snow to her first class in Adam House, ready to deal with the home life of the Macbeths. She opened the door only to find that the room was inhabited—infested—by Madame Carpentier, a Madame Carpentier whose tapestry bookbag rested on the instructor's desk and whose purple quilted coat hung on the coatrack. Madame had moved in and was busy writing on the blackboard.

For a moment Sarah stood and stared as the neatly slanted writing developed before her eyes. It was a quotation: "Quand *Madame Bovary* parut, il y eut toute une révolution littéraire . . . Le code de l'art nouveau se trouvait écrit" (Emile Zola).

It was a quotation that undoubtedly would be the subject of discussion for the next class period, her, Sarah's, very own class period. She took three steps into the room and cleared her throat. "Madame Carpentier."

Madame put down her chalk and turned. "Ah, Miss Deane. It is good you are ahead of time because you will be able to discover another room for your class, *n'est-ce pas?*"

Sarah squared her shoulders. "Madame Carpentier, I have twenty-two students coming for their literature class. In about ten minutes. And I will need to meet them and have the class in this room."

"*Ah, c'est dommage,*" said Madame. "A pity. My classroom has been, what is the exact word, excavated. Excavated by the police, who are so very busy searching for something of which they do not yet know the nature."

"Madame Carpentier," began Sarah, more forcefully this time, "you must find a place to go, because my students will expect to come here."

"But my students, my senior French Four students, will expect to find me also here. I have called to their dormitory rooms and given the message. You, Miss Deane, must stand at the door and warn your own students of this change in the plans. Perhaps," Madame said, a small smile moving her thin lips, "you could use the Adam House student lounge. You have noticed, have you not, that the student lounges are a place in which no work, no sensible activity, takes place. Your class in English will improve the atmosphere of the student lounge. *Eh maintenant*, I must now write out the homework, *les devoirs*, for the next day."

And Grace Carpentier returned to her blackboard and began to write in a firm hand: "*VOCABULAIRE: exaucer, exhumer, piger, pilule.*"

Sarah recognized a defeat when she met one; a fill-in teacher must certainly bow before seniority, before the head of the Language Division, no less. So with dignity she withdrew, stationed herself at the door, and directed her arriving students to the student lounge. She followed them, saying "bloody hell" under her breath, and then, since the remark came so aptly to the tongue, began her discussion of *Macbeth* by slapping down the paperback of the play on a coffee table and saying loudly, "Bloody hell!" This remark had the effect of waking up the sleepiest students, and even several girls passing through the lounge came to life.

Despite Grace Carpentier's usurpation of Sarah's classroom, the rest of the school community went about its daily Monday grind. Dr. Joanna Singer spoke by telephone to a number of concerned parents and managed with her smooth reassuring voice to calm the waters and describe the security measures being taken. Babette Leclerc introduced her second-year French class to *Le Petit Prince*, a story she believed dealt with life and death, though in a remote and unreal setting. Giddy Lester raced between the Nakatani Art Center and her drawing classes, and she met successively with two of Anita Goshawk's students to discuss Flemish painting and Greek sculpture. Carlo Leone handed out peppermints to his second-year Italian class and spent an entire period drawing Dante's vision of hell on the blackboard, even though with their scant knowledge of the language they would never be able to read *The Inferno*.

By noon, a sense of normality had returned. And although the Classic Club's trip to Boston to see a production of *Lysistrata*, escorted by Mr. Parsons, had been postponed until the following week, the Drama Club met at lunch to discuss a spring production of *Mrs. Warren's Profession*. Then, over the loudspeaker came good news for the sports teams that were due to practice that afternoon: a large number of the items collected over the weekend would be returned to Althorne Gym, where students could pick up their skates, skis, baseball bats, ice hockey sticks, and other such equipment. Of course, it didn't take a Doctor Watson to notice that the field hockey sticks were not mentioned by name and so were presumably still being scrutinized by the police laboratories.

"So now we're sure what the weapon is," said Zoë to her houseparent, Freda Cohen, who sat next to her at the luncheon table.

"You know nothing of the sort," returned Freda Cohen, who was sure that Zoë was right but thought a show of ignorance on the matter must be maintained; the girls were too upset as it was. And Freda began to plan a little gathering in her apartment sometime later in the week, with pizza, homemade cookies, and apple juice. Perhaps they'd rent a movie, something nostalgic, soothing. *The King and I*, perhaps. Or, more daringly, *Grease*.

The idea of a hockey stick as a weapon was not a new one; almost every girl at the school, after hearing by way of that mysterious underground grapevine that operates so effectively in any school that Anita was neither shot, poisoned, strangled, nor run down by a car, and had in fact been bludgeoned, began to speculate on the possibility that a readily available item, a baseball bat or a field hockey stick, for instance, had done the deed.

The students and faculty were, of course, not the only ones sure of this fact. In the Copeland Room of Radnor Hall—now a police home-away-from-home—Jake Markham and Hillary Mumford, with shirtsleeves literally rolled up, Jake's tie pulled off, and Hillary's sweater abandoned—the room was overly hot—pushed aside the pile of statements from the school population and fixed their attention on the latest lab reports.

"So the boomerang is out," said Jake. "I don't suppose even the dumbest killer would choose some one-of-a-kind instrument. Too bad."

"We've got a blood match on the hockey stick," said Hillary. "Actually, three matches for Anita's Type A-Positive blood."

244

"I said, didn't I, that some of these sticks would have been bloodied up. Anyway, we ought have the DNA report by Thursday. That ought to nail the weapon down."

Hillary put down one sheet of paper and picked up another. "Look at all this, will you? I didn't play field hockey, I played soccer, and I had no idea that there so many kinds of sticks. Long, short, heavy duty, every damned color of the rainbow."

"All made in Pakistan," put in Jake.

"Which is neither here nor there," said Hillary. "Any one of these could have done the job on someone's head. Particularly, according to this report, one of the ones used for defense, the fullbacks, I guess. They're heavier."

Jake reached over and skimmed down the sheet. "My God, some of them are graphite-reinforced, and some use Kevlar, polyethylene, fiberglass, multi-laminated hardwood, and mulberry."

"I hefted one," said Hillary. "It's got a terrific grip—feels like rubber, but it's polyurethane."

Jake grimaced. "So the killer's hands won't slip. How useful. And have you seen these names?" He ran his finger down a page of illustrations. "Falcon, Karachi-King, Gold Medal, Score Master, Max-Skor. And Day-Glo colors. If you own one of these babies, you've got something pretty classy."

Hillary sighed, gathered the papers together, and looked at her watch. "Presuming that the hockey stick is the weapon, we'll have to find out which ones came from what school building."

"We want the sticks that came from the houses nearest to the footpath, not the ones off on the rim."

Hillary shook her head. "You don't have kids, Jake. Or at least not ones I know about. Kids don't put things away. Katie goes to visit Clare in Madison House and leaves her stick, Megan drops in at Griffin House and dumps her stick there. Some of the sticks apparently turned up in the gym, the art center, and the science building, and one from the infirmary. The maintenance crew did a clean sweep."

"So hope the hockey stick has a girl's name on it and that she knows where her hockey stick was Friday night."

"Right," said Hillary. "Meantime, I've made a visit to our new friend, Georges Thibodeau. He's in a snit but absolutely denies selling anything but a pepper spray and a flashlight to Madame Carpentier."

"He can't admit selling a firearm—or giving one—because he'd be on a very hot seat," said Jake.

"I think," said Hillary judiciously, "that we may start having uniformed police make visits to the man's shop. For little chats."

"Sounds like harassment to me," observed Jake.

"Friendly concern," said Hillary. "And I'll tell him the truth. We're not so much interested—not now, anyway—in whether he's slipping firearms to friends. Right now we want to know if Grace Carpentier is armed so we can stop some crazy shootout she has in mind."

"Her room is clean. Too clean. She even showed Frank O'Mara a loose board and a little hideaway hole. Said when she goes away on a trip she hides her camera, her jewelry, and important papers, stuff like that."

"And he believed her?"

"Of course not, but what can you do? She volunteered to let us look at her room, but I can't go busting into her car or frisk her when she comes into the dining room. But we've alerted the state park people that if anyone hears gunshot sounds to get on it fast. And let us know."

Hillary stood up, reached for her sweater. "Got to get back to the lab people. See if we can speed things up with the DNA. Also—and this is a little weird—this Thibodeau character said something about Sarah Deane. Thinks she's at the root of all these questions the police are asking."

"Sarah drove me to his shop," admitted Jake. "Your car was running rough."

"Your note just said you took another car. Don't tell me she got mixed into it."

"The guy started running away when we were trying to get him to answer the door. I was around back and Sarah—"

Hillary's eyebrows rose. "Sarah what? Honestly, Jake."

"She tackled him. Actually, he ran off and Patsy—you know, that wolfhound of hers—and Sarah chased him. Knocked him into the snow. And then we had our little talk in the shop. That's it, and at least we found the guy."

"Let's hope this guy cools it. He should be worried about sneaking guns to friends, not suing anyone."

"Amen," said Jake, standing up in his turn. "Getting Sarah getting mixed into it—well, it's really my fault."

Hillary gave him a tight smile. "You said it."

Babette Leclerc met Sarah at the school cafeteria for lunch. "So," she said, "what about this afternoon? Strap on your skis and come on out to the state park. The school cross-country team is practicing, and the snow is wonderful. Do you good. You're looking a little pale."

"I always look pale in January."

"So, work up a glow. You did bring skis down from Maine, didn't you?"

Sarah nodded, hesitated, and then said, "Okay, I need to get out. Is Madame hitting the trail? Without Szeppi?"

"Sometimes with, sometimes without. But except for her dog, she skis alone. She doesn't like distractions like friendly chit-chat."

"Isn't that risky for someone who just might have been first choice for being banged on the head?"

"I told you she claims she's taken care of the protection

problem. She's a law unto herself. Her own *La Sureté*. Besides, the ski trails will be filled with people. Lots of school teams practice there. No one could lurk in broad daylight with skiers and hikers at every turn."

The Great Brook Farm State Park at two-o'clock that Monday afternoon was indeed, as Babette had predicted, a popular place. The ski center parking lot was filled with a number of heavy-duty vehicles of an upscale SUV variety, Jeeps, Explorers, Land Rovers, and Expeditions. Added to these were pick-up trucks, the usual number of family vans, and a scattering of sedans and small sport cars.

"You see," said Babette, "the trails will be packed. You don't have to worry about Grace."

Sarah opened her trail map—they had stopped at the Park headquarters before parking. "It says," she pointed out, "that the state park has nine hundred and fifty acres of land and water."

"What are you trying to say?"

"That it would be easy to get lost and to be out of sight of anyone. And that Grace Carpentier is a damn fool if she goes zinging off without someone in sight."

"And I thought *I* was a fidget about safety."

Sarah was about to remind her companion that certain moments in her own past argued for caution in the matter of solo trips, but then it was a beautiful day, the soft snowfall was diminishing, no wind stirred, visibility was excellent, and as Babette said, there did indeed seem to be a number of skiers moving toward the trails.

The day may have begun in an irritating manner with Grace Carpentier's usurpation of Sarah's classroom, but now, who the hell cared. Sarah breathed deeply, lifted her arm and her pole, pushed one ski forward with one pole into the snow, then the next ski, and before long worked herself into a satisfying, rhythmic arm and leg pattern. The snow was dry and light, and recent events faded before the wonder of moving almost soundlessly through the woods.

They kept on in silence until they reached a long downward slope. Here Sarah paused and looked about before pushing herself forward. "Where," she asked Babette, who slipped up beside her, "are these hoards of people we're supposed to be seeing? I mean, look at all those cars—so where has everyone gone?"

"That's what's so great about the place," said Babette. "Twelve miles of trails. You don't have someone breathing down your neck."

"You are contradicting yourself," said Sarah. "We were worried about Grace, remember?"

"There are probably skiers around the next bend," said Babette. "It's an illusion being alone. Look down there." She pointed to the bottom of the long slope, and sure enough there came a line of six skiers wearing numbers over their jackets.

"Ski team," said Babette. "There's probably a meet today. See, I told you. The place is packed. Do you want to go back?"

But Sarah didn't. The next few miles were covered with less vigor, perhaps, but with sufficient sightings of other skiers that Sarah ceased to worry about Grace Carpentier as a solitary target. In fact, as they turned and regained a view of the parking lot, she saw Grace emerge from a trail marked "Lantern Loop," followed by two teenage boys. "Pah!" exclaimed Grace, catching sight of the two women. "There are too many people altogether. I could not get myself loose of them. Persons at every turn. But the snow, it was excellent."

"You don't have Szeppi today," said Sarah.

"Ah, Miss Deane. No. Not everyday do I have Szeppi. The trails are too busy for my dog to enjoy himself." And Grace hurried off toward the parking lot.

Sarah followed the French teacher's progress, watching her scrape the snow off her skis and stow them along with her poles in her car. "I still think," she said, "that Madame Carpentier on skis doesn't fit my picture of her. I'd say she would be much more likely to be working on a loom. Or making pots, or visiting old bookstores. Anything but stamping around on skis."

"Or she should be in a kitchen making evil potions or building little guillotines out of Legos?" asked Babette. "I admit she's not the Nordic type, especially when she used to wear that cape. It always gave her a sort of vampire look."

"That quilted purple thing isn't very Nordic," said Sarah. "She looks like an eggplant."

"We should all be grateful she does ski," said Babette kicking her skis off. "Think of all the energy that's used up on the trails and not in the classrooms."

Sarah bowed her head in acknowledgement of a truth, and then she pointed out another odd figure, a tall man, at some distance. He was wearing a black and red lumber jacket, carried a canvas rucksack on his back, and had a wool cap with earflaps. He looked as if he had just skied down from the north woods of Maine.

"There," said Babette, "goes a sensible man. He probably sees no reason to waste money getting himself rigged up in expensive ski clothes."

They climbed into Babette's car, an ancient, rusty, red Buick, and headed back to the school, both in the glow that comes from exercise on a beautiful winter afternoon.

Giddy, waving her arms over her head, met them at the entrance to Gregory House. "Order of the day. Sports equipment and skis—even faculty skis—to be stowed in the owner's room or in the basement. Madam has spoken. Actually, Joanna Singer has also spoken, which makes it legit. Madame claims she single-handedly accomplished the cleaning of the vestibules and porches and front halls of the whole school, and things must stay that way. She is, I quote, 'most tired of falling into the junk that blocks the way.' "

250

Giddy paused, looked about as if to make absolutely sure that the three were alone. Then, lowering her voice, she said, "There's news. A field hockey stick has been identified. The one that killed Anita."

20

SARAH stared at Giddy. "You mean, they know—but how?"

Giddy cut her short. "I just heard. New report from the lab. There were a few fragments of hair found on her stick. Anita Goshawk's hair. They must have been embedded in the stick. Jake didn't go into details, but he said the DNA report will probably confirm the whole thing."

Sarah frowned, surprised. "Jake told you all this?"

"It's no great secret because he asked me to walk the owner of the stick over to Radnor, to the Copeland Room. She's to make the ID and answer some questions."

"But how do the police know the owner?" persisted Sarah.

"It was one of the sticks that tested positive for dried blood. And now the hairs. And the stick has the owner's name on it. Small print, in magic marker. H. Hoyt. Hannah Hoyt. She played right fullback on varsity this fall."

"Oh God," said Sarah, and as she said it, she realized that she had been hoping that the weapon—whatever implement that was discovered—would be anonymous, from some alien planet, or at the very least part of the anonymous, unlabeled school collection.

"Because Hannah plays defense," Giddy went on, "she uses one of the heavy sticks. And she's from Gregory House, which places the stick in a convenient place for the attacker to grab it from the vestibule and hightail it to the footpath."

Babette, listening, began shaking her head. "Poor Hannah. To think that something you owned did that horrible thing. She must feel awful."

"She doesn't know yet," said Giddy. "I was just to say she was wanted. If she asks, I'm to tell her. As for 'poor Hannah,' she's made it very clear she detested Grace Carpentier. It complicates things. But now that you two are here, could one of you walk her over? I'm supposed to be over at the art building right now, meeting a student."

There was a pause and then Sarah nodded. "I'll do it if you want. I've gotten to know her pretty well."

Then Babette said in a tone of great distress, "Hannah doesn't mean half what she says. And let me bring her down from her room. I'll tell Freda and Joel Cohen so they can be ready with sympathy." Babette hurried up the steps and vanished into Gregory House.

"I'm sorry about Hannah," said Giddy. "She's a great kid. But she really does hate Grace. She's tried a hundred times to get out of French and switch to another language, but it's her parents. Her family's moving to Paris for a few years—business reasons—and they want her to speak French."

"And she listens to her family?"

"Some kids do. Especially if they want their parents to help with college expenses. Like pay tuition, room and board, and transportation. Okay, here she is."

It was obvious from Hannah's wary look, first at Giddy and then at Sarah, that Babette had indicated that the coming interview was not of a general nature and that it might well have to do with a certain article of sports equipment.

"Hannah," said Sarah, "I thought I'd walk over to Radnor with you. If you'd like."

Hannah, usually a poised young woman, faltered, possibly wrestling with a desire to appear entirely mature and an equally strong wish to have human company. Comfort won out. "Please, Sarah," she said as they started down along the snow-packed drive that led past Radnor Hall, "come with me. And see if you can stay in there with me. I mean, if I'm going to get the third degree. I suppose it's about my hockey stick, isn't it?" she said bleakly.

Sarah said that it might indeed be about the hockey stick, but it might be only a matter of Hannah's identifying it so they would know which building it had come from.

"Like Gregory House is pretty close to the footpath," said Hannah.

And Sarah said yes, and when they reached the door to the Copeland Room, she put a restraining hand on Hannah's arm. "Let me go on in and see if it's okay for me to sit in with you. Stay right here."

Hannah grimaced. "You mean I might hop a taxi and get myself to Logan and fly to Tibet for a better life."

Sarah smiled. "You'll do fine. A sense of humor greases a lot of wheels."

"That's a pretty lousy metaphor for an English teacher to use," said Hannah, smiling back.

Jake Markham was feeling used, bruised, and in serious need of sleep, as he pushed himself through statement after statement, arguing with Hillary, Frank, with whichever state policeman approached with a suggestion or a new bit of evidence. But now, at least, they had the weapon; they had the field hockey stick, and the owner was on her way to Radnor Hall to acknowledge ownership and, if they were lucky, to perhaps fill in a few gaps.

"So what do you know about this Hannah Hoyt?" asked Hillary Mumford, pulling a file front and center. "I mean, besides her original statement. And about the fact, which she naturally didn't mention but everyone knew, that she couldn't stand Grace Carpentier."

"From what I've seen of Hannah around the school, she seems pretty steady. One of the older girls, eighteen in December. Giddy Lester reports that she's got talent, hopes to go to a university with a strong fine arts program. And it's possible that she was involved in those scarecrows of Grace Carpentier that turned up in the fall. Maybe drew the picture of Grace as a rattlesnake."

"But not the paper puppet hanging by the neck?"

"Probably not. Sarah Deane says Hannah was shocked and then frightened when they found it. Thought she'd be accused, and so she buried it. Was unhappy when Sarah dug it up and turned in."

"What about Hannah and Anita Goshawk?"

"No trouble there," reported Jake, pulling the file toward him and flipping over a page. "Anita's comments on her report card say positive things. Good insights, an imaginative student. Things like that."

"I suppose," said Hillary thoughtfully, "that it's possible for a good, steady student with talent to go after a teacher that's making her miserable. It's done all the time, isn't it? Adolescents with AK-47s spraying the gymnasium, picking off kids in the cafeteria, nailing them as they come out of the school door."

"You're saying the school is probably lucky that only one person was killed and that the weapon was a field hockey stick?" said Jake.

But now Sarah Deane stood at the door, Hannah Hoyt at her side.

"May I come in just for a few minutes before you talk to Hannah?" asked Sarah.

Hillary nodded, and Jake looked up in some surprise as Sarah approached the long, library table that served as a desk and holding tank for folders, papers, paper cups of coffee, and a plate of soggy-looking doughnuts.

"Three things," said Sarah, determined to make it short. "Hannah wants me to sit in with her. She's a little edgy, I've gotten to know her, and it might be helpful if it isn't against rules. And I've been thinking about that file card I found on the tree. I think I told Jake that the printing looked unnatural. It reminded me of the writing of someone who is right-handed but using the left hand to disguise it. I used to try that in school when passing notes, thinking I was fooling my teacher."

"Handwriting experts," said Hillary, "say that certain characteristics remain constant. Left- or right-handed."

"Assuming our writer," said Jake, "was an amateur at writing obscene notes, he wouldn't know what experts think. Damn, I wish we had those famous postcards that Grace Carpentier has hidden. Or flushed down the toilet."

"We'll be looking into handwriting samples. Left-handed and right-handed ones. Okay, Sarah, what else?"

"It's not much of an idea. In fact, it may be completely stupid."

"Listen," said Hillary, "we can use any idea you have up your sleeve."

"It's that the person who printed the file card used the abbreviation for Madame. You know, 'Mme.' It seems to me that most of the girls not taking French would print out the whole word. But French students—or faculty, or adults, anyway—would use the short form. I know this is trivial . . ."

"Actually," broke in Hillary, writing busily on her notepad,

256

"it's not a bad idea. I hate to think I'd have to get samples from the whole school community—getting parental permission and lawyers involved. So, maybe we can start with Madame Carpentier's students. So, let's have Hannah in. And Sarah, yes, hang around. We'll be asking Hannah a few questions and see what she thinks about giving us a voluntary handwriting sample."

Sarah went to the door and found Hannah sitting on a bench, her gaze fixed on her feet.

"Okay, you're on," she said to the girl. "And relax. They don't bite."

"Come in, Hannah," said Jake. "Take a seat. Miss Deane will stay here and make sure we don't use rubber hoses. Hey, Hannah, just joking, it's okay."

"Honestly, Jake," said Hillary. "Hannah, we called you because we've had word from the lab people. Apparently a field hockey stick was used to kill Miss Goshawk."

Hannah appeared to shrink inside her heavy jacket. "You're saying it's my hockey stick, aren't you?"

"Yes," said Hillary. "The lab has evidence that your stick was used. This is where we need your help. I know you're an adult, you're eighteen, but we've called your parents, and they say that it's all right for you to talk to us if you want to. You can make a call right from this desk if you want to confirm that. Remember, you don't have to answer a single question. But you're not under oath, you're not testifying to anything, and nothing is being taped. It's all very informal."

Here Hannah nodded dumbly, a sign Sarah took for assent.

"Good," said Hillary briskly. "Now, see if you can remember when you last saw your stick. Where you last saw it and when you last used it to practice." Hillary patted a leather library chair next to the desk. "Come on, this won't take too long."

But Hannah remained on her feet. She stood, eyes wide, looking from Hillary, to Jake, then to Sarah, who had taken a

257

chair at the other end of the table. Then she covered her face with her hands, and a long shudder shook her body.

"Hannah, Hannah, I'm sorry," said Hillary. "I know it's a shock, something like this. But we want your help. We need to know where you think you left your stick. It's important. And please, please sit down. You're making Officer Markham nervous."

Hannah gave a tremulous smile and took a seat on the extreme edge of the chair. And began, in fits and starts, to talk, to explain that the field hockey season was over.

"I mean," she said, "it's been over since the fall semester. We don't play field hockey in the winter."

"Not even to fool around on the field?" asked Jake.

"No, we're really into other things. Skiing, basketball. Ice hockey."

"So," Hillary said, nudging Hannah forward, "you haven't used the stick lately. Just left it somewhere?"

Hannah gave a gulp and nodded. Yes, she had just left it, dumped it, in the Gregory House vestibule. Along with all the other junk. "Everybody does, " she explained. "We just come in and leave the sports stuff there. It's, well, convenient. We don't need those things messing up our rooms."

Jake, remembering the condition of the student rooms he had seen, allowed himself an inward smile. "When do you remember last seeing it?" he asked. But Hannah didn't remember. She supposed it had been there along with all the other things, but she hadn't checked. But now that there'd been this cleanup, Hannah wasn't sure where anything was.

"Your stick had your name on it?" asked Hillary.

Hannah looked at her in surprise. "Yes, it's an expensive one. I didn't want to lose it." Then, hesitantly, "Is it evidence, or do I get it back? Though I'm not even sure I want it back if it killed someone."

Hillary explained that yes, at the moment it was needed in

the investigation, but the police would make a note about ownership. "And one more thing, Hannah. Just a routine matter, and it's entirely voluntary, but could you go over to that desk over against the wall and copy on this sheet of paper a couple of sentences. With your left hand and your right hand." Hillary indicated a small writing desk of extreme age and fragility, no doubt the gift of some student from the Civil War period.

"But I'm left-handed," objected Hannah.

"It doesn't matter. And don't use cursive. Please print, and use this pen. If you don't want to do this, we understand. If you'd like to get hold of an attorney, fine. And you can refuse. Whatever you decide, we do thank you for your help."

Hannah bit her lip, appeared to be considering, and then shook her head. "Honestly, I don't feel like it right now. Maybe later. The hockey stick thing is enough for one night. Okay? I'd really like to go back to my room. Besides," she added in a shaking voice, "I haven't done anything, so what's the point?"

Hillary thanked the girl again. "I know it hasn't been easy, Hannah." Thus dismissed, Hannah, face reddened, with tears almost ready to fall, walked to the door; Sarah followed, and the door closed behind the two women.

"Okay, Jake," said Hillary. "I think we've just talked to a person with something on her mind."

Jake's expression was grim. "I hate to say it, but bingo!"

Hillary rubbed her eyes and leaned back in her chair. The day had stretched into night, and the night was getting longer by the minute. "Okay, so maybe we've found the file card person. Maybe not. But a match for the file card doesn't mean we've got the field hockey stick user."

"No, but here's something in from the lab. About those pieces of the paper puppet cut-out of Grace Carpentier."

"And?"

"They were cut out by a right-handed person who knew exactly what she—or he—was doing. A tidy piece of work."

"But not by left-handed Hannah," said Jake.

"No. Are you saying we've got at least three people acting independently to do in Grace Carpentier?"

"Or Anita Goshawk."

Hillary gave a deep sigh, a sigh all the way up from her high-laced winter boots. "Or Anita Goshawk *and* Grace Carpentier."

Jake and Hillary stared at each other. The idea that more than one person planned to eliminate two of the school's most prominent teachers was a bit much to swallow.

Jake caught up with Sarah at the entrance to Gregory House. At five-thirty it was dark, and the lampposts that stood at intervals around the building illuminated small circles of soft, falling snow.

"Hannah make it back okay?" said Jake.

Sarah nodded. "But something's really eating her. More than just having her hockey stick involved."

"Something should be eating her," said Jake. "Everyone knows she's the captain of the Hate Grace Carpentier club."

"But not the Hate Anita Goshawk club," said Sarah. "It really is double trouble. And there's Grace—next victim presumptive—who doesn't seem to have a worry in the world. Driving around town, cross-country skiing."

"It's driving the police crazy," said Jake. "She makes such a great target."

But at that moment, the storm door of Gregory House was flung violently open and Hannah Hoyt, followed by Giddy Lester, came down the steps. Hannah saw Sarah, saw Jake, skidded to a stop, and grabbed Jake's arm. Even in the dim lamplight, Sarah could see that Hannah's face, her hair, and her person were even more disordered than they had been leaving Radnor Hall.

"Jake," shouted Hannah. "Officer Markham. Come on. With

me. Before I lose my nerve. I can't stand it anymore. Take me back to Radnor. I want to tell the police I wrote that file card because I just wanted to tell everyone what a shit Madame Carpentier was. I had to get it out of my system, so I printed with my right hand so no one could tell who wrote it. I thought, what the hell, everyone's going around making fucking scarecrows and cutting out fucking puppets, why not get into the fucking act."

"Easy, easy," said Jake.

Hannah tugged on his arm. "I said, come on. Let's get it over with. Hell, who wants to graduate anyway. They can tar and fucking feather me. But I didn't hit Anita Goshawk over the head with my hockey stick. If I ever hit someone, you can bet it wouldn't be her. You can bet it'll be—"

"Whoa," said Jake. "Easy. Simmer down, Hannah. We're all nice people, and we all want to come to your graduation. Let's go." And the two of them, Jake being hustled by Hannah, departed at a quick jog.

21

"WHEW," said Giddy. "I found Hannah stomping down the hall and asked what was going on, and it all came out in a flood. I think it'll be okay. Kids do these things. Even eighteen-year-old seniors. Dr. Singer may not throw her out. If Hannah's lucky, it'll be a good, old-fashioned detention—or suspension. After all, murder is the problem, not some stupid file card tacked to a tree by some pissed-off French student. And now I'm dying for food. And drink. Come on over to the dining room, and let's grab some tea. Or hot chocolate. And some hunk of carbohydrates, like a doughnut or pie. My fridge is empty."

"Better yet," said Sarah, "come up to my room. I've got all sorts of killer foods."

The women settled in Sarah's two armchairs, cocoa and tea at the ready, lemon-filled doughnuts on the side. For a while they talked over the murder and about the members of the Hate-Grace society, and then Sarah expressed what was probably a universal wish.

"I hope," said Sarah, "that the murderer isn't someone we know. I hope it's some slime who dumped the field hockey stick, left town, and now has fallen into a snake-infested bog in Brazil. End of case."

"I'm with you all the way," said Giddy, pushing herself to her feet. "Maybe before the killer jumps into the snake-infested bog he'll mail the school a confession so we can get back to normal. And Jake will have some free time. I thought he might be Josh's replacement, because he's a lot nicer than Josh. Just what my doctor ordered. You know, take one at bedtime. But I want someone who comes home at night for at least four hours."

Sarah rose, picked up the mugs, and headed for the little kitchen. "From what I hear," she said over her shoulder, "Carlisle isn't Murder City, U.S.A. The last murder was years ago. The town probably has nothing more going on than small-town stuff: barking dogs, breaking and entering, car theft, vandalism, a few drug deals, drunks, a spot of arson, and car smash-ups. Jake will probably have plenty of leisure time after this is over."

Giddy turned to leave, but Sarah stopped her. "Wait up. I've got a question. It may not mean a thing, but do you know who Rosemary Streeter's advisor is? I've been wondering."

Giddy frowned. "You, Sarah, don't just wonder. You're like a mongoose. Or a mole. Something that goes down into things or hangs on to things with its teeth."

"Is that an answer?"

"For what it's worth, her advisor is Babette Leclerc. I remember because we expected she might choose one of the African American faculty, but Rosemary said she needed help in understanding—and this is an exact quote because I heard her make it—'the devious mind of white people.' Or, more particularly, a white woman. Although Babette isn't any more devious than a cocker spaniel, a loveable cocker spaniel. If Rosemary wanted the white man's skewed point of view, she should have chosen someone else. I mean, Babette! Come on."

"So," said Sarah carefully, "it wasn't ever Adrian Parsons, or Carlo Leone, or even Anita Goshawk?"

Giddy stared at her. "What are you getting at?"

"Nothing," said Sarah stoutly. "Nothing at all. Forget I ever asked."

"Do you want to share?"

"You'll just think I have a poisoned mind, so no thanks, I won't share. See you around, Giddy." And Sarah stepped up to her apartment door, yanked it open, and retreated inside. And, without bidding, the restaurant scene rose in her mind again. Carlo Leone's hand laid across Rosemary's hand. Their two heads inclined toward each other. Each looking intently and closely into each other's eyes.

Then Sarah shook herself. Students were perfectly free to seek counsel from faculty members other than their advisors. Babette, Rosemary's chosen advisor, was a sweet and sympathetic woman. But perhaps too much so. Giddy called her a loveable cocker spaniel. So, maybe Rosemary needed something more stringent in the way of advice. Something said with an edge. Then why not Adrian Parsons? But no, perhaps he had too much of an edge. Carlo Leone would be approachable. Casual, non-conformist, easy-come, easy-go. And—why hadn't she thought of it before—Rosemary had probably been in some of Carlo's classes, and a familiar teacher would be a logical person from whom to ask advice. He might be a compassionate listener, for all Sarah knew, even though this side of the man had never been made manifest to her.

No more speculation. No more guessing. After all, what did she know about these people? The personalities around the school had only just begun to show themselves. For all she knew, Dr. Joanna Singer was a closet motorcycle racer, Adrian Parsons played in a rock band, Carlo Leone cross-dressed, and Freda Cohen was a world-class mud wrestler. And Babette Leclerc was Grace Carpentier's step-daughter—not as unlikely a thought as it first seemed—Grace would do nicely as a wicked stepmother.

Okay, back to work. Shakespeare, Dickens, and T. S. Eliot. Sarah settled into the task of preparing for her three Tuesday morning classes. For her freshman *Macbeth* class, she decided to give in to Grace Carpentier's usurpation of her classroom by having the students spend the period in the library compiling a bibliography for an essay she would assign on the subject the following week.

But the image of Carlo Leone's hand over Rosemary's hand returned, insistent and provocative. And Sarah stamped on it, banished it. Slammed the door on it. Angrily, she snapped open the *Selected Works of Thomas Stearns Eliot* to "The Waste Land" and pointed out to the poet that as far as she was concerned, January, not April, was the cruelest month. A month mixing freezing weather with murder and suspicion. And, just possibly, desire.

Tuesday, the twelfth of January, dawned with a continuing feather-light snowfall, mere fluff gathering in corners, blown under cars, and softly frosting the trunks of trees. The sharp angles of the white clapboard and brick school buildings became blurred with white, and the whole scene, the low, gray sky and the dark, reaching branches of the bare trees, all gave the sense that the school had been put into a glass globe and been shaken by some giant hand.

Sarah rose, wrapped herself in winter layers, and took Patsy for his walk. And as she pushed her way through the soft piles of snow and saw the glint of sun striking the icicles on the roof lines of the houses, she thought that even the nine o'clock sight of Madame Carpentier in Sarah's own classroom could not shake her pleasure in such a beautiful day. She would deal with her classes and hit the ski trails by two, and after this glorious exercise she could face whatever further disturbances were in store for the school community.

After a breakfast designed to bolster the faint—juice, tea, and oatmeal—she stationed herself at the entrance to her classroom in the lower reaches of Adam House with the intention of re-routing her students to the library for their research. This plan went smoothly; Sarah's students went their way, and Madame Carpentier's class filed in. Sarah was interested to see that Hannah Hoyt was among those present; she hadn't noticed her on the previous day. Hannah's shadowed eyes suggested a sleepless night, but her walk was steady and her head was up. Then, as Sarah turned to go, she found her left elbow taken in a firm grip.

It was Grace Carpentier, just arrived for her class. And Grace was clad in the glory of her black wool cape, complete with its high collar and the hood hanging from the back.

Sarah gave a short jump. "Oh! Madame Carpentier. You startled me. But you have your cape back. Or, or is it a new one?"

Grace began divesting herself of the garment, hanging it carefully over her arm and revealing herself in a black silk jacket, a purple wool skirt, and high black boots. Madame's nose was red and sharper than ever, her black brows blacker, and altogether here stood Richard the Third in his feminine incarnation.

"Ah, Miss Deane. Yes, I have my cape. *Grace au bon Dieu.* But no, it is not the cape taken without my knowledge by Miss Goshawk. It is new. I called that little shop in Albany, and I made a very strong urging that they immediately make me another, and they have now sent it by Federal Express."

"It's very handsome," said Sarah, picking up her briefcase and preparing for flight.

"Wait, Miss Deane. I thought you might find it, shall we say, useful, to come into my class and observe it in action, as they say on the television programs. I think you may learn something, because I have sometimes walked by the open door of your classroom and I have said to myself, this Miss Deane, she is allowing the students to take the upper hand with her and so is losing some of her concentration. And her grasp of what she is saying."

So overwhelmed was Sarah by the idea of Grace Carpentier looking in—make that spying—on her that for a moment she couldn't speak. And by not immediately protesting, she found herself pulled into the classroom and directed toward a seat at the back of the class. She felt like a fourteen-year-old with a C minus average.

"You do not, Miss Deane, have to stay the entire period. Especially if your French is a little out of the practice. How do they say it—on the rusty side. But I think you will find that my classes, for which I receive much student criticism, are very smooth, and that the students, even if they do not wish it, learn to speak the French language." And Madame Grace marched to the front of the room, now filled with twenty girls, and reached in her briefcase for a book and a ruler. The latter she whacked down on the desk, looked up, and said in a voice that might— and probably had—shattered glass, "*Attention, mes étudiants. Nous avons ici Mademoiselle Deane. Elle veut écouter vos récitations aujourd'hui.*"

Sarah never knew why she stayed frozen on her chair. Hypnosis was a possibility—Grace Carpentier had the sort of eye associated with Coleridge's Ancient Mariner. Or perhaps staying put was simply taking the easiest way, going with the flow. Or was it curiosity? Yes, she decided, never mind other forces at work, curiosity could usually be counted on to win her over. Besides, it was only too true that every now and then things got a little out of hand in Sarah's classes. She encouraged chat and argument, sometimes to the point of noisy confusion and time-wasting. Okay, let's see how Madame did it. And maybe, just maybe, get a handle on why this female was so feared and hated. And, in some few cases, admired and envied. She got the results she apparently did. Why she was kept on, year after year, at Miss Merritt's School? And, bottom line, why would someone want to kill her?

Sarah's grip on the French language had never been strong. Now, as she tried to follow the class through a rapid question and answer session, she gathered that they winding up the tangled affairs of Emma and Charles Bovary, and that Charles had, in the words of M. Flaubert, *"tomba par terre. Il est mort."*

"Eh bien," said Madame Grace, *"Charles Bovary, il est mort. Et pourquoi? La fatalité? Un coeur lourd? Une vie sombre et triste? La faute de Rodolphe? Repondez . . ."* Madame searched the room and pounced. *"Repondez, s'il vous plaît, Mademoiselle Hannah."*

Hannah, eyes down, voice low, began an incoherent mumble, a mumble cut short by Madame. *"C'est ça. Vous ne comprenez pas mes questions parce que vous n'avez pas fini le livre.* I will say it in English so you can remember what I am saying. You have not understood the questions because you have not finished the book. I will ask Mademoiselle Streeter. *Eh, bien, Mademoiselle Rosemary Streeter."*

Rosemary picked up the questions, juggled them neatly, and returned them to Madame in what seemed to Sarah to be almost flawless French. Madame, by a bob of her head, acknowledged this feat and then tossed out another question. And another. And the students, according to their degree of understanding, fended them off or responded in kind.

Madame in the classroom reminded Sarah most powerfully of a symphony conductor dealing with an insufficiently rehearsed orchestra. Who was the legendary conductor who inspired such fear and exercised such control that the final performance stunned even the exhausted players? Toscanni perhaps? Fritz Reiner, Serge Koussevitzky? Because somehow

Madame, pointing a long finger, stamping her foot, and flourishing her ruler, got answers, even discussions, and at the end of the class, some of the students, reluctant as they were, had been forced into near-fluency. Not that she reformed her opinion of Madame, but a modicum of respect crept into her view of the woman.

"Ah, Miss Deane," said Grace, catching up to Sarah in the hall, "you see, one cannot be always kind in the classroom. The students will not learn so very much if you do. Some of these girls are, *bien sûr*, good children, but they are spoiled. They have gone to schools that have allowed them too much freedom. And they have been given too many things because their parents have no time for the discipline. I am the antidote for all this. It is, how shall I say, my mission at this school."

And Madame stepped to the door to Adam House, opened it, marched down the steps, and as the wind caught the corner of her cape and billowed around her, she looked to Sarah's eyes like some great black bird of ill-omen. A crow perhaps, or one of the ravens that were said, in ancient verse, to hover over bloody battlefields.

Sarah took off for her next two classes, and then, with her encounters with *Bleak House* and the first lines of "The Waste Land" behind her, she prepared herself for something hot and savory for lunch. Lasagna again, perhaps.

But to her astonishment, at the portal of the great dining room stood Georges Thibodeau. He was dressed in a suit of black wool, looking like yet another crow, another harbinger of evil. Seeing Sarah, he bowed slightly from the waist.

"This is a pleasure," said Georges Thibodeau. "I was hoping to find you here."

"How did you get in here?" demanded Sarah, astonished at the man's appearance. "The police are checking everyone."

"Madame Carpentier has vouched for me," said Mr. Thibodeau complacently. "I will make a visit with her later but it is now you to whom I must talk. I have some things to say. About our recent encounter."

Oh Christ, he's come to sue me, thought Sarah wildly. She looked around the cafeteria, saw Jake Markham at a nearby table, and relaxed. Let Jake throw the man out.

"Please, a few minutes," pleaded Georges Thibodeau. "Then I will have said what I wish. Could we perhaps eat while I talk to you? This is the cafeteria, yes?"

Sarah was torn between grabbing Jake to begin the ejection process and listening to what the man had to say. The idea of a lawsuit was a little scary, but perhaps she could dash some cold water on the plan—if that's what the man had in mind. Fighting anger, Sarah indicated a table in Jake Markham's orbit and informed Georges that a cold had made her slightly deaf and would he speak up; Jake then could not fail to overhear if skullduggery was to be on the menu.

They settled at the table with two steaming dishes of pasta and tomato sauce in front of them. Sarah thought that Mr. Thibodeau seemed anxious. His narrow face was pale—no miraculous thing in the dead of winter—but his black hair was mussed as if he had been shoving his hand through it, his brow was creased, his napkin was crushed into a ball, and one hand was shredding his slice of Italian bread into bits. If threat, blackmail, or announcement of a lawsuit was his game, it was making the man decidedly nervous. Sarah decided on maintaining silence. She wasn't going to help him by saying a single word. She bent her head over her spaghetti, twirled a mass inexpertly in a spoon, and poked it into her mouth.

"Well," said Georges Thibodeau, finally. "I wanted to talk about this incident. And other things, too."

Sarah raised her eyes briefly and then returned to her meal.

"It's that I have an emotional kind of a disposition. Being jumped upon like that. And the big dog. It is not something that should happen outside one's very own shop."

This remark Sarah ignored, but she asked herself if this man actually sold hunting equipment. Did he actually go out into the great outdoors to test his products? She tried to picture Georges Thibodeau tramping through the woods, his shotgun under his arm, or marching along by the side of a rushing stream, ready to cast a fly. She couldn't. Sarah shook her head and twirled in another mouthful of spaghetti.

"I do not want," said Georges Thibodeau, abandoning his mangled piece of bread, "to be a person who is difficult."

Sarah lifted her eyebrows.

"I am a most reasonable person. Perhaps you would be good enough to join me for dinner some evening. So that we may talk this matter over in not so crowded a situation."

This remark Sarah had to answer. "We can talk right here, Mr. Thibodeau."

"Georges. Georges Thibodeau. Let us be friends. It is so much better because I do not bear you any ill will."

Sarah's jaw tightened. "Please, Georges Thibodeau, say what you have to say. I am sorry I frightened you. And I'm sorry that my dog frightened you. But I'm not sorry I chased you because you were trying to run off and Officer Markham wanted to talk to you. We were trying to help your very great friend, Madame Carpentier."

"Ah, yes, Grace. Such a wonderful woman. But you know, Miss Sarah Deane . . ." Sarah could see that the man was actually perspiring with the effort of explaining himself. "You know," he repeated, "Madame Carpentier is an older woman. A most admirable woman who is the age of one's mother. But one does not wish always to be with one's mother. One might wish to have a companionship with a person close to one's own age. A person with education. A teacher, perhaps, at this very school at which we are now eating our lunch."

Sarah stared at the man. Christ Almighty. Now she got it. He was making a deal. A proposition. Go out with me, play with me, and I'll forget all about suing the pants—no, that was an unfortunate thought—suing you for all you've got."

"The first time I saw you in the snow," said Georges, lowering his voice, a drop of perspiration now running down the tip of his nose, "I thought that you were this attractive person. You remind me of many handsome French ladies I have known. Do you have, perhaps, a mother or a father who is French?"

Sarah put down her fork. "Mr. Thibodeau, I am married, and I love my husband. I do not go out with other men. Why don't we say goodbye, and if your coat got dirty when you fell into the snow, send me the cleaning bill."

But to her astonishment Georges Thibodeau began waggling a finger at her face. "Ah, Miss Deane. That is not quite so true. I saw you having dinner with a gentlemen Sunday evening. The man had his hand over yours. Was this your husband? Because he is here in this dining room. Over there. And you have not asked him to join us." And Georges pointed across the room to Adrian Parsons, who was eating by himself at a table near one of the long windows.

Sarah stood up, her plate with its half-finished mound of spaghetti in one hand. She briefly wondered if she could actually throw it and have the satisfaction of seeing limp strands of tomato-soaked pasta slip down his face. Then, trying for control, she informed Georges that although it was none of his business, she had been having dinner with a colleague, which was something faculty members did all the time. And goodbye.

But Georges Thibodeau wasn't finished. "But I hope to see you again when you are calm, Miss Deane. So we can finish our little talk. I do not want to take any action about your pushing me into the snow. That was what one calls a pretense. I only want to know you so much better." And again Mr. Thibodeau bowed slightly from the waist, reminding Sarah powerfully of a waiter in a French comedy, and was gone.

22

SARAH, in a state close to a boil, watched Georges Thibodeau depart. Then, carrying her plate of congealing pasta, she stormed over to Jake Markham's table, banged down the plate, and flung herself down on the chair facing him. "That slime Thibodeau. I think he's trying to blackmail me into going out with him."

"Want me to warn him to stay off the school grounds?" asked Jake.

Sarah frowned, swallowed, and shook her head. "No, no. Let the guy go. I think he's harmless. It's because I look French or something. But I can take care of myself."

Jake grinned. "You want a small automatic weapon?"

"I'm thinking about putting in a supply of Bear Beware pepper spray. Something no woman should be without. Never mind, let's change the subject. How goes the investigation—about which you are not allowed to speak."

Jake shook his head. "It comes. It goes. If anything for public consumption comes up, you'll hear about it. But what I've heard is that you and Mr. Adrian Parsons had a cozy dinner together in Bedford. Dayla's, wasn't it?"

Sarah scowled at him. "My God, Jake, isn't anyone safe from the Carlisle KGB? That weasel, Mr. Thibodeau, says he saw me there and made little noises about unfaithful wives. And in case you want to know—"

"But I don't want to know. I don't give a damn who you ate dinner with. But any impressions about friend Adrian you want to share with me, go right ahead."

Sarah subsided. "Small towns can really do a job on privacy," she said. "But since you ask, I was trying to get away by myself, but first I ran into Carlo Leone and Rosemary Streeter, so I ducked out and ran right into Adrian Parsons. Who wanted company and understanding. And sympathy. The guy is a wreck. I'd say he was really smitten by the fair Anita and can't begin getting over her death. And yet some of the teachers were talking about how angry they both were at each other after the breakup."

"Yeah," said Jake cautiously. "I think we've dug up evidence suggesting that it wasn't always sweetness and light between those two."

"I really hate gossip."

"Gossip," said Jake, "is the oil that makes a case like this run. We miserable police are forced to feed on gossip because we haven't that many facts to work with."

"I," said Sarah, "am above such things." She grinned at Jake, rose, took her plate over to the dish bins, and started for the door. And walked directly into that interesting couple, Monsieur Thibodeau and Madame Carpentier. Georges Thibodeau, looking flustered, backed up a step, but Madame Grace hailed Sarah in the manner of a teacher recognizing a promising but slipshod student.

"Ah, Miss Deane. You must meet my friend, Mr. Thibodeau.

We are members together in the Middlesex County Alliance Française." She turned to Georges Thibodeau, her expression, to Sarah's eyes, bordering on the coy. "Miss Deane and I share a classroom, and she has been observing my teaching methods, have you not, Miss Deane?"

Georges Thibodeau had now pulled himself together and extended a limp hand. Which Sarah, after a moment's hesitation, took. And discarded. "I've met Mr. Thibodeau on a—" Sarah fumbled for the right words. "On a hunting expedition," she finished lamely.

"Yes," said George. "She was with a policeman."

Grace inclined her head. "We are doing very much business these days with policeman. They are all over the school like insects. Like locusts. It is a plague, *n'est-ce pas*, Miss Deane?"

Miss Deane acknowledged that it was indeed a plague and that now she had to go. She flung her coat over her shoulders and stepped outside Lockwood Hall and breathed the frosty air deep into her lungs. Feeling somewhat cleansed, she headed to the English office for an appointment with the two students who felt they were mired beyond recall in the depths of *Bleak House*. After which, by God, she would take to the trails. She would go skiing in the state park and clear her mind of the noxious gossip, insects, and locusts that buzzed about Miss Merritt's School.

Sarah decided that half the county had taken a look at the blue skies and the soft falling snow, cut their day short, headed for Great Brook Farm State Forest, put on skis, and hit the trails. The parking lot was jammed with cars and school buses disgorging students, teams, coaches, and ordinary mortals like English teachers.

Sarah parked, shoved her boots into the toe clamps, and took off in a herd—it was the only word for it—of skiers. There were toddlers on short skis, oldsters wearing heavy wool sweaters and knitted hats with pompoms, and the de rigueur costumed Nordic skiers gliding along, arms and legs moving like pistons. And even, as Sarah could see in the distance, that same figure she had noticed on the previous visit, the tall man who looked as if he came from the lumber camp. Now that he was closer, she could see that besides his black and red wool jacket and the hat with the earflaps, he also sported a drooping walrus mustache and horn-rimmed glasses. But he was a cheerful soul who waved at anyone who passed. If he hadn't been so slender, Sarah thought, he might have passed muster as a latter-day Paul Bunyan; all he needed was an ax.

She hung back, and then seeing that a majority of the skiers ahead were heading down the Acorn Trail, she took a sharp right and began working her way along Lantern Loop. The snow was perfection. A base had built up over the weekend, and the new-fallen layer lay like swansdown on the trail.

Sarah skied as if her life depended on every push of her pole, every swing of her arm, every glide of her skis. By the time the shadows deepened into darkness and she arrived back at the ski center entrance, she thought that she had a better grip on life than she might have thought possible when the day began.

All that week, afternoon skiing on the trails of Great Brook State Park became the thing to do for those who could free themselves from the workplace. The temperature stayed in the twenties, and the snow fell softly every night. The skies cleared briefly during the day, and then in the evening, as if responding to a heavenly signal, a new dusting freshened the woods and trails, softening the angles of rooftops and street corners and keeping the whole town in a state of whiteness.

Of course, the investigation into the murder of Anita Goshawk, the reviewing of statements, the re-examination of fragments from the murder site and from the wound, and the checking of timetables could not yield to the pleasures of the outdoors. Jake Markham stalked about the school with his folders, papers, and re-measured distances, met with his fellow investigators, and even found time to investigate the nature of the Middlesex Alliance Française, which turned out to be made up of a heterogeneous collection of former and present French citizens, all in all about as dangerous as a ladies' quilting circle. However, Georges Thibodeau continued to be a person of interest, and he and his shop were kept under low-profile surveillance.

Naturally, none of Miss Merritt's teachers dismissed classes ahead of time and told their students to go out and enjoy the snow. It took a proclamation from on high—from Dr. Joanna Singer—to declare that if the snow held, classes would be cancelled on Friday and buses would take students to the state park, to the downhill skiing facility in Nashoba, or to one of the skating rinks in the area. "Even if you've just come back from vacation," said Dr. Singer, "this has been a troubled period at Miss Merritt's, and I think we all need this extra day, this long weekend, of refreshment."

Hallelujah, thought Sarah, when the announcement was made at Thursday's dinner. A day off and Alex coming on Friday sometime. Possibly by noon because, as he had told her on the phone, Dr. Zim and others of the investigating team needed to review the finding of Anita Goshawk's body. Of course, Alex told her, he had sold his soul to a brother physician to get weekend hospital coverage, so what did an early departure from Maine on Friday matter.

Sarah pushed the distasteful part of his visit to the back of her brain and concentrated on the simple pleasure of her husband's arrival. She felt, not for the first time, that her worries and ditherings about the boarding school scene needed a quenching by her husband. He was a noted skeptic. A realist. A no-nonsense character. In short, he was a man who could be relied upon to tell her to stop stewing about events over which she had no control. Naturally, Sarah would argue back, disagree, stamp her foot, shake her fist in his face, and then feel a great deal better. And they would spend wonderful hours on the ski trail. Yes, Alex should make it to Carlisle by one or two, depending on the volume of interstate traffic. He could meet the investigators and then join her at Great Brook State Park. She would leave a note telling him which trails she would take and that she would ski until dark, all the while keeping an eye out for him.

Alex made it to Carlisle and the planned meeting in the Copeland Room in Radnor Hall by one o'clock. There he found, as expected, Dr. Harold Zim, Officer Jake Markham, and unexpectedly, his cousin, Giddy Lester.

"It's okay, Alex," said Giddy, seeing Alex's eyebrows raise a fraction of an inch. "I'm legal, I'm invited, at least for the first bit."

"We're going over several scenarios," explained Jake, "and we thought Giddy would be useful in discussing a student who might—or might not—be involved."

"It's the field hockey stick business," explained Giddy.

Alex nodded, pulled off his parka—he was already prepared for skiing—dragged a chair up to the long table, and waited.

"First," said Jake, "we're making some assumptions. That the murderer was acquainted with Anita Goshawk and/or Grace Carpentier. That he or she knew the way around the school property, including the footpath entrance and exit."

"And," put in Giddy, "where he or she could put his or her hands on a field hockey stick."

"Right," said Jake. "So, Alex, let's go over your statement

278

about the body. She was dead when you examined her, you say."

"I didn't do a real examination. Just felt for a pulse and thought about CPR, but after I'd had a hard look at the head injuries—they showed even in that dim lamplight—I knew she couldn't have survived those multiple blows. That she was gone."

"And you thought she must have just died? But within the hour, the half hour, ten minutes?"

"Maybe between ten and fifteen minutes. After all, she was still warm, even when the outside temperature had gone on a real downward skid."

"You're sure?" asked Jake.

"I'm not sure, it's just a guess," said Alex. He turned to Harold Zim. "You're the one to calculate the speed at which the body could lose heat on a cold night. She wasn't a large woman, quite slender, even thin. That would factor into the loss of body temperature. But, of course, she was wearing that damn black woolen cape."

"It's not an exact science," said Dr. Zim. "Too many factors operating, but I'd say your ten or fifteen minutes is in the ballpark."

"Okay," said Jake, breaking in, "only fifteen minutes at the most from time of death to being found. The killer had to hustle. He had to leave the art lecture and be at Radnor Hall in time to see Anita swipe the cape and take off back toward the footpath to get her slides."

"Or be on the footpath, see a woman in a cape, and think it's Grace Carpentier," said Alex. "Follow her through the woods, not on the path, and attack her when the time's right. When she's by herself."

"You're forgetting the field hockey stick," said Giddy. "The killer had to see the woman going back down the footpath, zip over to Gregory House, grab the hockey stick, hide it under a coat, race back, and do the thing."

Jake checked a page in his folder. "It's a fast-moving thing. Sarah and Babette met Anita almost running."

"You're not saying that the murderer was doing a four-minute mile," said Alex.

"Close," said Jake. "He had to grab the stick, do the deed, get back to the school, wash up, dispose of or hide any bloody clothes, and get to the reception—or go somewhere to be seen and counted as present."

"Not everyone thought that Anita was Grace in a cape," remarked Alex. He leaned back in the chair and calculated how much time he could devote to this affair. He had contributed his little bit, and now it was time to hit the ski scene and catch up with Sarah.

"Yeah," said Jake. "Your wife and Babette Leclerc met Anita going along the footpath and recognized her. Actually, they're probably the last ones to see her alive. But also we've got testimony from Zoë Fountain and Rosemary Streeter that they saw Anita near Philipi House, walking fast, and wearing Grace Carpentier's cape. They knew it was Anita, knew whose cape she was wearing. Which brings us to the girl who *didn't* see Anita in the cape. The girl who hated Grace. And who owned a heavy-duty field hockey stick. Hannah Hoyt. Giddy, it's your turn. Do you think . . ."

But Giddy interrupted. "For Christ's sake, Jake. Are you saying Hannah thought she saw Grace in her cape heading toward the footpath, ran to Gregory House, and chose her *own* hockey stick to kill the woman? Come on, be real."

Jake picked up a pencil, twirled it, and dropped it. He looked directly at Giddy. Who glared back. "We've got to start somewhere. Build a case, then see if it falls apart when you blow on it. You've been at the school for three years now, and you know Hannah. She's one of your art program stars, and

280

she's in Gregory House this year. So listen to how it might play out."

"I'll listen," said Giddy in a grudging voice, "but I think you're out of your skull."

"Facts. First, Hannah was a member of the crew that put up the two scarecrows, one on the soccer field, one on the school sign. We have kids' statements on this. Second, Grace was attacked by snowballs outside the art building when Hannah was around. Third, a picture of a rattlesnake turned up in the art building. It was well drawn, and Hannah is a gifted art student. No one knows who did the drawing, but Hannah is on the short list. Fourth, Hannah finds—accidentally on purpose, maybe—the paper cut-out of Grace, hanging by the neck. But which we now know was not cut out by Hannah, who is left-handed. Which is a plus for Hannah."

Giddy leaned over and pounded her fist in front of Jake. "I know Hannah hated Grace, but you, Officer Markham, are pushing this. You're really teeing me off."

Jake looked up. "Hold it. What is it? Alex?"

Alex and Dr. Harold Zim had risen with one motion. "You don't need us for this scene," said Alex. "Harold and I are going to do something wholesome, like get out of here. If you have any questions later, I'll be at the state park. On skis. Pursuing my wife." And with that, Alex and Dr. Zim took hold of their jackets and departed, leaving a purple-faced Giddy and an expressionless Jake Markham.

"Giddy, you can shoot it all down, but let me finish. Hannah, by her own admission, wrote that file card and nailed it to a tree. 'Mme. Grace Carpentier you piece of shit. Go rot in hell.' That isn't even close to a joke. It's sheer hate."

"It's sheer temper," said Giddy. "Hannah has a temper. She doesn't mean half what she says. And she confessed. Came to you and confessed."

"After her hand was forced."

"She's very sorry she ever wrote the thing."

"The murderer may be very sorry he clobbered someone he took for Grace Carpentier. Let me go on. Those three Gregory House seniors in the breaking-and-entering scene—"

"Not breaking in," said Giddy. "They were returning Grace's dog."

"But they stayed in the apartment."

"They thought someone might have killed Grace."

"And since there's no body, they open up a desk and find a batch of unstamped postcards with obscene messages, all featuring art scenes. Just like the cards in the art department files that Hannah has easy access to."

"Everyone has easy access to them. The kids use them for papers or projects. Instructors borrow them and make slides out of them. The whole school can get its mitts on the things," said Giddy, her voice rising again. How had she for one moment thought that she liked this guy? He was a piranha.

"And since Madame seems to have flushed or burned them, we just have to note that once upon a time the things existed. Face it, Hannah had a motive. And I don't think it's peculiar to grab your own hockey stick. People—murderers—acting on impulse who see a sudden opportunity don't always act logically. One more thing. Hannah is a tall girl. Over five ten. The blow to Anita came from above. Tall person attacking a short one. Now, it's your turn, Giddy."

"It's Ms. Lester to you," said Giddy. "Now, listen to me." And Giddy, shoving previous doubts about Hannah aside, held forth on her virtues. The girl was bright, sound of mind, and absolutely incapable of physical violence.

"You," shouted Giddy, "are so out of it, it's pathetic. Hannah is worth two of you."

Jake thanked her calmly for her opinion, said she could leave, and welcomed in Detective Hillary Mumford, who arrived shaking snow from her person.

"The stuff came right off the roof," said Hillary. "Some maintenance person told me not to leave a wet coat in the cloak room, so I'm bringing it in here to drip on all these Persian carpets, which will serve them right. So, how did accusing Hannah Hoyt go? Did Giddy come through?"

"Giddy," said Jake, "turned partisan witness and has something of an attitude. But she's firm about Hannah. Wonderful girl, wouldn't hurt a flea—or a French teacher."

"We'll have to think about downgrading Hannah's status as a suspect," said Hillary. "So what else do we have?"

"Those two guys who haven't any witnesses to where they were after the art lecture. Adrian Parsons and Carlo Leone, both with scratches on their faces. Adrian was checking mail and making a phone call—he says. Carlo was loading whiskey in his flask—he says. But I've just dug up a witness who says he might have seen Carlo giving someone a snort before the lecture."

"So he has to refill," said Hillary.

"Yeah, that makes sense. Anyway, as far as Grace goes, Carlo seemed to get along with her, even though he enjoys a few jokes at her expense. But he never showed dislike of Anita. As for Adrian with Grace, he's Sir Walter Raleigh."

"You mean he sucks up to her," said Hillary.

"Not exactly. It's in his interest to get along with her. Besides, everyone knows Grace treats men better than women. And we keep forgetting, Anita was the person killed. We have all those letters from Anita's apartment—the ones Parsons wrote after their breakup. Pretty sharp stuff. Adrian was very unhappy about the whole thing."

"Well, I have news for you," said Hillary. "Hot off the press. Adrian came to my office this morning and admitted entering Anita's apartment the other night. As we guessed. He had a key left over from the days of wine and roses. Says he wanted to find the letters and didn't want a lot of hurtful—his expression, not mine—material to become public. Said he wrote the letters in a temper. Lots of people around seem to have tempers. Anyway, he claims he really loved her. Madly, truly, deeply, et cetera. So is he playing the honest helper or the wily fox? He looks like hell, but is it some sort of a put-on? Done with smoke and mirrors?"

"Because she was killed or because he killed her?"

"Or—and I like this one—he made a god-awful mistake and killed the wrong person. And is now suffering."

"Except," Jake pointed out, "You don't just mistake your lover for the French teacher. As we've pointed out."

"But the others who recognized Anita had the benefit of being fairly close to her and were helped by lights from the houses and parking lot. The footpath was on the dim side, and it was sleeting. I wish we could come up with the murderer's clothes. They should be blood-stained and not that easy to get rid of."

"Probably in the Charles River. Or closer, in the Concord River. What about the raincoat switcheroos?"

"With all the fuss about the cape, we've neglected the raincoats. Carlo Leone claims someone swiped his coat, so he helped himself to another, saying they all look alike and who's to care. He's right, they do look alike. So the murderer might have seen Anita turn around at the entrance to Radnor, grabbed a coat as protection against blood spattering, taken off after her, and made a quick detour to pick up the hockey stick."

"Carlo showed me the kind of coat," said Jake. "It's a generic mackintosh affair, like the kind Humphery Bogart wore in *Casablanca*. Popular around here. Adrian Parsons, when he's not in camel hair, has one, ditto Joel Cohen, the dean, and even Joanna Singer has one. I've got one. Thought I'd look suave, but I only look like a used clothes rack. God, what a comedy. A cape mix-up, raincoats switched, plus two men with almost identical scratches on their faces from falling into bushes. Both of them. Yeah, right."

Hillary stood up. "All this, and guess what? The school's got an alumnae weekend coming up. I'd sort of hoped Dr. Singer would cancel it, but she said she's trying for normality. Things should go on as planned."

"Good luck on that one."

"It's not a major affair. Not like the big reunion scenes in the fall and at graduation. This is just class reps, trustees, and a few strays. Some may bring their families, but most will be staying at Alumnae House, and that place is just off campus. Winter activities are encouraged. They do it every year."

"They'll have a lot to talk about. Nothing like a dead body turning up on the hallowed grounds."

Hillary, engaged in working her arms through her jacket sleeves, paused. "Something I've said before, and I'll say again. Grace Carpentier might have set the whole damn thing up. Chew on that for a while, Jake."

"Hell, the kids have already thought of that one. Besides, I'd rather chew lunch. Or go skiing." Jake shuffled his papers into a neat pile and began to pack them into his briefcase. "The whole school and half the town is out hitting the trails. That's where the action is."

"Wrong," said Hillary briskly. "Miss Merritt's School is where the action is and don't you forget it."

But as sometimes happens in the affairs of men and on the pages of mystery fiction, Detective Mumford was wrong.

23

ALEX made it to Sarah's apartment on the double, inserted the key, greeted Patsy, and picked up a trail map of Great Brook Farm State Park together with Sarah's note. If he came before two o'clock, she'd be hanging around the cross-country ski center area. After that she was going to escape the crowds by trying out the trails at the end of Wolf Rock Road—map of park enclosed. She'd stay near something called Heartbreak Ridge. And if he wanted, he could bring Patsy. Patsy needed an outing. Okay?

Not okay, said Alex to himself. He eyed the large, gray dog. Cross-country skiing with the world's largest canine might have problems. But, what the hell. He snapped on Patsy's leash and took off. The way these meetings usually worked out, Patsy would get loose and scare a small child, he'd miss Sarah entirely, and he'd end up with Grace Carpentier instead—Sarah reported that the French teacher was a demon on skis. "And,"

Sarah had added, "she's got a new cape and looks just like a stingray in it."

He checked his watch. Twenty minutes past two. He'd grab a sandwich and then start going in circles on the Wolf Rock Road trails. On his drive out from the Gregory House parking area, he noticed a number of rather dressy females with small, white pin-on labels fixed to their coats, many clutching folders in their gloved hands and trudging along in the direction of the Nakatani Art Center. For a minute he wondered whether the group had anything to do with the homicide investigation team. Counterspies, or moles, perhaps? But then he remembered Sarah had said something about a high-powered alumnae group coming for its customary January meeting and that she had expressed doubt as to the wisdom of the thing.

But now, food. A pit stop at Daisy Market, the local bakery and deli, yielded a homemade chicken salad sandwich and a Coke, and then the turn off Lowell Road into Wolf Rock Road proved that Sarah wasn't alone in choosing the road less traveled. Some ten or so cars filled the small parking circle, and only with difficulty was Alex able to wedge the Subaru into a narrow slot. And yes, there was the Jeep. He got to work, unloaded his skis, and hit the trail. And almost immediately—and literally—hit Madame Grace Carpentier. Who, as Sarah had suggested, in her famous cape strongly resembled a land-based and mobile stingray. Her hood was down, her head circled in a pointed purple wool turban, her sharp nose a notable crimson.

"Aha," said Grace. "You must look where you are going. It is fortunate I am firm on my skis." She peered at him and then said, "But I see it is the husband of Miss Deane. You have come back to Carlisle to ski? And you are at this Wolf Rock place because you have seen that the ski center is filled with too many people so that it has become a circus. One does not want to be part of a circus, *n'est-ce pas*? And," she noted, shuffling back on her skis, "here you have the dog belonging to Miss Deane. I suggest you keep him away because he has an interest in my boots." This was said as Patsy, recognizing a familiar Gregory House scent, nosed down toward Carpentier's ankles.

Alex reined in the dog, but Grace had turned. "*Je vous laisse*. I shall ski alone, it is the only way for one to concentrate. I left my dog, my Szeppi, at home, because I believe there should be a rule about dogs in this park. But it is good to see you again, Dr. McKenzie. We need persons, men of sense, to visit the school because everyone has gone just a bit crazy. *Fou, affolé!* It is this murder. Every moment one's privacy is being invaded. *À bientôt*"

And Madame, with a shove of her poles—state-of-the-art touring poles—began moving away in a southerly direction.

Alex consulted his map of the park. Sarah had mentioned Heartbreak Ridge, but it was anyone's guess whether she would have taken the northern spur or the southern loop. This last route rolled around something called Tophet Swamp, ending in Tophet Loop—an area marked ominously, *Warning: Deep Mud—not for horses*. All right, he would give the search his best shot. Go north for forty minutes or so, then reverse and head back toward Tophet Loop. Then back again, and if Sarah hadn't turned up somewhere, he and Patsy would retreat to her apartment and wait in comfort.

The Heartbreak Ridge trail seemed lightly populated. Alex set out in a northerly direction, where the map promised, in capital letters, a gravel pit, a cabin, and another trail called Pine Point Loop. He looked at his watch. Two-thirty. He had about two, three at the very most, hours of light left before he'd have to give up the search. But the snow was perfection, the ski trails clear, the wind a whisper, and he needed fresh air and exercise. With or without Sarah. He gave a tug at Patsy's leash and took three or four steps, then he realized that an attached dog makes any sort of efficient forward motion difficult. Although not exactly an obedient animal, Patsy, who played Sarah for an easy mark, usually listened to Alex.

Alex unhooked the leash, and the dog, as if he were in a film on dog training, placed himself close to Alex's left hip and lifted his gray, shaggy legs into a long, striding trot. And off they went, moving fast enough to overtake a couple with a small boy, three teenage girls skiing side by side and talking a blue streak, and two small boys a few feet off the trail who were fencing with their ski poles. The only people he met headed toward the southern route were an older man and woman who wished him a good day and said that they had done their stint and were leaving. Then behind them, heading south and moving with energy, Alex saw a tall man in a black and red wool jacket and a hunting cap with earflaps. His backpack was khaki canvas, his trousers were wool, his boots were real work boots, his skis were antiques with outdated metal clamp bindings, and his poles were made of bamboo. Altogether, as he approached, Alex was reminded, as Sarah had been earlier, of a woodsman come down from the northern reaches of Maine. Even the man's red face, with horn-rimmed glasses and a walrus mustache, fitted in with the costume. When he came up to Alex, he lifted a pole in greeting, said something incoherent about great snow, and shoved past and disappeared from sight.

Alex gave the Heartbreak Ridge and a small stretch of Pine Point Loop his best effort and then reversed direction to the south, with Patsy continuing his role as model dog. By now the afternoon light had dimmed, and a sense of closing day seemed to have overtaken a number of skiers, particularly those in thrall to small children who were making loud demands for pizza, cocoa, and soda pop, all the while complaining of cold feet, cold hands, and cold ears.

But no Sarah. Alex skied back to the parking area, saw that the Jeep was still in place, and returned to the trail. The temperature had dropped slightly and a thin crust had developed along the well-skied trails, so the going was quicker, if a little more treacherous, on the downhill runs.

Knowing Sarah, Alex now decided that in one of her independent-from-the-world moods, she, like Grace Carpentier, might have chosen Tophet Loop and the "Deep Mud—Not for Horses" area. Well, if those two bumped into each other, he could bet that Sarah would shake loose from the French teacher, hurry north, and leave Madame to ski in peace on the southern loop trail.

Alex found that these speculations had slowed his pace. Coming to a stop, he surveyed the landscape. A number of lightly wooded steep banks and snow-filled ravines lay on the sides of the trail, but as long as the light lasted—and it was going fast—there was little chance of going astray and down into one. And, despite some wind drifting, the snow wasn't really deep enough to trap a skier, even if he ended up at the bottom of some minor gulch. Alex put himself back into motion, and just as he slid his right ski forward, Patsy, the model dog, with a great woof followed by a throat-filled howl, leapt into space, ricocheted off the back of Alex's knees, and bounded off. He disappeared around a bend and was gone. Cursing, Alex hauled himself to his feet, retrieved a pole, and set off, yelling for Patsy to come back.

Two skiers, coming toward him heading north, pointed behind them. "A dog's loose," said one. "He's as big as a house. I think it's a wolf."

"Or a giant coyote," said the other.

Alex thanked them, shoved in his poles, and began a modified sprint, slipped on an icy patch, cursed, picked himself up, caught the toe of a ski under a tree root, slipped, got up again, and skied ahead, all the while shouting loudly for Patsy.

*　　*　　*

Sarah had completed her tour of Tophet Loop and decided that she and Alex must have missed each other entirely by each going in the opposite direction. So, reluctantly, she had begun the trek north to Heartbreak Ridge and home. Then, with about a hundred yards to go, she paused. Stopped, and listened. It wasn't exactly the sound of skiers. More like the cracking of a branch. Or a trodden piece of brush. Curious, she edged toward a small clearing on one side of the trail and peered down a bank that sloped some fifty feet into a ravine. There was something there that she couldn't quite see.

She leaned forward on her ski poles. As she did, a a hand or a flat object hit her back with tremendous force and gave her a forward shove. Sarah had a sense of revolving in space, seeing the sky by her feet and branches in her face, all whirling and turning. She plunged down, tobogganing in a cloud of snow, feet and hands flaying, her body slammed into small trees and bounced off roots, one ski snapping off, the other twisting her leg and her knee, and still revolving, she came at last to rest in a heap at the bottom of the bank, her shoulder supported by a large granite boulder.

For a few moments—or was it hours or years—Sarah lay in a tangled heap. Somehow, it seemed easier to keep her eyes closed and imagine that all was well, that every muscle didn't ache, that her nose wasn't bleeding, and that her face wasn't criss-crossed with scratches. That she really wasn't slowly freezing to death. But suddenly a dog barked, almost in her ear. And then the bark stopped and was replaced by an eerie, high whine that started, stopped, and came again. Groaning, she pushed herself up, waist-deep in snow, to a painful sitting position and sat blinking in the increasing dark. And was suddenly beset by a large and familiar animal, a dim shape bounding through the snow and now standing over her, anxiously nosing her face, licking her damaged face.

"Patsy," said Sarah weakly. She reached over to take hold

of his collar. But to her surprise, he wrenched away and turned toward a dark fragment of something, a fragment thrusting out from the snow.

Then Alex came sliding and slipping, from drift to branch to bush and finally, to an awkward stop by Sarah. "My God, Sarah! What in hell are you doing!"

"I'm not here for the fun of it," Sarah snapped. "I got shoved. Pushed. I think I've lost half my face."

Alex extended a hand, pulled Sarah to her feet, and gently turned her face to what was left of the afternoon light. "No real cuts, just scratches. You'll probably have a great black eye tomorrow."

Sarah, grabbed a low hemlock branch for stability. "Look, Alex, I'm okay. Got my wind knocked out. But grab Patsy. He's got something. He sounds like he's about to eat it, and it's probably a horrible dead animal with rabies or something." She reached down to her ankle to loosen the toe clip on her remaining ski, lost her footing, and slid almost directly into Patsy's hindquarters.

Sat up swearing. Peered into the shadows. Reached for Patsy's rear paw. And gave a yelp. Or a scream. She never knew which.

Patsy did indeed "have" something. Or rather, he was tending something. Now softly nosing it, pushing it gently. An arm. With a ski pole still looped around its wrist.

And now Sarah saw that here and there poking through the drifted snow was: A second arm. A foot with a ski boot. A large triangular section of black material. A small strip of purple quilted cloth—the purple dark in the failing light. And, marring the perfect whiteness of the perfect snow, spatters, droplets, small pools of something wet, something looking appearing almost black, something that, coming from a warm and living— or recently living—body, had melted small holes in the snow's surface.

292

And Alex was kneeling beside her. "Let me see. You hang on to Patsy."

Sarah took hold of the dog's thick, gray fur hide, pulled, wrenched, and found his collar, and pulled him away from the body. If it was a body. But it seemed to her as if she were viewing the scene from some half-remembered collage: a black paper scissor cut-out of a body. A cut-out partly covered by snow. Or part of a scarecrow in a black robe. Or something a giant with great, long scissors had severed into many pieces, like the dark wings of a raven. Or, more accurately, the fragments of a giant stingray.

Oh, God. She must have said it aloud because Alex, now leaning over the far end of the half-hidden body, swiveled about. "She's still alive. Breathing's pretty shallow. But regular. Do you think you can climb back on the trail and get help? Call 911. One of the skiers may have a cell phone." He stripped off his jacket, scooped snow from around the shape so that something partially human began to emerge, and laid his jacket over it.

Sarah, as if launched into an unrolling nightmare, found her other ski—it would be quicker on the trail if she could ski—and, aware that her head was pounding, her face stinging as from a hundred lashes, began to clamber back up the slope. And with Patsy now obediently loping beside her, she skied north toward the Wolf Rock Road parking lot, shouting and waving her poles.

She was in luck. The fourth skier ahead of her did have a cell phone. He called the emergency number, identified himself as a physician from Emerson Hospital and, after offering her help for her obvious facial injuries and being refused, hurried back to help Alex.

And for the second time in two weeks Sarah found herself waiting for the rescue squad. She stationed herself by the opening to the parking circle and put an "X" on her map where she thought Alex, his helper, and whatever might be left of Grace Carpentier were located.

There had really never been any doubt. Grace Carpentier, her new cape about her, lay at the foot of the ravine. Bloody, bludgeoned, and half-dead. Or, by now, all dead. What did shallow breathing mean? Was it good? Wasn't any breathing good? But shallow?

Sarah gave up and instead fixed her mind on an imagined abyss, a deep, dark, bottomless cave. A cave in which black ravens circled and called in hoarse voices. A cave in which dogs whined and howled and reared up and snapped at a paper puppet that hung from the cave roof by its neck. A cave where a choir of black-robed scarecrows circled about, calling in French. And her mind began to play an incoherent jumble of little children's songs. In French. *Sur le Pont d'Avignon, Frère Jacques, Dormez-vous? Au Clair de la Lune, Il était un bergère, Et ron ron ron, Petit patapon.*

So, balanced unsteadily on the near side of tears, her body feeling as if she had spent a lifetime in a cement mixer, the skin of her face on fire, Sarah waited. And waited.

Then lights, action. The processional. The rescue squad. The stretcher. Alex and the second physician creaking and shuffling behind the stretcher. Mumbled talk about head trauma. Blunt head trauma. Intercranial pressure. Cervical spine immobilization. IV fluid protocol. The possible need for intubation. The hospital destination. The Lahey Clinic decided upon. The ER alerted. Departure of all parties, the vertical and the horizontal. Lights, sirens. The snow gently beginning to fall.

And then the police. A squad, a team. Men with boxes and cameras and lights. Yellow tape. And Jake Markham. Hillary Mumford. Sarah, standing by her car, Patsy at her side, stared at them as if they had reared up from another world. "What do you want me to do?" she asked Jake, stopping him as he started for the Wolf Rock trail entrance. "Shall I go on back to school and tell someone?"

"Good idea," said Hillary, who appeared behind Jake.

"What should I say?" asked Sarah, puzzled on this point. Should she report that Grace Carpentier was ill, hurt, attacked? Dying? Critical? Or just that someone from the school, identity uncertain, had an accident. Had to go to the hospital suddenly. Very suddenly.

Hillary, standing under the street light, her wool hat down over her forehead, her jacket collar pulled up over her chin, frowned. "Stick to the truth. Find Dr. Singer. She'll handle the news. Tell her that Madame Carpentier has had an accident skiing and has been taken to the hospital. A possible head injury. That the cause of the accident is being investigated. And, for heaven's sake, put something on that face of yours. You look awful."

"Betadine, lots of Betadine," said Jake. "And please take charge of that dog of Grace's and put a notice up that her weekend appointments have been cancelled. That might keep kids away from her door."

Sarah nodded. "And I suppose you'll want to talk to Alex and me, because we found her. Well, to be exact, Patsy found her."

Jake eyed her. "I think we should put a tail on you and Alex. It'll save time in the long run."

When Sarah located Dr. Singer in the Old Library in Radnor Hall, she was surrounded by what Sarah understood to be the Alumnae Association movers and shakers, trustees, loyal Miss Merritt class representatives, parent committee members, and the like. A dressy group. The ladies in dark winter colors; the men in pinstripes and blazers.

It was sherry-*cum*-tea time. And Sarah, with her scratched

and bloodied face, her rumpled ski gear, and her hair standing in electric spikes, felt like orphan Jane Eyre about to disturb Mr. Brockelhurst.

But Dr. Joanna Singer was all business. Once her attention was drawn to the figure of Sarah by the entryway, she left swiftly, closed the heavy oak door behind her, and raised one eyebrow.

Sarah delivered her message. Except for one deep intake of breath, Dr. Singer, for a moment, said nothing. Then she bit her lip, tightened her jaw, and nodded her understanding of the news. Sarah, waiting, felt she could almost hear the whirl of beautifully balanced wheels. Dr. Singer ought to be in government, the Supreme Court, possibly. Or some area where dignity and restraint were desperately needed. Congress, perhaps.

"Thank you, Sarah," Dr. Singer said. "This is a blow. I shall have to break the news carefully to the Alumnae Association, particularly as they've just been digesting the sad news about Anita Goshawk. I think I'll ask you to tell the houseparents what you've told me, and they in turn can tell their students. Then at dinner I'll make a short announcement. We should know more about Madame Carpentier's condition by then. And please, check into the infirmary and let the nurse do something about your face."

Sarah said she would, and added that Grace had been taken to the Lahey Clinic. "Because of the head injury."

"Good. I'll get in touch with the people there." Dr. Singer paused, and then curved her lips in a grim smile. "I'll be announcing that the memorial service for Anita is set for Sunday afternoon in the chapel. I shall add that this will also give us an opportunity to pray for Grace's recovery."

But as Sarah left, turning her steps toward the Bertha Comstock Memorial Infirmary, the thought buzzed in her head that by Sunday the memorial service itself might, of necessity, be expanded to include Grace Marie-Henriette Carpentier, instructor in French at Miss Merritt's School.

24

SARAH, her face cleaned and daubed with Betadine, and with two extra-strength Tylenol under her belt, decided to delegate. Going all over the school hunting houseparents would take forever, so she decided to turn it over to Freda and Joel Cohen. These sensible people she found in the Gregory House laundry dealing with an overflow problem. They heard Sarah with distress. Freda promised to round up students for a Gregory House meeting, and Joel said he would pass the news to the other houses. This settled, Sarah asked for Grace's apartment key, saying that she had promised to take care of Szeppi.

Szeppi proved an amiable animal. Fed, walked, and watered, Sarah returned him to Grace's apartment, looked at her watch, and found to her surprise that it was only a few minutes after six. It had seemed as if weeks had slipped by, leaving them all stranded on the other side of February.

Well, she couldn't just sit there waiting. She made a cup of tea, changed her torn and besmirched ski jacket for a coat, and in minutes was driving through the lightly falling snow out of Carlisle. Toward Bedford, onto the Burlington Road, to Bedford Street, Cambridge Street, and at last turned right into the rising lamp-lit drive of the Lahey Clinic.

The clinic rose to her right like some miniature city of brick and stone. Automobiles, buses, and taxis, twirled, started, stopped, disgorged passengers, and accelerated. Sarah, following the flow, drove to the end of an outdoor two-level parking lot. But why was she here, anyway? Good question, because Alex wouldn't linger. He would have said his piece in the ER on Grace's admission—if she had been admitted and not gone straight to the county morgue—and then would have driven straight to the Carlisle police office to make his statement. Here at the hospital she would probably learn zip. Did desk people still give out those unhelpful statements: He is doing as well as can be expected; he is holding his own; the condition is critical, guarded, satisfactory, improving. She doubted that she would learn more than the time of day and the locations of the cafeteria, the ladies room, and the telephone booths.

Sarah got out of the car and began a long slog through salt-sprinkled sidewalks to the main clinic entrance. She had been to the clinic before, when a family member had been in for surgery, and always found the experience unsettling. She tended to prefer the small-town cottage hospital, or the mid-coast Maine's Mary Starbuck Hospital where Alex plied his trade, this having a fine view of the Camden Hills from almost any room.

Floating through the magically opening glass doors, Sarah stepped into an enlarged version of a busy hotel lobby. What was it about these places? They always reminded her of a vast commercial lodging catering to a convention of persons with unresponsive depression syndrome. All the amenities were there: cafeteria, reception desks, newspaper dispensers, and a gift shop filled with cards, magazines, and stuffed animals. But any thought of comfort was usually dimmed by the sight of dejected couples sitting huddled together, the passing through of men and women in blue scrubs or white coats, and the oppressive presence of large portraits of medical dignitaries hanging along the walls.

Sarah decided that first she needed the answer to certain essential questions. Was an alive Grace Carpentier in the ER, a dead Grace awaiting transfer or autopsy, or was she "clinging to life," as the media would put it, in some ICU? Or none of the above. She saw what might be an admissions desk and headed for it.

And was stopped cold by a hand on her shoulder. Alex.

"Good," he said.

Sarah spun around. Alex, still in his ski clothes, spatters of something dark on his blue ski jacket, black hair every which way, all in all an unsavory mess.

"Good?" she repeated.

He gave her a short push in the direction of the door. "Good, because you must be feeling okay or you wouldn't be here. And good, because I haven't a car. I came in the ambulance, remember?"

"But Grace," said Sarah, twisting about and facing him. "For God's sake, how is she? I mean, is she alive?"

"Alive. And semi-conscious, which is more than we hoped for when we loaded her on to the stretcher. She's being managed for blunt trauma to the head. Surgical ICU. But it looks like, and this is just a guess, that whoever hit her missed his aim. The weapon may have slipped so it wasn't a direct strike."

"You mean because she's alive?"

"Yes, and perhaps not that critical. It's too early to say. Neurologists are a cautious bunch when it comes to predicting about head injuries, but it's a good sign that she's semiconscious from time to time."

"And she can talk?

"I didn't say that, though Jake Markham has been hoping she'll suddenly open her eyes and say something useful—which, considering that she's been intubated and fixed up with a nasogastric tube, isn't likely."

"He wants one of those scenes where the victim flutters his eyelashes for 'yes' and wiggles his toes for 'no'?"

"Jake's left an officer from the Burlington police with her and gone back to Carlisle. He'll hear pronto about any change in her consciousness, though most head injury victims don't have immediate recall of what hit them."

"Were you so sure I'd turn up that you didn't grab a ride with Jake?"

"If I had to make a bet, I'd have said you would. Curiosity is your besetting sin. Anyway, here's my thought. Grab a quick dinner at that seafood place in the mall, and then we'll have to meet with Hillary and Jake to go over the scene of finding her."

Sarah sighed. "Poor Grace."

"I never thought I'd hear you say that," observed Alex, heading for the front door.

"Well, it took finding her buried in the snow for me to work up any sympathy, but now I'm sorry. If she gets well in a week and comes charging back to school biting everyone's head off, I'll withdraw the remark."

Dinner at the Legal Seafood Restaurant was swift and filling—salmon for Alex, haddock for Sarah—and then as they waited for the bill, Alex looked at Sarah. "You deserve a medal for hanging in when you must feel like hell after that fall. Your face is a royal mess. And you know what you're going to be asked—whether you have any idea at all of the identity of the person who pushed you down that bank? Concentrate on that question while I drive."

At something like eight o'clock, Alex and Sarah found themselves back at the familiar interrogation base: the Copeland Room of Radnor Hall. Hillary and Jake were there, looking scruffy and heavy-eyed. With a long day behind them, they now faced a long night.

"Just had a call," said Hillary. "No real change in Grace's condition, but it doesn't seem that bad. I mean, she's alive, and the latest report is that she seems alert enough to try to pull out her IV lines."

"Sounds like the old Grace," said Jake. "Anyway, here's something that will interest you. Grace wore a small waist pack when she skied, and guess what was in it."

"A folding Uzi," said Sarah promptly.

"Aw," said Jake. "You're no fun. Not an Uzi, a little Smith & Wesson number. So we'll have to nail Georges Thibodeau with that one."

"She never had a chance to use it," said Hillary. "Her waist pack was still zipped. But nearby in the snow they've picked up a cute little pocket model of bear spray. The kind with a belt clip. She must have gotten it out but didn't get a chance to use that either."

Jake spoke up. "The state police are handling the visitor center questioning, statements from people who have been out on the trails today. Hillary and I are doing the Merritt School scene. So, Sarah, who or what knocked you off your feet? Or did you stumble, lose your balance, and just *think* something hit you?"

Sarah didn't hesitate. "I honestly think someone gave me a big push or a giant shove. I'm sure it was a person. It took me by surprise, and I went ass over tea kettle down the bank. Never saw a thing. It all happened too fast."

"Okay, here's my question," said Hillary. "From the statements that have come in so far, several people mentioned that for the last few days they've come across this northwoods character. Sort of a lumberjack."

Sarah jumped in her seat. "I saw him. Yesterday and the day before. All he needed was an ax."

"And," said Hillary grimly, "he may have had one."

"Trouble is," said Jake, "there've been a hell of a lot of people in the park today. Even a couple of jokers—someone in a Superman suit and one in a raccoon coat, plus some old duffers with antique skis or snowshoes—and this guy might be one of those. So it's going to take a while to sift out who was where and what they saw. But we are going to see if we find this one guy."

"He was very cheerful," said Sarah. "Waving at everyone."

"Right," said Alex. "Waved at me, too. He passed me zipping along at a good clip heading south toward the Tophet Swamp area."

"See the guy again, afterwards?" asked Jake.

But Alex shook his head.

"Which is a kinda peculiar for such a high-profile guy," said Jake. "About two dozen people the state cops have talked to so far never saw him after about three-thirty this afternoon. Not on the trails, not in a parking lot, not in a car driving away."

"Well, I'm off," said Hillary. "Statements, statements. The whole blessed school. Sarah, you may be interested to know that Hannah Hoyt and friend Zoë Fountain were cross-country skiing in the Heartbreak Ridge area, but Zoë lost touch with Hannah sometime after two-thirty. I'll leave you two with Jake to go over everything again. And this is crucial—we need to know what time things happened. Sarah, you take care, your face is pretty scary."

And Hillary picked up her portfolio and left.

For a moment there was a heavy silence. Then Sarah shook her head vehemently. "Not Hannah Hoyt. I'm with Giddy on this. You can't tell me that girl stuffed a brick in her pocket and pursued Madame Carpentier on skis and slammed it into her skull. No way. That attack was brutal. Not the sort of thing Hannah could possibly do. Scarecrows, file cards, yes, but not this. This was like the attack on Anita Goshawk. Really savage."

"Savage is right," said Jake. "Someone at the hospital mentioned a length of pipe as a possible weapon. I mean, I doubt if a field hockey stick figures in the attack. But we'll wait for forensics. And listen, Sarah, no one's going to leap down Hannah Hoyt's throat. We're just taking note of who from the school was at the park."

"What about the Alumnae Association?" asked Sarah. "Did those people stay at school the whole day?"

"Most of them," said Jake, "went to meetings. Fundraising, stuff like that. But believe it or not, quite a few class reps and alumnae visitors came with family and did go skiing. And from what I've heard, some of those are not exactly members of the Grace Carpentier fan club."

Sarah had a sudden vision of hundreds of angry former students of Grace Carpentier on the ski trails. "That's all you need, an army of alumnae whose lives were blighted by their French grades."

Jake sighed. "You're right about that. Okay, you guys, we'll be getting back to you. Stick around."

Thus dismissed, Sarah and Alex made their way out into the softly falling snow and headed for Gregory House. And were overtaken by Giddy. Giddy wore her yellow and black striped scarf wound around her sweatsuit and had apparently just come from indoor soccer practice.

"Not that many kids turned up," said Giddy, "They've all been skiing today, and God, Sarah, look at your face! What meat mixer did you walk into? And can you believe it, Grace got nailed. I hear she's still alive, but God, what a shitty thing to happen. I'm not a fan, but I never wished her dead. Gone, maybe, but not dead. I suppose this means that not Anita but Grace was the target all along."

"Skiing in that black cape didn't help," said Sarah. "Talk about being conspicuous. People in ordinary ski clothes usually look pretty much alike. And if they're wearing scarves or face masks, they could be anyone. Grace could have blended right into the crowd."

Giddy stopped abruptly under a lamppost outside Gregory House and confronted Sarah. "Are you saying that Grace asked for it?"

"The cape made her easy to find," said Sarah. "But you know, she never struck me as someone who wanted to blend into the crowd. And now that we know she had a handgun and a can of bear spray, she must have thought she was safe. But what's going to happen to the school? One teacher murdered, another attacked. That isn't going to do much for Miss Merritt's reputation."

"Better than having something happen to one of the students," said Giddy. "Bad stuff does go on once in a while at schools. Then time passes, and people forget."

"That's true enough," said Alex. "Every so often, somewhere a teacher runs amok, drinks, and drives a student into a tree. Or molests a student. An instructor is found sitting on a stash of child pornography, a student gets pregnant and something happens to the baby, a kid jumps out a window, and another runs away and is found dead in a trailer park. Schools, even the safest and best regarded, and the most ancient and honorable, are human communities and bad things sometimes happen."

"Yeah, maybe," said Giddy. "But admit it. This is different. It's a double feature. *Two* teachers!"

"So," said Alex, "let's cross our fingers that Grace Carpentier recovers. And that school goes on."

"If I know Dr. Singer," said Giddy, "she'll make school go on. She'll keep the media, the TV, and newspaper ghouls off limits as much as possible and hang tight to a schedule. The Alumnae Association dinner is tonight—that's when the kids and teachers and alumnae mix it up. Then the memorial service for Anita is on Sunday, classes on Monday, and everything else that can be made to function, by God, it will function. I'll go on busting my butt trying to handle Anita's history of art classes plus my own art classes, not to mention indoor soccer practices. And poor Babette Leclerc will take over Grace's French classes, where she'll probably find a bunch of traumatized students. And then Adrian Parsons must get a grip on the Language Division."

"I wouldn't think Adrian would mind that," said Sarah. "He's always struck me as someone who likes to run things."

As Giddy predicted, so it was. The school, the students, instructors, and staff, might be in a high state of anxiety, but even with the presence of the police, the repeated intrusions of the fourth estate—including representatives from the *Star* the *National Enquirer*, as well as from the *Boston Globe* and the *Boston Herald*, school life continued. It may have stumbled forward, tripping occasionally, but still it went on.

The Alumnae Association dinner had been designed so that the visitors could be brought abreast of school affairs, and to this end they mingled and ate with the students and teachers. But anyone with adequate hearing would have reported that not much was learned about the normal school activities. The whole cafeteria dining room buzzed and rippled. The death of Anita Goshawk, the attack on Grace Carpentier were devoured over the soup course, the entrée, the dessert, and taken with the coffee.

Alex was huddled with Jake Markham and one of the Lahey emergency room physicians during the dinner hour, so Sarah found herself sitting between Miss Merritt alumnae members Margaret (class of '87) and Andrea (class of '94) listening to speculations on who, what, and why, and then with increased attention to the remarks centered on the school's most recent victim.

"She ruined my senior year," said Margaret. "I lived on restriction and tried to switch to another language, Chinese, Sanskrit—anything—but she blocked it. My roommate had Carpentier two years in a row and went to bed every night crying over her French assignment."

"I was skiing when I heard the news," said Andrea, "and I admit that when I heard she'd been attacked, well, I kind of brightened up and said 'way to go' to myself. I don't really mean," she said, looking around the large table at the interested faces of four junior students, "that I would have *done* anything, but if it had to be a teacher, well, Grace would have been my choice. And," she added hastily, "I just would have bumped her. Not killed her or knocked her out."

"Of course, you girls know," Margaret said without conviction, "Madame Carpentier is a really unusual and remarkable teacher."

"What she's saying," added Andrea, "is that you just don't forget a teacher like that."

But the point had been made, and even Dr. Singer's short speech at the end of dinner reporting that Grace's condition had slightly improved did nothing to dampen the impression made by these former students. Sarah and Giddy, meeting in the front hall afterward, agreed that the number of other alumnae who might have been willing accessories to the discomfiture or possibly the elimination of Grace Carpentier was remarkable.

"It's like that book about the Orient Express," said Giddy. "Agatha Christie. A cooperative murder."

"Are you thinking that the attack was a pre-planned job cooked up by the Alumnae Association?"

"The idea is sort of appealing," said Giddy.

"Forget it. Alex and I found her. And there weren't any signs of a mass attack. I don't know beans about forensics, but I'd say that except for Grace's fall down the ravine and my tripping into it, and Alex following, there just weren't any signs that a herd had trampled down the snow."

But the idea of some unhappy members of the Alumnae Association getting into the act lingered uneasily in Sarah's brain all through Saturday and all through a musical review presented by the Glee Club that night. Finally, she told Alex about it Sunday morning as Alex was packing up to leave— more snow was forecast and he was on call that night. Alex, who never liked extravagant ideas, told her firmly that she and anyone else who thought such a thing was completely crazy, and Sarah reminded him that crazy things did happen.

"Not that crazy," said Alex.

"You forget," said Sarah. "You've been up to your ears in a lot of crazier things than this. Remember our trip to Europe? People being pushed into Monet's pond and down medieval stairways all over Europe."

"Europe," said Alex, zipping his duffel bag, "is different. Odd things like that happen in Europe. Goodbye, my love, and go to that memorial service today. It will cool your brain. As your Grandmother Douglas would say, there's nothing like a few hymns to settle a person."

MISS MERRITT'S SCHOOL
M.M.S.
1861
SHE FLIES WITH HER OWN WINGS

25

THE memorial service for Anita Goshawk was held in the chapel of Lothrop Hall at two o'clock on the Sunday afternoon of January seventeenth. And, as Alex had predicted, the service did a great deal to rest a fevered brain. There is nothing like ceremony, Sarah told herself as she took her place by Babette Leclerc, to calm troubled waters. This thought she repeated to Babette, who nodded but added that forty hymns and a tour through the entire *Book of Common Prayer* wouldn't ease the fact that she was now teaching five classes of French.

"It may sound like a terribly selfish way of looking at things," whispered Babette, "but I'm glad they're not going to do one of those 'celebrations of life' affairs, because that would mean almost everyone at the school would have to get up and say uplifting things. Besides, celebration is all very well, but the poor woman was murdered and that does throw a damper. But Anita left a note in her will about having a traditional service, so that means we'll get out by three, hit the reception, and get back to work. Now, look over there at Adrian. He would have been asked to speak, and he's a total wreck. I used to think he was distinguished looking, but now he's the picture of a prisoner of war who's just been released."

Sarah looked up off to the right side of the aisle and saw that the classics teacher was huddled down inside his trenchcoat and that his head and smoothed-down hair gave a strong impression of a bare skull.

"Of course," said Babette, sinking her voice even lower as the minister in his black robe stepped forward, "Dr. Singer isn't looking too sharp. Circles under her eyes and thin as a rail. Even Freda Cohen acts like she's coming unraveled, trying to be mother hen and keep her students from going over the edge."

But now the organ groaned into life, hymn number two-sixty-six was called, and there was a general upward heaving of bodies and, aided by the school chorus, the assembly launched into "A Mighty Fortress Is Our God."

It was, Sarah thought, when the congregation began leaving the chapel and heading for the reception in Radnor, as Dr. Singer had foretold, an event with a coda. Anita's service held pride of place, but the minister was able to devote several minutes at the end to regretting the injury done to Madame Carpentier and asking for prayers on her behalf. "Bless we pray thee, thy servant, Grace Marie-Henriette, that she may be restored to health of body and mind, through Jesus Christ Our Lord. Amen."

"Of course," said Babette as they filed out, "Grace, being Roman Catholic, would probably have a fit being tacked onto a Protestant service."

"A prayer is a prayer, Grace should be grateful," said a voice. It was Freda Cohen, done up in Loden cloth and a black felt hat with a feather.

"Don't count on it," said Babette briskly. "I don't think Grace Carpentier has an ecumenical bone in her body."

And so the day wound down with the passing around of edibles and the restrained drinking of tea or sherry with the usual offers of additives from Carlo Leone, who circulated among faculty and Alumnae Association members, bringing, if not cheer, at least a jolt of an expensive whiskey.

"I haven't seen you around much lately," said Sarah, shaking her head at his offer to freshen her tea.

"I'm job hunting," said Carlo. "Went for a couple of interviews. My students are doing research papers, so I could take a few days off."

"You're leaving Miss Merritt's?" asked Sarah, surprised. Carlo Leone, even in his loose, casual way, seemed something of a fixture at the school.

"Time to move on. My contract's up, and I'd like to get a job at a college. Just as an adjunct, since I've only got an M.A., but I could work on my doctorate."

"Where are you looking?"

But Carlo only shrugged and said something incoherent about somewhere "around the East."

"Have you been cross-country skiing?" asked Sarah, to keep the conversation alive. "It's the 'in' thing to do."

"I wonder if Grace would agree with you on that," said Carlo, and then, as if he had seen someone in need of refreshment, smiled, and took off down the room.

Sarah was left with the distinct impression of someone who had something on his mind that was not suited for general conversation. And then she saw that he had traversed the length of the room and cornered Rosemary Streeter by the library door. He frowned, she shook her head, and suddenly they were both gone. And Sarah was brought back to that night at the restaurant. The instructor and his student? Or? But it had been a long day, and her brain, temporarily soothed by the somber funeral service, had begun to sputter back into life. However, she didn't need the aggravation of worrying about the likes of Rosemary and Carlo and whatever they might be up to.

The evening passed, the morning came, and the classes began, and when she had time to consider the matter, Sarah noticed that, in the interest of sanity, the members of the Merritt School community had begun to focus their attention on the various jobs at hand. Freda Cohen made cocoa and had extra Gregory House meetings, Babette Leclerc rushed about trying to keep up with her double load of French classes, the athletic schedule got back on track, the cast for *Mrs. Warren's Profession* began rehearsals, and plans were made for a Valentine dance in Concord with Middlesex School. And Sarah made the switch from bloody *Macbeth* to *The Tempest* with her freshmen, nudged her general literature class toward the end of *Bleak House*, and with her senior class exchanged T. S. Eliot for Wallace Stevens, with Gwendolyn Brooks on deck.

The police were a constant presence, and from time to time students, faculty, and staff members detached themselves from their school world and trudged through the snow to Radnor Hall to take another at their statements or to add to them. The forensic team searched and researched Grace's apartment, while Jake Markham gave Sarah the added duty of not only feeding the dog Szeppi but also walking and housing him, since Grace's apartment was now off-limits.

And, at a remove from these scenes, there was the Lahey Clinic hospital. At some time around the finish of the third week of January, the neurosurgical team in charge of Grace Carpentier declared that she would probably live to teach again. Her conscious intervals had much increased, and everyone was, as the phrase had it, "cautiously optimistic." In response to this cheering news, instructors, staff members, and Dr. Singer made ritual trips to the hospital to leave messages—she was still allowed no visitors—and some of Grace's students sent get-well cards with appropriate sentiments.

"How," demanded Hannah Hoyt, "can we put it that we want her to get well but not come back to school?"

"We could say," said Zoë, "that we hope she has a good rest and a long vacation."

"A vacation somewhere in Burma or New Zealand?" suggested Rosemary, who was putting the finishing touches on a homemade card cut out in the shape of France.

Zoë grinned. "We'll say we want her well by the beginning of next September, because that's when the three of us will be gone."

As for Grace Marie-Henriette, she had been in a world of her own. For ten days or so she drifted in and out of consciousness and had good days and less-good days. On her good days she was intermittently aware that over her bed the talk ran to indecipherable matters such as anticerebral edema measures, diuresis, intracranial pressure monitoring, CT scans, possible secondary neurologic deterioration, and the need for another MRI.

By the end of the first week in February, a period notable for days of alternating thawing and freezing and thus the ruination of the cross-country ski trails, Grace's neurology team allowed themselves the luxury of saying that all seemed to be going pretty well and that, although weak, she was now completely conscious and oriented to her surroundings and understood the cause of her being in the hospital. Of her attack she had no memory.

Jake Markham, Sarah, and Giddy (who had decided to forgive Jake), meeting by chance at the school cafeteria, decided to join forces for lunch—the lasagna was again featured. It was Friday the twelfth, Lincoln's birthday, and the beginning of a week's "winter break," a respite much needed by the harried faculty and staff. A few students lingered, but many had left after the noon classes, and the three were able to find a quiet corner in the half-empty dining room. The conversation turned immediately to the state of Grace Carpentier.

"Of course," said Jake, "she doesn't remember what happened. I had a talk with Dr. Fiero—he's the neurosurgeon who's running the show—and he said that amnesia's common after head injury. Of course, it's pretty damn convenient for Grace not to remember that she was packing an illegal handgun and can of bear spray. And she's lucky. No speech or motor difficulties. No personality changes."

"You call that lucky?" said Giddy. "We were hoping that she'd come back all warm and fuzzy and ready to hand out A's and B pluses to all her students."

"Sorry," said Jake. "But she is allowed visitors. Ten minutes only, and not too many in one day." He shoved his lasagna plate aside and pulled a triangle of apple pie front and center.

"But," said Sarah, seeing a gaping hole in this arrangement, "how are you going to know if one of her visitors isn't the one who tried to kill her?"

"Security. We've arranged to have someone from the Burlington police to sit outside her room, the door ajar so he can hear."

"A lot can be done in ten minutes," Sarah argued.

"Yes," said Giddy. "Mr. Killer goes in clutching a bunch of roses with a knife hidden inside and . . ."

"No flowers allowed. Visitors must take off their coats and jackets and are given the once over," said Jake.

"The visitor," said Sarah, "tiptoes in, offers to adjust Grace's bed or smooth her pillow, something like that, and pounces, smothers her with the pillow. No sound at all. Then he tiptoes out and tells the guard he didn't stay because she's asleep. Which she will be—for good."

Jake shook his head. "You've been contaminated by hospital sitcoms. Things like that don't happen."

"Want to bet?" asked Giddy.

"The Carlisle Police," said Jake, "the Burlington police, the Massachusetts State Police VICAP team—"

"The what?" said Sarah.

"VICAP, Violent Criminal Apprehension Program, and the Lahey security guys are all on top of this," Jake continued. "No one wants a Hollywood shoot-out on a hospital floor or a chase down the hall spattering IV stands and lunch trays and nurses against the walls. Everything's going smoothly. Grace has already had quick visits from Dr. Singer, Adrian Parsons, Babette, and Carlo with no blood shed. Also, our favorite sporting goods man, Georges Thibodeau, popped in. I was there when he came. He was going to kiss her—probably on both cheeks like the French do—but she fended him off. Anyway, if you two ladies want to visit Grace, it will be allowed."

Sarah nodded. "I could stop in and tell her that Szeppi is just fine and that he and Patsy are buddies."

But Giddy had moved to another subject. "How about that guy everyone says they saw skiing? The one in the red and black wool shirt? Everybody's talking about him."

"We're on top of that," said Jake complacently. "Or rather, the state police have sent some men who are trained to work the woods to look around. They've been at the park off and on for the last couple of weeks. Nothing so far. Maybe he was a visitor from out of town or another planet and he's gone home." With that, he turned to Sarah. "Your face is still a mess, do you know that?" And with these encouraging words, Jake took his leave.

Sarah grimaced. "I wish people would stop telling me that my face might frighten children. Okay, Giddy, what do you say? Shall we call on Grace? Alex is coming down for the long weekend, and we're going to ski around the area and do some theater in Boston. Grace likes Alex, so we can use him to break the ice. And she must want to hear all about Szeppi and his little tricks.

314

He's a nice dog, so maybe we've been misjudging Madame."

"That," said Giddy dryly, "I doubt."

"Let's go and visit. Alex will be here any minute, and you can bring Grace up to speed on the school scene."

Giddy grinned. "You mean tell her that Babette is making friends and winning votes with all her students?"

Sarah and Giddy met Alex as he pulled into the Gregory House parking lot some ten minutes later, Sarah having armed herself with a photograph taken the week before of Szeppi and Patsy sitting side by side. Alex locked the Subaru and climbed into the backseat of the Jeep, saying that he'd been driving for three and a half hours and it was Sarah's turn. "You face hasn't improved much but I love every scratch on it," he told Sarah. And then to Giddy, "How goes your plan to add Jake Markham to your string of scalps?"

"You know," said Giddy, "it's true. A policeman's girl is not a happy one. He's too busy, I'm too busy. Maybe in the spring, but not now. I feel sorry for anyone hitching their life to a policeman on a homicide case. And I feel sorry for a policeman like Jake who doesn't have time for a decent meal. Or have time to change his socks or go pee."

At which the conversation lapsed. Sarah drove slowly, the roads were icy. As they slid out of Bedford, she said, "I have this crazy idea. It's been building, and I'd like to try it out on both of you."

"Shoot," said Giddy.

"As long as it doesn't involve a chase through the ER," said Alex. "I'm beat."

"It's about clothes," said Sarah, trying to sort out her ideas. "Start with that black cape. Grace's cape. She always wore it, in the fall and winter at least. Right?"

"Hardly an earth-shaking observation," remarked Giddy.

"Let me go on," said Sarah.

"Or," said Alex, "we won't hear the end of it. Ever."

"Shut up and listen. Grace's cape was one of a kind. At the school, anyway. When you saw someone in a cape go by, you thought, hey, there's Grace Carpentier. And when those scarecrows were put up and when that cut-out puppet was found, there wasn't any doubt about who it was meant to be, right?"

"You're boring me," said Giddy.

"Hold on. And it's safe to say now that Anita Goshawk wearing Grace's cape on a dark footpath got Anita killed." She paused and swung the Jeep into the Burlington Road and stopped at the red light. "Grace's cape is what someone called a 'signature garment.' But there are other ones. You always wear that black and yellow striped scarf, don't you, Giddy? The one you've got around your neck now that looks like a bumblebee, and no one at the school has anything like it. And, we usually recognize, even from the back, Adrian Parsons in that elegant camel-hair coat of his, or, like Carlo, in a Scotland Yard trench coat. And Freda Cohen wears those Tyrolean outfits that look like she's loose from *The Sound of Music*. And Dr. Singer wears those tailored power suits. With a silk blouse. Perfect shoes and handbag. And Babette wears those hand-knitted coats and vests."

"Where is all this going?" asked Giddy. "Because we're almost at the Lahey."

"I'm saying that this guy with his red and black jacket established, at least for those great snow days before the attack on Grace, a sort of presence. In a signature outfit. I've been skiing at the state park since the snow got really good, and he didn't turn up until that week. My theory is that the man—I'd swear it's a man—was there to establish a false identity."

"Huh?" said Giddy. "You mean like it was a disguise?"

"Yes. And one nobody could forget. The lumberjack look.

The classic red and black wool shirt. Baggy wool pants, and old-fashioned wooden skis."

"The natural man," said Alex. "Environmentally correct. We should all look like that."

"Thank you, Alex," said Sarah. "Now, just listen. Here's the hospital. I'll find a parking place, but please, you two, stay in the car until I finish. This guy not only wears the sort of clothes that make people remember him, but he's got a khaki hunting cap with earflaps, so most of his face is hidden—except for those horn-rimmed glasses and that big mustache. And he waves to everyone. Doesn't stop to talk, but goes on. So we remember him." Sarah swung the Jeep into a space at the farther reaches of the clinic parking lot and then said triumphantly, "You know why no one saw this man again?"

"You want us to say that he ceased to exist," said Alex. "He attacks Grace and strips. Changes clothes."

"Yes," said Sarah, "more or less. He may have attacked Grace, watched her roll into the ravine, found me coming along, and gave me a big push. And then switched clothes. Plenty of cover off those trails."

"But the police haven't found any stray clothes," Giddy reminded her.

"Say he stuffs the jacket and pants into his backpack. Probably has cross-country tights and a nylon parka under the heavy clothes. Then off come the horn-rimmed specs and the mustache, and on go dark glasses and a Nordic cap, and he waits off the trail until the coast is clear. And skis off. Gets out while Alex and I are finding Grace. But now he's wearing everyday cross-country gear, which no one would look at twice."

"How about those old-fashioned skis?" demanded Giddy.

"It's almost dark. He skis on the edges of the trail where the snow is thick and covers the skis. Besides, I'll bet no one would look twice at his skis since he now looks like everyone else. The only reason the skis were noticed before was because of the whole outfit. And it was daylight. Anyway, he leaves the trail, stows his skis in his car, and off he goes. Mission completed—except it wasn't, because Grace is still alive."

"You're saying no one sees this guy leave the parking area at the Wolf Rock Road?" asked Alex.

"No," said Sarah stubbornly. "The cars aren't lined up. They park around a circle, with trees in the middle. You don't get much of a view of anyone. And I'll guess he isn't driving a bright red BMW or a vintage MG. Just an ordinary car. Then, picture this. Alex and I find Grace, and I run to the trail and find a skier with a cell phone, who calls 911. In comes the Rescue Squad ambulance, lights blinking and siren wailing. No one is going to notice a nondescript person packing away his skis and leaving."

"So now," said Giddy, "all we have to find is a man who looks exactly like everyone else and ask him if he likes to dress like a lumberjack so that he can slug French teachers?"

"What we do," said Alex, "is congratulate Sarah on a gripping scenario, get out of this car, call on Grace Carpentier, and hit the road and head back."

"You are rotten, ungrateful people," said Sarah, turning off the ignition and reaching for her handbag.

The three trudged along the sidewalk toward the clinic entrance, and then Giddy broke the silence. "Are you thinking what I'm thinking? About what men at the school fit the bill? Could pass themselves off as a lumberjack?"

Sarah made a face. "Adrian Parsons and Carlo Leone. Not Hannah Hoyt, even though she's tall and could have done the job. But it's not in her. And it's not Joel Cohen. He's too short. And too nice."

"Adrian Parsons," said Giddy, "must want Grace's job and must hate being number two. And Carlo's always been a wild card. And I've heard he's looking for work because the school didn't renew his contract for some reason."

Sarah remembered Carlo's talk about sending out job applications and his dinner meeting with Rosemary Streeter, but decided that a liason with a senior student hardly added up to guilt for murder. Unless.

"Unless," she said slowly, "Carlo Leone was caught doing something he shouldn't. By Anita? Or more likely, Madame. And she was going to call him on it. She wouldn't be afraid of him. She isn't afraid of anyone."

"Maybe now she is," said Alex. "And with good reason. But I think you're trying to complicate something that's already in a tangle."

"Remember, both those men had deep facial scratches the day after Anita was killed, so maybe it was a two-man job," said Sarah. "Grace snitched on both men? Or worse, Grace and Anita snitched—separately or together—on both men."

"So Adrian and Carlo joined forces," said Giddy. "And it was always supposed to be a double killing. First get Anita, and then nail Grace. Although," she added doubtfully, "there was only one man dressed up as a lumberjack."

Alex stood back from the clinic door and allowed Sarah and Giddy to enter. "You ladies need a strong purgative. I suggest ten ounces of citrate of magnesia. It sparkles and has a pleasing lemon flavor."

26

THE three paused at the Lahey Clinic Gift Shop, a glass-enclosed space featuring the usual variety of items intended to cheer the hospital patient.

"I suppose we should bring a card," said Giddy.

"Madame Carpentier probably has a hundred cards," said Alex. "Our cheerful selves should be enough. A quick in-and-out. Visitors can set patients back for days."

"There speaks Dr. Friendly," said Sarah. "We're only letting you come because Grace likes you, and you can soften her up."

After the elevator trip to the seventh floor—Neurosurgery—they discovered Grace Carpentier was located in a room with a distant view of a small, enclosed garden. Alex went in first and found the lady sitting in a vinyl-covered chair by the window, a copy of *Le Monde* folded on her lap. She wore a burgundy housecoat with a mandarin collar, and this garment, plus the black sateen skullcap covering her partly shaved head, made Alex feel that he was some humble person calling on a potentate from an archaic Asian kingdom. Her injury had not softened her features—her nose was still sharp, her chin sharper, and the fading bruises on one side of her face simply enhanced the sense of a person who was not like ordinary mortals.

"Ah," said Grace, looking up. "It is the Dr. McKenzie. I am told that you made yourself part of the rescue effort. So, *bien sûr*, I am grateful. Now, if you have influence with this hospital and with this Dr. Fiero who is in charge of me but not always the most amiable, will you instruct him that I must return to school. I have a great fear that my classes will be in a sad state. Miss Leclerc does her best, but she has a most yielding nature. Also, it is that I must care for my little dog, Szeppi, who will be learning bad manners spending the day with the dog Patsy."

Madame, having firmly established that she was in full control of her mind and that there had been no detectable change in her personality, reminded Alex that she was limited in the time a visitor could stay and that he must not linger. However, she was willing to see Miss Deane and Miss Lester for a short time. She had seen their faces from the door.

Alex yielded to Giddy, who stayed only long enough to be chided for laxness in the art department and informed that she marked her students with, as Madame put it, "a higher grade than they deserve. It spoils them and makes them inattentive."

Then it was Sarah's turn. She stood facing Grace and listened to a list of things she should be doing or should not be doing for Szeppi. Sarah admitted to feeding him twice a day and switching him to ProPlan since the nearest grocery was out of Science Diet.

"You must always buy the Science Diet," said Grace. "My veterinarian says that it is the best."

"My veterinarian," said Sarah, briefly losing her cool, "says

ProPlan is just as good." But then, seeing fire in the Carpentier eye and fearing that contradiction might bring on untoward symptoms, she nodded. She would pick up a bag of Science Diet.

"*D'accord*," said Grace. "Thank you for coming. You must visit my class again when I have returned. It will be for you a great benefit."

Sarah took her leave thankfully, and in the interest of exercise, the three visitors decided to take the stairway down. Circling about on the concrete stairs, they had just reached the fifth floor when Sarah remembered she had forgotten to leave the photograph of Szeppi.

"I'll be right back," she said. "I'll meet you in the lobby, by the gift shop." She reversed direction and began the two-floor climb to the seventh floor. This reached, she pushed open the metal door.

And was met by a riot. Tumult and shouting. Objects, people everywhere. A woman in blue scrubs scrambling on the floor. A litter diagonally across the corridor. A man cowering by a fire extinguisher, clutching his walker. A woman trundling an IV stand backing into an open doorway. Someone shouting, "Stop him. Stop both of them. Call security!"

Sarah, holding the door open at the entrance, had hardly any time to focus on two figures, familiar figures who, one after the other, hurtled past her down the corridor, disappeared, and then returned. The first man, holding a hand over his face, plunged blindly into the litter, picked himself up, and galloped for the door. And, as he shot through the door Sarah still held open, he gripped her shoulder with his free hand and gave her a heavy push—the sensation was hideously familiar—and slammed her to the floor. Then he wrenched the door wide and headed down the stairway. The second man followed, leaping over Sarah's sprawled body, and disappeared in his turn down the stairs.

There was no time to think, to yell for help. Sarah scrambled to her feet, ducked under the reaching arm of a white-coated man, pulled at the door, and flung herself past the landing and hurtled down the stairs.

Seventh floor to the sixth floor, Sarah, clutching at the metal rail for balance, trying not to see down into the stairwell to the dreadful and distant basement, charged after the two figures; figures who, like strange, terrestrial birds, their open coats like wings flapping about their bodies, clattered and whirled and circled below her.

Sarah couldn't gain on them and the men stayed two floors below. Then, suddenly, they were gone. Out, one after the other. Oh, thank God, Sarah thought. It's the fourth floor, the lobby floor. They weren't going to the basement; the chase, the confrontation, shoot-out, or whatever was going to happen would take place in the civilized confines of the heavily populated lobby. Where, she hoped to hell, that among many others, Giddy and Alex waited. Ready for action.

She shot like a cork out of a bottle from the stairway exit, down a hallway, and into the lobby. At a dead run she brushed past a man clutching a newspaper to his chest, a woman rearing back in her wheelchair, and saw her first man running, right, left, bumping into low tables and chairs, and then in a final plunge flinging himself straight into the gift shop. Followed by his pursuer, followed by Alex, by Giddy. And also by a just-arrived taxi driver who knew action when he saw it, and by three alert nurses coming out of the cafeteria.

The hospital gift shop had never been designed for nine people all in random motion. Get-well cards, Snickers bars, magazines, bath powder, bottles of toilet water, small, pink teddy bears, and boxes of notepaper bounced off shelves and racks, flew into pieces, and landed on the counters and on the floor.

And landed on the tall, bony man in the camel-hair coat

who kneeled on the chest of the man in the trench coat, holding him with both hands fast by the throat. Adrian Parsons, his face a mask of rage, and Carlo Leone, his a burning crimson, contorted in pain, had both come to rest.

The arrival of security personnel, the disentanglement and restraint of both men, the comforting of the frightened gift shop volunteer who had ducked behind her sales counter, the picking and sorting of the gift shop detritus, all this business gave Sarah, gave Alex and Giddy, time to regroup. To step back, regain their senses, their equilibrium. And express their amazement at the recent events.

"Oh God, what an almighty awful mix-up," said Sarah. "All we needed in the gift shop was Grace hitting everyone over the head with her umbrella." She and Giddy now stood at the entrance to the clinic, waiting for Alex to bring the car to the door, a service he was rendering in recognition that Sarah and Giddy had, in an incoherent way, been almost right about Anita's murder as well as Grace Carpentier's very close call in the woods of the state park.

"I don't think I guessed," said Sarah. "Not all of it. You were closer with this idea of a double event."

"But it wasn't double. Not really," said Giddy. "Except that when he killed the wrong woman, he had to go on and get the right one. Grace Carpentier. I suppose she was the target from the beginning."

Sarah wiggled her shoulders and groaned. The fall on the seventh-floor corridor had left her feeling bruised and battered. "When I saw them coming at me, Carlo blundering into everything, it was pretty scary. He was a wild man, his eyes almost closed, his hand covering his face. Then I thought I might fall down the stairwell, or that one of the two men—or both— would go over the rail. And in the gift shop I honestly thought

Adrian would strangle Carlo before anyone stopped him. I mean, my God, I think his eyes were bulging."

"Here's Alex and the car," said Giddy. "Let's rehash when we get back to school. Right now I need to lean back and breathe deeply."

Fifty minutes later, as the late afternoon sent dark shadows across the Persian rug of the now all-too-familiar Copeland Room, Giddy and Sarah, each holding a tumbler of restorative spirits—rum and orange juice—met with Detective Hillary Mumford and that long-suffering head of school, Joanna Singer, who appeared to be drinking straight Scotch. Alex would be joining them later but was now meeting with doctors at Emerson Hospital, where Mr. Leone had been sidetracked to be treated for the damage caused by taking a blast of Bear Beware pepper spray full in the face.

Jake Markham, too, was expected, but at the moment he was busy arranging charges against Carlo Leone for assault with intent to kill Grace Carpentier—murder charges for the death of Anita Goshawk being for the time on hold pending solid evidence. And it had indeed turned into a double-header, as Jake was also preparing charges against Adrian Parsons for assaulting Carlo Leone.

"So, let's kick this off," said Hillary, looking around the table. "I think, Dr. Singer, you've been holding out on us."

Joanna Singer, looking almost as haggard as Adrian Parsons, frowned. As a woman who habitually took charge of procedures, meetings, and decisions, it was hard to find herself on the defensive, a subordinate to this slip-of-a-girl detective. Now she hedged. "I don't understand what you're driving at."

Hillary sighed. If Dr. Singer stalled, it was going to be a long session. "About Carlo Leone. His contract had not been renewed. He wasn't coming back to Miss Merritt's."

"That's general knowledge," said Dr. Singer. "And the reasons are confidential. It's a matter of protecting private sources of information."

"Not in a murder case," said Hillary in a tight voice. "More information might at least have prevented the attack on Grace Carpentier."

Joanna Singer looked about the room and fixed her gaze on the large portrait of founder Claudia Merritt as if seeking guidance. And she gave in. "Anita Goshawk and Grace Carpentier, whose words I didn't doubt, came to me—separately—and told me that Mr. Leone was handing out liquor at school functions. And that he was involved with a student—not having an affair, perhaps, but it was a close thing. Mr. Leone was pressuring her. She came to me two days ago and said she was disturbed by the relationship and wanted out."

Sarah sat up. "You mean Rosemary Streeter, don't you? I saw them having dinner together. But I wasn't sure it meant anything. And about the liquor, didn't everyone know he was slipping whiskey into punch glasses? For the adults."

"And for the students," added Dr. Singer. "First it was faculty members and visitors. I was very late in finding this out; he was extremely quick with his hands, but lately, this fall I've been told by Rosemary, he's given drinks to students on hikes, on field trips, and when he sees them off-campus. No hard drugs apparently, but the alcohol is bad enough. Unfortunately, Grace, who is absolutely fearless, let me know that she told Carlo she was going to report him."

"And look where that got Grace," said Giddy. "And where it got Anita, dressing up in Grace's cape."

Dr. Singer licked her lips, drew in a breath, and stood up. "I have to go. A meeting with some of the faculty to rearrange the teaching schedule, so many losses. I'm sorry," she said, sounding incoherent perhaps for the first time in her life. "I, we, try to keep this sort of thing quiet and deal with it privately. Just let the inner circle of the trustees know. Because parents, well, they are always so ready to pounce. I made a mistake. I won't do so again."

"Let's hope," said Hillary sharply, "there won't be any need for you to do it again. One murder and one assault ought to take care of the next fifty years."

Dr. Singer departed, Giddy followed, Giddy pleading her double class load.

These two were almost immediately replaced by Alex and Jake, arriving one after the other.

"Bear Beware spray in your face does quite a job," said Alex. "Carlo Leone is plenty miserable."

"Which he deserves to be," said Hillary. "But how did Grace get hold of the stuff? She was in the hospital. A patient in the hospital, for God's sake."

Alex grinned. "Never underestimate the long arm of the Alliance Française. Georges Thibodeau to the rescue. He slipped her a little canister when he visited. *Semper paratus*, right?"

"We should give them to hospital patients, you think?" said Hillary. "Okay, here's the story. Jake, you break in if I lose you along the way." Hillary turned the page of her notebook, pressed it flat, and began.

"As we've learned a little too late from Dr. Singer, Grace Carpentier and Anita Goshawk, by reporting Carlo's off-the-wall behavior, to put it mildly, screwed Carlo out of his job at Merritt's and probably out of any decent references for another job. But Carlo only knew that Grace was the villain because she told him up front what she was doing. Carlo liked it here—not too much pressure, he enjoyed the girls, and, apart from anything else, he fell for Rosemary Streeter."

"Hey," interrupted Jake, "I met with Rosemary this afternoon about some holes in her statement. She told me something about the two of them. He was hanging around too much, making her nervous. And that Leone also wanted to get a job at whatever college she ended up going to."

"Another victim," said Hillary, "except Rosemary seems pretty with it. She must have had a tough time saying no—he's pretty persuasive—but I gather she did. Anyway, back to the murder. Just before I came over here, a report came in from the Carlisle transfer station and that Swap Shop shed the town keeps there. We've been keeping an eye on it. People leave all sorts of odd stuff, chairs, toys, and beat-up sports equipment there. Well, a pair of old wooden skis appeared. They've gone off to the lab, and we're betting that traces of blood will turn up, maybe embedded in the bindings. A pretty dumb move on Carlo's part, I'd say."

"We always figured it had to be one of the two guys, Leone or Parsons," put in Jake. "Those two late to the reception and had no one to back up their stories about how they spent the time after the lecture. Hannah Hoyt didn't fit the murder time slot and Giddy and Sarah were right; she wasn't the violent type. File cards and scarecrows, yes, field hockey sticks, no."

"It goes like this," said Hillary. "Carlo is mad as hell and he wants to get Grace. He sees Grace—only it's Anita—leaving Radnor Hall and heading back toward the east edge of the campus toward the footpath. Carlo grabs a raincoat for a cover-up and then picks up Hannah's heavy-duty field hockey stick—Gregory House is on the way to the footpath. He's a fast mover, in every sense. He ducks through the woods, and bang, bang, bang, Anita—as Grace—is finished."

"But he must have known when he'd killed her that he'd gotten the wrong woman," said Sarah.

"Yeah," said Jake, "I agree, but this is one cool character. He probably rinses off the hockey stick in that pond, races back through the woods, puts the stick back with all the other sticks in the Gregory House vestibule, and gets rid of the bloody raincoat and his clothes—where, we don't know. Gets himself over to the reception, making sure he spends a few minutes with Rosemary Streeter. He needs a witness that says he was nowhere near the footpath close to the time of the murder."

"So," said Hillary, taking up the tale, "he hangs around the reception for a while so that people can see him, then leaves, putting on his own raincoat, which he's left in the cloakroom. So he didn't snitch a stranger's coat as he claimed, because his own had been hanging right there in the cloakroom during the murder period."

"And," put in Alex, "he scratched his face in the bushes while he was dealing with Anita."

"I hate to think that Adrian got his scratches honestly," said Sarah, "because he made such a good suspect. Suave and snobbish. Except."

"Except what?" said Hillary.

"After my dinner with him, I began to believe that even after the breakup he still loved Anita and was stricken by her death. And would have known her, cape or no cape."

Hillary looked up at Alex. "What I want to hear is what happened on the seventh floor of the Lahey Clinic. And how those two men ended up in a wrestling match in the gift shop."

Alex leaned back and smiled. "That I can tell you. I've been on the phone to my dear friend, Madame Carpentier, and she has given me the low-down. Carlo Leone came to the Lahey as a visitor—he'd come before, so no trouble with the guard. He apparently engaged Madame in conversation, got closer and closer to her chair, reached out to do something—who knows exactly what—smother her or strangle her. But Madame had been waiting for this very event, though she didn't know who her enemy would turn out to be. After all, she has quite a collection of enemies. Well, she whips out the bear spray—kept it in her dressing-gown pocket, at the ready—and gives him the works. Carlo yelps, backs up, and smacks right into Adrian, who is arriving as a visitor."

"Adrian never connected Carlo with Anita's death?" asked Hillary.

"No," said Jake. "It came as a complete surprise. A real shock. Adrian told me at the station. If he had known, we might have had that nasty scene a lot earlier."

"Adrian responded like an old war horse," said Alex. "Sarah's told you about the chase, with Carlo half-blinded by bear spray, crashing around, blundering around the lobby, trying to get out of the hospital, and crashing into the gift shop. And I think that Adrian would have throttled Carlo for good if he had a few more minutes."

"Another revenge scene," said Jake. "Which we didn't need."

"Here's another piece to the puzzle," said Hillary. "But it's one we couldn't find before because we couldn't get a search warrant for the whole faculty. Forensics has come up with some art postcards in Carlo's apartment. Mostly illustrating Roman sculpture, ruins, and Italian painting. After all, he taught Italian, and probably used them for his classes before he got the bright idea of sending them to Grace."

"Oops," said Sarah. "When the girls told me about the postcards, they did mention that they seemed to be scenes of Italian and Roman art."

"We can't prove he sent them, but the Italian connection is interesting. We're going to try the idea out on Grace and see if she can remember if the handwriting seemed familiar, and I think—"

But Hillary was stopped cold as the door to the Copeland Room flew open and Giddy reappeared. "I've got news," she announced.

All four at the table jerked to attention, and Jake said suspiciously, "What now, Giddy?"

"Don't be such a wet blanket, Jake Markham," said Giddy. "This is good. Guess what turned up during the rehearsal of the spring play?"

"I give up," said Jake.

"The kids were trying to find clothes for the spring play in the costume room, and among the men's stuff there was this red and black wool lumberjacket and a pair of heavy wool trousers and a hunting cap. Zoë Fountain and Rosemary Streeter and Hannah—they're all in the play—recognized them because they've been skiing at the park. So they looked around, and mixed in with the props were some horn-rimmed glasses and fake mustaches. I told them not to touch anything, that I was going to hot-foot it over here and tell the police."

"Giddy," said Jake, smiling broadly, "I owe you one."

"You're dern tootin' you do," said Giddy, "so forget about this homicide kick you're on and be human. I'm starved for male companionship." She grinned and was gone.

Jake stood up. "I'll call the lab and have them meet me in the costume room. If they can pick up some fibers and hair and blood on the shirt and pants, I'd say we've nailed Leone on the Grace Carpentier assault. It makes sense for the skier to have been Carlo. Adrian may be tall and thin, but he isn't the athletic type, and lately he looks like he's going to pass out just walking to class."

"But what did he use it to hit Grace?" asked Sarah. "Not a hockey stick. And what about Anita Goshawk's murder? Bashing Grace is one thing, but you've got to prove he killed Anita, don't you?"

Hillary picked up her briefcase, opened it, and unwrapped a limp-looking sandwich with lettuce hanging from its sides. "No lunch," she explained. She took a bite, made a face, and put it on its wrapping. Then she looked at Sarah. "All in good time. We'll be looking around for the weapon. Forensics suggests a length of pipe. And Carlo Leone isn't going anywhere, so we can pull his apartment into a thousand pieces. These days, you don't pack up raincoats, wash yourself, and wipe your boots off without leaving something that will hang you. Or at least send you up for life."

"You mean," said Sarah, "blood will out?"

"You got it," said Jake. "Well, I'm outta here. Alex, what do you think? Would your cousin Giddy and I make a good combo? Or is she too much for the likes of me?"

Alex stood up in his turn and offered a hand to Sarah, whose aching body refused to stir. "With Giddy," he said, "you travel at your own risk."

Afterword

Spring came; it usually does sooner or later in New England. The cross-country ski trails returned to hiking paths and the Middlesex County Alliance Français gave a dinner to celebrate the return of Madame Carpentier from her long hospital stay. The classes of Carlo Leone, who was now held without bail in the Walpole State Prison, were taken over by a five-foot-eleven female, Signora Buonoparte. This lady, who wore tweeds and a necktie, ruled Carlo's classes in Italian and European literature with an iron fist, a fist that almost rivaled that of Madame Carpentier. Carlo's former students, to put it in their words, were "totally bummed out" by this development, much preferring the lackadaisical, humorous, anything-goes regime of Mr. Leone.

On the police front, the case against Carlo was strengthened by the discovery of a foot-long piece of pipe found in a pile of building materials near the Outing Club building. This object, examined in the forensic lab, showed satisfactory evidence of Madame's B-Rh negative blood as well as microscopic fibers from a black wool garment.

By the second Saturday in June, the terrors and tensions of the beginning of the winter term were overshadowed by the upcoming graduation ceremonies.

It was a beautiful blue and cloudless spring day. Sarah had finished packing. Her suitcase and her duffel bag sat by the door, and a box of groceries, destined for Babette Leclerc, sat on the kitchen counter. Patsy, wary, kept an eye on the luggage from his place on the sofa. Sarah's academic robes, complete with her new doctoral hood, lay across the chair; she had been invited to take part in the academic procession scheduled for two o'clock that afternoon. All that remained were the hails and farewells. She checked her watch. Just past noon. Almost time for the luncheon set up on the lawn outside the Nakatani Art Center. And now on the door came a familiar thump of hands. The threesome. Rosemary Streeter, now recovered from her uneasy association with Mr. Leone, was destined for Stanford. "Time to hit the west," she said, tearing up her acceptance from Yale. Zoë Fountain, taking a year off, was headed for a job at a veterinarian hospital in Nashua, and Hannah Hoyt, emerging from assorted restrictions and penalties connected with file cards and Madame Carpentier's classes, was flying to Paris in two days' time to join her parents and begin the study of art at whatever institute could be persuaded to take a student with a shaky academic record and a very unsure grip on the French language.

The girls were followed in quick order by Babette, Freda and Joel Cohen, and Giddy, who announced that she and Jake Markham might visit Maine in the summer if Jake could overcome a completely unnatural fear of ocean sailing. "Complete wimp," said Giddy. "He thinks I'm going to take him out and dump him. Which I probably will."

Giddy was replaced by Adrian Parsons, who held out to

Sarah a familiar-looking key chain fashioned as a black-robed witch. "I remember," said Adrian, "that you were much struck by this. Please take Hecate as a momento of your sometimes disturbed, but not, I hope, entirely unhappy semester at Miss Merritt's."

Then, as Sarah reached the door, ready for the graduation luncheon, she walked directly into Madame Carpentier, dressed for the occasion in a layered crimson affair, which gave her, Sarah decided, an unnerving resemblance to Alice's Red Queen.

"Ah, Miss Deane. I am glad to have caught you. An interesting semester, has it not been? We have all learned something of importance. I have learned that even with practice, one must not depend upon a small firearm. But also, one must never be without one's little pepper spray. And you, it is hoped, have learned something about classroom discipline. And about the proper care of a dog. So I say *au revoir* for the time. But not *adieu*. I am taking a year's leave of absence from Miss Merritt's and have been asked to teach a course in French literature at your very own institution, Bowmouth College, in Camden, Maine. So we will meet again in the fall."

And Madame Grace Marie-Henriette Carpentier, with a magisterial wave of her arm, turned and disappeared down the hall of Gregory House.